THEIR DOMME

QUEEN OF HEARTS BOOK THREE

SUKI WILLIAMS

Publication: November 2022

Editing by: Michelle Motyczka

Formatting by: Jarica James

Book Cover Design by: Everly Yours Cover Designs

Publishing by: Suki Williams

NOTE FOR READERS

Please check on my website for all trigger warnings for this book. Their Domme is intended for readers 18 or older. Also, readers will see familiar faces if you have read the Lies and Loves duet for Blake's story. If you have not read Blake's story then you might not know that Blake is non-binary and genderfluid, Blake uses they/them pronouns.

PLEASE NOTE

I would like to remind the reader that Blake, a side character in this series and main character of the Lies and Loves series, is non-binary and genderfluid. What this means for you as a reader is that I use the pronouns 'they, their, and them' when referring to Blake throughout the story.

You might be asking, what is non-binary and genderfluid?

Non-binary is an umbrella term for anyone who is not *solely* or *only* male or female. Some people use the terms bigender, genderqueer, or agender among many others under this umbrella. None of these terms mean the exact same thing, but each term speaks of a gender experience that is not simply male or female. In Blake's case they use the pronouns 'they, their, and them' and don't identify as either male or female.

Blake is also **genderfluid**, which is not the same as non-binary. Someone who is genderfluid does not adhere to one fixed gender and who may move among genders when it comes to their gender identity. A person's gender identity can change over time or from day-to-day. Blake moves along the gender spectrum throughout the book and the entire series.

If these definitions are wrong in any way or offensive please let me know and I will update or change it ASAP. My intent is to let readers know this information before jumping into Blake's story so you can fully enjoy it while being informed of what these words mean.

Please be aware these are very basic definitions for these terms. Gender is a very nuanced and personal experience for every individual. This story reflects Blake's experiences and views for themself.

Prologue

Unknown
Friday

"Please!" The woman's voice cracked. Tears ran down her cheeks, smearing her makeup and the blood on her face. "Please, just kill me."

"Kill you?" I asked her softly, a smile tugging at my lips as she flinched away from the hand that caressed her cheek. "I just got you. I thought you were made of sterner stuff, Nicholette."

Tears fell down her face. "Nicholette? I'm not—"

With a roar, I punched her, savoring her screams and sobs before I grabbed her throat, shaking her roughly. "You fucking ruined it! You stupid fucking whore. I don't know why I bother anymore with you bitches. Fucking worthless, the lot of you."

"Please, please—" she rasped, eyes closed as if that would make me disappear.

These women were all pathetic, nothing like my Nic. A few hits, and they were begging for it to be over. Saying they would tell me whatever I wanted, do anything I wanted... Nicholette would be cursing me, laughing and asking if that was all I had. Her blue-green eyes would sparkle with contempt and hate as I made her beg, made her come. Oh, it would be beautiful, not this whining, sobbing *trash* that was before me now.

A shudder passed through my body as the image of Nicholette being the one here with me made my dick harden. Licking my lips, I let go of the woman, ignoring her weak thanks and crying. Soon enough, she would figure out there was no escape for her.

My Nic should be here right now.

But she had decided to prolong our games instead. I'd been playing cat and mouse with her for too long. I needed her, and I needed her *now*. The only solace I had was that she wasn't with her *guys*, as she called them. Watching the bigger one, Vas, lose it when he discovered all her things were gone was priceless. I replayed it for days, his rage and pain making me come in seconds. They had scrambled to her old apartment and found my little present for them.

The sooner those assholes stopped making waves in Ashview, the sooner I would be able to find my woman. Nicholette disappeared a month ago, and they had put the city on fucking lockdown, searching and connecting with every person to find her. Any owed favors were called in, each of them digging down into the depths of their criminal ties to search for any lead. The bodies were piling up, and eventually, the authorities were going to notice a difference in the criminal underbelly of the city.

I was watching their every move; every update they got, so did I. It was the perfect part of my plan, and the best part was they had no fucking clue. Soon, I'd have her with me.

Reaching down, I pushed my pants down just enough to free my cock. Rubbing my hand slowly up and down my length, I approached my victim. Her eyes widened with fear, but that just made it all the more sweet when I slammed into her. She was tight, and her body tried to clamp down, almost like it could fight me off, keep me from claiming what was owed to me, but she didn't stand a chance. Pushing through her resistance, I brutally fucked her until l felt wetness easing my way. There was something about the slickness that told me I'd caused some kind of bleeding, and I began thrusting into her with renewed strength. It was different once blood was involved, so much slicker, easier, her body's way of fully giving itself over to me in a surrender that I, of course, had no choice but to revel in.

Screams gave way to pitiful cries, creating cracks in the almost zen-like state I'd found myself in. Why couldn't this bitch just let me enjoy a single moment? Was that too much to fucking ask? I grabbed a nearby knife and stabbed her in the stomach. The metal table she was strapped to became wet with bright red blood, and begging filled the air. I smirked down at her, stabbing her over and over again until she finally stopped making noise.

Tossing the bloody knife onto the ground, I continued to fuck her, enjoying her limp body as my blood-covered cock slid in and out of her, that natural lubricant turning every motion into a smooth, powerful glide. Her glassy eyes stared up at the ceiling, and I studied the blankness in them until a faint gagging sound drew my attention.

I gave my audience a fierce growl. "You better get a stronger stomach, Thomas. This is nothing compared to what I've done before. Besides, I could be fucking *you* instead."

The young teen hid his face, or at least he tried to hide. He was currently tied up in the corner of my work room, so it wasn't like he had many options in the way of shielding his face. He was clean, freshly showered, because I couldn't stand the smell of him anymore. And while I had threatened to fuck him, I wouldn't do it unless he pissed me the fuck off... or Nicholette did. Kids weren't my thing, no matter my involvement with the trafficking ring. I was in it for the money, and there was a lot of money to be had in this business.

But Thomas... He was part of something personal, so I'd make an exception if necessary. Nicholette liked her men rough. Well, I'd prove to her that there was no one like me. Our reunion would be something she would never forget. I threw my head back, cursing Nicholette's name as I came into the still-warm corpse.

Come out, come out, wherever you are, Nicholette.

I'll find you soon enough.

Sacha
Friday

Blood splattered along the tiled wall as the echoes of a gunshot rang in my ears. Vas must have tired of me asking the guy the same questions. In all the time we'd been looking for information, we'd gotten no answers, just more questions, and no sign of Nicholette anywhere. The others remained silent as I adjusted my grip on the bat in my hand, swinging it to hit the dead man over and over again once my anger and pain took over. I needed a release, an outlet, some way to get all these emotions out of me since Nic had disappeared.

Vas was back to being his usual quiet, calm self, but my anger had returned with a vengeance. Oliver and Bodhi had found some comfort in each other, but Oliver was struggling more than usual now that he had told us about his past, or what he remembered of it. We had all worked well together before Nic eased herself in through the cracks in our walls, but now... It felt like our lives had a distinct line down the middle—before Nic and after Nic. Unlike the aftermath of our breakup with Ava, we were not recovering. *At all.*

"Sacha!" Vas called my name harshly, pulling me out of

my thoughts. I stumbled back after he shoved me, glaring up at him, but he just yanked the bat out of my hand. "There's nothing left of him, brother. Go clean up before we have to scrape his fucking brains off the ceiling of the warehouse."

I snarled at him in frustration, but Vas met it with a bland look of his own, his muscles tensing as if he was ready to fight me. Oliver and Bodhi smartly said nothing as I grumbled, stalking out of the torture area and heading toward the showers. I could see Nic around every fucking corner, my life haunted by the woman who had stormed into our lives and stolen our hearts with wild abandon.

This damn warehouse, the apartment, my bedroom... All of it seemed so fucking empty without her mischievous smile or her smartass comments. The hint of vanilla and coffee had long faded from my bed sheets, which made me hate sleeping since I felt her absence more at night. Now, there was nothing but my thoughts to keep me company. The feel of her skin against mine, the way she deferred to me like she did with no one else, her easy acceptance of all of us and our broken pieces... Everything we had shared crossed my mind, making me hate and mourn and *love* her a little more in equal measure. Every part of me ached for her, and there was no sign of her.

She had fucking left us.

Fuck, I need to get my head in the game. Losing myself in thinking about her being gone wasn't going to get her back any faster. Ripping the door open with way more force than necessary, I immediately started stripping out of my clothes, just now noticing the blood and meaty bits all over my suit. With a curse, I tossed the clothes onto the floor, knowing I'd have to throw it all away.

I turned the knob and let the icy cold water pound into me. Part of me hoped the cold water would calm me down, but if anything, it solidified the anger and pain that had been building during the last few weeks. The mental image of two pink lines assaulted my mind, and I punched the tile wall, ignoring the sharp pain that shot up my arm. I let out a yell, hoping the scream would provide some kind of release, but just like with everything else since she'd left, there was nothing to catch me, steady my emotions, even me out. The scream continued, echoing off the tile, until my throat was sore. I closed my eyes under the now warm water as if that would somehow help me, my breath coming in and out in shaky gasps. I should really clean up because the only thing left to do now was to carry on. We'd find her one way or another, then she would never be free of us again.

"Sacha?" The quiet voice broke the whirl of my thoughts. I peeked through the long, wet hair that was obscuring my face to find Bodhi standing by the door, watching me carefully. I didn't sense any fear in him, which was interesting. How had he become the steady one during all of this? During all of this, Bodhi had somehow become not only Oliver's rock, but my own. "Vas and Oli are cleaning up the body. Oli asked me to come in here and make sure you didn't destroy the showers because he doesn't want to find a new warehouse."

A half smile tugged at my lips, the comment breaking through some of my melancholy. "Tell Oliver he can fuck off. If this place survived him chasing down you and Nic, it can deal with my anger."

"Those are two very different things," Bodhi pointed out, running a hand through his short honey-brown hair as his dark brown eyes studied me. "We will find her."

"It's been almost a month," I said gruffly, squeezing my eyes shut. "Rhodes and the others haven't found anything either. The stalker could have her, and we have no way of knowing."

"I don't think they have her," Bodhi replied with conviction as he approached, stopping right in front of me. The splashing droplets from the shower had to be hitting him, but he didn't seem to mind. "I think she did what she always does. Nicholette took matters into her own hands without talking with us, and now she's doing what's necessary."

"And the baby?" I asked as he reached up to push my wet hair out of my face. His fingers trembled for a minute before he could hide the reaction.

"I don't know," he answered honestly, his voice slightly shaky. "I don't know how I feel about it or if Nic would even keep it, to be honest. It's not exactly like we are all... prime parent material. I don't know if I can handle that even with the whole group of us there to take it on together."

"Guess we will find out when we find her again," I told him gently, feeling calmer now that he was close to me. Bodhi might be more confident in Nic's safety than the rest of us, but he rivaled Oliver with his uncertainty when it came to the pregnancy. Being the one who was more settled gave me back some of my control. I couldn't keep my shit together for myself, but I could tighten those reins now that I'd seen these little signs that Bodhi might need something from me.

I reached down, my fingers playing along the bottom of his shirt, enjoying the way his breath caught when my fingers brushed along his bare skin. "Join me?"

Bodhi nodded, a happy smile curling his lips as I pulled his shirt off. He threw his pants and boots toward the door so they didn't get soaked even more. Not waiting for me to take the lead, he wrapped his arms around me and pressed his lips to mine. I groaned, loving the sweet taste of him on my lips as I squeezed him. Strong fingers dug into my hips as he teasingly flicked his tongue along mine, taunting me to take control from him, a challenge I couldn't ignore.

Grabbing his face, I smiled against his lips when he whimpered, completely giving in to me as I backed him against the wall. I broke away and peppered kisses down his neck, loving the way he panted and cursed my name. He was so responsive to everything, so irresistible, but just as I started to go lower, there was a pounding on the door that made both of us freeze.

"Hate to interrupt, but Vas got an urgent message on our voicemail. We have a new client, top priority." Which meant that we had to go to a meeting tonight. *Fuck.* "No meeting requested, but Vas wants to get on it ASAP. He said we would understand once he shares the details."

So much for shower sex. Both of us cleaned up and hurriedly got dressed, though I didn't miss the longing glances he kept shooting my way. Everything was falling apart except my new relationship with him, and those traces of his desire made me smile more easily than anything had in weeks. We hadn't been able to spend much time together alone, not with all of us spiraling in Nic's absence, but he was always there, and it felt nice to have someone I could lean on.

As he slipped on his second boot, I reached for him, pulling him tight against me. I gently brushed my lips across his, wanting to claim one more soft moment for myself before I had to let that fire reignite within me. "Thank you."

"For what?" Bodhi asked breathlessly, and pure male satisfaction filled me. *I* was the one who'd made him react that way.

"For being you."

He swallowed hard, cupping my face in his hands as he rocked up on his toes to firmly kiss me. "Same back at you. Now, let's get to work. Maybe it will distract us for a little bit." Bodhi grinned, snagging my hand and leading the way to the torture space where Vas and Oliver had finished cleaning up.

"What are the job details?" I asked, all business, as we joined them.

My brother looked over at me, his dark brown eyes cool, calculating, probably trying to gauge how I'd react. Whatever he saw there must have satisfied him because, with a slight nod, Vas' hard face smoothed of all expression before he started talking.

"Listen for yourself."

He pushed a button on his cellphone, and a chill ran down my spine when Maeve's voice filled the line.

"Morozov, I have information for you. My contacts have said there is movement in Millfield, but they don't have any details yet. It looks like it's related to the trafficking ring Warren was involved in." There was the shuffle of papers in the background, then she cleared her throat. "There are rumors of members disappearing, more men than the ones I know you've questioned. One of my people was taken. I'll send Sacha the details. Find them. And Nicholette."

Click.

You could have heard a pin drop in the silence that followed the end of that voicemail. Next to me, Bodhi swallowed hard, and Oliver's face was practically gray as he slowly sat down on the bloody chair nearby.

When she'd said Nicholette's name, Maeve's cold voice had actually *cracked*. I hadn't thought the woman was capable of any emotion that wasn't geared toward manipulating others into what she wanted, but it appeared the bitch could experience pain. There was no other reason to explain the raw way she'd sounded; she was, undeniably, affected by her ex-lover's disappearance. I supposed it shouldn't have been any kind of surprise considering how she'd reacted weeks ago.

The moment we realized what had happened, I had gone to pay Maeve a visit. Maeve's shock was clear, and when we mentioned the pregnancy, she had almost fainted. An uneasy alliance had formed that night; we would share information when it came to tracking down Nicholette because, at the end of the day, we all wanted her safe. It definitely wasn't how I saw things going, but I wouldn't complain about the Madame of Ashview being an ally, at least for this.

"I never thought I'd hear that old bitch's walls crack." Oliver broke the silent tension, and even Vas' lips twitched in a mostly suppressed smile.

Bodhi looked over at me, brow furrowed. "She didn't name a price."

"Something I also noted," Vas added. Both men looked at me as I walked over and snagged my phone off the counter. I had placed it there earlier, so it wouldn't get covered in blood. Unlocking it, I opened the secured email app we used for jobs and saw Maeve's email there. I felt my brows rising in surprise as I skimmed its contents, then I forwarded it to Oliver.

"The file on the person we are looking for will be easier to see on the computer. Just sent it to you, Oliver." The younger man hummed in acknowledgment before getting up to grab his laptop. I thought that Vas was going to take Nicholette's absence the hardest, but Oliver was the worst. Bodhi had held steady that we would find her, never wavering in his conviction that she would come back. Vas' anger and rage grew with each day, but it was bottling up inside of him, just waiting for him to explode. Oliver... Maybe it was the fact that he had just shared his history with all of us for the first time, but it felt like he was barely keeping it together. He joked around, but there was more bite than there used to be. Our group had quickly become a powder keg ready to explode... not to mention my cousins and uncle... It would be a volatile reunion whenever we get Nicholette back.

"We should tell the others since it involves Nic," Oliver said as he came back with his laptop, collapsing on the navy couch. Bodhi looked at Vas and me before walking over to sit next to his boyfriend. Oliver didn't say anything to him, but he turned to press a quick kiss to Bodhi's cheek as his lover cuddled into his side.

The others.

I never thought we would have other people join our group dynamic, but while there were some rough patches at times, the three other men fit in fairly well. My and Vas' cousins, Alexei Volkov and Maksim Angeloff, and our uncle Rhodes Angeloff, were all dangerous men in their own right, and things had been nothing but interesting with them joining us. Rhodes and Alexei were obviously hurt by Nic being gone; both of them were acting off. Maksim was harder to read, and while I knew he did miss her, in his own way, most of the time I couldn't tell. It was mostly based on Alexei that I believed my more standoffish cousin was suffering in Nic's absence. Given how close they were, I took his word for it.

Vas settled down on Oliver's other side, looking over the screen as I opened the group chat.

Sacha: We got a new job from Maeve. Related to the trafficking ring Nic's stalker is part of.

I didn't have to wait even a minute for a response.

Rhodes: Come to the compound.
Alexei: Maksim and I are already here. We'll wait for you all to get here.
Maksim: Bring food.
Alexei: He means it will be a long night.
Maksim: And I'm hungry.

I rolled my eyes as I locked my phone.

"That fun, huh?" Oliver joked, drawing my attention.

"Maksim said to bring food on our way to the compound."

Bodhi chuckled, not the least bit put out by Maksim's demand. "Ever practical."

"This is interesting, though," Oliver muttered, looking at the email again. "Her contact is a guy, and he's been working on this ring ever since Warren was killed."

"I noticed that too," I commented, absently running a hand over my face. "I'm gonna need coffee from wherever we get food."

"And there is no payment included in this since it's tied to Nic. Says to use it as a lead. Maeve just reminded us she wants to be kept in the loop," Oliver looked up at me, and I nodded sharply.

"No matter what we think of her, she obviously cared about Nic. And right now, I'll take all the leads we can get," Vas commented as he stood up and started for the door.

"Put in an order for pizza or some shit, and we can bring it with us. Your place has that coffee shop nearby."

"We'll get some on the way," I tacked on, following right after my brother, with Oliver and Bodhi not far behind me.

I hoped this lead was useful. We needed something, *anything*, to think about besides the siren haunting all of our thoughts. As much as I hated not seeing and being with Nicholette, I felt more than a small bit of respect for her ability to hide from us. Underestimating Nic was something I thought I had stopped doing after our first meeting, but she had more skills than any of us knew. That respect didn't do anything to dull the frustration of being so far behind her, though.

Maksim

THERE WAS a rough knock on the office door, then Alexei waltzed in without waiting for me to answer. I rolled my eyes at him, but I didn't bitch about it when he settled on the chair on the other side of my desk. Nic ghosting, the photos from the stalker, and the positive pregnancy test... It had taken its toll on him, which bothered me more than I wanted it to. We had all spent the last four weeks in fucking limbo, and I was goddamn tired of it. It was fucking exhausting keeping up with everyone else's feelings and what I should say and shouldn't. I'd never had to be this emotionally cognizant, and I didn't know how other people functioned like this. How did they live their lives when they had to spend so much time thinking about what other people were feeling or going through? This shit fucking sucked.

"Any new information?"

"No," I replied without looking away from my computer. "I've hit every lead I could find through the Lords. Every lead that was alive, at least. The cousins are thorough."

"I heard something interesting today," Alexei replied quietly, and I looked up to find his green eyes staring intently at me. He was leaning back, looking completely at ease if not for the deadly tone of his voice. "The trafficking ring is having a leak problem. High-ranking members are going missing. Most were never found again, but the few who were... My contacts didn't bother to explain the state the bodies were found in, but it was bad, considering the gray tinge to their faces."

I clicked my tongue and leaned forward, focusing on Alexei as I processed what he'd just said. He was dressed in his usual clothes, black slacks and a dark green button-up that showed off the muscles of the man in front of me. His curly hair was now cut short, not buzzed like my own, but still shorter than I'd seen him have it in years. With Nic gone, he had focused on the job given to us by our cousins with an intensity that would have been concerning for most men. He barely slept, ate like shit, and there were even a few times I saw him smoke a couple of my cigarettes, something he had always said he hated. Rhodes had kept his calm most of the time, though that was a bit of the pot trying to care for the kettle. He had started drinking more the longer Nic had been gone.

I wasn't really sure how I felt about her absence. She was smart, with a wicked sense of humor. Her body was made for sex, and if I thought hard enough, I could still remember the way she cried while riding me, begging for an orgasm. Her being gone sucked, but she had been gone before and came back. My days were more boring without her, and I kept thinking about the horror movies she watched, the way she'd laugh when I bemoaned the villain's inevitable defeat. Alexei told me that probably meant I missed *her*. I had explained my thoughts to him during one of our nights together. It was somehow easier to talk in the dark without looking at him. I trusted him to not use my ineptness at emotion against me.

But mostly... Nicholette got me, that was what I missed most. Alexei got me, and Rhodes did most of the time, but everyone else... Hell, I needed a break just thinking about it.

"Sacha and Vas have been going through all the people associated with the trafficking ring that they can find," I said slowly, reining my wandering thoughts back to the job at hand. "Or the ones we find."

Alexei inclined his head slightly. "As has Rhodes, but none of these names are familiar."

"The Förstner Family had a change of leadership recently. Emmerich is taking over. He could be making his mark," I suggested, making Alexei hum in thought.

"Maybe. You think he would share information with us?"

"Doubt it since he has put off face-to-face meetings with Rhodes since coming back to the East Coast. All his recent deals have been done with representatives coming in his stead," I replied with amusement. "Rhodes has been very irritated because he can only rock the boat so much with the man now that he's the head of the Germans. It's obvious he's prioritizing fixing his own house before worrying about anyone else, even if that someone else is Nicholette. Too many repercussions if he pisses them off or pushes too far. Fucking politics."

Alexei had opened his mouth to say something else

when an alarm beeped on my computer. Opening up the security footage, I saw Sacha and the others driving up. "They better have brought food. I'm fucking starving."

"Just try to not start shit with Vas tonight," he muttered as he stood up.

"That sounds like a boring as fuck night," I joked, laughing when he shook his head. I followed him out of the office. Quietly, we walked down the hallway and got downstairs just as Rhodes strode out to the first floor to meet us. My uncle's long hair was slicked back as usual, though I had noticed more lines to his face than there had been a month ago.

The ground level was a large open space that used to be the factory floor. Now it featured groupings of sofas, coffee tables, and pool tables, and in the back was where some of the members did work on their bikes. It was a nice space overall, thanks to its many uses, from club meetings to orgies to a torture room.

While I was looking around at our place, the brothers walked in with Bodhi and Oli behind them, both men carrying pizza boxes.

"What did the ice queen say?" Rhodes asked, not bothering with a greeting or small talk of any kind.

Bodhi and Oli laughed a bit at the nickname, putting the pizza boxes down on top of one of the coffee tables. The rest of the club had been cleared out by Rhodes as soon as Sacha had texted us.

"One of her contacts was investigating the ring when he disappeared," Sacha informed us firmly. "She gave us his information and all the information he had gathered before going silent."

"I have news as well," Alexei said as we walked over to join them, him settling on the end of the couch as I sat in the middle, grabbing three slices of pizza. "Higher ups in the ring have been going missing, but no one knows who is responsible. Brian only said two names, but neither of them are ones we've questioned."

"Who?" Vas asked him as Sacha grabbed a seat. Bodhi sat next to me, with Oli sitting on the arm of the sofa beside his boyfriend. Rhodes pulled up another chair, his steely gaze studying all of us intently.

"Karen Ellenburg and Tim Johnson. He didn't give any other information though."

"I'll look up the names after I eat this slice," Oli said when Sacha glanced in his direction.

"I'll search for Karen, and you take Tim?" I offered, and the younger man gave me a thumbs up as I took a bite of my food.

"What about Maeve's informant?"

"A guy named Gabriel. We figured we'd look at it all here together. Make things easier," Sacha said easily, drinking the coffee in his hand in favor of ignoring the pizza on the table. "He worked for her for a while, then he opened his own boutique in the city. Olive and Grove."

Oli choked hard enough that Bodhi reached up and smacked his back a few times until his boyfriend could breathe. "Did you say Olive and Grove?!"

"You know it?" Rhodes asked. Oliver nodded, but the movement was immediately followed up by a shake of his head.

"Tell us," Sacha ordered.

"Never been there. But after our apartment was broken into and all of Nic's stuff was destroyed, she went there to get clothes. I remember seeing the name on some of the bags."

All the men around me stilled. I took the last bite of

pizza and stood up, wiping my hands on my jeans. "You all look at the shop. I'm going to check into the bitch's name." Without looking back, I walked upstairs and back to my office, snagging my pack of smokes off the desk. I lit up a smoke before unlocking the computer. I'd start with the easy legal shit like Google. Karen Ellenburg was an older suburban grandmother. There were tons of pictures of her with grandkids, nine adults that looked like her kids, and other posterworthy family photos. A fucking lie if I ever saw one.

"Where is your dirty laundry?" I muttered, blowing smoke out one side of my mouth while I kept scrolling.

Sixty-eight years old, mother of nine, and grandmother to twenty-seven grandkids. She was the president of a local homeowners association, a widow, and she'd just sold her florist business a few weeks ago. Karen had gone missing two days ago, and the family was beside themselves. A fifty-thousand-dollar reward had been allocated for leads, but nothing had come to fruition yet. The police had nothing—no leads, information, or even ideas for suspects. From what I saw in the news articles, their best guess was that she'd walked away.

Nothing fucking useful.

Taking another drag of my cigarette, I savored the nicotine filling me as I pulled up another website and typed in her name. *Still nothing.* No police record. Nothing about her would even hint at being part of something as horrific as a trafficking ring.

"Let me guess..." Oliver's voice had me jolting, and I found him walking in with his laptop in hand. "Clean record. Wholesome image. Nothing about her would suggest that she's a criminal?"

"Same for Tim?"

"Yup," he replied, sounding resigned, as he sat down in the chair Alexei had sat in earlier. "I'll need to go off grid to look deeper. I'll have to do it tomorrow."

"Not tonight?"

"Nah." He shook his head, looking up at me with tired hazel eyes as he ran a hand through his tousled dirty blonde hair. "Better to do it early in the morning. For some reason, people expect hackers to hit at night. Plus, last time I went in was at night. I like to change it up to keep people on their toes. Want to join me?"

"Sure," I answered slowly. "I need coffee though. I'm used to going to sleep at four in the morning."

"If you're good with cheap Dunkin, I got you. Otherwise, it's on you."

"As long as it has caffeine, I don't care," I told him honestly.

"I'll even bring you a fresh pack." He tipped his head toward my cigarettes. "I think you're going to need it, or I will at least."

"You don't smoke."

"Going back into my past like this... I might have to take it up." He gave me a wane smile before getting up. "I'll pick you up at five."

"Great," I drawled, making him laugh as he left the office. I wasn't looking forward to such an early morning, but the sound of Nic's laughter and her smile as she looked at me filled my mind...

For her, I could deal with an obnoxiously early morning. Fuck, if Alexei was right about me, about the things I could feel for her...

For her, I'd deal with a lot fucking more than that.

Nicholette
Friday

S creams filled the air as I wiped at the blood on my face, annoyance filling me, directed at the pathetic person crying out. She was an older woman who was part of the upper crust, one of the rich snobs from the suburbs of Boston. The reason she was graced with my company right now was that she was also a high-profile client of the Ashview Hills trafficking ring. Disgust soon took over when she began to whimper, begging me for mercy.

Apparently, the last two days hadn't clued her in that I didn't have any mercy left in me. *None.* I was void of mercy and morals. All the lines I thought I had were disappearing one by one the longer I was away from the life I had started to build for myself. I didn't know if it was just me or the raging pregnancy hormones that raced through my veins, but I felt cold, calculating. Sadly, I never reached that numb state that would make my separation from the guys any easier.

I considered the woman tied on the chair in front of me. She was naked, though you wouldn't be able to tell at first glance given the amount of blood all over her. Her nose was horribly broken, sitting at an unnatural angle after I had punched her. It had been a convenient handle to drag her over to the far corner of the room where I had her trussed up for a while. Torture session or not, sometimes a girl had to take a minute to get other shit done, ya know? The corner was where she had sat, whimpering and uselessly pulling at her constraints, until I tied her up on the chair she now occupied.

Her whimpering cut off into soft sobs and gasps when my steps brought me closer to her. Grabbing her chin roughly I yanked her head up to force her to meet my cool gaze. "Are you going to tell me what I want to know now?"

"I don't know!" she wailed, her entire body trembling. I tsked tauntingly, not believing a word of her supposed ignorance. "*Please,* you have to believe me! They don't share their identities. The anonymity is the entire point of the ring!"

"I thought the entire *point* was for you all to get children to take advantage of and abuse?" I asked, my other hand unconsciously resting on my still flat stomach. "Give me your point of contact. Give me *something,* and I'll *consider* giving you mercy in return."

"I-I-" she stuttered, and I dropped her chin, pulling back my hand to smack her hard enough to whip her head to the side.

"You should think very carefully about your answer, Karen. Because I know enough about you that I can make everything that happened so far seem like fucking child's play. After all, you have a lot of children that I hunt down. What would be more fun than killing them right in front of you? After I tell them your dirty little secrets, of course. How long will it take you to break then, hmm? I don't think you'd last long."

"You're insane," she whispered raggedly.

"I'm pissed, pregnant, and in pain," I hissed, walking away from her, my bare feet silent on the concrete floor. "Someone thought they could take my brother to get to me —a *very* stupid mistake, so if you're going to continue playing dumb, you'll become my message. Your other colleagues took me up on the offer of mercy. So, bitch, it's your decision. By all means, give me the fucking chance... I've had dreams about using this."

Ending my taunts, I grabbed the cattle prod from the corner, zapping it so I could revel in the growing fear on her face. Those faded blue eyes of hers had widened in shock, which almost sent a little shiver up my spine. With all my guys safely away from me, I needed to get my kicks somehow. Walking back over to her, I raised it up, holding it on her exposed pussy, and waited. "What will it be?"

"Joe!" she screamed, her voice cracking as she tried and failed to wiggle away from the weapon. "Joe Graves! He's my contact. I know he's high ranking, higher than myself, but that's it. Him and his wife. Miranda."

Hitting the trigger, I basked in her wails and screams until they echoed in the space. It almost drowned out my whirling thoughts, but it didn't quite do the trick. Her answer was too shocking for me to avoid thinking about it for long.

Joe Graves. Miranda Graves. My parents.

They'd thrown me out for being bisexual, but they were involved in a child trafficking ring. Where the fuck did they get their righteous sense of superiority from? Had my brother even been safe at home? Had I failed him so completely by leaving him behind in what passed for their "care"? If I thought I'd felt cold before, that was fucking nothing compared to the ice rushing in my veins now.

Many people said their anger ran hot, scorching through their veins until they had no choice but to explode, trying to get that heat out from under their skin. But mine was often cold, a source that had once numbed my inhibitions until the day I'd long run out of those. Right now, the icy anger gave me a hint of solace, letting me put aside the family baggage I would need to deal with in order to finish taking care of my guest.

Moving the prod to her chest, I electrocuted her again, the scent of burnt flesh making me drop the cattle prod to the ground. I enjoyed the pain it inflicted on this woman who so sorely deserved it, but that would never be a pleasant smell. Grabbing the knife I always kept strapped to my thigh, I stabbed her in the eye, the warmth of her blood and the gel-like liquid from her eye covering my hand. It centered me somehow, knowing that the pain I felt was being experienced, given life—just not through me.

In the month I had been gone from my men, I had been searching for answers. It wasn't just my safety hanging in the balance; it was theirs, and the baby's. I hated being away from them, and I knew they would give me hell when I came back... because I *did* plan to come back. I just hoped that they understood after they worked through their anger.

They would burn down the world to save me. How could I give them anything less?

Pulling the knife out of her, I shook it, flinging off the fleshy bits, as I walked over to the cabinet. This blade deserved a careful cleaning. It was the one Vas had given me after carving his name into my inner thigh. It was my connection to him, to all of them, besides the baby growing inside of me, and I always kept it close.

Right now, I couldn't let myself get lost in the yearning I had for my men. I had to deal with the news Karen had shared with me, but my father's name, my mother's... They meant that the place I had been avoiding was where I would need to go. Millfield, Vermont was where this was going to play out, or at least some of it. My hometown had answers, and as much as I would rather raze the place to the ground than set foot back on its soil, I needed those answers first.

But I can't do it alone.

I wasn't ready to go back to my men yet. The puzzle of my stalker was something I hadn't figured out, and everything I had done so far, I couldn't throw it all away. My friend who had helped me stay under the radar had been MIA for the past four days, which I knew meant trouble. This way of life was hard, brutal, and mostly short-lived, so I needed to think of other options.

My brain immediately started running through my connections. I knew it was time to call them, or at least *some* of them. Ignoring the dead woman and the cries from my waiting victims in the other room, I walked upstairs, not caring that I was naked and covered in blood and other bits. Within seconds, I was standing in the kitchen, dialing a number on my burner phone.

By the second ring, a smooth, professional voice answered, "Roderick."

"Is Em back in Boston?" I asked, my voice empty. I was sidestepping the small talk, I knew that, but I just didn't have it in me to play that game right now.

There was a long pause, then the man on the other end cleared his throat. "Nicholette. It's good to hear from you again. Emmerich is back on the East Coast, yes. He's busy setting up business contacts now that he is the head of the Family."

"The king is dead, long live the king." I laughed, threading a bloody hand through my hair. "Congrats to him.

Any updates on what's going on?" My question might be vague, but he would know what I was referring to.

"Your men aren't the only ones tearing apart the city looking for you. Detective Lewis is calling me for updates. He wants to question you."

"He's still on the force?"

"Yes." Roderick sounded frustrated, and I heard papers rustling on his end of the line. "His union rep was really good. Besides a slap on the wrist, nothing was done about his conduct with you."

"Not surprising," I sighed. "Prostitute's word against a detective's."

"Detective Allen has also reached out to speak with you about some murders that happened." I swallowed hard at that, flashes of the pictures plastered all over my old apartment flickering across my mind's eye.

"Set up a time. Next week at your office. I'll stop by and get details soon."

"I can do that."

"Thanks."

"Nicholette? If you need any help, I'm here."

"A full-service lawyer?" I joked, but Roderick just hummed.

"I am for those on the list." I chewed on my lip, heart pounding in my head as I placed a hand over my stomach. It had started to turn during this conversation. *Please don't get sick.* "If you need me to pick you up, or if you need a place to stay, let me know."

I turned the offer of help over in my head. Would this backfire on both of us if I took him up on it? "I'll keep that in mind for the future. Thank you."

Click.

I hung up the phone without waiting for him to say

anything else, then I turned the burner off. I couldn't take the chance of someone tracing any of my calls. Coming out of my hideaway wasn't something I was looking forward to. I had kept myself isolated but informed while hunting down connections in the trafficking ring, starting with William and working my way up the ladder.

My stomach turned, and I reached for a nearby drawer, pulling out the box of saltines I had gotten yesterday. The sleeve was ripped open with care, then I shoved a cracker into my mouth to help settle my nausea. I thought over how I would handle leaving, trying to figure out what needed to be done before I could head out. I still had a few more people waiting downstairs. I'd heard their screams and crying while questioning Karen, but the sounds were more annoying than anything. Padding through the kitchen, I went to the bathroom, and as I washed my hands, I looked myself over. My hair was a tangled mess, there were black circles under my eyes, and saying I looked sick was an understatement. Ever since I had left, my sleep was shit. I wished I could blame it on morning sickness, but in reality, it was because sleeping alone didn't hold the same appeal it used to.

As my nausea settled, I clenched my hand on my stomach. I still couldn't believe that I was pregnant, much less that I was *still* pregnant. I remembered walking into the clinic and what had followed. The impersonal doctor had swiftly removed the IUD with a small warning about me having a chance of miscarriage due to the procedure. Needless to say, life apparently had other plans for me because I stayed pregnant. Morning sickness became all-day sickness. There was nothing like throwing up on people to get them to give you answers. It had been disgusting... but it worked. I wrinkled my nose, remembering how I'd had to hose the body down before I disposed of it.

A cry from downstairs had me back to the situation at hand. I'd question all of them back-to-back then clean up before heading into the city. Before I met up with anyone, I needed to fix myself up. Haircut, new clothes, a spa day for self-care so I could introduce everyone to the ruthless killer I had been shaped into. I always thought motherhood would make someone more caring, empathetic, soft... I was wrong. Any morals I used to have, any limitations, they had gone out the window. Now, my only priority was to protect everyone that mattered to me.

Heading back downstairs, a small smile curled my face. I didn't need to see it to know it was terrifying. I felt cold, clear headed, as I ignored the body parts tossed around the room and headed for the locked door. It was time to get more creative because I had better places to be than sitting here with these freaks. My stalker had started a battle, and I doubted they were ready for the hellfire I was going to rain down on them.

They wanted a fight?

I was going to bring them war.

Nicholette
Sunday

The building was a typical brick condo building, or that's what it looked like on the outside, but I knew that behind those rows of small windows was the infamous Förstner Family. Finishing the last bit of my coffee, I approached the door and reached for the security pad, punching in the pin while I graced the camera with a smirk that was all me. I let myself inside the building. *Em should really get that changed.*

Industrial loft-style was the first thing that came to mind as I looked around at the exposed brick and ventilation along the ceiling. It hadn't changed since the last time I had been here. Light hardwood flooring flowed throughout the space, and the only sound in the building was my heels clicking on the hardwood as I walked toward the kitchen. The room was huge, the kitchen featuring a sprawling island with modern cabinets and appliances that would make any Ikea catalog jealous. I hummed, throwing away my coffee as I settled on a barstool at the island, content to wait for someone to find me. *I wonder if they have any food...*

I'd had a bite to eat in between my makeover and purchasing new clothes, but I was so fucking hungry —again.

After I sat there for twenty minutes or so, I said fuck it and got up, rifling through the cabinets. Of course, I didn't find anything that I could eat without having to cook. *Motherfuckers.* I let out an annoyed sigh just as the front door opened. Even, measured footsteps wandered through the house as if looking for something or someone, but the cadence was familiar, so I didn't bother hiding. I had a cocky, taunting smile on my face by the time Blake entered the kitchen with a grim expression and gun at the ready.

"You brat," they said by way of greeting, lowering the gun in their hand.

Not the least bit shy, I gave them a once, then twice-over, seeing how much they had changed since I last saw them. Long brown hair was cut short into something similar to a pixie with an undercut. The bit of hair on top was slicked back, giving the illusion of a more masculine cut. They had on a big black AC/DC t-shirt and gray sweatpants that looked way too fucking hot for the weather outside. One could probably say the same for my black pantsuit, but I needed to look good more than I needed to feel cool right now. The clothes made me feel more put together and in control, which was something I desperately needed.

"You look good, Blake," I told them honestly. Their brown eyes were sparkling with good humor as they approached me, switching the safety on then tucking their gun somewhere I couldn't see under their shirt. "But you weren't who I was expecting to run into, at least not yet."

"Emmerich is on his way," Blake replied, wrapping an

arm around my shoulders. They squeezed me for a minute before leaving it there. "I'm saving my questions until he's here, but I have plenty by the way."

"I'm sure you do, and Em, too. Not to mention my guys, who I'm sure have contacted you both."

"Your Russians are dedicated," Blake said with a huff of exasperation. "Sacha and Vas both showed up here as soon as we were back from Seattle, *demanding* answers from Emmerich and me. Very bold, I'll give them that. Not that we had anything to share with them since you had gone rogue."

I swallowed hard, hating the tears stinging my eyes at just the mention of their names. Fucking hormones were jerks. "Sounds about right," I rasped, clearing my throat as I pulled away from their side. "I need food. Sooner rather than later. You don't want to see the rage of a pregnant woman needing to eat."

Their gaze flicked down to my still-flat stomach, then up again, before nodding a few times. "Sit down. How the fuck you're even wearing heels is beyond me."

"It makes my legs look longer." I shrugged, glad they were letting me change the subject. "As you know, they are one of my best features."

"That and your psychotic mind," a smooth voice said. I turned, then froze. A man with shoulder-length wavy blond hair stared at me with intense blue eyes. *Atlas.* He looked so fucking familiar, yet not. I couldn't put my finger on exactly why that was. Maybe it was his longer hair? I could be reading into things though, or it could be hormones. I'd only met him a handful of times before he ghosted like Blake had.

I hadn't heard him enter the room, him or the men

behind him. One looked to be almost thirty, with dark buzzed hair and haunted light blue eyes that studied me with equal parts curiosity and suspicion. Two older men were behind him, near the entrance to the living room, watching me carefully. Both had dark brown, almost black hair, but the one that was slightly older had hints of gray.

"I'm glad you appreciate my favorite asset." I moved my focus back to Atlas, who laughed sharply at that. "Are they all with you, Blake?"

"Yes. Unlike you, I don't need to collect every person I come across, so that's all of them," Blake deadpanned, and I laughed, not the least bit insulted. I mean, they were right. I *had* been adding to my group of psychos at a rate that should have alarmed me.

"I didn't do it on purpose." I shrugged then walked around the island, settling onto the stool I had left just a few minutes ago. "But why would I complain? They fuck me like they want to kill me. Girl's gotta have standards."

"Has one of them actually tried to kill you during sex?" Atlas asked, claiming an open seat beside me before giving me a quick side hug. I leaned into it, then pulled back, meeting his curious gaze. His blue eyes were intent on me, but I could hear Blake moving around in the kitchen while the men behind Atlas shifted a bit.

I hummed, thinking it over, and shook my head after a minute. "*Actually* kill me? No. Could they have, though? Hell yes, and the possibility alone is delicious. Like I said, standards, Atlas. If you aren't bleeding and bruised by the end, what's the point?"

"You think they offer a group therapy discount for the mafia?" Atlas asked, making the older men and Blake chuckle. Even the guy with buzzed hair smiled a little bit.

"I'm not mafia." I waved a hand, dismissing his joke. "I'd probably scare them away with my issues. Besides, if I work through everything, where will my edge of mystery go? Do I get an introduction?"

Blake, who had been going through the cabinets and fridge, getting food together, turned and pointed to each man. "Atlas, you know. Wulf is the one trying to figure out how to ask me who you are. Robin, beside him, has figured it out and is trying not to show that he has figured it out. Conrad is the one with the buzzed hair. Keep some boundaries there. Guys, Nicholette."

I flipped my hair over my shoulder as I rolled my eyes. "I see your introductions haven't changed since we last saw each other. Hey, guys."

"How else should I have introduced you to Emmerich?" Blake asked, laughter in their voice as they looked to the side.

"Literally any other way than how you did would have been great." Emmerich's sassy voice filled the room as he sauntered in and beelined right for me. He scooped me up, grunting when I looped my arms around his neck and held him tight. I gave him a quick warning to not spin me, so he just squeezed me instead. "I'm *so* beating your fucking ass, Nic. Where the hell have you been?"

I pulled back to meet his glare with a wide-eyed, innocent expression. "Busy."

"Busy could mean a lot of things," Em said dryly as the others relaxed a bit. I could tell Wulf was still trying to figure out how he must know my name, but he'd lost some of the stiffness in his shoulders.

"Do I want to know how they know my name?" I asked, gesturing at Blake's men.

"Oh, they might have heard about me walking in on you and Blake fucking," Em said easily. "Guys, meet Nic, the prostitute-turned-call-girl and one of the most prolific serial killers on the East Coast."

"I don't know if *prolific* is the word I would use. I'm a little young for that particular title. Besides, there is so much competition around to compare me to," I protested even though I felt a warm sense of pride at that declaration. "Anyway, a girl has to have a hobby."

"Killing people?" the guy with buzzed hair, Conrad, asked softly.

"Blood and lust make the world go round," I replied casually as Emmerich slowly set me down. He didn't leave my side, and I knew that spoke more to the way he felt about our friendship rather than any lack of trust in his sibling's partners. "Is that food ready? I'm starving."

"If you aren't cooking, no bitching."

"If you still want a kitchen, you don't want me to cook," I snarked back.

"Then shut it," they commented, starting to throw together what looked like hamburgers, which luckily didn't make my stomach turn.

"You said you were busy. With what? I'm not taking another deflection," Em warned.

My face smoothed out, and I purred, "I have a business proposition for you, Emmerich."

"A business proposition? With you?" Emmerich arched an eyebrow, but he stood there waiting for more. From someone else, I would have smacked them for the implied insult, but right now, it gave me an advantage so I let it slide.

"*Me*. The woman who is intimately tied to very close business partners of yours... and the person who has found an in with your trafficking rival." I didn't blink when

Emmerich's mouth dropped open in shock. The others froze, their attention focused on me, but I ignored them all for the man in front of me. "You just took over after your uncle's... untimely demise. I might have been hiding out, Em, but I still kept tabs on what's going on. I can help you show everyone your iron fist and your strength as the new leader of the Family by taking care of the rival your uncle could never touch."

"A bold claim," he said softly, his sharp, cold green eyes searching my face. I couldn't tell what he was thinking, but I had my game face on as well. This was business, not two friends talking or me calling in a favor.

"A true one. I had everything taken from me, Em. *Everything.* My life, my future, and my *brother.*" I felt Atlas jerk at that, but I didn't look his way to see what was going on with him. "I've spent the last month hiding and working my way through names associated with the trafficking ring in Ashview to find my stalker and Thomas."

"And what's the price for this information?" Blake asked.

"The contacts I found... Their deaths are mine. And I want you all to help me find my brother, like we originally discussed. But this time it's not part of the favors you owe me. I'll hold on to those."

"And your stalker?" Emmerich asked.

"How far are you willing to go?" Blake added on.

"There is nothing I wouldn't do to protect what is mine. *Nothing.*" A cruel smile curled my lips. "It's funny, you know. I thought being pregnant would make me more cautious, but they chose the wrong bitch to play with because it's just made me even more bloodthirsty."

"Pregnant?!" Atlas asked, his voice cracking.

"It's not yours," I joked, glancing at him again. "Relax,

Atlas. Do we have a deal, Em?" I held out a hand, waiting to see what he would do.

After watching me for a minute, he grasped my offered hand, sealing the deal. "Name."

"Joe and Miranda Graves. They're in the inner circle of the ones running the show."

"Nic..." Emmerich's eyes widened, his hand letting go of mine, but I shook my head.

I tsked at him, lightly patting his cheek. "You'll need to work on that poker face, sweetheart. It seems I get to do something I never wanted to do. I get to go home."

"And the Russians? When are you getting them involved?" Blake asked, breaking the tense silence.

I just chuckled, amused by their question. "What makes you think they aren't already involved?"

"What does that even mean? If they saw you, there's no way you would be here right now," Em shot back, his brow furrowed as he tried to read between the lines.

"Is someone going to fill the rest of us in on what's going on?" Robin asked dryly, and I bit my lip, trying not to laugh any more. "Half conversations are only informative if you know everything to begin with."

"I have a stalker. They kidnapped my brother and said they would sell him to the highest bidder if I didn't dump my guys," I responded blandly, moving my focus from my best friend to one of the men I had just met. Out of the corner of my eye, I saw how pale Atlas had gotten, but I kept my focus on the one who had asked. Something about all of this was really getting to Atlas, and from the concern on the other men's faces when they glanced at him, they could tell as well. "As for the Russians, they're the men I'm with, the ones I had to leave behind to deal with all this bullshit."

"Which ones?" Wulf asked, rubbing his fingers together in a way that reminded me of Rhodes and Maksim when they started craving more nicotine. "I've met a few in Ashview on business over the years."

"All of them," I replied with a sad smile. "Oh, I also have a meeting with Allen next week. I don't need to deal with the police on my ass along with everything else happening. There were a few other names I wanted to track down before I came back, but others got to them first."

"Your men have been very thorough," Em said gruffly. "I told you they would tear the city apart to find you."

"And as a heads up..." Blake didn't turn to look at me as they spoke. They just kept flipping the burgers like all of this was no big deal. "They know you're pregnant. To be honest, I'm surprised you kept it."

"I am too." A broken laugh escaped me. "Besides getting my IUD out at some clinic, I haven't been able to deal with anything else. Getting it removed meant there was a chance I would miscarry, but I guess life decided this would stick."

"If you had gone to the safe house we set aside for you..." Em started, finally taking the seat beside me as the other men joined us in the kitchen. Conrad and Wulfric went to a far window, cracking it open and each lighting a cigarette. Robin came to a stop beside Atlas, his body pressed against the younger man's side. Atlas leaned into him, seeking comfort, and some of his tension drained away. "You would have had a doctor to see."

"But Sacha and Vas came to see you right when you got here," I told him. "Sacha would have known you were lying, and given what they've done to look for me, I knew he wouldn't hold back just because of who you are."

"How the fuck do you know they came here?" Em asked.

"I told her," Blake said to their brother before changing the topic. "So, where did you go?"

"A friend's. His name is Gabriel. Used to work for Maeve until he retired, at least from sex work. He was part of her network of contacts. He put me up in one of his hideouts and stopped by a few times to check on me, but there's been nothing but radio silence from him for the past few days." Emmerich hummed as Blake slowly nodded.

"Who is Allen?" Conrad said from the other side of the room. "You said you have a meeting with him next week."

"He's a detective in Ashview, a contact of ours," Blake answered.

"And he needs to question me about the murders in Ashview, I'm sure. Maybe about the whole rapist thing as well." I waved a hand, not really worried about that right now. "As long as Lewis isn't there, I'll be fine. Regardless, Roderick will be with me the entire time, so I should be fine."

"Roderick?" Emmerich asked, his body tensing.

"Who do you think confirmed you were going to be here?" I smirked when he started to curse. "You put me on his list, Em. He's my lawyer for this, and after my last run-in with Lewis, all questioning and communication with me happens through him. But enough about me. How did things go in Seattle?"

"We settled the score and left the city in shambles," Blake replied after a beat of heavy silence. They turned around with a plate full of burgers then tossed a bag of buns on the table beside it. "If you want condiments or something, you can get it yourself."

"Someone after my own heart." I sighed in happiness, reaching for a bun and a burger. "I'm too hungry to worry about anything being on it." My phone beeped right before

I could take my first bite. Switching the burger to one hand, I reached for my inner pocket, reading the text before locking the phone and digging in. *Fuck, it's delicious.*

"I'm going to get some fresh air for a minute." Atlas stood up without saying anything else and walked past the others to go into the small backyard. Robin took a step forward before Conrad motioned him to stay; he turned to follow Atlas outside. The latch of the closing door was the only sound for a few minutes before I felt a sharp stare from Blake.

"Don't push them, Nicholette. Conrad *or* Atlas."

I arched an eyebrow but changed the subject all the same. "I wasn't going to. Anyway, when are we going to Ashview to get started?"

"In a few days. There are some things I need to settle first." Em rubbed his chin.

"That's perfect. I need to reach out to a few more people while we're here," I replied between bites. "Get a few things lined up and in progress before I show back up."

"You need a doctor visit," Blake said softly. "We should do that before we go down there. We have some people up here, so it won't leave a paper trail for your stalker to find." My mouth was suddenly dry, nerves making it hard to swallow the food I had been chewing. I nodded, not trusting myself to talk just yet. "And you didn't ask," Blake continued without missing a beat, "but your guys? They look like shit. Even Rhodes, who was beyond pissed off that I went to our last business deal instead of Emmerich."

"As they should be. I did leave them," I quipped, pushing away the twinge of guilt tugging at my heartstrings. "Thanks for the burgers, Blake. I'm going to go throw up half of it then sleep. I'll see you all later."

Finishing up my second burger, I stood up, ignoring the

stares on me. I was just about to leave the kitchen when Emmerich broke the silence. "You don't need us to show you where to go?"

A grin spread across my face as I stopped and looked over my shoulder. "You should change the code for the keypad, Em. It's still the same one Frederick gave me when I came up here."

The way Blake's face grayed, I knew they'd filled in the blanks of what that meant. Not saying anything else, I made my way upstairs to a guest room I had used before, wanting a space with an attached bedroom. I didn't know the history between Frederick and everyone in his Family, but I knew he had been a complete fucking asshole. He might have been a monster to the people under him, but he was utterly boring and disappointing in bed—a fact that I ignored because he paid me well and had introduced me to his brother. And his brother... Fuck, there was nothing even remotely vanilla about *him*.

As the first wave of nausea hit me, I kicked my heels off and made it to the toilet to throw up. I knew this was just the beginning since morning sickness was a fucking bitch. Just then, my phone beeped again with another text message.

Private number: I cleaned up the mess you left behind, and I saw your message.
Private number: I'll be in Boston tonight.

Well, this was going to be fun. I wasn't sure how to give Emmerich and Blake a heads up about the company coming our way, so I decided to not say anything at all. Might as well keep everyone on their toes with the amount of favors I was prepared to call in to save Thomas and get rid of my stalker. I wanted my life back.

Lightly, I rested a hand on my stomach as I heaved again, bile making my mouth bitter. Tears ran down my cheeks, the privacy of the room meaning I could let my walls down. I wished the guys were here, so I didn't have to do this alone. Sacha and Alexei wouldn't care about holding my hair out of the way. Vas would be overprotective to the point of annoying, while Oli and Bodhi would be trying to figure out how they felt about all this. Maksim and Rhodes would be practical to a fault when it came to helping me with pregnancy stuff, but I thought they would appreciate the added curves that would be coming thanks to my changing body.

Well, that's how they would react if they took the news well. What did they think when they figured out I was pregnant? Did they understand why I left? Did they hate me? I wasn't sure if I was ready for those answers. Regardless, I knew our reunion was going to be explosive no matter their thoughts about the baby.

My body and heart ached for all of them. Vas and Sacha's controlling, dominating ways. The crazy laugh of Oli's that always made me burst out in laughter along with him. Bodhi's sweet and mischievous expression. Rhodes' possessive command of me when we were alone. Alexei's unfailing patience and Maksim's bluntness... God, I missed them.

I wiped the back of my hand across my lips as I flushed the toilet and sat down on the floor. *Alone.* I'd been alone so much of my life. Even as a child, I'd been surrounded by people but alone all the same. I had never felt as lonely as I did right now, pregnant and puking, and the emptiness of the room beyond the bathroom almost mocked me.

Sleep. That's what I need. These emotions and nostalgic thoughts wouldn't get me back to them sooner. I needed to get my fucking shit together and kick some ass. I'd need every fucking guard up and steady before I went back to the place I never wanted to revisit.

Home.

Oliver
Sunday

"Well, Maksim and I found some really fucking interesting and sick things during our search yesterday," I said by way of greeting as I walked into the compound. Maksim was beside me, being his usual bubbly, talkative self. Surprisingly, we had worked together pretty well. He listened to my bullshit commentary as I dug into the trafficking ring and stayed silent, focused on the task at hand. It worked out for both of us.

We had gone to one of my hiding places off the grid to hack and reach out to darknet contacts about the names we had gotten. But it had taken so long, and both of us hadn't slept at all the night before, so we ended up crashing on the couches in the rundown apartment for the day. Luckily, I had managed to text Bodhi to tell him the change of plans before I couldn't stay awake any longer.

"What did you find?" Rhodes and Sacha asked at the same time. Both of them were sitting in Rhodes' office. Rhodes was leaning back in his chair behind his desk while Sacha was in the chair across from him. The older man had a glass in hand, though it didn't look like he had drunk much yet, which was good. It looked like they had been discussing something, but as soon as we walked in, they had quieted, their gazes fixated on us.

"They are definitely part of the trafficking ring here in Ashview," Maksim started, running a hand over his buzzed hair. "Both had similar cash withdrawals around the same time and bookings at the hotel you guys found in Millfield."

"There were also phone calls and texts between the same three numbers for both Karen and Tim," I added, grabbing the free chair beside Sacha and flopping down. "We checked out the numbers, but they were burners, and we couldn't find any info on them. From the looks of things, there's a website for this ring. I couldn't find it while we were gone, so I honestly think I'll need to go underground for a while to get it. I'm sure they have crazy security, but if we find even a *hint* of the trail to get there, then I can get in."

Digging into them would cost me. Hell, even this small dive had made me grab a few of Maksim's cigarettes— thankfully something he didn't care about. The walls I'd had up for so long were dust now. Memories of my captivity were slowly coming back, and I hated it. I'd do this for Nic, which showed how much I felt for her, but that didn't mean I wouldn't make her pay for it later.

"But there's something else. They're both missing," Maksim dropped our biggest bombshell with his usual bluntness. "They both went missing around the same time, and their families are frantic. Thousands are being offered as a reward for information."

"Interesting," Rhodes murmured, carefully setting the glass down on his desk as he thought that over.

"That's all we get? *Interesting*?" I snarked, arching an eyebrow.

Rhodes didn't take offense; humor flashed through his gray eyes as he stared at me. "That's how you described it when you came in here. I was just agreeing with you. How many is that now? Ten people from the trafficking ring that we've tried to get ahold of only to find them missing."

It took a minute for my brain to catch up to what he was hinting at, then my jaw dropped. Lust hit me with surprising strength. The thought of what was happening to those sick fucks shouldn't turn me on, but fuck, it *really* did. "You think Nic is responsible?"

"She ran," Sacha said softly, staring off in the distance. "For the boy in the picture, who may or may not be her brother, she left all of us behind, and she might be pregnant. All of those things could make her snap. Not that she needed to snap to be able to do this... but so many big things, so fast... She had plenty of motivation."

"Or she could just be really, really fucking pissed," Maksim said dryly. He was a man of few words, but us all working together to find Nicholette was making him more comfortable around us. Now that we'd spent some time together, we were getting more than one-word answers and snarky commentary. Well, Vas didn't, but I'd come to realize that that was just how they were with each other. "But we have no proof as to who took them. Maybe the trafficking ring raising their security is because of what's happening with the Förstners? Emmerich took over the Family recently, so he could be sending a message to not mess with him."

"Possibly." Rhodes inclined his head slightly. "He has been too busy to pick up his own shipments. Apparently."

A throat clearing made us all look up to find Razor, one of Rhodes' men, standing in the doorway. "We just had a delivery. It has all of your names on it."

"What?" Rhodes questioned as he stood up.

"It's not just for you, Pres. All of you that are with Nicholette, your names are on it," Razor said, his stoic expression breaking for a minute. That only showed how concerned he really was. "It's not going to be good."

We all shared a look and hurried out of the office, following Razor downstairs and outside to find Alexei, Vas, and Bodhi joining us. Bodhi walked over to stand between Sacha and me, concern in his honey brown eyes as he pushed his long hair out of his face.

He brushed his hand against mine, but we kept our attention on the small box in front of us. It was about the size of a small cooler, and I instantly knew that Razor was right. It wasn't going to be good. Vas stepped forward, flicking open a knife and opening the seals, then he pulled the lid off. Since I was standing, I could see a flash of flesh as soon as the lid was out of the way, and I grabbed Bodhi's hand. He was already trembling, so I pulled him close just as Sacha started letting out a string of what I assumed were curses in Russian.

"Well, it's not a boy's hand, at least," Alexei said evenly. "Could be Gabriel's? Who else would they send to us?"

"I wish that was reassuring," Vas commented darkly, tilting the cooler to show us the dismembered hand. There was no note inside, but it didn't need one. It was a right hand; every single finger was broken in multiple places, and the raw edges on the stump made me think it had been removed with some kind of handsaw. The cold detachment I felt as I assessed the hand should concern me, but I was more worried about what would happen once the cold thawed.

"Rhodes!" a familiar woman's voice yelled out. There was fear and anger in the woman's tone, though neither emotion seemed to be aimed at the man she was addressing.

"What the hell is going on today?" Rhodes cursed as we all turned to see Wrenn rushing over. She had been another surprise. The moment she found out Nic was missing, she was determined to help us find her, keeping an ear out for rumors for us to look into and checking in through Alexei and Rhodes for updates. She wasn't afraid to get her hands dirty, willing to do anything we asked if it helped Nic. Even Bodhi was slowly starting to trust her, a feat to be sure. Was she trying to join this fucked up group of ours, or was she trying overly hard for redemption because of her past with Nic? Or was it something else entirely? I had no idea, and right now I was cautiously waiting to see how it all played out.

"What happened?" Maksim asked curtly.

Wrenn's face paled as she got closer and saw the cooler, but with a deep breath, her expression smoothed out. "There's another body right outside the compound. One of the ones that's made up to look like Nic. The dye job was horrible, and... it's the worst one."

"Who found it?" Alexei asked her as he and Maksim headed in the direction Wrenn had come from.

"Me and one of the other girls. She ran back to the women's quarters. It's only going to be a matter of time before they all know."

"We should check the security footage for the compound," I said, pulling Bodhi with me. "I'll get started on that. Bodhi, you can help me look."

"How is it that Nic can make my life a shitshow without even being here?" Rhodes griped as he pulled out a cigarette and lit it. "You two take care of the hand. Get whatever you need, then dispose of it. I'll look at the body."

Razor joined his president as he stalked after his nephews. Bodhi didn't say anything as I led the way through the compound, upstairs, and into Maksim's office. I had gotten the login info for the security system a few weeks ago, both of us spending nights combing through everything to find any hints as to who had infiltrated the Lords of Chaos to take all those pictures. Nic's stalker was good, though; we never found a hint of them or saw anyone suspicious.

Walking into the room, I sat down and got the security footage pulled up. When Bodhi didn't bring over a chair to join me, I looked up to find him standing by the door, staring at me. He was worrying his bottom lip, a sign that he had a lot going on inside him.

"What's up, Bodhi? You want to go with Sacha?" I asked. Concern tugged at me when Bodhi didn't respond for a minute. Was any of this bringing up his trauma with his mom and sister? Did I get so caught up in my own shit that I'd missed that Bodhi needed me?

"No. Sacha and Vas can handle disposing the hand without me." Bodhi stepped inside and shut the door. Before I could ask what he was thinking, Bodhi knelt in front of me. He stared up at me as he ran his hands up my legs. "You're wound so tight, Oli. I'm worried about you."

"I think we all are," I said gruffly, threading my fingers through his long hair and pulling, loving the way he whimpered at the hint of pain. Him using Nic's nickname for me made me hard as hell. I missed her, every fucking thing about her, until I felt like I was going mad without her. It was stupid to feel like everything was almost less without her here, but I knew I wasn't alone even if we didn't talk about it. Had I, being lost in my heartache and flashbacks of my past, pushed Bodhi away again? Was I pushing aside my relationship with him and making him feel less? That's something I would never want to happen. I loved Bodhi, more than he probably even knew. He'd saved me. "Have I been neglecting you, Bodhi? Is this your way of saying you need me?"

"Always," he whispered breathily. "But I think you need me more, Oli. Let me help you get some of this tension out."

"I don't think Maksim would appreciate us fucking in his office. In fact, I think he'd kill us slowly and painfully if we even dinged his computer setup, much less came all over his desk."

Bodhi laughed, the most carefree laugh I'd heard from him in a while. "I wasn't thinking anything that intense." He shuffled on his knees until he was under Maksim's desk then pulled the chair to the desk again. Before I could blink, he was undoing my jeans, pulling my cock free, and licking at the pre-cum on the head of my dick.

I groaned, my thighs tensing thanks to his teasing, as he swirled his tongue around the head before licking me from root to tip. Bodhi grazed his teeth along my length before he opened up and took me into his mouth. He didn't take me far though, giving me a few playful swirls of his tongue along my piercings.

Fuck.

He pulled away for a brief moment to tell me to get to work then put me back inside his hot, wet mouth. The fucking menace was going to suck me gently, cockwarming my dick as I worked on the footage. I felt my cock thicken, and he hummed in response, making my dick jump.

"I'll get you back for this," I hissed at him, the warning turning into a moan when his long fingers freed my balls from my jeans. "I'm checking this, then I'm fucking your throat until you can't talk for a week."

I felt his laughter vibrating along my length and squeezed my thighs around him. Fucking brat, he must have taken notes from Nic when I wasn't looking. With a deep breath, I tried to steady myself and center my thoughts. Bodhi stopped his teasing touches, resting his cheek against my thigh as he gently sucked on my dick while I started digging through files. With Bodhi on his knees at my feet, me working on a computer... It was the most centered and normal I had felt in weeks.

Once I found the camera that showed everyone crowded around something on the ground, I enlarged that screen and a few others nearby, looking back an hour or so to see if I could find anyone hanging out or dropping the body. A few cars drove by, and some pedestrians passed, but no one lingered near the compound. Everyone knew this was Lords of Chaos territory, and they didn't give warnings to trespassers. A few guys in the club entered and left, but there was no one suspicious.

One second, the body wasn't there, then it was, the corpse splayed out on the ground like a rag doll. I rewound the footage a few times before I spotted it—a glitch in the corner of the screen, almost imperceptible but still there. Someone had messed with the footage or camera. On a hunch, I started checking out the other cameras, looking for another glitch to help me trace a path.

Bodhi flicked his tongue along the underside of my cock, making me groan and jerk my hips to push my cock deeper inside of him. He sucked on me harder until I reached down, tugging his hair just enough to get his attention.

"Behave, Bodhi," I warned. "I think I found something."

He tried to pull off of my dick, but I pushed him down, keeping him right where he was. "No footage of who dropped the body, but I saw a glitch in the video. Someone messed with the security feed. I'm trying to trace the glitches to see how our guy got here."

Bodhi nodded slightly in acknowledgment, but he didn't try to move when I removed my hand from his head. Concentrating on the screens again, I lost myself in the hunt for this asshole who kept evading us. He, or she, was the reason Nicholette had left us without a word. No goodbye, all her stuff gone, a copy of what Ava had done to us, minus a goodbye letter.

A vibration caught my attention, and I checked my phone to find Sacha and Vas messaging that they'd taken care of the hand and were going to talk to Rhodes. I had shot back a text, letting them know I was still watching the cameras just as the door opened. Bodhi's rhythm faltered, and I squeezed my thighs around him, holding him in place. Maksim was stalking toward me, the usual glower on his face.

"What did you find?" he asked curtly, coming around his desk to stand behind me, his gaze focused on the computer screens. Thank goodness the desk wasn't open, so unless Maksim looked down, he wouldn't see Bodhi kneeling there with my dick in his mouth.

"There is no footage of the drop actually happening," I told him, "but watch this."

As I played the footage for Maksim, Bodhi started playing with me, his tongue toying with my piercings as he took me further into his mouth and down his throat. I clenched my hands into fists, determined to not react with the other man right at my back. *Yup, he definitely took notes from Nic.* I was going to kick his ass, then hers.

"Someone messed with the footage," Maksim said, forcing my attention back to what I was showing him. Thankfully, he knew shit about computers, so I didn't have to point out the small jump in the video during the playback.

"Yup. Either on the inside or the camera itself," I agreed with him. "I'm trying to trace our steps through the other cameras, see if I can spot a pattern or path of travel based on glitches in the other screens."

"Any luck?"

"Some," I told him, hitting a few keys and bringing up the other cameras for him to see. Just as I was about to explain what I'd found, Bodhi pulled off my dick and moved down to tease my balls. Biting my fist, I tried to stifle my groan so Maksim didn't know what was going on just a few feet away from him.

"It looks like they could have come from either the south or the west," Maksim said.

"I still need to check the rest," I told him roughly as Bodhi started jacking me off. It took everything in me to keep from crying out. "If they are smart enough, they could have fucked with all the cameras, and this would be all for nothing."

"Maybe, but it can't hurt to look. Besides, at least you're getting a blow job during it. I'll have to remember that the next time I get stuck doing this job," Maksim commented with a trace of humor in his voice and a small smile that was gone in a blink of an eye. "Don't get anything on my chair or desk. If you do, I'll drag you both back here to clean it with just your tongues until the mess is gone."

Bodhi whimpered, which made me clench my jaw, the sound alone getting me ready to blow. "This wasn't the plan when we came up here."

Maksim let out a bark of laughter as he stepped back and pulled out a cigarette, lighting it with a quick flick of a lighter. "I don't give a shit. Just clean up after and don't break anything. I've done a lot more than just gotten a blow job in this office."

With that, Maksim left just as quickly as he'd appeared. Before the door even closed, I pulled the chair out, grabbing Bodhi and pulling him up by his hair to give him a glare.

"You did that on purpose!"

"We like an audience, and he likes to watch," Bodhi gasped.

"You want him to watch as you choke and cry around my cock? You want me to bend you over this desk and force you to stare at him while I fuck you? Maybe I'd let you beg and plead with him, let him decide when you're able to come... if you were allowed to at all." Bodhi cried out at that, the fantasy making him come in his pants, his hips jerking in the air before I slammed him back down on his knees and shoved my throbbing cock down his throat.

I didn't bother being gentle, knowing that Bodhi loved it when I used him like this. Fucking his mouth with abandon, I slammed into him until I lost my rhythm, coming down his throat with a growl. He desperately tried to swallow my cum, and I savored every skip in his breath that said he was choking just the slightest bit.

Letting go of my hold on him, I collapsed back in the chair, my heavy breathing the only sound in the room until Bodhi pulled back. He looked up at me with bright, happy eyes as he licked his lips.

"Fuck, that was hot," he croaked, his face twisting a bit. It must have hurt a bit for him to talk, but that was something he liked, so I didn't have any regrets about how I'd handled him.

"When did exhibitionism become a big thing for you?" I asked lightly, my curiosity getting to me. "You usually like *watching*, not being watched."

A flush covered his cheeks, and he looked away from me. I smirked, propping my chin on my hand, waiting for him to get over the embarrassment and give me an answer. Oh, this was going to be good, I knew it.

"When you walked in on Nic and me," Bodhi mumbled. "At the warehouse. It was... Fuck, it was hot. Plus, I like watching you with her."

"So... Maksim? Out of everyone in the group?" I arched an eyebrow.

Bodhi froze, his hands twisting before he let out a shaky breath. "He likes to watch and direct. I know Sacha likes to be in control, but I don't think he'd want—"

"A show?" I finished for him with a small smile. "Unless it was with Nic, you're probably right. Though you'll never know unless you ask him. I wouldn't mind sharing you with him one night to try it out, in case you wanted to know."

"Really?" Bodhi asked, his voice cracking with surprise. "What about Maksim watching?"

I tilted my head, considering my boyfriend and the nervousness in him as he waited for my answer. "Two questions. How involved would he be? And are you doing this because he would remind you of Nic being with us? That level of control, I mean."

Bodhi shook his head a few times. "I like your fantasy, him watching and deciding if I finish or not. I mean, he's not unattractive. I wouldn't be opposed to more, but..."

"Really? Maksim, not Alexei? Out of the two of them, that's who I thought would pique your interest." I reached down and tucked myself back in my pants before cupping his face. "You didn't answer my question about Nic though, sweetheart."

"He wouldn't be anything like Nic." A sad smile pulled at his lips and my heart strings. "I wouldn't want him there as a substitute for her."

I pressed a quick, hard kiss on his lips and stood up. "We should go, Bodhi. Wouldn't want Maksim to make us lick up the ground because of a mess we didn't make. Though I'm sure you wouldn't mind it."

Bodhi roughly laughed, then he gasped in pain, grabbing his throat. "You wouldn't mind either, Oli. I wasn't the only one who finished quickly just now."

"Shut up," I told him in a sing-song voice as I pulled him up to stand with me. "Now, let's go meet up with Vas and Sacha before the cops show up."

Reaching for the door, I opened it to reveal a man I'd met once before, a smirk fully in place on his face.

"A little late for that," Detective Lewis informed us. "You'll both need to come down to the station with me for questioning."

Well, shit.

Nicholette
Monday

After some phone tag, I had an appointment with Allen, courtesy of Roderick. Seven in the morning though? I hated even the thought of that time, but I couldn't really complain since Roderick would be the one driving. I had wanted to do the interview at Roderick's office, but he couldn't convince the detective to go along with that. *Wonder if I can convince him to stop for coffee if I pay for it?*

"I think you have to limit how much coffee you're going to have if you're pregnant." The bland voice made me jump. Whirling around, I pressed a hand over my hammering heart. Blake was leaning against the door to the bathroom with a smirk on their face and their dark eyes guarded.

"What the fuck, Blake?" I hissed, shaking my head before I opened the shower curtain and stepped under the hot spray. "Next time, a little warning would be nice. What are you doing here?"

"I can't come check on you?" they asked innocently, and I pushed back the curtain to give them a 'give-me-a-break' look. Of course, they did nothing but chuckle when they saw my face. "Fine, you caught me. I wasn't checking on you. I'm coming with you today."

"I don't need an escort," I refuted firmly. "Roderick is going to be there."

"Yes, but Emmerich asked me to come, so I am. I stopped by to see if you needed anything."

"Clothes?" I half joked. "The only thing I have are the clothes I wore here yesterday. I left everything at the guys' apartment like you and Em suggested, so I don't have anything."

Blake didn't say anything for a minute, then I heard the rustle of clothing. "Let me go find something that will fit."

"Thanks," I called back as they walked out.

Slowly, I lathered up, washing my hair and body thoroughly. I needed the extra time to mentally prepare myself for today. Going back to Ashview after leaving was huge, and it felt wrong. I wasn't going straight to my men; I had plans I needed to put in motion before I went back and faced whatever I had coming to me.

I recalled the texts from last night. My friend had been delayed, and he hadn't given me an update as to when he would arrive. Knowing him, he would show up exactly when he thought best. I just hoped I agreed with his timing because although his arrival was going to cause a stir no matter what, certain situations would be better than others.

"I'm leaving stuff on the bed for you," Blake yelled out from the bedroom. "Roderick is going to be here in thirty minutes. Meet me at the front door."

"Okay!" I acknowledged before finishing up and turning off the water. Stepping out of the shower, I grabbed the towel off the rack and dried myself off before tossing it on the counter. I was curious to see what Blake had left out for me, so I padded out to the bedroom.

Sitting on the bed was a pair of black leggings and a white button-up shirt that looked too big to be theirs or Em's. Checking the tag, I saw it wasn't the cheap brand that Frederick always bought. It was a Tom Ford shirt, the quality of the fabric made more obvious when I ran my hands along the soft cotton. Ansel's shirt. Tom Ford was one of his favorite brands.

I bit my lip, trying to keep myself from yelling out to ask why they had given me one of his shirts. Would it be a better fit? Or were they trying to avoid me wearing something that belonged to one of their partners? That was probably it.

Shaking my head to get myself focused, I slipped on the black cami Blake had also included before throwing on the too-big white shirt. The cami would clearly show beneath it, but it covered my breasts, which was likely Blake's goal since we were headed to a police station. Next, I slipped into the leggings, going commando because it was comfortable. I let out a deep sigh when I realized there was no makeup. *I really want my stuff back.*

My phone beeped right then, and I walked over to the bedside table to see a text from Roderick.

Roderick: Just talked to Allen.
Roderick: He needs to reschedule. Something about Lewis going on a rampage and not wanting you to be exposed to that.

Oh shit. Thank fuck Allen mentioned something. There was no way I could deal with Lewis' bullshit right now. I had too much on my mind.

Nic: I'll let the others know. Thanks.

Slipping the phone into my cami, between my breasts, I hurried back to the bathroom to brush my teeth and put on some deodorant I'd found under the sink. Frederick's cleaners had always kept the spare rooms stocked with essentials, and I was glad Em hadn't changed that. I knew I wouldn't be able to go back to sleep, so I was going to be as ready as I could be before I went downstairs. *Not that I slept that much last night.*

Checking myself over in the mirror, I tried to ignore the dark circles under my eyes. Sleeping alone wasn't something I liked anymore. The feel of someone beside me, or multiple people, was the only thing that would soothe me. The few months we had been together had taught me the safety I could find in the arms of my boyfriends... something that had been absent for way too long now. That, and my morning sickness going away, but that wasn't happening anytime soon.

"I don't see Roderick yet," Blake said as I came down the stairs.

"He just messaged," I told them. "The meeting got postponed. Something about drama at the department."

"The one day I fucking get up early," Blake grumbled before stifling a yawn. "I'm going back to sleep. I'll see you later at a normal fucking wake-up time."

I chuckled, moving out of their way so they could hurry back upstairs in their sweats and large t-shirt. They were probably going to jump back in bed, curling up with someone to nap... or more. Fuck, I hated Blake right now. My dry spell sucked, and I hated every damn moment of it. I was going to make up for lost time, pregnant or not, when I met back up with the others.

I wandered through the downstairs until I settled on a couch in the living room with a bagel and coffee in hand. A broken laugh had escaped me earlier when I had gone into the kitchen only to find a normal coffee maker sitting there. I could hear it in my mind, knowing exactly how Sacha would bitch about the "cheap ass machine." The man really was a damn diva, no matter what he said. But at least Blake knew coffee, so the beans were good quality. So long as the taste was good, I didn't care what machine brewed it. I was mostly grateful that the morning sickness hadn't ruined my enjoyment of coffee.

"Getting so lost in your thoughts you lose awareness of your surroundings is dangerous," a cool voice reprimanded just before hands clamped down on mine. I jerked, but his hold kept my coffee from spilling.

None other than Ansel Förstner was standing in front of me, watching me with an arched look. "You're late," I sassed, ignoring the pounding of my heart from him sneaking up on me. "One would think you'd be more punctual, ya know, given the whole hitman thing."

We stared at each other for a moment before a small smile curled his lips, though it faded much too quickly for my liking. He loosened his hold on my hands and settled down beside me on the couch. I shifted to face him, tucking my feet under me, and we each studied the other. We hadn't seen each other in a while since life had a nasty habit of keeping us both busy.

He'd gotten older, obviously, with a few more lines around his eyes, but he had no gray in his dark black hair. Ansel wasn't as put together as he used to be, his clothes a bit more askew and worn than normal, but they were of the same high quality that he typically liked. There were dark circles under his eyes and a tightness to his mouth that told me he was hurt somewhere, but I couldn't tell right away where the injury was. Gray eyes took me in silently, and it made me wonder what he saw when he looked at me. The young woman he had met a few years back? Somewhat innocent and untested? Life had made sure I didn't stay that way.

Ansel was just as handsome as the first time we had met. I had been gifted to him by his brother for a job well done, and the rest was history. We had become unlikely friends, sporadically reaching out and talking, nothing consistent considering the nature of both of our lives, but we'd shared enough that I trusted him more than I did most people.

"You look terrible," he said with a hint of dry humor.

I rolled my eyes and took a small nibble of my bagel. "Aren't you the charmer? I blame morning sickness and my inability to sleep alone now. Both things I lay firmly at my men's feet since their stupid penises made me this way."

Ansel blinked slowly, his gaze traveling down my body until it zeroed in on my stomach. "You're pregnant?"

I nodded, my throat thick with nerves before I sipped some of my coffee. When he turned his focus to my cup, I held it close to me, glaring at him. "Em made me look it up. I can have one cup of coffee, so you can fuck right off. If you try to take this from me, I'll gut you."

"I see you're handling the hormones well," Ansel deadpanned, making me flip him off. A bark of laughter burst free before his face twisted in pain.

"What's wrong?" I asked him, concern filling me. I'd never seen him react that way. Not once even in all our violent and physical times together.

"Nothing," he said, dismissing my concern, then he shifted his seat so he was further away from me. "I got your messages and cleaned up the mess you left. Who were they?"

Silence reigned between us until I decided to let his avoidance go—for now. I'd get my answers later, that's for sure. "Members of the Ashview trafficking ring," I told him before pursing my lips in thought. "My stalker is part of it, so I've been working through names to find my brother."

"Any progress?" he asked with no outward reaction to my admission. I wondered if he already knew who they were. After all, they were direct competition to the Förstner Family.

"I found out the names of two of the ring leaders," I said, biting my lip as I turned over the information in my head. "But I want more information before I take any action. Better to be sure before doing anything that would hurt Thomas." Ansel silently propped his chin on his hand and waited for me to continue. "I just don't know how it happened. Since I've been on my own, I've wondered how my stalker had gotten ahold of my brother. I mean, even if they hated me, my parents loved Thomas. I can't imagine them just letting him go without trying to protect him."

"Did you go back there to see what had happened?" he asked after a moment of silence.

"No." A broken laugh fell from my lips as I finished off my coffee and set it, along with my barely touched bagel, on the coffee table. My chest burned, and I rested a hand on my rolling stomach as if that would help anything. "I don't want to have to deal with my hometown until I'm ready. There are a few more things I need to get in place before I take a trip down trauma lane." Ansel didn't say anything. He just sat there, watching my battle to keep my coffee down.

"You should eat," he said gently, slowly leaning forward to pick up the bagel and offer it to me. "It will help."

"I don't think I can stomach it."

"Part of the reason you're nauseous is because you need food in your stomach," he argued. "The coffee is acidic, which will just make getting sick worse."

"Either way, I'll just puke it back up," I countered.

"Try ginger after you eat a little bit. It helped my wife when she was pregnant with both Emmerich and Kat— Blake," Ansel corrected himself before pushing the bagel at me again.

After another moment of hesitation, I grabbed it and took another small bite. "When I throw up again, you're going to clean it up."

His lips twitched, but his serious gaze was shadowed with sadness. His wife had been dead for years, yet every mention of her had him reacting the same. Ansel had loved her; I could see it whenever he mentioned her, even in passing, though that was rare. It was as if every time cut open the wound all over again.

"No, I'm not," he replied blandly, pulling me from my thoughts. "How far along are you?"

I shrugged. "No idea."

"*What?*"

"What?" I asked, my brow furrowed at his sharp question.

"You have no idea how far along you are?" he asked, speaking slowly as if he were confused.

"I got my IUD out... That's all I've had time for. I don't want my stalker to find me and realize I'm pregnant," I told him. I knew he would get it even if he didn't like it. "I don't know what they would do to me or the men if they found out, much less the baby."

Ansel's expression became grim as he stood up, looking around the living room. "Where are the others?"

"Asleep." I replied. "I was supposed to talk with Allen today, but it got pushed back. I haven't been sleeping, so I figured breakfast would help. What are you doing?"

"You need to see a doctor," he said firmly, reaching down to grab my wrist and pull me up. I didn't fight him, feeling almost grateful that someone was taking charge of this for me. His eyebrow arched when he got a good look at what I was wearing. "Is that my shirt?"

"Blake gave it to me," I said, shifting my weight. He stared at the shirt then met my gaze again, but I had no idea how to read him right now. "I can change—"

"No," he cut me off as he snagged my bagel from me. "I'll call the doctor on the way."

"Wait, we're going right now?"

"Yes," he replied, dragging me along after him.

"I think Em was going to call..." I stopped talking when he shot a glare over his shoulder. Before I had another chance to think, we were outside and headed to his car. "Nevermind."

A few moments later, I was sitting in the backseat of his car while he drove through Boston, talking to someone on the phone in German. After a pointed look in the rearview mirror, I took another small bite of my bagel, hating it and hating even more that he was right. My stomach was settling with every bite I ate.

Ansel's protectiveness was sweet, though I bet he would hate to hear that word. I should be annoyed at him for barging in, taking charge, and dragging me around to a doctor's appointment without even pretending to ask me, but my guys would approve. If I was being honest with myself, I did too. Like he'd said, he'd been through this twice before with his late wife, so I trusted him to know at least a little bit about what I needed to do. I, on the other hand, had no idea what I was doing. None.

"He's going to take us right back when we get there," Ansel announced as soon as he hung up the phone. "Eat up. We will be there in a few minutes."

Ansel

TWO HOURS LATER, we were back in the car, and Nicholette was noticeably quiet. She hadn't said anything for the past hour, giving only soft murmurs of acknowledgement and a few nods to what Dr. Fischer said before he took about six vials of blood for tests. He gave her medicine to help ease the morning sickness, saying it would need a day or so to take full effect. After that, she shouldn't throw up as much and would be able to keep food down. Even that good news hadn't garnered more than a soft thanks. Before we left, he'd directed a concerned look and a silent order to keep a close eye on her.

"Nicholette—" I started, but she shook her head. My eyes narrowed, and I quietly hummed before starting the car. "Buckle up."

This time, she sat in the front passenger seat, and while I drove through Boston, I let the silence hang between us. She needed to process everything in her own time, and as she did that, I contemplated how much she had changed since I saw her last. It felt like it hadn't been that long, but she had changed so much. Her blue-green eyes were as calculating and sharp as ever, but I could sense a hint of warmth underneath. I had known her for years, having first met her when she was barely eighteen, thanks to my brother. He liked them young and used prostitutes often, and I typically didn't even give them a second glance... until Nicholette. Even then I could sense something different in her, and for the first time since my wife died, I felt something stir in me.

Then Frederick paid for a night with her and dropped her off to stay with me. I hated him for forcing her on me and her for rousing my interest. I didn't touch her once that night, but when Frederick had gifted me with another night on the memorial of my wife's death, I lost control. I sought to break her, grind her under my heel. Nicholette surrendered to it, reveling in the pitch-black well of my desires to the point that she pulled me in with her. Even while covered in bruises and shaking, she checked on me when we were finished. After that, I figured out how to get in touch with her, and somehow I found myself becoming friends with and occasionally fucking someone younger than my youngest child. *By a year, but still.*

"Penny for your thoughts with that expression?" Nicholette's comment jolted me from my thoughts as I stopped at a red light.

"Just remembering when we met," I responded honestly, looking over to find her studying me. Her face softened at that, and a small smile pulled at her lips before it faded.

"The night you didn't touch me at all or the night we first had sex?"

I let out a gruff laugh. "Both."

"Where are we going?" Nicholette asked after a beat of silence.

"You look like you need some time," I told her briskly. "You won't get any at the Family house."

"And you won't either," she said dryly, and I could hear her amusement. She wasn't wrong; I wasn't quite ready to see Blake again after the revelations that had come to light in Seattle. Tension between us was the norm, but this was something else entirely. What I had learned about them, Atlas, Frederick... The guilt I felt for not being able to protect Blake from my brother weighed heavily on me. I'd let Blake down, and I knew I'd never forgive myself for it.

"With my children, there is no such thing as calm," I deadpanned, forcibly redirecting my thoughts before I let them take me in a direction I didn't want to go.

She threw her head back, laughter spilling from her and lighting her up. It took my breath away. Nicholette, everything about her, brought life back into my life. Her laughter was always something that drew me to her. "Blake and Em don't know anything about calm, unless you mean the calm before the storm."

"And you know about calm?" I arched an eyebrow as I turned into a neighborhood and reached out to punch in a security code for the community gate.

"Depends on who you're comparing me to," she replied flippantly, curiosity clear as she arched an eyebrow at me before turning to look out the window. The thick woods near the roads made it impossible to see the homes in the community, which I preferred. We were just outside the city, and everyone here valued their privacy more than anything else.

We took care of our own if something were to happen, and most importantly, people kept to themselves and minded their own business. The police weren't even allowed on the premises unless the residents were forewarned. It was the perfect place to settle down. I'd moved here after Blake left, needing the memories of the old house gone.

Nicholette stared out the window as we moved down the driveway, turning to me once my house came into view. Her eyes were bright, and her jaw had dropped. It was a modern home with wood, concrete, and black accents, surrounded by open land that sprawled in all directions for half a mile. The huge windows were bulletproof for security. Parking right in front of the house, I got out and went around to open the door for Nicholette. She kept her gaze on the house as she took my offered hand.

"Welcome to my home," I told her gently. "No one will bother you here until you're ready."

"Do Em and Blake know about this place?"

"Emmerich does," I answered, then let out a hard laugh. "Which I'm sure means Blake does as well. But no one else, and let's just say the people who live here... There's an understanding of how things are taken care of."

"So, basically, this is where criminals come to retire?" she asked, looking up at me with humor dancing in her eyes.

"If not for the doctor's visit, I'd make you pay for that commentary," I said as I led her up the stairs and into my home. "I'm nowhere near retirement, Liebling."

Her amusement changed to awe as she looked around inside, and a spark of pride warmed my chest. The place wasn't perfect, more rooms were empty than I cared to admit, but there was enough space to run away from my thoughts when I needed to. A big fireplace, brown couches, and a big TV made up the living room. The kitchen was clean, industrial, and had just a few things on the counter since I hated clutter anywhere.

Nicholette wandered through the open downstairs and came to a dead stop by the wall of windows facing the back of the house. There was a large deck that connected to an infinity pool overlooking the forest. It was one of my favorite views... at least until I saw her standing there at the windows taking it all in for the first time. *First time?!* I shook my head. *I can't let myself get drawn into her webs of chaos. Too many people, too many plays at political machinations that have never been my forte.*

"Can I swim?" she asked, not glancing back at me as she opened the sliding glass door.

"Of course." Before I knew it, she stripped out of her clothes, dropping them on the ground and jumping in completely naked. Only Nicholette would turn her back on me and strip like it's nothing.

She glided through the water, and I could almost *feel* some of the tension inside her draining away as she swam to the other side of the pool. Reaching down, I gathered the clothing, folding it and placing it on one of the chairs before sitting back to watch her.

Nicholette lost herself in the water, swimming laps for about thirty minutes before she stopped by the edge of the pool closest to where I was sitting. I raised my eyebrows, waiting, curious to see what she was going to say, and it wasn't anything that I expected.

"You should swim with me." She wiped at the water on her face. "You're wound as tightly as I am."

"I am *not* wound tight."

She leveled a glare at me. "Ansel, you've been sitting stiffly since the drive to the doctor's office, and it's only gotten worse since we got here. Whatever injury you're hiding is going to give you a shit ton of problems if you don't do something."

I didn't try to deny that I was hurt. In fact, my shoulder and arm hurt like a motherfucker, but that wasn't anything new. After I'd found out what my brother had done to Blake... I lost it. Killing Frederick would have been a mercy he didn't deserve, so I was going to give him to Blake to handle. I knew that they would have no mercy for him. In true coward's fashion, he pulled the trigger before I could even open my mouth, but the idiot was no hitman. The bullet hit my shoulder, tearing through muscles, but the pain wasn't enough to stop me from doing what needed to be done.

But the injury and its lasting effects were starting to show. The arm would always ache, throbbing with pain at times, and the doctor said it was a miracle I could still use the damn thing considering the damage the bullet had done to my nerves. However, that *miracle* didn't make me feel any better about the situation or the reminder of my age as I watched her heave herself out of the pool and pad over to me.

"Come on, Ansel. I promise it's not holy water. See? I'm perfectly fine."

"You make it seem like we're the same, but we aren't," I said coolly, not taking the hand she held out. I was too focused on trying my damndest to not check out her naked body on display in front of me. But I was no saint; all I could picture was her curves and the memory of her skin against mine as she cried out.

"We aren't. You're a hitman for the mafia. I'm a prostitute-turned-call-girl who kills people to relieve stress." She put her hand on her hip, staring me down in challenge. The movement drew my eye, and I stilled, my eyes zeroed in on the name carved on her inner thigh. "You've seen me naked before, Ansel—"

"Someone carved a name on you," I growled.

"He did." Her gentle, vulnerable tone made me look up

at her. Tears were in her eyes as she brushed her fingertips over the name. "He's going to be so fucking pissed when I see him again."

"You *let* someone do that to you?"

"Says the German whose Family brands people," she shot back, but there was no real heat in her retort. "He was jealous, mad about me dancing with my ex and going off to do stuff without telling him... He wanted to remind me who owned me." A shiver ran through her body, and I saw goosebumps cover her skin while she licked her lips. "Come on, Ansel. I know just what I need to help me relax enough to face what I just learned."

"What is that?" I tilted my head to the side, curious as to what she was going to say. "Sex?"

"I'm not opposed to sex." She grinned, running her hands up her body. I'd like to think it was because she was teasing me, though, knowing Nicholette, it was probably just a habit. "But I was thinking of swimming, then we could find someone to chase through these woods. I need some exercise to get my blood pumping and someone else's blood spilling over me. You said people keep to themselves here... Let's have some fun."

"Who are we killing?"

Nicholette smirked before turning around to head back to the pool. "I don't care as long as they fight back and make it interesting. If I need more stress relief, you can fuck me afterward. Now, come on. Get in with me. We can plan our little game of hide and seek before we get someone to join us. Unless you're too old to keep up with me." With those final words, she jumped back in and started swimming toward the other end of the pool.

A snarl curled my lips before I stood up and slowly undressed. Folding my clothes, I placed them on the chair and joined her. The water was refreshing, so I slipped under and pushed off, heading right for Nicholette. I came up for air right in front of her. This section of the pool was only five feet, letting us both stand up. Her gaze went right for my shoulder, eyes widening for a second before she hesitantly reached out to touch it. Funny how she had never reacted to any of my other scars, and I had plenty of those all over my body, like she was with this one.

Had something changed between us, or was there just something different inside her?

"A gunshot?" I nodded in answer to her question, and her fingers ghosted over the injury before she met my gaze. "Frederick?"

"What makes you think it was him?"

"Because Em and Blake wouldn't have missed. If they had, you would have been pissed." She chuckled, the sound soft. "You missed the kill shot?"

"What makes you think I would have missed?" I asked, challenge sparking something inside me. Did she truly think that I would miss? Without warning, I grabbed her throat, applying enough pressure for her to feel the strength in my hands.

"You weren't aiming to kill him, or you wouldn't have been hurt at all," she said confidently, only the slightest hint of strain behind her voice. Her hand rested on my chest, showing she wasn't the least bit bothered by my hand on her throat. "Or your emotions got the best of you."

"Emotions?" I scoffed.

"Yes, even you have them. Try as you might, you're not a sociopath." Her eyes were bright with laughter as she stared up at me. "You're just insane."

"You're with seven men, Nicholette," I pointed out, and she dropped her hand from my chest. "I think insanity applies more to you than me. Plus, you're in a pool, naked, with someone who *isn't* one of those seven men."

She waved dismissively. "We're friends." My chest tightened at her easy dismissal of me, but I wouldn't push it. Hell, I couldn't be with someone who was with seven other people. *What the fuck am I even thinking? How is that even the damn line? She's been with Blake, Emmerich, Frederick... Fucking her was one thing, but being with her is something else altogether.* "Now, do you have someone in mind for our playmate, or am I going hunting on my own?" she purred, pulling me from my thoughts.

I studied her face. There was a hint of a smile playing at the edge of her lips, but the vulnerability in her eyes made me pause. She was putting on a brave face, maintaining her damn walls as long as she could, and I respected the hell out of her for that. Stepping back from her to get some distance, I ignored how hard I was in favor of looking out at the forest in front of us.

"I have someone," I told her after a longer-than-necessary pause. "You should tell Emmerich where you are so he doesn't come banging down the door."

"He will anyway," she said with a snort. "He's bossy like that."

We let the quiet settle between us. Instead of our normal, easy silence, it was charged, or at least it was for me. My awareness of her was keeping my senses on high alert, and I wasn't sure what to do about it. I was fighting with myself, trying to figure out my next steps, until there came a loud banging from my front door.

What the hell? Who could that be?

Nicholette
Monday

Ansel looked surprised and annoyed by the interruption, throwing a glare over his shoulder, and I chuckled before grabbing the edge of the pool and pulling myself out with ease.

"I'll get it," I told him, curious to see who was here.

"Nicholette..." Ansel growled behind me, and I picked up my pace, knowing he wouldn't be far behind. Sometimes it was just fun to make men chase after me, especially when I got to poke fun at the ones that weren't used to someone questioning their demands.

I snagged his shirt on my way past and slipped it on as I walked up to the front door and opened it. My eyes widened in shock, my mind racing as I tried to figure out why he was here, not to mention the man behind him. The two men had similar expressions, so I quickly schooled my mine and stepped back to wave them in.

"Ansel, you have company!"

"I'm right here, Nicholette." His hands landed on my shoulders, pulling me tight against his chest as Christopher then Detective Allen came inside. Ansel had put on his undershirt and pants since I had taken his button-up. "What are you doing here?"

"We have a problem," Christopher said, his gaze flicking from my face up to Ansel. His eyes narrowed as he studied us, especially Ansel's hands on my shoulders. "Did we interrupt something?"

"And if you did, what business is that of yours?" Ansel crooned, the promise of violence clearly written in his tensing muscles. I looked between the two of them, confused about the entire situation, really.

"Why is it always like this with you, Nic?" Allen asked, pinching his nose and releasing a long-suffering sigh.

"Because I'm like the daughter you never had?" I guessed, tapping my chin with one of my fingers as if lost in thought. I tried and failed to suppress a smile while I tried to think of some good reasons. "I like to keep things interesting? Making up for the monotony of my childhood?"

"I know more about you than I would ever want to know about a daughter," Allen retorted, though I saw the spark of humor dancing in his light blue eyes. Running a hand through his graying brown hair, he focused on the man behind me who was still having a stare-off with Christopher. "But we do have a problem. Otherwise, we wouldn't have come by."

"You work with the Förstners?" I asked Christopher, tilting my head. I had known him for years, but I was suddenly realizing I didn't know anything about him at all. Turnabout was fair play, I supposed, but this new revelation made me feel like I was on uneven ground since I knew a lot of the Germans.

The older man looked down at me with a half smile. "Yes, but that's all you're getting from me, Delilah... Fuck, Nic. That will take some getting used to. But you should know your Russians won't be happy about all of this." He motioned at Ansel, and something in me was irritated at how he worded that.

"I'm no one's property," I retorted coolly. "In case you missed that memo, *Christopher*. What I do and don't do isn't any of your business. If you're here to talk Family business, I'll just—"

"Actually, since you're here, Nic," Allen interrupted before I could step away, "there are things I need to speak with you about."

"Should I call Roderick then?" I asked lightly, not about to back down on that, not even for Allen.

"Of course you know Rorik," Ansel muttered, and I glanced over my shoulder to look at him.

"Rorik? Oooh, I like that nickname." Ansel rolled his eyes, but as I let my body melt against him, I felt him soften just a little bit. I needed every bit of comfort I could get because something inside told me that shit was about to hit the fan yet again.

Allen shook his head. "No, I'll leave talking about that for when I'm fully on record, so Lewis doesn't try to get back on the case. I need to talk to you about some other things that came up recently."

"You two talk, then. Allen, come join us after," Ansel ordered. He squeezed my shoulders one more time before he walked off, gesturing for Christopher to follow him back out by the pool. Christopher followed at a slow pace, shooting a look over his shoulder that told me his lecture wasn't over yet—a bit of a pot-and-kettle situation considering what he was apparently involved in.

"How are you, Nic?" Allen asked, and I turned to give him my full attention. He had more gray in his hair since I had seen him last, and the lines on his face appeared deeper. He was studying me with nothing but purely fatherly concern, which was a change for me. It was... nice. My eyes teared up before I could stop it. How many times had I wanted someone to look at me like that? With no expectations about what they could get from me, just genuine concern *for* me. "Nic?"

"I'm staying busy." I sniffed, forcing myself to push away the emotion welling inside of me. "But plausible deniability on your end and whatnot. What do you need to talk to me about?"

"Lewis is on a rampage," Allen said after a long pause. "He is looking into you. Your past, your associates. He's trying to figure out everything about you. After getting pulled from your case, he wants blood. Be very, very careful with whatever you have planned. He isn't the only one trying to follow you. Your boyfriends are turning the city upside down to find you, and more than a few people have gone missing during their efforts."

"Detective—" I started, but he cut me off.

"Two of them are currently in police custody," Allen said grimly, "being questioned by Lewis. He's had them in custody since yesterday, and he can hold them for another two days. He was called in when another body was dumped at the Lords of Chaos compound."

"One of the women that looks like me?" I asked softly, shivering thanks to the cold chill running up my spine.

"Yes, actually." Allen's voice grew rough before he squeezed his eyes shut. "It's bad, Nic. Really fucking bad. Whoever is looking for you is spiraling. All of your guys were there when Lewis arrived at the compound. I don't know if he legitimately came up with reasons to question and hold them or not."

"Who is he holding?" I asked.

"Oliver and Bodhi." My anger had already been ignited, but now that I had his answer, it exploded.

That asshole had Oli and Bodhi stuck at the police station? And from what Allen was hinting at, he had no intention of letting them leave anytime soon. He was determined to use the entire seventy-two-hour hold. Speaking from personal experience, he'd probably spend the time insulting them and annoying them with questions. A flashback of Oliver handing me over to Lewis popped into my mind, but I shook it off. Things done in anger were one thing, but this... I would never leave them to deal with his insanity if I could help it.

Not saying anything for fear I would lose it, I walked out to the pool where Ansel and Christopher looked to be in the middle of an argument. They stopped at the sight of me, so there was no way of knowing what they were discussing. "Nicholette?" Christopher asked, his brow creasing in concern at whatever he saw.

"I need a phone, Ansel. Now. I left mine at the house."

He considered me for a moment, searching my face, before looking behind me at Allen. Ansel nodded, reaching into his pants pocket and handing me his cell phone.

He didn't have a lock on it, which was bold but completely in character for him. Flipping through his contacts, I found Roderick's nickname, Rorik, and hit to call him. While it rang, I let my rage simmer until I heard Roderick say Ansel's name in greeting.

"Hello, Roderick," I purred. "Or should I say *Rorik?*"

There was a weighted pause, then the lawyer on the other end cleared his throat. "Nicholette, this is an unexpected—"

"I need you to do something for me," I interrupted, turning to face Allen with a serious expression. "Call Allen and tell him I can't reschedule the questioning. It needs to happen today. We can just meet him at the station."

"From what he told me this morning, that's not a good idea," Roderick advised in an even tone. "But if that's what you want..."

"It is," I told him firmly. Allen's eyebrows shot up in surprise, and I could feel the weight of Ansel's and Christopher's stares on my back. "And I need you to do something for me when we get there. I'm assuming you know where to pick me up?"

Ansel reached over and took the phone from my hands. "My place, Rorik. She'll be ready when you get here." With that, he hung up the phone. "What the hell are you planning?"

"This speeds up my timeline a bit, but I can work with it." I clicked my tongue, my thoughts whirling as I tried to rearrange my plans. I wasn't willing to divulge everything I had planned or up my sleeve yet. "I'll leave you to your business and get ready to take care of mine." Pushing past him, I grabbed my clothes and made my way inside. I wandered for a bit before I found a downstairs bathroom, but luckily I got there without a second to spare. No sooner had I opened the door than I rushed to the toilet, vomiting twice before I sat back, wiping my mouth with the back of my hand, and flushed the toilet.

"Emmerich called." Ansel's soft voice startled me, making me jerk and whip around to find him standing by the open door. *Shit, did I forget to lock the door?* "Some of Blake's men are going to meet you at the station."

I nodded a few times, praying my still-rolling stomach would settle soon. Ansel stepped into the bathroom, shutting and locking the door behind him. "Shouldn't you be out there with Allen and Christopher?"

"They are leaving, and they know not to linger," he said, grabbing a small cup by the sink and filling it with water before offering it to me. "Here. You can rinse your mouth when you're done."

"Well, this reunion was fun. Guess I'll see you around," I joked, taking the small paper cup from him, but when I tried to pull it to me, he didn't let go. Looking up at him, confused, I found him smirking down at me.

"Oh, I'm coming too. I told Rorik, so he knows to expect me. Trying to taunt your stalker with this little excursion back to Ashview?"

"I don't need you to come with me," I protested, refusing to rise to the bait. I wasn't going to reveal my plans to him. There was too much on the line right now and not enough firmly in place to share what I was thinking.

"I wasn't asking, Nicholette."

"I'm the one in charge of this, Ansel. This is about my brother, my men, my... children. If you or any of the others have an issue with that, then you can go fuck off right now," I told him as I carefully stood up. I rinsed my mouth with the water and spat it out in the sink before I focused on him again. "Am I clear?"

Ansel blinked slowly, arching an eyebrow. "Perfectly clear, Liebling. Finally facing that revelation from today?"

I swallowed hard and thought back to the ultrasound photos the doctor had handed me while Ansel sat beside me, letting me squeeze his hand hard enough that I was surprised I didn't break any bones. *Twins.* My men, always the overachievers. *Fucking twins.* "My guys aren't going to be happy after I do this. Not that they're particularly happy with me right now anyway..."

"I would expect nothing less from one of your plans."

I snorted, a half smile tugging at my lips before I

sobered up. "I still want our murder plans for later, though. I bet Em won't care if we do it at the Family house."

"You're coming back here afterward," Ansel said, eyes narrowing.

"Well, be ready for company then because I don't see Blake or Em letting me just run off again," I warned him. *If others don't join us as well.* "For someone who wants to be so damn cold, you raised children with more emotion than they will ever admit to. Soft hearted, all three of you."

"They care about you," Ansel said. "As do I," he added after a slight pause. "Get ready. Rorik will be here soon, then you're filling us in on what the hell you have planned."

Ansel exited the room just as quickly as he'd appeared. *They care about you... As do I.* His words echoed in my mind, threatening to overwhelm me. He cared as a friend like the others did. Right? I was too vulnerable and unsure about everything in my life right if I was reading into things Ansel said to reassure me. That's all it was. I needed these hormones to level out and stop fucking with my brain and emotions. Considering I had fucked pretty much every member of his family, it was a surprise he even wanted to be friendly.

I slipped back into my leggings and cami, but I decided to keep the button-up shirt I had taken from Ansel instead of slipping back into the one Blake had given me. *This one smells like him—rum, vanilla, and a hint of lemons.* Rifling through the cabinet, I saw he had a spare toothbrush and toothpaste underneath, and I tried to ignore the shot of jealousy that hit me. Why did he have extras in a random bathroom? Did he regularly have someone stay over? Why that bothered me was something I wasn't interested in thinking about right now. *One plateful of bullshit at a time, Nic.* I brushed my teeth super quick, making sure to get all the throw-up residue out of my mouth before tying my hair up in a messy bun.

Walking out to the main entrance, I saw Ansel sitting nearby, fully dressed in one of his usual suits, his hair roughly styled, focused on the phone in his hand. "Rorik will be here any minute."

As if right on cue, there was a knock at the door. Roderick opened it a breath later, letting himself inside as if he was completely comfortable in Ansel's space. He was just as tall and broad shouldered as I remembered. He was still clean cut, without even a hint of a five o'clock shadow on his chin. His black hair was purposefully messy, styled just so to match the business casual look he had going on with navy blue slacks, white button-down shirt, and a matching navy blazer that he'd left unbuttoned. The color worked well with his dark tan complexion and dark brown eyes. He looked at Ansel, who pointedly stared at me as if they were both waiting for me to take charge of what was going to happen. *What a refreshing response.*

"Lewis is going to be livid when I show up to talk to Allen, even if you're with me," I said, addressing Roderick first. "We are going to use that to our advantage to get something I need. And I need you to get something to Oli or Bodhi while we're there."

"That means leaving you alone in the police station."

"With Ansel." I tilted my head to indicate the man watching me like a hawk. "Besides, I can listen to whatever is said and not respond until you get back. I'm sure Allen knows the routine, and I can ignore whoever comes in with him. Ansel, what guys are meeting us at the station? Did Blake say?"

"Conrad and Robin."

The man with buzzed hair who Blake said I needed to

be cautious around and one of the older men—not the one that smoked if I recalled the introductions correctly. *Interesting*. They would work for what I had in mind. "Perfect. Roderick, may I use your phone?"

"Why mine?" Roderick asked, not moving.

"I'm not going to do anything illegal," I told him with a smile, not the least bit put out by his cautious question. "I just need to call an old friend."

"That sounds terrifying considering who you're currently with," Roderick muttered after Ansel ordered him to give me the phone without asking more questions.

I chuckled and began dialing a number from memory. I was relieved when her cool voice filled the phone after the second ring. "Maeve, long time no see."

Silence.

"Nic?" Her voice cracked before she roughly cleared her throat. "Nicholette, where the *fuck* have you been?"

"I learned from the best," I replied softly, ignoring the tears that pricked my eyes. Fuck me, everything was just hitting me in ways that I really couldn't deal with right now. Why should I care about how she'd sounded when she said my name? That chapter of my life was done.

Ansel and Roderick had both stilled when I said Maeve's name; they were so quiet I wasn't even sure if they were breathing. "I've been preoccupied with getting some things ready to go. I take it my boyfriends reached out?"

"More like showed up on my doorstep, knocked down the door, and demanded answers," Maeve replied coldly, and a wild laugh escaped me from picturing that. *Vas probably stared Maeve down, just waiting for her to do something shitty so he could hit her.* "It's odd they are the ones you picked, Nicholette. I had pictured you with someone with more... class."

"Really?" I asked, shrugging even though she couldn't see me, then I moved to sit down in an open armchair. "They might be rough around the edges, but they're honest about it. Besides, Sacha is plenty fancy enough for me when it's necessary, and when it's not, he's just as bloodthirsty as the rest."

"More honest than you are," she said evenly.

"Perhaps," I allowed. "Meet me at the Ashview station this evening. Roderick will message you the time."

"Is this the favor I owe you, then?" Maeve asked, and I heard papers rustling in the background.

"No," I replied in a clipped tone. "I'll pay you for your time, Maeve. You paid me for mine."

Click.

I ended the call before she could say anything else and held the phone out to Roderick. "We should go, or we'll be late."

"Allen asked for me to let him know when we're five minutes out," the lawyer commented, slowly taking his phone back.

"What are you planning?" Ansel asked again, but I just gave him a secretive smile.

"I need your real reaction, Ansel, so I guess you get to find out when everyone else does." Not bothering to say anything else, I grabbed my shoes and made my way outside and into Roderick's SUV, a completely different ride from the silver coupe he had driven previously. I slid into the back, happy to let the men take up the front seat. Roderick and Ansel followed at a more sedate pace, the latter getting into the back with me and holding out a piece of candy as Roderick started up the vehicle.

"It will help with your stomach," he said when I didn't take it. "Ginger."

"Thanks." I remembered he had mentioned trying ginger this morning, but I couldn't recall him stopping to get some for me. Though, to be fair, I was pretty sure I had zoned out during part of the drive to his home. As I opened the candy, I scrutinized his face, but I was met with that stoic mask of his that didn't give me even a hint of what he was thinking.

"Your men will be there," Roderick said after a few minutes of silence. "Allen said the two brothers have been there all day, trying to get them to release Oliver and Bodhi."

"Sacha and Vas?" I asked, but Roderick surprised me with a quick shake of his head.

"No. Volkov and Angeloff are there. Volkov is trying to get them to release the others if there are no charges happening. Angeloff is apparently scaring the shit out of the cops just by sitting there and smoking."

"Alexei and Maksim?" Ansel and I asked at the same time.

"Curious," he muttered as Roderick said it was them.

"It is," I hummed in agreement, drumming my fingers on the door as I mentally tweaked my plan. The cousins were getting along a lot better than they had before my disappearance. *At least that's some kind of silver lining.* "I can work with that."

"Which one are you trying to talk to?" Roderick asked.

"Neither. I just need them to see me."

"They won't just let you go," Ansel said, pointing out the obvious.

"If they take me, let it happen," I ordered them both, ignoring the growl of displeasure from the man beside me. "I can deal with them just fine on my own."

"That's not how this is going to work," Ansel said. His

hand landed on my thigh, making me very aware of his strength when he squeezed me hard enough that I gasped. The pain made me *very* fucking aware of the bra I hadn't bothered to put on under the cami and his shirt. "You came with me, and you're leaving with me, too. No exceptions."

"That's not—"

"It is now." Ansel tightened his hold until I whimpered. He was rough enough that I knew I'd have a bruise later. "You. Are. Leaving. With. Me."

"I will go back to the house, yes, but I'm not leaving with you," I responded, holding my ground and fighting the arousal growing in my body. My already high sex drive had only gotten more voracious since becoming pregnant, and with no release besides my own hands, I desperately needed some sex. "This is *my* show, Ansel. Get with the program, or Blake's men will."

His hand wrapped around my throat, pinning me to the seat, before he got into my face. "Be very careful about how you talk to me, Nic."

"I was." I swallowed hard, giving in to his hold even as I glared up at him. "But I'm in charge right now, as I've said many times. My brother was taken and is being used by a crazy person who has stalked me for *years*. There's also the fact that you are in no position to try to dictate what I can and can't do. We are friends, Ansel. You're not one of my guys, so fuck off."

"Rorik. Get out."

Belatedly, I realized the SUV had stopped moving, and I looked over to the side to see we were outside of the station. Roderick commented that he would let Allen know it would be ten minutes, then the door slammed shut behind him, leaving me alone with Ansel.

"The only boss I have is Sacha, and you're not him," I

told him, not the least bit intimidated by the man still holding my throat. "I get that this might bring up some stuff for you, but this is *my* life and *my* shit to sort out."

"I think you are underestimating a lot of things right now," Ansel warned me. His face tightened for a moment as if he were in pain before his empty gray eyes met my stare.

"Like what?" My brow furrowed, and my mind was racing to figure out what he could possibly mean when he claimed my mouth in a kiss. It was deceptively soft, a stark contrast to the hand pinning me to the seat.

He didn't deepen the kiss, but it was jarring all the same. Ansel pulled back when I didn't respond, his gray eyes studying mine, and whatever he saw there made him smile. "You had no idea?"

"You've never even tried to kiss me. Plus, given *when* we always meet up... I wasn't... How the fuck would I have known?" *Well, this is certainly not my best moment.*

"What do you mean?" he asked huskily.

I licked my lips. "Nevermind."

"Nicholette," he warned, tightening his hold on my throat until I moaned.

"The anniversary of your wife's death. That's when you always called me for sex," I rushed out, staying still when he stilled. *Did he truly not realize?* When he didn't say anything in response, I chewed my bottom lip, studying his expression for any type of reaction, yet I found none. "I shouldn't have said anything."

I pulled back from him, and Ansel's hand loosened enough for me to slide away. Ignoring the way he practically whispered my name, I climbed out of the car. Roderick didn't comment when I straightened my shirt, nor did he say a word when I rubbed a hand on my neck as if that would make the handprint go away.

People milled about on the sidewalk, everyone heading about their business. A few cops were sitting around, watching the station, and I knew the moment Ansel joined us because a few of them went completely still in the way prey freezes when it senses a predator in its midst. Ansel's role in the Family wasn't public knowledge, but the fact that he was a Förstner was well known.

"Nicholette..."

"Not now, Ansel. We can talk later," I told him firmly, discreetly indicating our surroundings. Plus, who knew where Alexei and Maksim were. *At least Vas isn't here. This is already going to be a shit show of epic proportions.*

"Stop fucking dismissing me," he snarled, grabbing my arm and forcing me to spin around to face him.

"I'm trying to fucking focus," I hissed, instantly pissed off by his tone. "Plus, like you said, I'm with seven people. Why would—"

He grabbed the back of my neck, yanking me toward him to claim a kiss despite my protests. I moaned when he nipped my bottom lip, and I instinctively pushed my body against his when our tongues tangled together. I wrapped my arms around his neck. It felt like hours had passed before we pulled away from each other even though I knew it had barely been minutes.

"You're an idiot," I told him hoarsely. I hated that I had responded to him, and I couldn't even blame it on pregnancy horniness. I had always felt safe with Ansel, something that he had called me an idiot for previously, but it had always been true. When we were together, he put me through hell—physically, mentally, and emotionally, and I loved that he challenged me that way. Mercy wasn't something I wanted when he called me.

"Rhodes' nephews look pissed." Ansel sounded amused

by that, which was definitely not a good omen for how the rest of my day was going to go. I squeezed my eyes shut and took a deep breath, listening to the sound of approaching footsteps from the safety of Ansel's arms. "Conrad. Robin."

I opened my eyes to Blake's men standing beside us, their serious gazes set on Ansel and me, especially how close we were, before looking toward the station where Alexei and Maksim must be standing. *If I look at them now, I'll never be able to walk away.*

"Welcome to the party," I told them with a grin. "It's about to get really fucking interesting."

Alexei

WE HAD COME to the police station to try to get Oliver and Bodhi out of custody. Sacha and Vas had been here most of yesterday, and they'd reported back that the cops had largely ignored them. I was honestly surprised that they hadn't gotten arrested since neither man was the type you could just ignore. When the detective had taken the two men from the compound, Sacha's anger had been something to behold. Vas, somehow the surprising voice of reason, had managed to keep his brother outwardly calm enough to prevent him from being arrested, so Maksim and I had volunteered to take the second shot at figuring out what the hell was going on.

It had been an uneventful and frustrating day until I felt Maksim tense up beside me. I glanced over only to find him staring out the window beyond him and felt my heart jump into my throat.

Nicholette.

She was standing there talking to Ansel Förstner. Whatever was being discussed was intense, which was almost enough to have me striding forward, but then my jaw dropped when he grabbed her and kissed her. As if that weren't enough, she didn't knee him in the dick or push him away and knock him out. No, she actually responded, kissing him back. *Oh hell no.*

We were on our feet and out the door in seconds, but we both stopped short when they broke apart as two other men joined them. I swore to god if we didn't kick Nic's ass, Vas was going to the moment he heard about this. The memory of him chasing Nic down at the club after the bullshit with Finn and Lacey flashed through my mind.

"Think the baby will stop him?" Maksim asked dryly, his eyes flicking over to meet mine. Although he was showing his trademark smirk, it didn't reach his eyes. I wasn't surprised he was thinking the same thing I was.

"No," I replied with a rough laugh as I ran a hand through my hair. "We need to tell them she's here."

"And find out who the fuck those other guys are," Maksim growled. He pulled out a cigarette and lit it before he grabbed his phone. "I'll call Rhodes."

"Thanks so much, brother," I snarked, ignoring the heat that filled me when his smirk warmed in response. *Asshole.*

Walking away from him, I selected Sacha's name and waited for him to pick up, keeping an eye on Nic as she talked to the men around her. Right before the voicemail picked up, the call was answered, though it was Vas, not Sacha, who spoke.

"Did you get Oliver and Bodhi out?" I couldn't say I minded that he cut right to the chase.

"No," I replied. "But you both should get down here. Now."

"We are a little busy at the—" Sacha tacked on, his annoyance coming through.

"You're not now," I said, firmly cutting him off. "She's here."

A heavy pause.

"Nicholette is there?!" Sacha asked. The hair on the back of my neck stood on end at the promise of violence and pain in his voice.

"Is she under arrest?" Vas added on. A gunshot sounded in the background, then the shuffling noise told me they were moving.

"No," I said quietly. I wasn't sure how they were going to take this next part, but I knew I couldn't keep it to myself. "She isn't alone."

"Don't tell me, Maeve?" Vas guessed.

"Ansel Förstner," I said grimly. "And a few others I don't know. Maksim is talking to Rhodes right now."

"We will be there in ten," Sacha promised, then he disconnected the call.

"Rhodes is on his way," Maksim said from beside me, blowing out smoke along with his words.

"Did you mention the kiss?"

"Fuck no." Maksim inhaled deeply. "That's on Nic, not me."

"You don't care?" I asked, surprised, yet not, as I waited for his answer.

"She's alive, and she came back. Even if it's not permanent yet, she'll be back for good. Or did you really think she just happened to show up while Bodhi and Oli were here?" I paused and stared at him. He just shook his head at me like I was being slow. "Nicholette is a schemer, Alexei. She has plans upon plans in that brain of hers. Keeping us guessing is part of her fun. The question is whether she'll share some of it with us, or is she just here to save those two?"

"And Ansel?" I asked.

"Don't know about that one. Besides, he kissed her first, not the other way around. But, like I said, that's on her to explain. Her being with someone else doesn't affect her being with me or us being together, so why should I care?" It was jarring to hear him mention our relationship out loud and prioritize it. I'd done so much denying when it came to us that even while it warmed me, it gave me pause. He took another long drag of his cigarette just as the front door of the police station opened to reveal Detective Allen.

"Nicholette," he called out, raising a hand. "Glad you could make it."

Nic turned around to face him, her cocky smirk firmly in place as she pulled away from Ansel's hold. Roderick offered his arm to her, leading the way. Nicholette didn't glance our way as she came up the steps and made her way inside. Every part of me ached to reach out to her, to kiss her, scream at her, wanting fucking anything other than to be ignored.

"If she looks over here, she won't be able to follow through with it," a smooth voice commented beside me. I glanced over as Maksim did the same. Ansel Förstner was standing beside us watching Nicholette disappear, the two men I didn't know following them inside. "But I think it's time I caught you up on what I do know."

Nicholette
Monday

"Where were you Saturday night and Sunday morning?" Allen started, his serious face staring me down from across the interrogation table. He hadn't brought anyone in with him, so it was just the two of us and Roderick in the small space. If not for the horrible beige walls and two-way mirrors, it could have been almost cozy... which, when I thought about it, was a whole other set of issues in itself. I really had spent way too much time on the streets and in police stations if I was considering the coziness of a goddamn interrogation room.

Roderick nodded, indicating I should answer. "In Boston with some friends. Hung out a bit, ate, went to sleep."

"Anyone who can verify that?" he asked, writing something down in his notebook.

"Blake and Emmerich Förstner."

Allen nodded a few times before looking at Roderick. "I assume I need to go through you to speak with them as well?"

"Yes," he replied smoothly. "I can reach out to my other

clients after this if you need a verbal statement. If you need something in person, I will need to talk with them before setting something up with you."

Allen let out a long sigh before he roughly rubbed his face. I could see the deep lines on his face, and it took everything in me to not reach across to ask what else was going on.

"Nicholette—"

Just then, there was banging on the door, drawing all our stares when it was followed by the sound of arguing. Suddenly, Detective Lewis burst in, his gaze on me.

"You," he hissed. His face was bright red with rage, and there was a faint tremor in his body that told me he had actually begun to shake at the sight of me.

"You can direct all communication with my client to me, detective," Roderick said sternly. When the man began to advance toward us, Roderick stood up, putting not only his words but his body between Lewis and me.

Allen stood up a second later, angling his body toward the interloper. "Lewis! This is my interview." He stopped the other man when he got closer, and Allen's white-knuckled grip on Lewis' arm told me how much strength he had to put into that.

"It's mine now," Lewis snapped, leveling a glower at Allen. "Talk to the chief. She put me back on the case."

"We can talk to her together. After the last time you spoke with Miss Graves, I'll need more than your word to allow you to be in the same room with her," Allen retorted, gesturing toward the door. Lewis growled and stomped out of the room. Through the open doorway, I caught a peek of Robin and Conrad outside before the door slammed shut. Both of them watched the tantrum-throwing detective stalk away with concerned frowns on their faces.

"Well, that was interesting," I commented before turning to look at Roderick. He tipped his head, subtly pointing out the cameras in the room, but I was well aware of their presence. "I know. You'd think Lewis would be taken off my case completely considering the harassment from last time. Does this mean I need an escort to go to the bathroom, or will I be fine on my own?"

Roderick took a deep breath, but I saw the hint of a smile on his face before he started to rub his face. "I'm sure you can go to the bathroom without a police escort. Get one of the guys to walk you."

I slowly got up, wishing I had another ginger candy when my stomach began to roll. When I got to the door, I knocked until a police officer opened it. His nerves were clear in his pinched face as he glanced at the two men closely watching us from either side of the door.

"I need to pee." He opened and closed his mouth, almost as if he were taken aback by my directness, but I just arched an eyebrow and stepped past him out of the room. "No need to show me around, officer. I know the way. Just wanted to let you know where I was going in case the detective comes back."

I strode down the hallway, heading for the closest restroom, and someone fell into step beside me, making others around us give us a wide berth. I looked over to find Conrad nearby, his hard gaze scanning the people around us. He never took his eyes off them to look at me, but I knew he had noticed my scrutiny.

"Yes?" he asked gruffly.

"Just curious to see who was walking with me. But I do actually have to pee," I told him as we arrived at the bathroom. "Can you do something for me? See if you can figure out where the others are being questioned."

"Your... guys?" he asked, focusing on me. I could practically see him weighing my words, judging my sincerity, as I met his serious light blue stare with my own.

I nodded. Not waiting for him to say anything else, I went to the bathroom, quickly took care of my business, and headed back out. I probably should have stalled a little longer, giving Conrad some time to poke around, but a girl can only think so clearly when dealing with a lack of sleep and morning sickness.

Before I even realized that Conrad wasn't nearby, likely doing what I had asked, there was a hand clamping down over my mouth and an arm dragging me back into the bathroom. I instantly knew who it was thanks to the familiar, comforting smell of cigarettes. I hadn't seen this coming, but I wasn't going to fight it.

Rhodes closed the door and turned the lock before he let me go. I backed up a few steps, not sure what reaction I was going to get from him. *Or what mine is going to be if I'm being honest.* Just our close proximity made me want to run into his arms, but I knew that I'd never find it in me to walk away. Shit, if this was how I felt seeing Rhodes, seeing Vas and Sacha might just kill me. It wasn't that I loved them more than I did Rhodes. My connection with them had just burned so brightly and intensely from the start, and the rest of our relationship had followed that trend.

It was silent between us, and I stood there, watching him carefully, waiting for him to say something to me. Instead, he remained still with his back to me. He was wearing his usual black leather boots, black jeans, and his leather jacket with the Lords of Chaos patch on the back. I was equally sad and happy I couldn't see his face yet.

"Rhodes—"

He shook his head and held out a hand. "You could

have come to us," he said roughly, still facing the door. "You could have come to us instead of taking off without a damn word like you always do."

Tears stung my eyes, but I refused to let them fall. "I did what was necessary—" I believed those words, I truly did, but now that I was saying them out loud to one of the men I'd left behind, they tasted like ashes in my mouth.

"You did things your own damn way, fuck the rest of us!" Rhodes shot back. He finally whirled around, his gray eyes dark and stormy and a shaking finger pointed directly at me. "You fucking walked out on us. You should have trusted us to help you!"

"It's not about you, Rhodes!" I shot back, my anger getting the better of me. "Did you ever think about that? It's not about you or me. Maybe I fucked up, but I did the best I could with what I knew. Sorry if you couldn't handle that."

"Leaving us was the solution you truly thought was best?!" he hissed, stalking forward. His hand shot out, grabbing me by the wrist and walking me backward until I was pinned against the cold tile wall.

"I left so I could come back," I told him. I twisted my hand in his hold but he held steady, I wasn't trying to escape his hold; I was craving more contact between us, wanting to feel the warmth of his skin against mine. "You don't trust me? After everything, hotshot?"

Rhodes' arm shook, and I could see his emotions warring for control until he slammed his lips on mine. I whimpered, kissing him back and wrapping my arms around his shoulders to pull him closer. Pressing myself against him, I savored every hard line of his body as he nipped my bottom lip and my blood sweetened the kiss. Relief filled me. I knew the guys would be angry, understandably so, but I was hoping they would listen before they lost it completely. If he was holding me, kissing me, then that meant I hadn't completely broken things between us. I actually had hope that my relationships would make it through. There was no way they'd be unscathed, but if we could survive, scars and all, I still wanted a future with these men.

He broke the kiss, pressing his forehead to mine. "Ansel said you have a plan."

"You talked to Ansel?"

"He mentioned you were staying with the Germans these past couple of days," he said dryly, his hands stroking my sides as if he couldn't believe I was here. "I didn't catch the rest because I came inside to find you."

"Allen is questioning me about things, including the newest dead girl," I told him softly. "I can't be gone for too long."

"Just answer one thing for me, Nic, and I want the truth." He put a finger under my chin, forcing me to look up and hold his gaze. "Why did you take your stuff?"

I furrowed my brow, my eyes searching his face. "What?"

"Your things. From the apartment. You could have just—"

My eyes widened. "Rhodes, what are you talking about?"

He froze, realization dawning on his face. "You didn't..."

"I never went back to their apartment. In my mind, the ghosting was enough," I whispered. My heart was breaking as what they must have thought hit me. *Did they think that I was really leaving them? Oh, god.* Then anger came in. Someone had gone into my safe space, their apartment, and taken my things. "I left everything behind so Sacha and them... I didn't want them to think I was just like Ava. Rhodes, that means they were in their apartment!"

"We can tell them—" he started, but I leaned back, violently shaking my head as I grasped at his leather jacket.

"If they were taking pictures of us at the compound, maybe they're doing more than that. Think about it... If this person or people have been in the apartment, they might even have cameras set up too. I wouldn't put it past them at this point. It's not safe for me to go back, Rhodes." My voice cracked, tears coming way too easily. No matter what they might have thought, leaving them behind hadn't been easy for me. All that had gotten me through it—the separation, knowing the hurt feelings waiting for me, the loneliness— had been the knowledge that I'd be with them again, that this wasn't permanent.

"Nic," he breathed, closing his eyes, but not before I saw the sheen of tears.

"It's not just about us anymore, hotshot. I *can't* go back yet."

"Bodhi found a test. At your apartment..." Rhodes rasped. He opened his eyes as his hands cupped my cheeks. He stayed silent, waiting for me to answer his unfinished question.

I hummed, looking anywhere but at him. "I had an IUD, Rhodes. It was never supposed to happen!"

"Nic..."

"I swear! I didn't mean... I don't even know what you all think! Hell, I don't know what *I* think most of the time. Fuck, I can't—" He slanted his lips over mine in a searing kiss. It was so different than the kiss just a few minutes earlier; the hardened man against me was being so fucking gentle and understanding. He didn't demand I respond; no, he *coaxed* me into it. I lost myself in him, leaning forward to slide my hands under his jacket. I needed to feel him under my hands. He broke the kiss and pulled back the barest distance, long pieces of his black and gray hair brushing my face.

"Love..." He wiped my cheeks with his thumbs, making me realize I was crying again.

"Please don't," I pleaded, hating the way my voice cracked. "I can't go with you right now, and if you're being all understanding, I won't be able to do what I came here to do."

"Get Oli and Bodhi out of custody?"

"No," I managed with a half smile, "but I certainly gave Lewis a distraction so they could get a break. Plus, I'm sure Roderick is advising them of a few things right now since Conrad probably found them while we were in here. I passed him a note on the way inside."

"Then what's the plan, Nic?" he asked, slowly stepping back from me. "Give me something to tell the others. If not, I guarantee they will shoot their way through this police station until they get their hands on you."

"That seems a tiny bit extreme," I deadpanned. "But completely in line with how Vas and Sacha would handle things. I needed to talk with a friend, and this is the best way I could go about it."

"Then you're going back to the Germans? Is that where you've been this whole time?"

"Maybe, and no," I answered him, unwilling to elaborate when I heard a bunch of people running by the bathroom. "What is going on out there?"

"If I had to guess, Vas is here. He made a scene yesterday."

"So fucking dramatic," I huffed, rolling my eyes even as

my heart ached. I wished I could run to him, not away, when I opened that door. "I have to go."

"Nic—"

"Please, hotshot. Trust me." I looked up at him with bright eyes. "I promise I'm doing everything I can to come back home."

"I'm fucking your ass when I see you again. Lube is *very* fucking unlikely the longer you take," he promised me roughly, his fists clenching and unclenching, but I only grinned.

"Promises, promises, old man."

"I'll show you old," he growled, pulling me close to kiss me one more time. My knees buckled, but he caught me, holding me tight. I grabbed the envelope I had stashed away inside my cami and stuck it inside his jacket with a whispered order to look at it when he knew he wasn't being watched.

Unable to stomach the idea of goodbye, I let him go and walked to the door, stopping only when he said my name. Glancing over my shoulder, he gave me a fierce look. "Give them hell, love."

"Oh, hotshot, it's the only thing I know how to dish out, which you know first hand."

With that, I walked out, not letting myself look back. I hurried past the interview room, and Robin fell into step beside me as I approached the back entrance. Conrad joined us right before we stepped outside.

"Did you find them?" I asked, scanning the vehicles parked nearby.

"Yes. Oliver was yelling through the closed door of his interrogation room to talk to Bodhi, who was set up in another room across the hallway. Something about cheap pizza and a game of hide and seek when they got out? I think they were having a blast. Some of the nearby cops looked exasperated but amused once Oliver moved on to describe how he was going to fuck Bodhi when they got out of there. He took a break from oversharing when Roderick came by."

I snorted as Robin chuckled. "Glad they're doing well."

"Those look fresh," Robin said softly, gesturing at his mouth, and I sighed. Rhodes must have nipped me harder than I realized. Reaching up I brushed my hand across my mouth only to find small drops of blood on my fingers.

"Yes, I had a little... chat with one of my boyfriends who had managed to sneak inside. Which reminds me... We need to get the fuck out of here, or they're going to drag me back before I'm ready."

"Isn't this going to make them even more pissed?" Conrad asked. I was about to answer him, but then I caught sight of something that sent me hurrying down the steps— Maeve's car.

"Definitely. But the guys like a good chase, and their anger will just make things more fun when we do get back together. Anyway, this is where we need to go our separate ways, boys. Thanks for the escort."

I waved at them both, tugged the car door open, and slid inside before they could react. Maeve pulled away from the curb, expertly weaving through traffic while I consciously kept myself from glancing in the mirrors to see who was standing around. My guys might have convinced me to stay but leaving is what I will always be best at.

"Nicholette," Maeve purred.

"Maeve," I said coldly, shifting my full attention to the woman beside me.

Her white-blonde hair was neatly pulled back in a chignon, not a single wisp out of place. She was in a cream pantsuit, and the white shirt beneath her blazer featured a deep V-neckline that bared the swell of her breasts. Her makeup was perfectly applied; honestly, everything about her just made me feel like a complete fucking mess.

"What information do you need from me? Tell me, and I'll give you my price for it." I nervously licked my lips, wanting, no, *needing* to trust her with this task because I knew I couldn't do it myself. But there was just something holding me back from answering her question. I must have been silent for too long because Maeve repeated my name with uncharacteristic softness.

She turned into a parking garage and pulled into a stall before she twisted in her seat and grabbed my chin, forcing me to face her. Her hands were slender, soft, a complete contrast to the men who had claimed me so thoroughly. *Not to mention Ansel... which is so not helpful, brain.* I met her curious and cautious bright blue eyes and drank in the face of the woman who still stole my breath away, even after everything that had played out between us.

"I need you to look into Joe and Miranda Graves," I told her roughly, allowing her to maintain her hold on me. "Give me everything you can find about them. You have twenty-four hours before I'll be going to Millfield."

"You want information on your parents?" she asked. The tone conveyed her confusion more than anything else. The woman had perfected the emotionless mask that she used often enough.

"Parents is a very loose term, Maeve, but I suppose they did raise me, for better or worse." I huffed out a humorless laugh as I moved my chin away from her hand. "Where do you want me to meet you for the drop-off?"

"What is going on, Nicholette? You ran off with your men only to ghost them," she asked instead of answering my question. "I've known you to be a bit unpredictable when it suits you. They didn't tell me everything, but I want to know. That's my price for helping you."

Of course it was. *Information, the best kind of currency.* I wouldn't agree to this deal from just anybody, but with our past and what I was asking her to do, I'd pay it. This once.

"I had more than one stalker," I told her, facing forward to stare at the empty cars around us. "There was Warren ramping up, spiraling to own me, and a second stalker, who had been following me since I arrived in Ashview. They killed old johns of mine and even some clients you set up for me. They're escalating now, dropping dead bodies of women they've altered to look like me." I looked over to find Maeve watching me intently, showing nothing but patience. "They took my little brother. Said they would sell him to the highest bidder if I didn't follow their instructions and leave."

"So you left?"

"Yes."

Maeve nodded a few times, searching my face. "What else?"

I squeezed my eyes shut and pressed a hand to my stomach when it rolled. Maeve followed the movement and paled, her eyes shooting back up to meet mine. After a small shake of my head, she held the words back, not voicing what she'd realized.

"It's not simple anymore," I whispered roughly. "There's no place that's safe until this person is gone. I might put myself in constant danger without a care, but now I'm protecting not only my partners, but innocents. Maeve, there is nothing I won't do to protect what's mine. *Nothing.* Get me that information."

"Nic," she murmured before taking a deep breath. "I'll

get your information. And a bit of unsolicited advice from an old friend? Ask Roderick to make a will... just in case. You have enough assets from your work. You will want to make sure you have things in place."

I blinked back tears. "I know. I'm going to talk to him about it soon."

"I'll get started on retrieving your information and get in touch for a drop-off. I have Ansel's number. If I need more than twenty-four hours, I'll let you know."

The car doors unlocked, and I reached for the door, but instead of opening it, I faced the woman I loved and hated in equal measure, someone who had helped shape me into the woman I was today. "Maeve?" She hummed, and I leaned over, pressing a soft kiss to her cheek. "In case I don't get a chance to say it later, thank you. For everything, even if I hated it at the time. I could only hate you so much because of how deeply I love you. Maybe if things had been different... There will always be a part of my heart that's yours even though you never wanted it."

Maeve slowly turned, tilting her head to gently brush her lips against mine. "Goodbye, little one."

She hasn't used that nickname in years. Tears filled my eyes, and I rushed out of the car, moving as fast as I could until I strode toward the exit of the parking garage. Apparently, this was going to be a thing now—saying my goodbyes just in case this all went to shit later. I was under no illusions about my possible survival rate. Making over women to look like me, then killing them... that was a whole other level of depraved.

A warm breeze hit my face as I stepped out of the parking garage. I glanced around and realized I was only a few blocks from the police station with no ride nearby, no cell phone, and no idea of where I was going. But fate had other plans. A black car pulled up, blocking my path, then the back door opened. Before I knew it, I was being hauled inside, someone's hand covering my mouth to keep me quiet as the car peeled away.

"So glad you decided to join us, Nicholette," Sacha purred dangerously from the front seat. Vas let go of me just long enough for him to grab duct tape and press it over my mouth before winding it around my wrists as well. *Thank goodness he kept them in front of me.* "I've been thinking about this reunion for the past four weeks, twelve hours, and thirty-six minutes... in a lot of detail. I hope you're ready."

A muffled whimper escaped, then Vas pulled a bag over my head, letting the darkness take over.

I was so fucking screwed.

And horny.

Fuck, I hope I don't throw up.

Vas
Monday

Holding Nic in my arms felt fucking surreal after a month of her being away. Sacha didn't say anything else after threatening Nic. He was focusing on driving around, taking a meandering route with extra turns to disorient her. Nic didn't try to fight or escape, but she didn't lean into me either, so I hauled her up, holding her tight to my chest. She had *left* us. Right now, when I finally had her back in my arms, I wasn't going to put up with even a tiny attempt at some defensive kind of distance.

Sacha had spiraled during Nic's absence, his hair-trigger temper back at full force, replacing the calm man he had become with her around to balance him. My rage, however, had cooled. I became more quiet and calm, at least outwardly. Inside, I was hurt and *so fucking angry* that Nic had just left. She'd walked out of our lives at the drop of a hat, taking everything with her, without so much as a glance back at what we had together.

I knew it might be a little more complicated than that, but the fact that someone was stalking her, the same someone who had possibly taken her brother, somehow didn't matter right now. If she had thought for even a second that I wouldn't track her down and drag her back to me, then she hadn't been paying attention when I carved my name into her. *Maybe I need to think of another way to get my point across.*

"You have so much to answer for, slut," I told her. She didn't respond, though I could feel her shiver in my arms. "First, though, I want to know whose shirt this is so I can fucking blow his brains out." I ran my hand along the men's shirt she had on, not giving one fuck when I tore it off of her, ripping it apart to leave her in just the cami she had on underneath. Fuck, I couldn't let myself think of all the people she'd walked by today, looking like this, on display for everyone. It would just piss me off more.

Reaching around her, I cupped her breast, enjoying the muffled moan she couldn't contain, then I squeezed her hard, needing to make her feel a fraction of the pain she'd put me through. My dick throbbed with her cry, and I was being overtaken by the feel of her soft skin against mine. Fuck talking. I just might need to fuck through my anger before we could get to the talking part. A glare from Sacha told me he knew exactly what I was thinking. *Such a fucking prick... but maybe he's a little bit right.* I needed to keep my shit together.

"Don't worry though. Right now, I might be the least of your worries, to be honest. Sacha is *pissed*, slut."

"I'm so fucking beyond pissed off, brother," Sacha drawled from the front seat, and part of me wondered if I would need to police not only my anger, but his, once we got to our destination.

Nicholette tried to say something, but I couldn't make it out. She started getting more worked up, so I reached under the hood to loosen it. I wasn't willing to take it off, but I wanted to make sure she could breathe. We wanted to send her a message, not kill her, so I tore off the tape. She took a shaky breath and mumbled something about our destination.

"It doesn't matter," Sacha responded sharply.

"Not the warehouse, the compound, or your apartment," she retorted vehemently, gaining back her usual strength.

"What makes you think you get any say in where we take you?" I asked. The anger that I was keeping a tight rein on flared, pulling at my control. She had the audacity to mouth off to us right now?

"Because *I* didn't take any of my stuff out of your apartment when I left," she said with a slight hitch in her breathing. Hearing those words made me feel like I'd gotten the wind knocked out of me, and even Sacha glanced back, but Nic wasn't done dropping bombs on us. "Which means they were in your apartment."

"Cameras?" I asked. My mind was already racing at the idea of someone having been in our place; that shouldn't be possible. The building had its own security with a front desk and surveillance cameras all around, and Oliver had set up his own measures inside of the apartment. If someone had been inside, we should have known about it.

"I wouldn't put it past them considering all the pictures they had plastered all over my apartment. Cameras would be the next logical move," Nic said calmly, seemingly unbothered by her tied-up state. "But if you could take the hood off—"

"Why the hell should we do you any fucking favors? It's not like you listen to us," Sacha ranted.

"Shut up, Sacha. Take the fucking thing off, Vas!"

Something in her voice sounded off, so I ignored Sacha's

bitching and took it off. Not a second too soon either because she puked in the cloth hood until she was dry heaving. Her entire body shook from the force of it. When she tried to wipe her mouth, she stopped mid-motion as if she'd just remembered she was restrained.

"Nicholette—"

"Be prepared for a lot more of that in the coming months if my experience over the past four weeks has anything to say about it," she deadpanned, spitting into the hood before wrinkling her nose. "Ugh, that's fucking awful. I need to get that medicine."

My heart pounded in my chest with the realization of what she meant. Sacha must have had the same thought because he swerved the car over and parked, his hands clenching and unclenching around the steering wheel before he managed to speak from between clenched teeth.

"Does that mean you're..."

"Rhodes said you found the test, boss," Nic said softly, keeping her eyes away from his. "You should call him."

Sacha slammed his hands on the steering wheel while cursing her out in Russian, complaining about how she didn't listen and promising he was going to kick her ass, pregnant or not. Nic chuckled beside me then looked over, her blue-green eyes bright with tears. "I don't know Russian, but I get the gist of the tone. He knows that, right?"

My lips twitched despite my best efforts. With a sigh, I dug around in the car until I found a napkin and wiped her mouth for her. I threw it in the hood and tied the whole thing up before opening the car door to toss it out, not wanting the puke smell to fill the car. "Why should we call Rhodes? I think it's safe to say that Sacha and I want to hear this from you, Nic. No, we *deserve* to hear it from you, not Rhodes."

Just as she opened her mouth, Sacha's phone rang. He glared back at us through the rearview mirror before answering on speaker.

"Sacha. Meet me in Shadowglen Estates. I'll meet you at the gate, and we can all go in together. The others are already on their way. I have information," Rhodes said. The flick of a lighter came over the line after his claim.

"This have anything to do with Nic?" I asked, staring down at the woman in question.

"Yeah, and some other people. The Förstners are going to be there in force. All hell broke loose today."

Nicholette let out a loud huff of annoyance. "Is Ansel there?"

There was a moment of tense silence. "Nic?!"

"Tell him we need a little bit, then we'll be there," Nic said, glancing between my brother and me. "We have a bit of catching up to do. He can yell at me later."

"Why would Ansel be yelling at you?" Sacha crooned.

"Is this really the best time—" Nic shot back. I cut her off by wrapping my hand around her throat, squeezing lightly in warning.

"I swear to god, slut, if you kissed one more goddamn person, I'm going to lose my everloving shit."

"I need to know the answer to that too before I hang up, love," Rhodes added on, inhaling deeply.

Nicholette didn't say anything for a minute, taking a deep breath before visibly bracing herself, but she didn't say what I thought she would. "I talked to Maeve. That's who I saw before you kidnapped me. You're not the only one with updates, so let's all play catch-up together at Ansel's place in a few hours."

I'm going to kill her.

I'd just gotten her back, but I was ready to throttle her.

"I kissed her before I got out of the car," she tacked on like we needed the clarification.

Rhodes whistled. "Ansel must be really fucking important if you're using Maeve as a way to side-step talking about him. I'll remember that when I talk to my old friend while we wait."

Click.

The silence was deafening. We all sat there, no one willing to break it, until Sacha took a deep breath, unbuckled his seatbelt, and got out of the car. The slam of the door behind him shook the car with its force, and Nic didn't try to follow him.

"You always come in like a wrecking ball, don't you?" I murmured, running my fingers through her hair.

"Well, you smacked me the last time I made this big of an entrance. I guess it's Sacha's turn." I knew it was her attempt at a joke, but her voice cracked. It was that little sign of emotion from her that made my heart start to tremble. I buried my face in her hair, unable to process everything that had been thrown at me in the last few minutes. God, I missed her and the whirlwind of chaos that followed in her wake.

"I hate you for leaving, Nic. I get it and hate it all at the same time," I whispered into her hair.

"If it had been Sacha, you would have done the same thing." She sniffled, rubbing her face with her restrained hands.

"So it was your brother who was taken?" I asked, and she said it was. "Fuck."

Nic leaned back and looked up at me. I reached out, tucking loose strands of hair behind her ear as I met her stare, noting the sheen of unshed tears as she swallowed hard. "You said you'd burn the world down for me, big guy.

Did you really think I wouldn't do the same for all of you? Walking away almost killed me, but this is about my brother, us... more than us. This time, I'm the one calling the shots. I need to be."

"As if you haven't been calling them most of the time already," Sacha deadpanned, startling both of us. Apparently, he had rejoined us. How I'd missed the car door opening and closing, I wasn't sure, but I was glad to see some of the anger had faded from his eyes. "But this time, you're telling us the plan, Nic. No more going around behind our backs and figuring shit out on your own. That's over with."

"Does that apply to you as well, boss? Or just me?"

"All of us," I answered on his behalf. I wasn't going to let their dick measuring contest get in the way of things moving forward. "But we deserve to hear some answers from you first, Nic, not just bombs dropped on us in front of everyone."

She bit her bottom lip and looked out the window, probably thinking over everything she had set in motion since she left. Nic let out an unsteady breath then shifted away from me, putting her back to the door so she could face us both.

"What do you want to know first?"

"You're pregnant?" I asked before Sacha could speak. I needed to hear the words from her for it to be real. Sacha watched Nicholette like a hawk as we both waited for her to answer.

"Yes." Nic licked her bottom lip, her face scrunching up in disgust, probably because she could still taste the bile from earlier. "And no, I have no idea which one of you did it."

A bark of laughter fell from my lips at her dry tone as I

rubbed my face. Fuck. *Pregnant.* I had no idea what to do with that or how I felt about it. Over the past month, the thought of it had been an abstract idea, but with her confirming it, I had no idea how I felt.

Sacha broke through my spiraling with his next question. "What have you been doing the past month?"

"Probably the same thing you have, boss." Nic smirked. "You kept killing people I was trying to track down, and I have a feeling I did, too."

"Did you kill Karen Ellenburg and Tim Johnson?" I asked.

"Yes," Nic purred, rage flashing in her eyes. "They died too quickly for my liking, but I got information from them. It's why I needed to meet with Maeve. She's going to confirm what they told me."

"Where have you been this entire time? In Boston with Emmerich?" Sacha asked blandly. Nicholette blinked, and for the first time, she looked nervous. "Don't you dare fucking lie to us right now. Were you with *Ansel?*"

"I've been here. In Ashview," she practically whispered, curling up like she expected us to lash out. Sacha froze beside me, and I knew that he had seen her recoil. His deep breaths filled the moment of silence before I spoke.

"You've been in Ashview this entire time?"

She looked at me when I asked that, though she kept glancing at Sacha, aware of his every movement. "Yeah. I stayed with a friend for a few days at a time before leaving again. Can't really question and kill people in a city apartment. People get nosy. And I owe you answers for a lot more, I know I do, but everyone should hear them. You all know how I am with emotions and shit. Can I just tell you all at once? They won't be watching us at Ansel's place."

"How confident are you of that?" I asked her, reaching

out for her wrists to rip the duct tape off. She didn't flinch as I did it, calmly rubbing her wrists once they were freed.

"Very, very fucking sure," she replied. "Think we can stop and get some shit on the way? I cannot sit here just tasting this crap the entire way up there."

The hint of a smile on Sacha's face made Nic grin back at him before it crumbled away. "I can't say I'm sorry because I'm not. Not about leaving to protect what's important to me, including all of you jackasses. But I missed you all, every damn second of every damn day."

I didn't even have to think about it. I grabbed her, hugging her to me, and she broke down. Every damn ounce of anger I had left. Hot tears splashed on my neck as she fell into me, sobs making her body shake, and wrapped her arms around my neck. She mumbled things I couldn't understand while I ran a hand through her hair. Sacha watched us with a serious expression until he couldn't wait anymore.

With a much more gentle touch than I had been expecting from him, he touched Nic's arm. She pulled back and moved toward Sacha without so much as wiping her face. He pulled her through the small gap between the front seats to sit her in his lap. She held onto him tightly, mumbling incoherent things into his neck as he crushed her to him. Sacha's stoic expression fell away, and I saw every moment of pain and sadness since Nic had left flicker across his face before he squeezed his eyes shut, letting himself sink into her.

I was glad she was home. And even though this reunion had gone a lot smoother than I thought it would, so far at least, I knew it wouldn't stay that way. Nic had a lot of secrets, and, to be honest, Sacha and I weren't the ones she needed to worry about seeing again.

Oliver was going to be something else when he saw her.

Not to mention who knew what everyone's reaction to the baby would be... Hell, I didn't know *my* reaction to the news. Bodhi... I didn't think he was going to take it well, and Maksim... The only person who could even begin to guess how that fucker would react was Alexei. I guessed there were just some things that I had to wait to see how they unfolded.

Except Ansel.

I was going to punch him the moment I fucking saw him.

Ansel
Monday

"Probably a good time to warn everyone that Nic's men are... different," Emmerich said from where he was sprawled in an armchair in the living room. One leg was thrown over the side, and he slouched down, not caring that he was wrinkling the black slacks and white button-up he was wearing.

Blake snorted at that and looked at their men; some silent conversation happened between them before they all nodded.

"Meaning?"

"That I honestly wouldn't be surprised if they physically dragged her out of here at the end of the night. No matter what anyone else wants, especially Nic."

"Not to mention a few bruises for the stunt she pulled," Blake drawled, leaning their head back against the sofa. I could see a hint of a smile on their lips despite their words, but the men looked concerned, particularly Atlas and Conrad. I wasn't surprised by my children's comments; the need to wring Nic's damn neck after what happened at the police station was strong, so I could only imagine how the others felt about her up and disappearing for a month.

Of course, they are actually with her unlike myself...

The thought twisted me up inside in ways it definitely shouldn't. But I wasn't left to myself for long because the front door crashed in right before my name was bellowed out.

I arched an eyebrow and remained in my chair, watching the entryway as one of my oldest friends, Rhodes Angeloff, stormed inside. Apparently, he'd decided he wasn't going to wait for Nicholette like he had said in his texts. His long black and gray hair fell into his face, but I had no trouble seeing the glint of promised violence in his gray eyes. We had similar builds, but where I usually dressed nicely, Rhodes wore jeans, t-shirt, and his Lords of Chaos jacket. The scars on his cheeks stood out even more when he glared at me.

"You!"

"I'm afraid I'll need more context, Rhodes," I deadpanned, not the least bit intimidated. His nephews walked in behind him, staying out of the way. Alexei Volkov and Maksim Angeloff were dangerous and powerful men in their own right. Alexei had a razor-sharp mind, and even I found Maksim's taste for pain impressive at times. With links to not only their mercenary cousins but the Lords, they were feared among many. "I've done a lot of things for you to yell at me for. What did I do this particular time?"

"I think he means to say..." a man I couldn't see started to speak. He sauntered out from behind Rhodes with a taunting smirk firmly in place. Another young man trailed behind him, pushing his longer brown hair out of his face. "What the fuck were you doing with our woman?"

Surprise hit me the moment I got a good look at him—

short dirty blond hair, gauges in both ears, and tattoos along his arms. His hazel eyes searched my expression with predatory intensity. His face, though... I'd seen it many times before. It was familiar in a way that I would never forget, and from the sudden stillness in the room, I knew I wasn't the only one who had noticed the resemblance. *Does Nicholette know too?* Anyway, now was not the time to bring it up.

"I think you should remember whose house you're in," I retorted coldly as I slowly stood up. "You don't own her, and all I did was help out an old friend."

"That's not all, though, was it?" Rhodes crooned, and before I could say anything, an icy voice cut through the building tension.

"Glad to see you're all getting along," Nicholette called out as she waltzed into the room, her cocky smile firmly in place. Sacha and Vas Morozov slowly walked in behind her, their faces unreadable and gazes locked on Nic. The shirt she had been wearing, *my* shirt, was gone, leaving her in just a cami with no bra underneath. I thought I could see a hint of redness around her mouth and her wrists, but she didn't seem concerned about it.

"We deserve an explanation—" the man giving me a hard time started, but the glare she leveled in his direction instantly cut him off.

"Sacha said we should share some information," she said briskly, completely focused on business. She walked past the Morozovs, dodging the hand that Vas shot out to try to stop her. Nicholette didn't look back when she got closer to me, and I took a step to the side, letting her take the chair I had vacated like a fucking queen. I moved over to stand behind Emmerich's chair, ready to see how this unfolded. "So where should we start?"

"Oh my god, Nic," Blake muttered with a shake of their head. There was a spark of admiration in Blake's eyes as Nic stared at her people with an expectant expression.

"Oh, I don't fucking think so," the blond man glared at Nicholette.

The man who had followed him in said his name and reached out for him, but *Oliver* pulled away from him.

"No. She fucking up and disappeared for a month! Instead of choosing to come to us for help, you ran off," he snarled, pointing a finger at Nic. She didn't react beyond propping her chin on her hand, a patient expression on her face, but that only enraged him further. "I'm going to fucking slap that expression off your damn face, Nic. I swear to god."

"I see you took on some of Vas' anger while I was gone," she replied, seeming not the least bit surprised by the venom in Oliver's voice. "Is everyone else going to keep it together so we can get business done, or are you going to let your emotions get in the way too?"

A whistle escaped one of the others, but everyone else remained motionless, wanting to see Oliver's reaction to Nicholette's taunt. Blake's men kept a close eye on the newcomers, shifting closer to Blake to protect them if shit hit the fan. Well, except Atlas. He had left at some point during the confrontation.

Emmerich hummed and pulled out a gun, idly switching off the safety as he played with it. I shifted in place where I stood behind my son, a little surprised by how fast he'd moved to protect Nicholette. Just how close were they? *Not the time to think of that.*

Alexei made the first move by snagging a kitchen stool. His grip was tight enough that I heard the wood creak under his hand before he settled it beside Emmerich's chair with a distinct thud.

"We should get the business done then, Nic." His dark green eyes met hers with a bland expression. "We have a lot of things to talk about when we're finished here, and you're going to listen to every damn one even if I have to string you up by the rafters to keep you from running away."

"I see foreplay isn't out of the question then," Nicholette quipped, but I didn't miss how she paled. "Did you clear your schedule, Em?"

"Yes." He nodded slowly, his attention zeroing in on Nicholette. "And it looks like my new partner will be here tomorrow to help out."

"Partner?" she asked curiously, eyebrows raised.

"Cosimo Ricci."

Nicholette hummed before glancing at Blake. "I feel like there's a story there for later." Blake grinned, and Nic let out an abrupt laugh before sobering up.

It was Sacha who jumped in next, though he directed his words and his focus at Nicholette as if there was no one else in the room. "You said you had information."

"So do you, boss," Nicholette said lightly. They stared at each other in a silent battle of wills that had everyone on edge until the young man whose name I didn't know spoke up.

"We've been looking for people connected to the trafficking ring," he said, ignoring Oliver when he started cursing. "But it seems *someone* got to a few of them before us."

"I've been hunting on my own." She inclined her head, and I scoffed. I remembered the bodies I had cleaned up for her; she had done a lot more than *hunting* on her own. Rhodes narrowed his eyes at the sound, but Nicholette kept speaking without looking in my direction. "And I found out the names of the top leaders of the ring. Maeve is getting more information on them before I leave tomorrow."

"*We.*" Everyone in the room corrected her at once, including Blake's men, which only made her shrug.

"Fine, *we* leave tomorrow."

"To go where?" Vas asked.

"I want the names," Alexei said, leaning forward as if that would keep her from ignoring his request. "Now."

"I'm not giving them until I hear from—"

"That's no longer an option, love," Rhodes stated, cracking his knuckles. "Whether you like it or not, you aren't playing this alone."

"I'm the one in charge here, Rhodes. Not you, Sacha, or anyone else," she shot back heatedly, blue-green eyes flashing in warning. "Remember that."

"You aren't the only one with important people on the line. Maybe *you* should remember *that*," Alexei countered calmly, but his words hit the mark despite their lack of volume or vitriol.

Nicholette looked down, twisting her fingers nervously. "I know."

"Then maybe you should fucking act like it," Maksim said with a quiet viciousness that made everyone look at him in surprise. I saw a hint of respect in the other men's gazes before they turned back to Nic again.

For her part, Nic didn't look surprised by their hostility. If anything, she seemed to revel in it. A hint of a smile raised her lips before it faded. Then she shifted back, curling up as if to protect herself, and given how Emmerich tensed, I wasn't the only one who'd noticed her position.

"Graves," Nicholette said evenly into the growing

silence. "Joe and Miranda Graves are two of the leaders of the Ashview trafficking ring."

Shock rippled through me. My job had never been to try to figure out information for our Family rivals. Sure, I'd killed a few people here and there associated with them, but my job as hitman was to follow orders, not question them. At least that was what Frederick had always told me when I questioned him. I glanced at my kids, noting the surprise on both of their faces.

"As in..."

A hard laugh ripped from her throat. "My homophobic parents who kicked me out were leaders of a child trafficking ring. Glad to know where their lines were. Maeve is getting information on them before we go up there to see what else we can find."

"Your *parents?*" Oliver asked before stumbling back a few steps.

"Oli—"

"No." He shot out a hand, cutting Nicholette off. "Just no." He spun on his heel and stormed out. The man I didn't know immediately went after him, and I heard yelling before the front door slammed shut.

"Well, that went well," Blake said dryly as they stood up, stretching their arms above their head. "Seems there is plenty for you all to sort out that you don't need me around for."

"I have more questions," Emmerich interjected, talking over them. He tilted his head and made a show of looking at me, then Nic, dramatically shifting his gaze. "You two? Really?"

"There is no us," I said dismissively, waving my hand as if the idea was ridiculous. Nicholette was absolutely no help. All she gave Emmerich was a blank stare as if that would throw him off the scent.

"The kiss at the station didn't make it seem that way," Alexei countered. He looked between me and Nicholette, whose expression remained completely empty. "Especially since she kissed you back."

"Or the fact that Nic decided that telling us she kissed Maeve was a good way to avoid talking about kissing *you*," Vas growled, his flushed face and clenched jaw showing just how jealous he was.

"Maeve? After everything?" Maksim sounded more curious than anything.

"Yes," Nicholette answered hoarsely. "But that doesn't matter."

"The hell it doesn't—" Vas started, but his brother reached out, physically stopping him.

"Why not?" Sacha asked. "What are you up to, Nic?"

I had no idea what Nicholette was thinking as she slowly shook her head and stood up. Instantly realizing what was about to happen, I moved aside so she could rush past me, getting to a bathroom just in time to puke. The sound of her heaving filled the living room until she managed to shut the door behind her.

"Fuck," Maksim groaned as Alexei ran a hand through his hair. The latter sat there without saying a word, the strain of this reunion showing in the lines of his face.

"While she gets herself together..." Emmerich said, shifting in his seat. "You never shared your information with us, so start there."

"Why should we share with you?" Sacha asked coolly, assessing Emmerich with a hard gaze. "You might be the new head of the Förstner Family, but we don't answer to you."

"Unless it's for the right price," Blake countered from where they were standing, Wulfric and Robin on either side of them. "Nicholette has our assistance in dealing with this problem of hers, which means we all share information."

"And resources?" Rhodes asked, glancing at me. I inclined my head, though I couldn't stop the narrowing of my eyes. It wasn't like they'd presented themselves as willing to be reasonable so far.

"Good, because we have a lot of dead bodies made to look like our little psychopath, and we need to figure out who is doing it before they take her. Nic is all caught up in finding her brother, so we need to make sure that the asshole doesn't take her in the process," Rhodes grumbled, his defenses falling. He ran a hand over his beard then sighed, his shoulders dropping with the exhalation.

"Are there more that I don't know about?" Nicholette asked as she walked back in, exhaustion making her move slower than normal. She didn't look good, and the others must have thought the same because Alexei started to move toward her. Unfortunately for him, I got there first, wrapping an arm around her waist right before she passed out. I was instantly surrounded by people asking questions left and right.

"She's going to need water," I said, and someone stepped away while Blake cleared the couch for her. Not caring about what anyone else wanted, I pushed through the men around me, carrying Nicholette to the couch to lay her down. She didn't stir, and her face remained pale. When I brushed a few strands of hair off her face, her skin was clammy. The fact that she wasn't immediately coming around was concerning, but I wasn't going to let anyone else, especially Rhodes, see that. Alexei, Vas, and I stayed close to her, though I remained standing, whereas the other two men knelt beside the couch to be close to her.

"What's wrong with her?"

"Knowing my girl," Rhodes replied dryly, "she probably hasn't eaten. That could be part of it."

Sacha started cursing, then he switched to rambling in Russian as he stalked out of the living room. A few minutes later, I heard cupboards opening and closing with more force than was necessary.

"I'll call the doc just in case," Emmerich said as he put his cell phone up to his ear and stepped out of the room.

"Help Sacha, Blake, before he tears apart the kitchen," I said dryly, stepping back to let Vas, Rhodes, and Alexei settle near her. Maksim kept his distance, though I knew his attention was completely focused on Nic. Blake followed my order without complaint.

"Long time no see, Wulfric," Rhodes said to one of Blake's men.

The older man gave him a small smile. "Rhodes. It seems you have your hands full."

"So do you." Rhodes chuckled, earning a half-grin from Wulfric as he looked toward the kitchen where Blake was talking to Sacha.

"Someone should check on Oliver and Bodhi," Maksim noted.

Nicholette started coming around then, groaning, and when Alexei reached for her, she flinched back, making the man still instantly. She turned away from him, curling around her stomach as if to protect herself and the babies. Alexei's face crumbled before he stood up, his hands trembling as he combed through his curly hair, trying to calm down.

"I'll go. I need some air." He stalked outside without looking back.

Vas didn't let her retreat from him like she did the other man. He scooped her up and sat back down with her on his lap, holding her despite her rigid posture. Nicholette didn't look at anyone, staying curled in on herself. The question was why.

Fainting could be disorienting, but the color returned to her face as she slowly relaxed into Vas' arms. Before long, I heard soft cries as she finally broke down, wrapping her arms around the man holding her. Vas squeezed his eyes shut, pulling her even tighter against his chest, giving her permission to let loose. Maybe it was pregnancy nerves, or fear, or just the weight of everything hitting the fan right now... probably all of the above. To be honest, if it were anyone else, they would have broken already.

"The doc will be here in twenty to look you over, Nic. And that wasn't a suggestion," Emmerich stated firmly as he walked back into the room. "And for the love of everything, just don't call Ansel Daddy or some shit when I'm around. I don't have enough bleach to erase that from my mind."

I rolled my eyes because of course he would say that, but Nicholette wasn't about to be outdone. She shifted in Vas' hold enough to peek out at Emmerich, her blue-green eyes showing the toll today had taken on her. Thankfully, a sparkle of mischief was still alive.

"No can do, that nickname is already claimed."

"Nic," Vas warned, but Emmerich had no such boundaries.

"Oh thank god."

"That's Blake's nickname."

"For fuck's sake!" Emmerich bitched as Nicholette chuckled, a grin tugging at her lips. I just shook my head, trying to dislodge that from my brain, as Blake burst out laughing in the other room. Vas and Rhodes let out matching sighs of fond exasperation that showed just how unfazed they were by Nic's particular brand of humor. Wulfric and Robin shared a look, both amused by what was happening, though their expressions iced over when they noticed my attention. They weren't ever going to like me, but I could live with that. I was living with much worse things than being hated by them.

"You asked," Nic mumbled, yawning.

"We aren't leaving tomorrow until you talk to us more, Nic," Rhodes told her, keeping his distance.

"I've shared information with you all, but none of you have shared anything with me," Nicholette countered without any heat, not moving from where she was snuggled into Vas' chest. "So you all have plenty to talk about tomorrow. Did you open the envelope I gave you?"

"No."

"You should," Nic mumbled, going from awake to sleeping in just a breath. She was exhausted, her body pushed beyond its limits. My arms ached, wishing she was with me, but I knew there was no way that was going to happen now. Her men were here for her.

I was back to being excluded, dismissed, something that was ever-present in our interactions together. That just made me think of earlier today and Nic's revelation of me calling her on the anniversary of Iris' death. I hadn't even realized it was that time every year, though maybe I should have. I loved my wife even though she had been gone for almost twenty years now. Parts of her lingered in me, whispering to pieces of my soul I knew I'd never fully put back together again. Losing her had broken me and helped shape me into the twisted and cold man I was today. There was no going back to who I could have been.

Nicholette made me feel alive again. She didn't meet my gaze with fear or run away when I approached. No, Liebling met me head on, always ready to challenge me in and out of the bedroom. Nicholette had never balked at what I did for a living; she always had questions about it, wanting details most would never want to know or dare ask. There were other men around, vying for her attention, but I wasn't as bothered by that as I would have expected.

"This?" Rhodes' question broke through my thoughts, and I glanced over in time to see the envelope the doctor had given her just this morning. *Oh, you certainly don't do things by half, do you, Nic?* When he saw that she was asleep, he sighed and ripped the envelope open. The ultrasound picture fluttered to the floor, and Rhodes grayed, his hand shaking when he bent over to pick it up.

"Rhodes?" Maksim asked, uncharacteristic concern in his voice as he stepped toward his uncle.

Sacha came in and immediately noticed the tension. "What's going on?"

"She—" Rhodes cleared his throat, but the shaking only seemed to get worse before he simply surrendered the paper to Sacha.

Sacha took it with a concerned look, and Maksim stalked over to look over his shoulder. Both men stared at it with shocked expressions, then they switched to looking at Nic and Vas.

"Someone better tell me what the fuck is on it," Vas growled. The front door opened, and Bodhi and Alexei walked in, though both men stopped in their tracks the second they got a glimpse of the others.

"What's going on?" Alexei asked, his face carefully blank. "Maksim?"

"Twins." Sacha's voice cracked slightly. "Nic's pregnant with *twins*."

Emmerich whistled loudly before heading out of the room. "Remind me to thank Blake for setting me up with Cosimo. At least I don't need to worry about that."

"You're welcome!" Blake shouted, and I couldn't help but shake my head at their antics. *They are impossible, both of them. I guess that means they're my children.*

Alexei took the paper, though Bodhi stood still, an odd look on his face. "Oliver walked off, and I can't find him. I think he just needs some time to cool down."

Sacha ran a hand through his hair. "It won't be good when he gets back."

"Good thing you have a lot of rooms," Vas drawled as he looked in my direction. "We aren't going anywhere."

"I presumed," I deadpanned, amused by the challenge in his gaze. "Take whatever guest rooms you want." Rhodes was still standing in the middle of the room, his skin practically gray, while the others started to talk around him. Alexei walked over to Maksim, speaking to him quietly, then they both walked out the front after saying they would look out for the doctor. I took a step closer to my friend, drawing Rhodes' attention, and inclined my head toward the back of the house where the pool was. He followed me, accepting the unspoken invitation.

We didn't say anything at first. Both of us settled into seats at one of the tables, and he lit a cigarette after a few shaky attempts to make the lighter work. He inhaled deeply, the lines of his face deep as he desperately sought out some nicotine to help calm his swirling thoughts.

Rhodes and I had been friends since childhood, both of

us having vastly different yet similar violent upbringings. There were only a few people that I actually counted as real friends, and Rhodes was one of them. We knew things about each other that most people would never be privy to, secrets both personal and business related, including the fact that Rhodes had almost been married once. After she died unexpectedly, he never talked about her again, which was no real surprise. His grief had spilled over at the funeral, completely consuming him until he lost it. When he was done, he had been hollow.

Not many had known about Lia at all, much less the baby she had been pregnant with. Complications from the pregnancy had killed both mother and child, leaving Rhodes alone with no outlet for his rage. I was with him through it all, unable to imagine the pain of his loss because I had lost my wife, but I still had Blake and Emmerich... even if they hated me.

"You went with her to the doctor?"

"Dragged her there this morning," I said slowly, aware he was listening to everything I said and didn't. "She had gotten her IUD out, but that's it before now. I took her to the Family doctor. No questions asked and the best care possible."

"Tell me everything." Rhodes didn't look at me as he deeply inhaled, the burning end of his cigarette bright in the dark.

"He took some blood for tests, like normal checks. Everything that came back while we were there was normal," I replied, staring out into the night. "After a few measurements, he estimated she's about eleven weeks along, almost out of the first trimester. He also did an ultrasound, and that's when he saw the two sacs. Fraternal twins."

Rhodes didn't say anything right away. He kept taking

long drags of his cigarette, lost in thought, until he suddenly spoke again. "I knew she was pregnant. Bodhi found the test when we were trying to figure out what had happened."

"That's different than facing the reality of it," I commented.

"It is."

"Nicholette isn't Lia. She's strong."

Rhodes shot me an angry look. "She just passed out, Ansel!"

"After running around all day, being highly stressed, and seeing all of you again, which hasn't been exactly smooth sailing," I listed, arching an eyebrow. "It won't be easy. Hell, a pregnancy with one child isn't easy, but twins... I bet it's something else. But you aren't alone. The others are there to help bully her into taking care of herself. As much as she will allow you to, anyway."

A broken laugh escaped him at that, then he shook his head. "And you? You'll be there."

"Nic and I are just friends," I told him, dodging the question.

A hand clamped on my shoulder, tightly squeezing where I had been shot, making me hiss. Rhodes glared at me. "That's not what I meant, and you know it."

"I'm not with Nicholette," I told him, rolling my shoulder to get him to release me. He did, but he gave me an expectant look that said he wanted me to keep talking. "Nicholette and I are friends, and that's it. We've had sex, sure, but it's never been more than that."

"True, but you aren't going to leave her alone, are you? From the sounds of that kiss, you both are avoiding talking about it even though it seems like it could be more."

"It was a kiss," I insisted with a shrug and a sigh. I leaned back when he shot me an annoyed look. If it were anyone other than Rhodes, I would have stuck to my guns, but I wasn't some unfeeling monster. My friend was hurting, and he was scared. I could give him this truth if he needed some small distraction that badly. "Fine, am I interested in her? Yes. But that doesn't mean anything is going to happen. She has plenty of people on her plate, and there isn't room for anyone else."

"As Nic would say if she were awake right now, you can't tell her what she can and can't do with her life. Body, heart, or otherwise." Rhodes grinned before it fell away. "You two need to figure it out because I could feel the tension between the two of you even in the little time that I've been here, so I'll ask you again. You aren't going to leave her alone, are you?"

"No," I said with a chilling tone, staring at my oldest friend. "No, I'm not. She makes me feel something beyond the mind-numbing coldness that took over when my wife died."

"I swear it's like she's trying to collect people on fucking purpose," a new voice complained from the doorway. Sacha stood there with a fierce expression on his face, though I wouldn't quite call it angry. He seemed more determined, focused, though I wasn't sure of the decision he'd come to. "The doctor is here."

"Are the others back?" Rhodes asked, putting out his cigarette before standing up.

"Yes, even Oliver. The doctor said she could only have two of us in the room, but Nic said she didn't want anyone in there with her after Vas woke her up." He clicked his tongue, showing his annoyance at her decision.

"So you're all loitering outside for updates?" I asked, amused.

"Where else would they be?" Rhodes huffed as I joined

them. All of us headed inside because that was just the effect Nic had on people.

"The others aren't going to be happy with this." Sacha gestured at me. "But that hasn't stopped Nic before."

Rhodes laughed, but the sound turned into a cough as we approached the group of men waiting outside of the guest room Nicholette had claimed. Bodhi and Maksim studied me curiously, while everyone else shot me hostile glares. But if they thought I was going anywhere, they had another thing coming. I had no idea what I was doing when it came to Nicholette or what she was thinking, but I wouldn't figure that out if I didn't stick around.

Maeve Cabott. I grabbed a nearby glass and threw it at the wall with a roar of pure rage.

My Nicholette, *my* woman, had kissed her in the parking garage after escaping those idiot men at the police station. The fact that Nicholette had gotten into the car with Maeve had set my blood boiling, but when she had voluntarily kissed her ex... I was beyond pissed off. Her willingly leaning into that viper's grasp... The longing expression on the old cunt's face when my woman had strode away without looking back... It had taken every ounce of self control to not attack her right there.

And there was also Ansel Förstner.

She had been all over him too.

Her other men were killers, but not like him. Das Gespenst, a brutal assassin known for being so thorough there was no body to find when he was done. Ansel was so unassuming, so normal looking, that most people had no idea of the devil lurking behind his charismatic smile and stone cold gray eyes.

But I knew... I knew him and what he was capable of.

Their comfort around each other had chipped away at the last bit of my control and then that stunt with Maeve... I felt myself snap inside.

No one else was going to claim my woman.

No one.

Nicholette might sell her body to the highest bidder, spreading her legs for the rabble of Ashview, but she wouldn't have to resort to that soon. The ones she claimed as her own had let her continue doing it, which I would never understand. She was mine, and when she finally realized that, she'd learn real quick that the only person she would be with was me. I'd erase every single memory of those other men and women even if I had to beat every touch out of her.

A muffled cry filtered in past my anger, and I glanced over at Thomas, the young teenage boy I had taken. He was huddled in the corner, crying, trying to make himself as small as possible, almost like he could sense my wrath. My lips curled in a disdainful snarl.

"So fucking weak," I taunted him, my disgust at Nicholette, her men, and this shivering boy rising even higher. "I saw your sister today. She never mentioned you once, you know that? You weren't even a passing thought in her mind. If Nicholette could see you right now, she would be so fucking disappointed in the weak child you turned out to be."

Thomas just hid his face in his arms until I stalked over, grabbed him by the arm, and dragged him up. He cried out at my punishing grip, but he didn't try to fight me. Tears and snot covered his face, and I saw his eyes were wide, fearful, even as he tried to avoid my gaze. *Pathetic.* I threw him against the wall and started to undo my belt.

"Wait- please don't," he stuttered, scrambling as if he could somehow get through the wall and away from me.

"I'm not fucking you, bitch," I hissed. "Like I'd mess up good property before I sold it. But I do have a lot of frustrations to get out, and that means letting off some steam. Not to worry though, these *will* heal. They just take time. It's better than anything you have waiting in your future, so you'll have to thank me afterwards, or I'll start over again."

His fear restrained him better than any rope could have. Folding the belt, I pulled back my arm then started raining down hits on his back, ass, and legs.

Every whimper, cry, and plea that fell from his lips aroused me. I pictured Nicholette crouched down there instead, her body showing me just how much she loved the rough treatment. There would be a delicious tinge of fear in her eyes as she wondered if I'd go too far this time. God, the rush.

I wouldn't be fucking him because that would take away from my bottom line when I sold him, but I'd be fucking someone later to finish riding this high. A cruel plan filled my mind, making my rhythm falter. I knew exactly who was going to get the real brunt of my anger, and it wasn't the sobbing boy in front of me.

It was time I paid the Madame of Ashview a visit.

Nicholette
Monday

"Everything looks fine," Dr. Fischer said confidently as he packed up his bag. "You need to remember to drink plenty of water and eat. The anti-nausea medicine will help with that. I brought you a bottle to start since I'm sure you didn't get around to filling the script I gave you this morning. I'd tell you to take it easy, but I doubt you'll listen."

I didn't respond to the pointed comment, guilt eating away at me as I recalled my reaction to Alexei when I woke up. It hadn't been anything personal; something in me had immediately needed to protect the babies.

Fucking babies.

Multiple.

Only with my damn luck would it all play out this way.

My phone started to beep, and I looked over to see Maeve's name on the screen. Glancing at the doctor, he inclined his head and started for the door as I leaned over for the phone, answering right before the call would end.

"What did you find?"

Pause.

"Good to hear from you—"

I cut her off, rubbing my face, not caring that I was being vulnerable with her. "Maeve, now is not the time for our games. I'm exhausted and on my last fucking thread. Just tell me."

She didn't say anything for a moment, probably hearing everything I wasn't saying, then I heard papers shuffling in the background before she delicately cleared her throat. "I found some information on Joe and Miranda. It's not good."

"They weren't good people," I told her blandly. If she was trying to warn me, then I definitely wouldn't like what came out of her mouth next. "Besides, aren't we supposed to meet up for you to give me—"

"Miranda Graves was shot in her home almost a month ago. Joe and Thomas Graves disappeared, according to police reports. No signs from either of them since the murder occurred, and it's an open, active case in Vermont."

"Meaning I'm going to be questioned when I get there?" I asked, trying to ignore the way my heart pounded in my chest. My mother was dead. Gone. My father had fucked off somewhere, and this was confirmation my brother was missing.

"That is very likely," she agreed.

"The only person I give a damn about is Thomas. Give me what you can on Miranda and Joe for now. I need everything else when you drop off the files tomorrow." Maeve didn't say anything in response, but she didn't hang up the phone either. "Maeve?"

"Did you take my advice, little one?"

I swallowed hard, tears pricking my eyes, loving and hating that she'd used the nickname affectionately. "I will. I haven't had time since I left you."

"The Russians got you?" She laughed delicately, but

there was a touch of sadness there. "What am I saying, of course they did. You need to be careful. From what I'm finding out, you are going toe to toe with some very dangerous people, and I'm not saying that idly."

"They have my brother," I rasped, ignoring the tears that spilled down my cheeks. "This person is trying to destroy my life and everything that matters to me. I'll play power games with gods to protect what's mine, Maeve. They'll realize that soon enough. They picked the wrong girl, and they'll burn for it."

Maeve hummed. "That sounds like my Nicholette. Just... be careful, okay? Oh, have you seen Gabriel by chance? I tried to stop by, but his shop was closed."

I shook my head even though she couldn't see me. "I haven't seen him." It was a lie, but it rolled off my tongue easily enough that I thought she bought it.

"If you do, let him know I'm looking for him. He has something of mine."

She hung up before I could ask what she meant by that.

Gabriel had kept me safe when I was hiding in Ashview, trying to figure out my next move. I hadn't fully lied to Maeve since Gabriel had gone radio silent days ago. I hadn't heard from him, but that didn't mean I couldn't guess why he was so quiet. If he wasn't dead, then he was probably wishing he was. *I'm so fucking sorry, Gabriel.* Tears stung my eyes, but before they could start to fall, there was a loud knock on the door before it opened.

It wasn't one of my men like I had expected; it was Blake. They waltzed into the room with a plate filled with hot food that made my mouth water and stomach turn. Blake shot me a stern look as they settled down beside me on the bed and held out the plate.

"Eat. Or Sacha is going to come in here and force it

down your throat." Their brown eyes sparkled with amusement. "His words, not mine."

"So damn pushy." I sighed and reached up to grab one of the rolls on the plate, taking a small bite. If I started with something like that, maybe my stomach would settle. The meds the doctor gave me should start working tomorrow, at least according to him, and I couldn't fucking wait.

"The doc said everything looked fine." I nodded silently, not sure where they were going with this. Blake stood there silently, watching me slowly eat the food they had brought me, with a stern expression on their face. "Your men are all standing outside, and it won't take long before they break down the door to get in here. Do you want me to take care of it?"

I paused, giving them an incredulous look, and they burst out laughing.

"I don't mean kill them, Nic! I mean, I could, but I don't think Ansel would appreciate the mess." They paused, tilting their head as they considered me. "But they aren't going to let you push them away for much longer. Your fear that they would just walk away from you wasn't true."

"Yeah, I guess so," I replied roughly, taking another bite of bread since it was helping calm my stomach. "Everything is just so complicated, Blake. I don't know what to do."

"You could talk to them," Blake suggested with uncharacteristic gentleness.

"Pot, kettle, Blake," I told them dryly before sobering up and meeting their stare. "Can you do something for me?" They raised their eyebrows, silently asking me to continue. "I need to talk to Roderick, alone. Can you ask him to come here?"

Blake contemplated me quietly. "What are you up to, Nic?"

"There's a lot going on, Blake." I averted my gaze and realized I had finished the roll. I grabbed the second roll from the plate, not quite ready for anything else that was on there. "I just want to make sure everything is straight... just in case."

"Nicholette—"

"I have to do this." I cut them off, not willing to hear any false reassurances. "We can't guarantee what's going to happen. Besides, you should know how serious trafficking rings are about keeping their secrets hidden. If we all make it out of this, that would be the damn miracle."

Blake didn't say anything after that. They simply sat beside me as I finally took the plate and dug into the food. Sacha, because it had to be him, had fixed me a plate with some rolls and what looked like a savory turnover. It was crispy and flaky, and the moment I bit into it, I moaned. *Definitely Sacha's cooking.* It was too good to be anyone else's. There was a mixture of beef and chicken, maybe some onions. It was filling but not too much. Absolutely perfect. It was probably a Russian dish that I didn't know the name of, so I'd have to make a point to ask. If I did, he would make it again.

It reminded me of the time Vas had brought me one of Sacha's sochniki as part of aftercare for a session. It hadn't been that long ago that he'd chased me through the woods, the two of us only a call girl and her client. Things had changed so drastically in a few months.

I ate every last thing on there, and exhaustion hit me as soon as I put the plate down. It was the first real meal I'd had in a month, and as I slid down, snuggling into the pillow, I felt safe. Blake reached out, playing with long strands of my hair.

"Who do you want to be in here with you?" they asked

quietly, concern bright in their gaze as they stared down at me. "Or do you want to be alone?"

Being alone would be easier, but I knew I wouldn't get any sleep if I did that. Restless sleep had plagued me for weeks, and this episode had shown me how badly I needed to stop running on empty. While I could normally handle it, I couldn't right now.

"Alexei and Maks," I whispered. I wasn't sure why I made that choice, but I needed the two of them more than anything at this very moment. Even if I would've asked for them all, it wasn't like they'd puppy pile and share nicely. "I want them."

Blake's hand stopped for a second, then they let out a low whistle. "An interesting choice... and Maks? I like the nickname."

"It's just for me to use," I warned them. I knew Maks wouldn't let anyone else use that nickname, or any nickname for that matter, but I was too exhausted to keep the sharp warning to myself. "So tired."

Blake chuckled, not the least bit irritated by my tone. A moment later, the bed shifted, then they headed for the door. It opened with a soft snick, and I caught them all standing outside, waiting for news, even Ansel.

How the hell did I go from being completely alone in life to having eight men waiting for the news that I was okay?

Maksim

WHEN BLAKE HAD COME out with an empty plate, I could practically feel Sacha's satisfaction. I swore I would never understand his obsession with food. I ate what I needed to survive; that was the whole damn point. What difference did it make what kind of food it was or who had prepared it?

I shook my head, switching my focus to Alexei instead. He stood beside me, staring off into space until Blake said our names. We looked over at them at the same time, matching expressions of confusion on our faces.

"Excuse me?" Alexei's shocked voice filled the now silent hallway.

"Nic said she wanted to sleep with you two." Blake arched an eyebrow at us when we stood there, rooted to our spots. "I mean, I think she's already out, so you don't have to, but she asked me to get you two before she passed out—in a good way this time. She managed to keep all the food down."

"Why us?" I asked as I glanced at my lover. "She flinched away from you earlier."

"Yes, thank you for that reminder," Alexei responded dryly, rolling his eyes at me.

"I'll go then." Vas pushed off the wall, and I instantly pulled my gun, aiming it at him. Vas barely blinked, and Sacha let out a long-suffering sigh as Blake and Ansel froze in place.

"The fuck you will."

"Then go, or I will. I'll record it when I fuck her then send it to you so you can see I had her first."

My face screwed up in a grimace. "Like I'd want some video of your small dick."

"Small?!"

"I swear the two of you!" Rhodes complained as Bodhi started to laugh and leaned into Oliver, who had a hint of a smile. There was a stiffness to Oliver that showed he still was upset about the day's earlier revelations, but a bit of it seemed to have faded.

"I'll kill him." Vas started for me, but a breathy laugh stopped us all in our tracks. Nicholette padded out of the bedroom to stand beside Blake. Both of them were similar in height and had dark hair, but that was where the similarities ended. Blake had short brown hair, while the black hair that Nicholette brushed over her shoulder was longer than ever. Blake was in nice, but loose, men's clothing, looking relaxed and comfortable. Nic's curves looked amazing in the leggings and cami she was wearing. In fact, she seemed a touch softer than before, the pregnancy already changing her body.

Dark circles rested beneath her careful eyes, and her smile faded as she leaned into Blake's side. "You guys don't have to—"

Alexei shook his head and stalked past Vas, Sacha, then Blake, to grab Nicholette around the waist and throw her over his shoulder. I followed at a slower pace, stopping right before I entered the room to glance over my shoulder at Vas.

"Don't worry. I'll send you a video of how my big dick looks like as I make her scream for me."

"Motherfucker," Vas growled, lurching forward as if he were going to grab me, but Sacha threw his hands up to block his brother. I happily slammed the door in his face. I thought there would always be some kind of tension between us, but at this point, pissing him off was one of my favorite things.

"Provoking Vas of all people?" Nic called out softly. "Somehow I'm not surprised."

I turned to find Alexei sitting on the side of the bed, Nic cradled in his arms and his face buried in her hair. She had her arms wrapped around him and her chin propped on his shoulder so she could see me. Her eyes were bright in the dim room thanks to the sheen of unshed tears.

"I'm sorry," Nicholette murmured quietly. "For pulling away earlier... It was disorienting to wake up, then you were all there, and I just... It was just instinct, I guess."

Alexei didn't say anything at first, but he eventually let out a long shaky breath, his shoulders dropping as if heavy tension had been released. "That makes sense. It just... You've been gone, and without a word... It was the longest month of my life."

"Something we will talk about in great detail," I said as I sat down beside Alexei, watching him and Nicholette together. Part of me wished I was the one holding her, but I knew that out of the two of us, Alexei needed her in his arms more than I did. I let him hold her close while I watched, trying to figure out when would be too soon to fuck her, him, or both because that video was definitely being sent to Vas one way or another.

"Tomorrow, Maks," Nicholette said. I focused on her in time to see her yawn big enough to make her jaw crack. "I need sleep."

"Doctor's orders?" Alexei tried to joke as he pulled away, cupping her face.

"I haven't been able to sleep since I left," Nic admitted, trying to look away, but Alexei wouldn't let her. "All of you ruined my sleeping abilities."

Alexei shot her a small grin. "You mean spoiled you?"

"No," Nic huffed as she rolled her eyes. "Maks? Save me from his teasing." She turned to me and leaned over, then Alexei loosened his hold enough that she could slide onto my lap. Nic tucked her face into the crook of my neck as Alexei shook his head, a tender look of affection, exasperation, and love on his face as he stared at our woman.

"You're the only person who would ever ask me to do that," I deadpanned, wrapping my arms around her waist to hug her loosely. "I knew you'd come back."

"You did?"

"You came back before." I shrugged, leaning back until my back hit the mattress so we were sprawled out on the bed with her across my chest. "It took a while, but you did. Of course you'd come back this time."

Nic hummed, running a hand up and down my chest. I felt Alexei shift and grab my gun, saying he'd put it on the bedside table for me. "Starting tomorrow, you and Oli need to tear apart the apartment and the compound. Maybe a few other places, too."

"Why?" I asked, tugging her up my body so I could look into her face.

Her blue-green eyes were tired but serious. "Because I never took my stuff when I left a month ago. All my things... Earlier today, Rhodes mentioned that they had been taken. I didn't go to their apartment before I left, Maks." I stilled, studying her face before glancing over at Alexei. His anger flared at the implications of what Nicholette had revealed. Someone had been in the others' apartment. When Sacha and Vas found out, they were going to lose it. "Tomorrow," Nic coaxed, shifting so she laid on her side with her ass scooted back into me. "Alexei?"

He didn't bother responding with words. Instead, he climbed onto the bed and laid down beside her so she could snuggle her face into his chest before instantly falling asleep. The three of us were more in the middle of the bed than up near the pillows, but I didn't care about that. Being with Nic and Alexei made me feel content, at home, like I was understood in a way I hadn't experienced with anyone else. Not on this level, at least.

We both watched her for a bit, our hands wandering her body, over and under her shirt, as if we were starved for the touch of her soft skin and needed reassurance that she was back with us. Not to mention an unsettling fascination with the idea of children growing inside of her. Whose were they? The idea that they could be mine was... terrifying, so instead of focusing on that, I kept my attention on Nic and Alexei, the person who had claimed my black heart a long time ago. Our hands touched a few times in a graze of fingertips, making me very aware of the man who was only a short distance away from me.

We had officially gotten together in Nic's absence, her disappearance encouraging Alexei to seek me out. He wanted to lose himself, and I was only too happy to help him with that. There had been progress made between Alexei and me even though we weren't out. I didn't really care about what level of public acknowledgement our relationship received, though Alexei might. I didn't give a damn what everyone thought of what was between us. The only people whose opinion I even cared to hear were in the room with me right now.

"It's going to take a long time to sweep through all those places," I said, trying to shift my wandering thoughts to something more productive. I glanced up at Alexei to find that he had been watching me with a serious look on his face. How long had I been lost in thought?

"If you do the compound and apartment, you might need to look at our clubs too," he eventually added on, and I nodded, agreeing with his assessment. I licked my teeth, wishing I had a cigarette. The prospect of how much ground needed to be covered was more daunting than I liked. That was a lot of fucking space.

"Probably need to ask the others what outside places they frequent," I thought out loud.

"I'm just glad she's back. Knowing Nic, she has more schemes and information she isn't sharing, but right now I don't care."

I snorted. "Yeah, this is as forthcoming as our girl gets. Maybe Wrenn will help with searching the clubs."

He wasn't thrown by my sudden subject change; he knew I wasn't good at letting shit go once I dug my teeth into it. Alexei looked thoughtful as he combed his fingers through Nic's hair. "Smart. She has stepped up a lot in the past month. We should mention Nic is back. Wrenn has been looking for her as well."

"Yeah," I huffed. "I can't wait to see how the others react when they get back together."

Alexei just shrugged. "Do you really think that'll happen? Their reunion wasn't smooth."

"Our relationship isn't smooth," I countered with some amusement. "Besides, they have history. Nothing will ever be straightforward when you have the past tugging at you."

"You'd think she'd be done... but no. Ansel, Wrenn..."

"Well, she added the two of us and Rhodes after she was with the others." I smirked, remembering how pissed off they all were when that came out and the way Nic had sauntered in, hell on heels. She was breathtaking, and that memory almost rivaled the sight of her kneeling before me, begging. "I'll call Wrenn. I need a cigarette anyway."

"Waiting until the morning to fuck her?" Alexei asked with a touch of amusement in his husky voice.

"I do have a video to send my favorite cousin," I joked,

and his rumbling laugh filled the room until I leaned over, covering his lips with my own.

He kissed me back readily, palming the back of my head and pulling me closer until I had to brace my hands on the bed, careful of the woman between us. I nipped his lower lip, soothing the sting with a quick flick on my tongue before I deepened the kiss. We stayed locked together for a few minutes, and when we broke apart, his green eyes were warm with enough emotion to make me swallow hard.

"Go smoke and come back, Maksim. We'll be here."

"She isn't the only one I'll be fucking, Alexei, so be ready. Though I guess I'll wait 'til tomorrow, so she doesn't miss out on that. I remember how much she loved it last time you both submitted to me."

"Fuck," he groaned, though he curled around Nicholette without complaint, holding her close while I stood up. When she muttered something and snuggled further into his chest, he smiled.

Not bothering to look back, I walked out of the bedroom to find some place to smoke, though I didn't get far. Ansel was standing there, leaning against the fall wall, with Rhodes beside him. The two of them stopped talking when the door closed behind me.

"What are you two doing out here?"

"What are *you* doing out here?" Ansel countered.

"Need to make a quick call and have a smoke. Nic shared something else before she passed out."

"Not inside," Ansel said dryly as I pulled out my pack of smokes.

Without breaking eye contact, I pulled out a cigarette and lit it, blowing smoke in his direction before turning to my uncle. "I'm calling Wrenn."

"Smart." Rhodes rubbed the back of his neck. "Let's go out back. Everyone else is out there, I think."

"Almost everyone," Ansel said as he reached forward, calmly snagging the pack of cigarettes from my pocket and crushing them before dropping it on the floor. "Not in my house. If you decide not to listen again, I'll make you eat the pack by shoving it down your throat."

"My mother did that once," I told him coldly as I inhaled again. "Threw up everywhere. After that, she was fine about the smoking because it was better than the puke."

My nonchalant response made him stare at me with cold eyes before he spun on his heel and strode down the hallway, into the living room, and out to a pool. Vas and Sacha both looked up when we walked outside, while Oliver's eyes were trained on the laptop he had somehow magically gotten ahold of.

"What's wrong?" Sacha asked, his laser focus starting on me before his eyes glanced behind as if Nic might appear in my shadow.

"She's asleep, and Alexei is with her." I took a long drag of my cigarette and unlocked my phone. "Need to make a call."

"That's more important than being in there?" Vas snarked as I hit Wrenn's name. I didn't bother to answer Vas as I listened to the phone ring before she picked up.

"Where the actual fuck have you all been?" Wrenn bitched by way of greeting. In the background, I heard a bunch of people talking amidst the wail of sirens. "Shit has hit the fan big time, and no one has been able to get in touch with any of you three."

"We have Nic," I told her, my eyes narrowing as I exhaled. "What's happening there?"

"Do you have Rhodes there?" she asked, and I arched an

eyebrow. I wouldn't normally put up with this shit, but I was somehow okay with the fact that she was comfortable around me, or maybe just that exasperated enough, to talk to me that way.

"Yes."

"Good, 'cause he needs to hear this shit too." There was some shuffling and yelling before she ordered, "Speakerphone, Maksim, we don't have all night."

"You're getting mighty bold," I crooned, amused that she thought she could order me around.

"Put the phone on speaker, Maksim, before you don't have a dick to fuck Nic with," she threatened sweetly, and I let out a bark of laughter before hitting the speakerphone button.

"We can all hear you."

"There's a fire at the compound." Wrenn dropped the bombshell like it was nothing, and Rhodes' face became red with rage as he started to move toward me and the phone. "Don't come down here. The place is crawling with cops. The fire mainly affected the women's quarters. Most of them didn't make it out."

"What?!" Rhodes hissed.

"The children did." Wrenn kept going, words pouring out of her like she was on a time crunch. Maybe she was. "Social Services is placing most of them. The majority of the club made it out fine, a few issues with smoke inhalation, but Razor has been keeping everything together since the cops showed up. They're asking where the three of you are, which I am very specifically *not* asking you about."

"Noted," I interjected.

"But it's bad. When you do get back here... I hope nothing too important was here because they're still fighting the fire, and it doesn't look like there will be much left once it's done."

Rhodes let out a string of curses before he kicked one of the chairs. Ansel eyed him before he stepped closer to the phone I was holding out.

"Did you hear what kind of accelerant they think was used?"

Wrenn didn't answer for a moment, though we heard her breathing over the line. Sacha looked at the older man and rubbed a hand over his beard. "Why does that matter?"

"Because I know a lot of people besides you Russians who enjoy it," Ansel said coolly.

"Answer him, Wrenn," Rhodes ordered roughly.

"Old-fashioned gasoline," Wrenn replied with a hint of amusement. "Or that's what they're speculating from the few conversations I've overheard." There was a momentary pause before she exhaled, the sound shaky. "Is Nic okay?"

"For now," Vas growled, and Wrenn burst into laughter.

"She must be good if you're that pissy about it. Razor and I will keep you up to date with shit on our end, but I better go. I see a few people eyeing me since I've been on the phone for so long."

"We'll call you tomorrow. There are questions we need to ask you," Sacha added on.

Click.

Wrenn hadn't bothered to respond to Sacha's statement, but then I got a text.

Wrenn: Cops were coming. Talk to you tomorrow.

"Cops were coming her way," I told Sacha. He glanced at me, acknowledging silently that he heard him, his expression thoughtful. A few steps away from me, Rhodes roughly rubbed his face before lighting his own cigarette and starting to pace.

"I'm going to kill every motherfucker behind this," my uncle muttered, promises of murder and revenge dripping from every word.

"Could it be connected to the trafficking ring and Nic?" Oliver said, surprising me, though I guess I should have expected it. I'd rarely seen the man without a computer, but his mind was often split between the task in front of him and everyone else.

"Maybe." Vas replied, leaning back and sharing a glance with Sacha.

"We won't know for sure until we have more information," Sacha replied then he turned to me with an intent look and propped his chin on his hand. He studied me for a minute before he looked at Oliver. "You and Oliver get to go back to Ashview tomorrow. Search our apartment, your apartments, rip everything down to the studs if you have to."

"She told you?" I started.

"About her never coming back to get her stuff? Yes." Sacha ran his fingers through his hair, pulling until it fell out of the bun he usually had up. "Who the fuck is this guy?"

"It's a good thing you have some more people to help you with that now." Ansel smiled, and the sight of it made a chill run up my spine. Not many things or people could shake me, but Ansel Förstner was one of those people.

Nicholette
Tuesday

When I woke up the next morning, both Alexei and Maksim were gone and the bed sheets were cold. *How long have I been here alone?* Shoving down the pang of disappointment, I sat up, stretching until I noticed the angry man sitting in the corner of the room. He silently stared at me, his expression guarded.

Oliver.

His dirty blond hair was a mess. The scruff along his jawline told me he hadn't shaved in a few days. His hazel eyes didn't move from me as the tense silence thickened between us, but I didn't know what to say. I knew he was angry about more than just me peacing out a month ago... The news I had dropped yesterday had been awful. Hell, I didn't know what to think of my parents being part of the trafficking ring. They had been terrible, true, but I didn't think their sins included selling children.

"You're not going to say anything? No smartass remark this time? Are you sure you're my Nic?" he asked, the dark circles under his eyes betraying just how exhausted he was.

"Would you like me to?" I quipped, tilting my head. I was trying not to tear up at the implication that he still thought of me as his. Part of me hadn't been sure that would still be true when I came back. "Would that make this easier?"

"What would have made this easier if you had stayed! Come to us!" Oli lashed out, his face flushed in anger. "Instead, you go off on your own—"

"I'm not some fucking damsel in distress!" I shot back heatedly, instantly riled up.

"We could have helped you. But no!!! Not you, Nic, *you* always have to do things on your own while damning the rest of us."

"Just like you?" I asked pointedly, not about to let him get away with pinning this all on me. "I do shit on my own because the only person I could ever rely on was myself, something I know you can relate to. Before you point all the fingers at me, saying how could I do this or that, think about that for a minute."

"My shit only dealt with me!" Oli yelled back, jumping out of the chair.

"And mine had to deal with more than just you guys and your fucking delicate male egos," I shot back, pushing myself up to kneel on the bed. I wasn't going to let him intimidate me. "My brother, all of you, these babies, fuck, even my own goddamn self are on the line, Oliver. It's not just about you or me. Have you thought of it like that? Did it ever once cross your fucking mind that I was trying to protect you from the asshole that's made my life hell for years. I'm sorry I love you all enough to try to protect you. So to hell with me for caring or giving a damn at all, I guess."

"That means you should have come to us." Oliver steadfastly held to his point, not swayed by what I was saying. "Don't give me some sob story, sweetheart." I tensed at his sarcastic use of the nickname, my anger making me tremble though I tried to hide it.

"Maybe I should have. I could have made a mistake, but I did the best I fucking could. So fuck you! Fuck you and your stupid, selfish ass. I hate—" I was interrupted when Oliver stalked over and grabbed my neck, pulling me into a heated kiss.

It wasn't sweet or loving. It was a punishment, a reunion of pain and blood, and we fought for dominance. He tilted us backward, covering my body with his own as I wound my arms around his neck. Teeth and tongues crashed together; we poured our anger and hurt into each other until he pulled back.

"I have to go back to Ashview soon to see if your stalker started watching us too," he told me gruffly, though he didn't move away from me. Maybe someone else would have expected an apology, but I knew both Oli and I hated those. Us moving on was more than enough for me right now. "More than he was before, anyway."

"Then we better be quick," I told him, leaning up to kiss him again. He let me pull him down, matching my urgency when I began to pull at his clothes. *So fucking happy I didn't wake up with morning sickness.* Part of me wondered where Bodhi was since they never seemed far apart, but then it occurred to me that he might be with Sacha instead.

Oli broke the kiss, trailing his lips down my throat before grabbing the cami I was wearing and tearing it off me. I pushed my leggings down as he took off his pants. Foreplay wasn't something I needed after going so long without sex, and he didn't seem inclined to give me any. We were barely undressed before he settled between my legs, lined himself up, and thrust inside.

A deep groan escaped him as he threw his head back, his jaw clenched. "You feel so fucking hot. Is this a pregnancy thing?"

"Probably. Now shut up and fuck me. It's been way too fucking long since I've had sex. I'm in withdrawal."

He smirked and rolled his hips so the barbells of his Jacob's ladder rubbed all the right spots inside of me. "Like that?"

"Yes," I breathed, snapping my hips up to encourage him to speed up.

Oli laughed softly before he bent his head down, latching onto one of my nipples and sucking hard enough that I gasped. My breasts were super sensitive now, and him playing with my nipple made my eyes roll back in my head.

"Nic," he whispered against my skin after he pulled back to move to my other breast. Teeth lightly scraped over me before he began to tease me with his tongue. "I missed this."

"I missed you too," I confessed with a cry. "Every damn second I was away, I missed you, Oli."

"Good." He pushed into me hard enough that my back bowed off the bed. "Because I missed you too. My past was colliding with my present, and then you were suddenly gone. Not to mention finding that test... God, Nic, I was terrified."

"Are you still scared?" I asked him, gripping his hair and pulling him away from me so I could watch his face.

"Yes," he ground out as he met my stare, snapping his hips forward with slow, hard strokes. "I went through hell and back so many times, and I just... I have no idea how to do this or make it work."

"Me too. For all of those things," I told him honestly, tears stinging my eyes as I searched his face. "But I have all of you, and it looks like we're going to figure it out."

Drawing his face closer, I brushed my lips over his, and he sighed. Our kiss was slow and sweet, a complete contrast to the way he was fucking me. My breasts bounced with every thrust, making me whimper, and he drank up every drop of it as his tongue slid along mine.

With a free hand, he reached between us to play with my clit, and it didn't take long. My month without sex made it so I came quickly. Breaking away from him, I screamed his name while he cursed mine, burying his face in my neck and nipping the skin there as I came again.

"Fuck, that was perfect." He looked down between us. "You soaked me."

"Is that a complaint?" I asked lightly, and he shook his head.

"Hell no." He smiled before pressing a soft kiss to my lips. "I'm still mad at you. I get it, but I'm still mad."

"That's okay," I replied. "I'm pissed too."

A knock on the door interrupted us, then it was opened to show Maksim and Alexei. Alexei raised his eyebrows at us, but Oli just curled up next to me, not the least bit embarrassed by them seeing him naked. Maks grinned at the two of us, openly showing his amusement.

"Glad you took care of my foreplay for me," Maks directed at the man beside me, and I burst out laughing. "Unless it's to punish her, it's no fun."

Alexei shook his head at the other man. "You know sex isn't a one-way street, right?"

"She likes how I fuck her." Maks shrugged.

"I'll let them know there was a delay." Oliver stood up, pulling on his jeans and grabbing his shirt before kissing me soundly one more time. "Have fun!" He shut the door behind him, and the brothers looked down at me, taking in my flushed naked body.

"We can punish you later for that stunt you pulled," Alexei informed me. "We don't have that much time."

"What's going on?" I asked, brow furrowed. "What did I miss?"

"After." Maksim cut Alexei off before he could answer me then reached back to lock the door.

Instead of arguing with Maks, Alexei pulled his shirt off and stalked toward me. I sat up and smiled as he crawled up the bed and urged me to lay down before he kissed me. Running my hands over his broad shoulders, I savored the hot feel of him under my fingers. As I dug my nails into his tattooed shoulders, I felt the bed dip down beside me, alerting me to Maksim joining us. Alexei pulled back to press kisses down my neck and torso while a slender hand roughly grabbed my chin, forcing me to look at Maks so he could claim his own kiss. Alexei cupped my breasts, roughly playing with my nipples. My body began to jerk with the sensations, and I whined into the kiss as arousal and pain twisted together.

"Fuck, do that again," Maks breathed as he broke the kiss. He held my chin in place, not letting me look away as Alexei did it again, and I gasped. Now that I was pregnant, the pain was so much more intense. "Hell, I might have to keep you knocked up if you react that way to everything."

"Fuck," Alexei hissed. Resting his head against my breast, he captured one nipple in his mouth and sucked until I felt tears sting my eyes. My back arched, but I couldn't get away from him, and my focus zeroed in on the combination of cum and my own arousal on my thighs. My sex drive had only increased with pregnancy, and I hoped they were ready now that we were reunited.

"Just imagine her stomach round..." Maksim painted the picture out loud for us as Alexei lightly nipped at one breast then moved to the other. "Breasts bigger, heavier. Every fucking curve you have, fuck toy, will be softer and even more fucking enticing than they already are. Your body will be so sensitive and responsive to every damn thing we do to you. I could come from the picture alone, and it seems Alexei likes it too."

"I'll just get another round of birth control," I countered, and Maks growled in my ear. Goosebumps covered my body, and I wasn't the only one affected. I felt Alexei shiver against me. Neither of us were immune to that dominant sound.

"I'll throw them away if you even try. And if you try to get one of those rods, I'll tie you up and make you watch as I cut it out of you. Then I'll edge you, and you can just sit there as I fuck Alexei until he passes out so you understand who owns this body. It isn't you."

"Shit," Alexei groaned at that, reaching down to grab his cock as I stared at Maksim with wide eyes.

I didn't see myself ever getting pregnant again, and I hadn't even gotten far along in my pregnancy. But the scene he painted, playing up a breeding kink, it turned me the fuck on. The possessiveness in his heated gaze and Alexei's jerky movements told me he was very into the picture Maks was painting. I could always get that rod put in for the sole purpose of Maksim fulfilling that fantasy.

"Fuck her now, Alexei. I'll go last and send Vas that

video I promised him yesterday. You'll just have to wait for me to fuck you later."

Without question, his lover lined himself up at my entrance and smoothly bottomed out in one slow, steady thrust. I inhaled sharply, my body needing time to adjust. I remembered Alexei was big, but somehow I had forgotten he was *this* big and so fucking thick he rivaled Vas. Even with Oli fucking me first, I needed a moment. Digging my nails into his shoulder, I pulled him into another kiss, but instead of meeting my lips, he pressed openmouthed kisses to my neck, interspersed with gentle love bites.

"It was torture without you here," Alexei whispered against my skin as he rolled his hips, leisurely fucking me at his own pace. "The smell of you faded from my bed days after you left, and I hated sleeping there after that. I spent most of my nights at Maksim's place because I kept thinking I heard you, only to find you weren't there. I thought I was going crazy."

"Alexei," I breathed, but he shook his head.

He didn't let me form a reply, fucking me faster, harder until Maksim's body was the only reason I didn't slam my head against the headboard. This sex wasn't meant for reconnecting; he was losing himself in me, not caring if I got off or not. He needed to know I was still here, and that was fine with me. Alexei played with my clit, making me come, and he followed soon after. Immediately, he rolled over so Maksim could take his place.

Maks didn't do easy either. He pinned me to the bed with a hand wrapped around my neck, lined up his cock at my entrance, and slammed home hard enough that I screamed. That was when he pulled out his phone, and I grinned when he held it at just the right angle, getting a good view of him sliding in and out of me before moving up to my bouncing breasts and his hand on my throat. *Men.*

He locked the phone before tossing it aside and using the hand around my throat to prop himself up, then he began to fuck me like a man on a mission. He didn't try to play with my clit or make it good for me, no, this was a reminder of who I belonged to, and I loved every damn moment of it. His hand tightened and loosened a few times, helping me ride that edge without going too far.

"Alexei. Knife. Phone." I blinked, trying to figure out what he was doing, and once I saw the blade come into view, I tensed. What the fuck was he going to do now? "Hold her down for me."

Maksim released my neck only for Alexei to take hold of it while Maks got his phone ready again. He pointed it at my inner thigh, and I suddenly knew what he was going to do. *He's going to do just as he promised.*

He was going to carve his name on me.

Sure enough, he moved the camera to my unmarked inner thigh and made quick work of carving his name into my skin. He was still balls deep inside of me, and as he finished carving the last letter, I came, screaming Maks' name while he recorded the entire thing. Alexei whistled as Maksim fucked me again, chasing his release until he let out a deep growl and spilled his hot cum inside of me.

I whimpered, feeling deliciously sore when he pulled out and reached between my legs to play with my pussy. When I tried to twist my body away from him, I found my legs pinned open, then he thrust his fingers inside me, his thumb playing with my clit as he stared at me in challenge. It was all I could do to whimper, turning my torso in an attempt to get away from his touch.

"Come again, fuck toy. Come all over my damn hand,

leaking cum from three different men, and know who owns this pussy. Who owns *you*."

I came when he curled his fingers, hitting that perfect spot inside of me, and clamped down on his digits, soaking him.

Darkness took over until I blinked a few times, trying to figure out where I was, and found a sight I had missed. Alexei and Maksim were naked on either side of me. Both of them were running their hands along my sides, watching me with smug, pleased expressions. Considering they had fucked me until I passed out, they had earned those expressions. Oh, Vas was going to be pissy, but I loved it. The marking, him filming it, getting to play with Vas' anger and jealousy... I was seriously fucked up.

Then my brain remembered what they had been talking about before they fucked me unconscious.

"What—" I licked my lips. "What happened? Why are a bunch of you leaving for Ashview?"

They shared a look over me before Maksim answered my question. "We're looking for cameras like you asked, but there was also a fire in the women's quarters at the compound. The children got out, but most of the women didn't."

"What?!" I sat up quickly, but when I tried to get out of the bed, Alexei grabbed my wrist.

"Nicholette—"

"I'm going," I told him stubbornly.

"It's not safe," he countered.

"My entire life has been unsafe," I told him evenly, but he didn't budge when I tugged against his grip. "Alexei, that could have happened because of me. I need to go."

"It's the Lords' compound," Maksim replied. "There are plenty of reasons why it could have been targeted."

"The women's quarters and not the clubs?" I asked him calmly. "Where's Rhodes?"

"Talking with Ansel the last we saw him." Maks rubbed his fingers together as Alexei released his hold on me. "What's going on with him?"

"He's a friend."

"That was some kiss at the police station for just a friend," Alexei challenged dryly. "You'd think both of you would come up with something better than 'nothing' and 'we're just friends' as denial tactics."

My cheeks heated, and I sat back on my heels to study the two of them. "What do you want me to say? We're friends. Have we fucked? Yes. Many times. Paid and unpaid. So it's not just something casual."

"I think you're both deluding yourselves. Ansel has more invested in you than you realize, and I think it's safe to say the same for you when it comes to him."

"I'm getting dressed. Don't you dare leave without me." I changed the subject, not ready to examine the kiss or what he had said to me. They were right; there was more than just friendship between us, but I wasn't sure exactly what our relationship had become, so I was going to avoid the topic for as long as possible. "I'll just get there another way, then you won't know where I'm at."

"Such a fucking pain in the ass," Maksim grumbled, but I saw a spark of amusement there as he grabbed his clothes and quickly got dressed. "I'm getting a smoke. I'm glad you're back, Nicholette."

He started to leave, but I reached out, touching his shoulder to get him to stop. I stood on my tiptoes, pressing my lips to his in a short kiss. This was the softer aspect of our connection. Would he ever be as tender, as gentle as the others could be? I'd wager a bet against that, but I didn't care. I'd appreciate these little moments for the gift they were, glimpses into another side of him that rarely took the reins. He wrapped an arm around my waist, pulling me close as he deepened it. I closed my eyes, falling into the moment as I reached up, running a hand over his short buzzed hair. The brush of his beard against my face made me smile until he pulled back.

"I missed you, Maks."

He rested his forehead against mine, nodding a few times before he kissed me and left the room. Maks was a man of few words, but I hadn't missed the slight shine of his blue-gray eyes when he spun away.

"Maksim always knew you were coming back." Alexei wrapped his arms around me from behind, the warmth of his skin now replaced by the soft cotton of his shirt. He kissed my shoulder softly. "Never once wavered on it. Him and Bodhi. I'm sure they were both upset in their own ways, but never once did they doubt you showing back up."

"The rest of you did?" I asked, running my hands over his tattooed arms.

"We were pissed, upset, and hurt that you disappeared without a trace. We turned the city upside down. Even Wrenn has been helping to track you down." I turned around in his arms and cupped his face, playing with his short beard.

"There hasn't been a single moment I didn't think of all of you," I told him honestly, my voice rough with emotion. "I tried my best."

"I know." He smiled gently and kissed my forehead right where Maksim had. "I'll see you down there."

He walked out, and I sighed before I went to the attached bathroom, cleaned up the best I could, and searched for some spare clothes in the room. No idea whose clothing it was, but I threw on a pair of slacks and a large black t-shirt. At least everything would be comfortable. My inner thigh was sore, but luckily there were some bandages under the sink. I had just finished cleaning up when a buzz caught my attention, so I hurried over to the bed and grabbed my phone out of the bedside table. I had a few missed messages and emails.

Reading through them, I replied to the email then switched to the texts.

Roderick: Blake said you needed to talk with me.
Nic: I want you to make me a will.

My phone vibrated in my hand right after that. I swallowed hard before answering with a forced lighthearted hello.

"Nicholette." Roderick's serious voice filled the line. "What do you need it to say?"

I let out a shaky breath, not sure how to say everything I wanted, though I knew where I wanted to start. "All my money should be put into two trust funds, all of it split fifty-fifty between the two babies. If they don't... If..." My voice cracked, and I forced myself to take a deep shaky breath. "I don't know what to do if they don't make it."

"That's okay," Roderick gently replied, his voice soothing and calm. "Who will you give custody to?"

"I don't know who the fathers are, I mean, you know what I mean." I waved a hand as if to dismiss what I'd said. "But I want them to be together."

"What name should I put down?" Roderick asked when I didn't speak for a minute.

"Sacha," I said without thinking, instinctively going with him. He would make sure they were safe and that everyone would be able to see the babies. He'd play it fair no matter whose emotions got worked up, and that made him the perfect choice. "Sacha Morozov."

Papers rustled on the other end of the phone. "I'll have something for you to sign the next time I see you—"

"I want you to be the executor, Roderick," I interrupted him firmly. "Make sure it all gets taken care of like it should. I'll get my account information to you as well so it's all on there." There was a beat of silence, and I chuckled, the sound strained. "Maeve said you were the best, and you also work for the Förstners. My shit isn't as crazy as theirs, so I know I can trust you to do this for me. If not, I'll just haunt your ass."

"That's sufficiently terrifying," he drawled, and I threw back my head with a laugh. "Consider it taken care of it. Do they know?"

"No," I replied curtly, quickly sobering up at the mention of my partners. "They don't need to know unless it's necessary."

"Understood. I'll see you soon."

Click.

I bit my lip and checked my other messages. Nothing from Gabriel. I hoped he would turn up soon, but I had no idea what had happened to him. Were there any updates on his whereabouts? That was something to think about another time because now I needed to face Wrenn, which, despite any seeds of reconciliation between us, had me a bit on edge.

I looked through the room and took another dose of the nausea meds the doctor had prescribed, a fucking godsend, then headed out to figure out what the plan was. There were loud, angry voices yelling downstairs and when I realized who it was, I grinned and hurried to find the source of the commotion. The living room was full, everyone standing and sitting around, watching Vas yell at Maksim, who seemed amused as hell by the outburst. Just as my feet touched the floor, Vas lashed out, punching Maksim. Alexei threw up his hands while Rhodes shook his head. Sacha rubbed his face with a decidedly resigned sigh, and beside him I saw Bodhi and Oli grinning. Maksim just laughed, not the least bit apologetic or regretful.

Ansel, who was standing by the stairs, looked over at me. "You sure about them, Nicholette?"

"Oh, angry Vas is one of my favorite people," I told him with a small smile that grew into a large grin when Vas spun around at the sound of my voice. "I take it Maks sent you his video?"

"Oh god, no, he didn't." Ansel sighed, but I swore I saw a hint of smile as Vas stalked over to me.

"He did. *Two* videos, actually. One where he fucked me and another where he carved his name into my thigh." Ansel jerked at my description, and Blake, who was close by, raised their eyebrows, but Vas scooped me up and held me close before they could say anything.

"No more sex!" Sacha yelled out, exasperation straining his voice, and Maks chuckled with a huge grin. "We'll never get back to Ashview if everyone fucks her before we leave."

"I could blow you in the car?" I offered Vas, trying not to laugh as I wrapped my arms around his neck.

"Nic, not helpful," Sacha muttered, though Bodhi was failing to hold back a smile. Vas set me down on my feet, but I didn't walk away. I let him hold me close instead. Actually, I leaned into him, savoring the closeness between us. "We're taking care of some shit in town then leaving for Vermont. No other distractions. And you are not leaving our sides. If you even fucking try, I will beat you fucking back and blue."

"With what?" I asked, unable to help myself.

"Oh my god, only you," Blake laughed, looking beyond amused. Their men very carefully said nothing, though Conrad's eyes were intrigued and just a little bit guarded as he looked between all of us.

"It's good to have the details beforehand." I shrugged lightly before sobering up. "But I heard about the compound. Any ideas on who could have done it besides my stalker?"

"Your stalker doesn't make sense though," Rhodes said, his voice and expression exhausted as he rubbed his face. "Why target women you barely know?"

"Because *you* know them," I replied softly. "You, Alexei, Maksim... You know them. Honestly, I'm surprised they didn't make sure Wrenn died to put the fucking cherry on top."

"She was there," Maksim commented matter of factly. "She got out with a few others and the kids."

"If this person is part of the trafficking ring, why not take the kids?" Blake questioned, glancing over at their brother. "I mean, even if that's not the point, they're there."

"True," Emmerich hummed. "Maybe they are devolving? That could be the cause of this total fixation on Nic."

"Or the 'CPS agents' who took the kids aren't actually part of Child Services?" Blake mused. "Quite daring since I'm sure the place was crawling with police and firefighters."

"But doable." Emmerich said, both of them looking thoughtful. Oliver looked sick to his stomach, and Atlas, who'd disappeared at some point last night, wasn't anywhere to be seen. *Where the hell is he?*

"That's not at all reassuring," I muttered before my

phone rang, which inspired a fresh wave of confusion. With a pit in the bottom of my stomach, I answered. "Yes?"

"Nicholette." Roderick's voice was hard.

"Why are you—" I asked, but he interrupted me.

"I got a call from Maeve. Meet me at her place. Alone."

Click.

Well, shit.

Nicholette
Tuesday

I chewed my lip as I locked my phone, knowing alone time was too big of an ask given everything that had happened.

"Who was it?" Sacha asked, a noticeable edge to his voice. "And don't even think about lying."

"Roderick. He needs to meet with me," I admitted, meeting his intent gaze with a calm expression. "I can't imagine it will take long."

"You're not going alone," he warned me, and Vas held me tighter against his front.

"I didn't even ask to go alone!" I replied tartly, arching an eyebrow. "I was going to ask who wants to go with me."

Sacha narrowed his eyes at me, probably questioning how agreeable I was being, but before he could reply, Blake spoke up. "You need Oliver and Maksim to tear through the apartments to look for cameras, yes?" they started reasonably. "I'll get Atlas to start looking at shit on this end since I don't think he's up to go to Ashview quite yet. Why don't Ansel and I go with her? Nothing will happen to her with us."

Ansel looked over at Blake, but his child's expression was blank, patient, and totally focused on Sacha. The others looked between Blake and Sacha, waiting to see what the decision would be. In that moment, I knew I had been right in my instinct to entrust the kids to Sacha. This alpha-filled group looked to him for leadership, freely giving him authority, and that was quite a feat. There weren't many in this group of killers and psychopaths that were the go-with-the-flow type—that only fell on Bodhi, and Oli when it suited him—but Sacha handled it all flawlessly.

"Take two of your men with you, Blake," Sacha responded sharply, a steely look in his eyes. "If she slips away, it's on your head."

"I have someone who can meet us nearby," Ansel added slowly, thoughtfully, and Blake and Emmerich both jolted. "And if you send me pictures of the compound, I'll look them over."

"I can do that," Rhodes said. He was continuously rubbing his fingers together, clearly needing a cigarette.

"Let's head to your apartment first." Maksim directed the comment at Oli, who agreed, and Bodhi beside him. "Get that cleared before anything else since the asshole was definitely there."

I sighed in irritation. "Which reminds me that I need new clothes... again."

"Nic," Bodhi said as Maksim and Oli headed for the door. "Speaking of clothes, have you heard from your friend Gabriel?"

I shook my head slowly. *Why would they bring him up now?* "No. Not for a while. Why? And how do you guys even know Gabriel?"

"We're looking for him," Bodhi replied, his gaze intent on me. "We have reason to believe he was taken by the trafficking ring or someone who knows about your connection with us."

"Why would you say that?" I asked. I wasn't sure where he was going with this, but I had a gut feeling that I wouldn't like it.

"We were delivered a hand at the compound," Rhodes informed me gently. "It was too big to be a child's or teen's, so we think it's his."

"Every bone in the hand was broken before it was cut off," Vas rumbled behind me, and I felt the blood drain from my face. Every bone was broken... They knew their target, that's for sure. They'd taken every possibility of doing what he loved away from him before taking the hand completely. *I'll kill them.*

"Are you sure it's not—"

"It was too big to be your brother's," Bodhi told me as he shook his head.

"Have you been given no proof of life?" Emmerich asked grimly.

"No, but I've been hiding. I don't want pieces of him to prove he actually has my brother."

"Giving you pieces would damage the merchandise," Blake replied blandly, their voice carefully empty. "That's how your guy or girl sees him, merchandise. If they're threatening to sell him to the highest bidder, keeping him whole and alive is a priority, which is a good thing."

"Tell that to the kids that have to live through it," Oliver muttered angrily before he stalked outside, Maksim close behind him.

"He was in the Ashview trafficking ring? A child of it?" Ansel asked, staring after Oli.

"Yes," Bodhi slowly answered after a heavy pause. "Why?"

"What are the chances?" Blake murmured before shaking their head. "Con, can you fill Atlas in and stay with him? Robin and Wulf can come with us and make sure Nic doesn't disappear again."

The younger guy with buzzed hair focused on Blake for a moment, blinking slowly when the older man spoke up. "I'll stay with Atlas."

"You won't be any help to him on the computer," Blake replied with a questioning glance.

"He doesn't need help with the computer things," Wulfric replied steadily, staring down Blake until they nodded.

"Works for me," Robin agreed. "We're ready when you are." Conrad remained silent, not protesting, as Blake looked down at their sweats.

"I'll change. Give me five." With that, they hurried upstairs. Ansel was texting someone, presumably his contact in Ashview, instead of chiming in on the conversation.

"We need to check in for our job," Vas reminded Sacha. "The client is going to want an update."

"It said messages only, no phone calls, so that should be easy enough," Sacha agreed. He strode over and gave me a firm kiss before he and Vas walked off.

Bodhi looked between Rhodes and me then nodded at the older man before walking outside, Alexei falling into step beside him. Part of me was sad I hadn't had a moment alone with Bodhi yet, but the chaos that was our lives apparently meant we'd have our one-on-one reunion later. Dealing with all of these people was an emotional fucking minefield, a delicate dance of who to check in on since there were so many people in a group. The others had said that Bodhi hadn't lost his faith in my return, but did he truly believe that down to his core? Or had he just been putting on a strong face for the others? Maybe there was some kind of forgiveness that needed to pass between us.

Emmerich and Ansel both stepped out too, probably to get their stuff together, leaving me with Rhodes. I took in his face and ragged posture and decided that there was no way to step around it. He looked like shit. When he realized I was approaching him, he exhaled a shaky breath. "Love..."

I wrapped my arms around him, pressing my face into the worn leather of his jacket, being mindful of the guns he had strapped to him. He swallowed me in a hug, breathing in deeply as he rested his chin on my head.

"I missed you, hotshot," I whispered. "I'm sorry about the compound."

"It's all gone," he replied roughly, squeezing me tight. "The fire tore through everything, and the firefighters couldn't stop it."

"Rhodes..." My words trailed off, unsure of what to say when he pulled back and tilted my face up. I rocked up on my tip toes and kissed him gently, then Rhodes fisted a hand in my hair, pulling me close as he kissed me back. I fell into it, hoping to comfort him in some small way before I had to leave. I cupped his face, my fingers tracing the scars on his face in a soft, gentle way that made him shudder against me.

"Go meet with Roderick and whatever else you have planned, then meet me at the compound," he ordered me huskily when we broke apart.

I licked my lips. "Okay."

"Are they going to find your little murder room?" he asked with a spark of humor in his gray eyes.

"Doubtful," I told him with a grin. "I put in a failsafe. If the entire compound burned, so did my space. The real question is what deal do I need to make with you to get a new one?"

A smirk tugged his lips upward, and he kissed me again just as I heard Blake come back downstairs. "I'll think of something for you, and I'll make sure it's *very* creative."

"I love the way you threaten me, hotshot."

"So fucking twisted, love. I'll see you soon." He kissed me one more time before he let me go and walked out. Before he got outside, he yelled out, "Keep her safe, Ansel."

"Hey, *I* can keep her safe!" Blake called back, sounding put out, just as Ansel and Em rejoined them in the foyer.

"Nic doesn't need help finding trouble," Rhodes replied dryly, making Em snort. Even Ansel's lips twitched, but Blake's men wisely stayed silent. *Smart men.*

"I'm picking up Cosimo at Logan, then I'll be joining you all. I'll call Blake to see where to go." Em held up a hand and left without waiting for commentary.

"The Chicago Family?" I looked over at Blake with a curious expression.

"You know Cosimo?" Conrad asked, his voice quiet.

I hummed. "We've met a few times. Anyway, are we ready to go? If there are any more emotions right now, I'll break out in hives."

"Maybe you should have thought of that before getting with so many people," Ansel replied, and I gasped, though no real offense was taken.

"Are you cracking a joke with me, Ansel?" I asked, pressing a hand to my heart before dodging his hands when he tried to grab me. "I like getting fucked six ways to Sunday, not the emotional entanglement side of things."

Conrad snorted at that, and I even earned a small smile when I winked at him before walking outside. I headed straight for the SUV, getting in the backseat. The others joined me soon after, with Blake and Ansel claiming the front while Robin and Conrad climbed into the back with me.

Robin got in on one side and Conrad on the other, safely tucking me into the middle. I shifted slightly closer to Robin, making sure to give Conrad space. Robin shot me a questioning look when I brushed against him, but his face cleared when he looked to my other side and put two and two together.

Ansel broke the silence as he started up the SUV. "Where are we meeting Rorik?"

"Maeve's place."

Ansel met my gaze in the rearview mirror as Blake whipped around to look at me. Their dark brown eyes were narrowed in suspicion. "Why?"

"I don't know. Roderick didn't say, and he's the one who called. I guess we all get to find out when we get there." I shrugged before looking at the younger guy beside me. "Just fair warning, Maeve is... intense."

Conrad slowly looked beside me to Robin, then Blake, before meeting my stare again. His light blue eyes were weary when he asked, "Why specifically give *me* that information?"

"Besides Blake's warning to make sure I maintain boundaries with you?" I tilted my head slightly, studying the man beside me. "You jerked when I mentioned my rapist and the detective questioning me about it, so it seemed prudent to mention it."

"Most people assume a man—"

"I was a prostitute," I interrupted him gently, "starting when I was seventeen, and I didn't become a call girl until I was twenty-one. Rape is something I have become intimately acquainted with given my life circumstances, so boundaries are something I respect, no details necessary."

"Maeve won't," Blake muttered, and I shook my head.

"Maeve won't do anything to you guys. This is about me and, if I had to guess, whatever she found when I asked her to look into my parents. I gave her twenty-four hours before I headed to Millfield. Guess she found something I can use."

"And Roderick will be there because...?"

"I have no idea," I responded, my stomach turning with nerves. "But it can't be anything good."

We remained silent the rest of the way to her place. Ansel parked the SUV and twisted in his seat to face me. "You're supposed to go in alone, yes?"

I nodded once.

"The Russians won't like that," Blake commented, but they didn't seem surprised by where their father was going with the conversation. I raised my brows, curious to see how this was going to play out.

"You go in, you come out, and get right in this car. If you go anywhere besides that, you won't have to worry about the Russians," Ansel warned, the chill in his voice lowering the temperature of the vehicle. Blake licked their lips, a sure sign of nerves, while the men on either side of me became so still I wasn't sure they were breathing.

I unbuckled my seatbelt and leaned forward until I could brush my lips against his in a barely there kiss, undeterred by his threat. "You still owe me."

"You follow directions, and I can arrange what I promised you before."

"Please don't speak sex code in front of me." Blake exaggerated a shudder, their teasing tone breaking the tension in the car. "It's creepy."

"Who said anything about sex?" Ansel asked, breaking our eye contact to look at his child with amusement. Everyone claimed they saw something more between us, but this was how we normally acted with each other. Actually, it was a little more tame than usual. He hadn't mentioned my revelation about calling me for his wife's passing, though I had only pointed it out yesterday, but there was now a slight distance in his gaze that wasn't there before. Soon, we'd be addressing whatever this was, our denials aside, but not right now.

"He promised me someone to kill to help with stress relief and exercise." I chuckled darkly, forcing myself to focus on the present. "Nothing like a good chase through the woods to get your blood pumping."

"Oh my god." Blake rubbed their face.

"I had a few ideas—" I started, but Ansel hit the unlock button.

"Go. Now. You need to earn the reward before you start trying to make demands for it," Ansel ordered. Conrad got out of the car, stepping aside so I could get out. He didn't move far from me when I just stood there, staring up at the house I had been to so many times before. This felt different, though. It felt... final. Something in my gut was telling me that once I walked in there, I would be changed. The same woman wouldn't leave this place, and I had to wonder what pieces of me would be left behind.

"Do you need someone to come with you?" Conrad asked softly.

"I can't ask that of you," I told him, forcing myself to shake my head. "I'll be fine."

"I offered." Conrad looked at me, and something in his light blue eyes seemed cautious but deadly.

"Anything that happens in there isn't leaving that

house," I told him, not wanting to be overheard with the door still open. "And that means to everyone."

Conrad gave me a ghost of a smile as he slammed the door shut. "Secrets are my specialty."

"Then let's go," I told him, squaring my shoulders before heading up the stairs with my unexpected companion right behind me

Why had she called Roderick instead of coming directly to me? What the hell is going on?

Not wanting to waste any time, I knocked on the door. Before I even finished the first knock, Roderick was opening the door and ushering us inside. He didn't even stop to chastise me for breaking his direction of coming alone. My lips parted in shock as I took in the state of Maeve's usually spotless home. The furniture was destroyed, with papers and broken decor scattered everywhere

"What the fuck is going on? Where's Maeve?" I asked Roderick, rounding on him even as I realized I didn't have Vas' knife. My hand clenched, missing the weight of it in my hand. Was it at Ansel's place? The Förstner Family home? *Fuck.*

"Nicholette. My office," Maeve's cold voice called from the back of the house. I studied Roderick's face, but he gave me nothing except for a gesture to lead the way.

I carefully stepped around broken lamps, shattered pictures, and my brow furrowed trying to piece together what the hell was going on. The destruction only got worse the closer we got to her office. Conrad was right behind me, and I heard the rustle of clothing, then the click of his gun's safety being switched off. I appreciated his caution, and even Roderick didn't dissuade him.

Maeve was standing behind her desk, and my heart dropped, my stomach turning enough that I thought I would get sick. This wasn't the woman I had met two years ago, with every strand of hair and stroke of makeup perfectly in place. Before me was someone I had never met before. This unknown yet familiar stranger had her white-blonde, slightly wavy hair loose and no makeup in sight. She wore a pair of high-waisted jeans and a t-shirt.

"You were supposed to come alone." Her voice was still the same, but there was a hint of exhaustion there. "Are you adding even more people to your group? I'd have thought it would be a woman."

"He's with Blake," I told her slowly, my mind racing to figure out what was happening. "And coming alone wasn't really in the cards considering everything that's going on."

"It wouldn't have stopped you before," she replied, keeping up the small talk as she looked down at the papers in front of her again.

"You know why it's different this time." I stepped forward, reaching out and placing a hand on her wrist to stop her. Maeve seemed to freeze at my touch, but I felt her small shiver. "What's going on, Maeve?"

"I found the information you wanted," she replied, gently pulling her wrist from my grip and handing me a stack of papers. "You should sit down."

All my complicated feelings for the woman in front of me stumbled to a halt when she gestured to the papers. Refusing to sit down, I flipped open the file. My hands started to tremble with the first few lines on the page.

Joe and Miranda Graves. Married for thirty-five years. IVF attempts for five years. Six miscarriages. A stillbirth. During all of this, there were arrests for Joe—assault, sexual harassment, stalking... It all happened outside Millfield while Miranda fought to have their child. Then something happened. Miranda and Joe separated for a few months before they got back together. But why?

Next up were adoption papers for... *me* and a birth certificate for Thomas dated thirteen years ago. *I'm adopted?!*

"Nicholette?" Conrad sounded concerned, and rightly so, since he'd barely uttered my name before my knees buckled. Strong hands caught me, keeping me from collapsing, and sat me down on a chair. Looking up, I met Maeve's stern blank stare, no pity in sight. She moved her hands to my shoulders, and the sensation was almost that of a ghost. Did she feel truly familiar anymore? The contact between us was the brush of something long past, a reminder of a connection that hadn't been severed, not exactly, but it was certainly no longer a vivid, living thing.

"Adoption papers?"

"Keep reading, little one," Maeve said gently, a contrast to her blank expression, and I knew this was only the tip of the iceberg.

With a shaky breath, I did as she directed. Adoption papers, photos of me as a small child, and a picture of me with them. It was odd to see the three of us playing, smiles all around. I had no recollection of these happy parents or the laughter in these photos. Pushing that all aside, I continued to flip through the stack and saw my dad had silently become a backer of Sacred Heart Adoption Agency, the same institution that had facilitated my adoption. He'd donated money to them throughout the years until he became a partner.

Does this mean...?

I looked up at Maeve's steady gaze as things started falling into place. She nodded, concern etched on her face, and my stomach lurched.

"Trash can," I managed. Maeve moved back while Conrad handed me the small office bucket, and I threw up, the bitter taste of bile making me gag. I heaved until my body hurt, unable to ignore the steady trickle of tears running down my face.

Maeve reached out and wiped my mouth with a tissue when I put the trash can down. "Little one—"

"Did you find out any more about the adoption agency?" I asked, my voice hollow.

"No," she replied, frustration flashing in her blue eyes. "I still have people digging through the layers of LLCs and dead ends to get more information, but it will take time. Your Oliver might be able to get through faster with his computer skills."

"I don't know if I can ask him to do that," I whispered, squeezing my eyes shut. "He was a child in the trafficking ring, Maeve."

"So were you." She broke it to me more gently than she'd ever shared anything, and I shuddered.

There was complete silence as that sunk in, and I shook my head, unable to handle this revelation right now. The only people privy to my breakdowns weren't here, and I wasn't sure I could handle one right now. My life was being torn apart at the seams.

"Did you find anything about Thomas?" I asked, forcing myself to compartmentalize.

"He is their child," she said while moving around to stand behind her desk. "From what we've found, all the doctor visits, ultrasounds, and birth records support that. Your records start at the adoption, and I can't find anything before that. The next important item to note is Miranda's murder. Thomas and Joe are missing, and they suspect Joe, but that isn't adding up since we know that he didn't take

Thomas with him. You'll probably be able to find out more when you go up there."

I nodded a few times, turning everything over. My mind was happy to have something else to think about. "Knowing him, he probably prioritized protecting himself."

"Meaning he left his wife there to get murdered?"

"His needs were always number one. Always," I said softly, flipping through the papers again.

"A few of Joe's charges happened in Boston and Ashview," Maeve said after a few moments of silence. "You might want to start there with finding him."

I looked up at her. "Will do. But why did you invite me here with Roderick to give me this? You could have given it to me whenever."

"The fact that even *my* contacts are having to dig *a lot* to get dirt on the agency is worrying. Getting information is my job, Nicholette, so if they're having such a hard time getting anything useful..." Maeve turned pensive, her jaw tightly clenched when she stood up and walked back around her desk. "You are going up against people that have a lot of power, resources, and influence, which means you need the same." I looked between her and Roderick, and Maeve continued talking before I could say anything. "Being a call girl isn't going to cut it anymore, and your men, while powerful, aren't going to be enough for this fight. I know you have contacts that you've never mentioned to me, people you've connected with on your own, like the Förstners, that can give you more leverage than I currently have."

"Maeve—"

She held up her hand, cutting me off before I could say more. My heart was pounding loudly in my ears, panic filling me when she paused, licking her lips as if she were fortifying herself to keep going.

"Their drive to help you isn't something that will transfer to me. It must be you calling the shots for this to work. We both know that. Things are already in motion, Nicholette." She gave me a sad smile, real regret showing once she let her mask down. "You need to sign things with Roderick while I finish up here, then you can get your paperwork in order. After that, walk out of here and don't look back."

"Don't do this." My voice cracked, and I stood up, letting the papers fall to the ground. Maeve speaking in riddles was something I was used to, but avoidance... She didn't *do* avoidance. There was only one way someone left a position like hers, and the thought of what she was about to do made me feel like she'd pulled the rug out from under my feet.

Maeve smiled indulgently at me. "Embrace how much you hate me, little one. Focus on the toxic relationship we had... It will make this easier. This is the last gift I can give you... and your children. My blessing and my goodbye."

I reached for her when she tried to walk by, and she let me stop her. I wasn't sure if I wanted to scream, cry, or lash out, so I was surprised when I pulled her into a tight hug instead. She wrapped her arms around me after a few seconds of surprise and held me tightly. Soft lips brushed my cheek, and if I didn't know better, I would have thought I'd felt tears on my face before she broke free.

"Why?" I asked just as her hand touched the door knob.

"Because you remind me of myself before life shaped me into the woman I am today," she replied, not looking back at me. "Ambitious, cunning, resourceful. You can do great things. And despite how bad we were for each other, little one, I love you. Maybe I never knew how to show it in any of the ways you needed, but I do love you."

"Maeve..."

She swiftly left, and I felt my heart shatter. Ice ran through my veins, the cold hardening with every fading click of her heels. A numb void consumed me until it felt like I wasn't even in my body anymore. Conrad moved in front me, and I blinked a few times when I saw his lips were moving. Eventually, his words started to register in my mind.

"Nicholette, do you need anything?" He looked so worried. I shook my head slowly, detachment taking over.

"What do I need to sign, Roderick?"

Roderick, who had remained silent from his post along the wall, stepped forward now. "Maeve named you her heir and beneficiary almost two years ago. The paperwork is all set. I just need you to sign everything. Conrad, if you could sign as a witness?"

"What is she planning?" I asked, not moving toward the pen he held out to me.

"I don't know, and I think it's best we all don't," he replied firmly.

My hand was somehow steady when I took the pen, but I didn't sign anything yet. I fiddled with the cool pen and looked up at Roderick, needing more answers even though I wasn't really sure I was ready for them. "What does being her heir mean? No legal jargon, just tell it to me straight."

"She left you all of her money, properties, everything in the event of her death," Roderick told me evenly, holding my gaze with a blank expression. "You will also become the next Madame and the head of her entire network of contacts. You will be one of the biggest players in the criminal underworld in the Northeast."

"The Madame of Ashview?" I choked.

Roderick shook his head. "She wasn't just the Madame of Ashview. Sign, then I can fill you in."

I signed the papers after another brief hesitation, then Conrad signed as well. He murmured something about getting rid of the trash can, and with a quiet order to wait for him, he left to dispose of it.

"Tell me everything. Now," I ordered Roderick sternly.

"Once everything is processed, you will now have access to all of Maeve's money. Last time I checked, it was about twenty million dollars. You are now the owner of quite a few businesses and about four different homes. We should discuss those at a different time when I can walk you through it all." He paused. I just stared at him, waiting for the rest because that wasn't what I was interested in right now. That was all her personal things, not the business side that she'd just said I would need to get my brother back. He let out a long sigh. "You had no idea, did you?"

"Then fill me in," I ordered him coldly.

"Not many people knew, though I thought you did since you were so close." Roderick rubbed his face, looking exhausted. "Maeve was *the* Madame. The head of a network that has ties and connections throughout the United States. I think she was starting to break into things overseas, but I'm not sure about that."

I looked back at him, not understanding, or maybe I just couldn't imagine that level of power. Why would a woman with that kind of power give a damn about *me*? Why leave me, a fucking prostitute who hadn't even graduated high school, the power to take over?

"This position will make you the target of many people, but it will also make you powerful enough in your own right to protect yourself," Roderick said softly. "The moment you walk out of here, you will be the Madame and one of the most influential people in the world."

I felt my lips tug upward, and a hysterical laugh filled the room as I threw my head back. Tears soon followed, and I curled in on myself, sobbing, when the meaning of all this truly hit me. Maeve was...

The door opened, revealing Conrad's concerned face as he hurried over.

A gunshot cut through the tension.

It echoed between us, and I knew what that meant.

Maeve was dead.

My enemy, my ex-lover, the woman that had been my everything had given me her everything to protect my children, my family, and myself at the ultimate cost—her life.

Fresh tears slid down my cheeks, and Conrad lightly touched my arm. I looked up at his grim-faced expression, shaking, while a distant part of me registered Roderick moving around us, packing up the paperwork. He handed the file to Conrad, then more words floated around me— Conrad saying we should go. But I couldn't move. My body just wasn't willing to leave just yet.

"The police will be coming soon."

Standing up on shaky legs, I took a few steadying breaths to get my bearings. Something caught my eye on Maeve's desk. Small jade bobby pins. She had used them whenever she put her hair up, and without hesitating, I grabbed them, needing a piece of her with me. I held them tightly and forced myself to walk out between the two men.

The SUV was sitting where we had left it, though it felt like a lifetime ago. Conrad opened the door, and I slid inside, him following after me as Roderick tipped his chin and continued on his way. The three people inside were quiet, though they looked at us with expectant eyes that spoke loudly enough. The concern on their faces only deepened with every moment of silence.

"What the hell happened in there?" I looked over at Blake, and whatever was on my face made them go very still.

"Maeve is dead. And I got the information we need."

Deafening silence filled the car, but it was nothing compared to how numb I felt inside.

"Are we going to the compound then?" Ansel asked, looking back at me in the rearview mirror.

"Yes," I told him softly. "Then we're going to Millfield. I need answers, and I need them now."

P olice cars were all over the place when I drove by.
Forensic teams. Crime scene tape. New reporters.

Maeve Cabbot was dead.

Murdered.

Anger made me slam my hand on the steering wheel.
That fucking bitch. Who the hell murdered this bitch
before I could get my hands on her?

My body trembled as I tried to calm myself down. I
needed to figure out what was going on before I lost my
temper completely. After a deep breath, I stepped out of my
car, determined to get some answers. Blending in with the
crowd, I listened in on the detectives and spectators talking
about what was going on. The security cameras had been
erased, leaving no evidence as to who had been by near the
time of the murder. She had been shot, and the house was
destroyed. Everything had been wiped down, so they had
nothing.

Given Maeve's status in this city, they were going to
turn over every stone to figure out what happened to her.

There was talk of forensics finding more, but they weren't hopeful.

This wasn't good. Not at all.

But as I turned to leave, something they said piqued my interest.

Her hair was dyed. Cut. Contacts. She was similar to the other bodies they had found throughout the city.

Irrational rage consumed me.

Someone had killed this bitch *and* thought they could pin it on me? They'd copied my murders as if they had any right to even think of my Nicholette.

Whoever had done this would pay. They thought they could be me. Thought they could try to get my Nic's attention like I was. Soon enough, they would know differently. Everyone would.

It was time to move up my plans.

First, I just had to find Nicholette.

I was tired of waiting.

Sacha
Tuesday

The police and firefighters were finally gone when I reached the compound, though I was sure someone would be around as soon as they realized Rhodes was back to check things out. As for the man himself, Rhodes looked outwardly calm, every action almost lazy with a swagger that put every part of my body on high alert. It was always the calm before the storm that you needed to worry about.

The compound was utterly destroyed. Almost every building had been burned, and while a lot of the structure was still standing, it didn't look salvageable to me. I knew he had gotten this place years ago, but I didn't know the full story behind it if there was one. Most clubs have their members live in the same space, though it definitely worked for the Lords. Rhodes clapped Razor on the back when he got close, and they started talking.

"Nothing from Nic?" Vas asked as he came to a stop beside me. I shook my head, not surprised his thoughts were straying to Nic. I was wondering when she'd be reaching out to let us know how things went with Roderick, but despite everything, I trusted Ansel and Blake to keep her safe and make sure she came home afterward. I shouldn't trust Ansel at all, but there was something about him that instinctively told me I could. I was probably an idiot. *God knows I just hide it well.*

Glancing at my brother, I was curious to see what his reaction was going to be when he realized what I had, that Ansel wasn't going anywhere. Of course, that wasn't the only person we'd been thinking about for the past month. I didn't see Wrenn or any of the surviving women nearby, not even the Lords' old ladies.

Refocusing, I zeroed in on my uncle and Razor. Rhodes was smoking while the two of them looked through the ashes of his compound. Razor was beside him, grim faced, speaking softly to his President. The other members were pissed off and ready to retaliate from what I could tell. It wasn't a question of *if* they would respond, but *when.* Luckily, they were off handling business shit right now, not pestering Rhodes about revenge.

"I wonder what they plan to do now," Vas said as we walked away to give Rhodes some privacy. We wouldn't go far in case he needed us for something. I had no idea what they would do for a place to live and operations, much less what would happen when they found the person responsible.

"Sacha, Vas!" The breathless voice interrupted my thoughts, and we came to a stop. Wrenn was running up to us. Her long blonde hair was in her face, and she brushed it aside as she licked her lips when she stopped in front of us. "There's something you need to see." Her face was pale, eyes a bit too wide, and she swallowed hard, looking behind us at Rhodes before switching back to us again.

"What is it?" Vas asked, his deep voice rumbling in his chest.

Her gaze scanned who was around us as my eyes narrowed, really noticing how pale she was. She shifted her weight from one foot to the other. She was nervous and scared, but determined as well, revealing a steel spine under that timid exterior that reminded me of Bodhi.

Wrenn shook her head. "It's something you should see for yourself. Rhodes too."

"Rhodes!" Vas yelled out.

I didn't break my stare until I heard Rhodes and Razor approach, the crunch of gravel under their boots loud in the tense silence. Wrenn nodded at the other men then spun around. "The women's quarters." She led the way to the building that had the most damage with swift, sure steps. Ignoring the caution tape, she made her way into the burned building.

"This place could collapse at any second," Rhodes grumbled, picking up his pace to get ahead of us and catch up to Wrenn. "I swear her and Nic have a fucking death wish."

Razor smirked before he hurried to catch up. Trying to make sure I didn't ruin my suit, I carefully followed them through the hallways until we got to what had been a large open room, maybe a community space. The three people ahead of us were all stock still, and when I noticed Wrenn pointing upward, it was as if time slowed down.

My stomach dropped, heart hammering, once I saw the body hanging from the burned rafters. My first thought was wondering how the dead weight hadn't broken the burned wood, but then my brain started processing the corpse itself. She wasn't burned, so the person hadn't been here during the fire. Despite that, she had been through her own trauma. Stab wounds, bruises, broken bones. Black hair hung around her in a messy tangle. Even from this distance,

I noticed something eerie. Her eyes were open. Even without seeing her up close, I would bet she had on blue-green contact lenses to look like my Nic.

"She wasn't here yesterday." Wrenn's soft voice cracked, though her brown eyes were hard. "Security cameras were destroyed in the blaze, so I can't look into how she got here. I was coming in here to see if anything could be saved for the kids, then I found her."

"Hanging her can't be a coincidence," Vas stated, rubbing his beard.

"What does that mean?" Rhodes growled, whirling around to look at us.

"Whore's Gallows."

Nicholette's voice filled the space, and we all looked over to find her standing across the room with one of Blake's men beside her. She walked over to join us, and the others followed after her, except for Ansel. *Where is he?* She came to a stop beside Vas and me, keeping enough distance between us that our bodies didn't touch. She stared up at the dead body, but I couldn't read her face. My Nic was shielding whatever was building inside her. Something about her seemed off, the distance in her face and stiffness in her body hinting that it was more than just her trying to concentrate on business. What the hell had happened?

"Not many people know about that detail of my life, so it could narrow down the list of who could be doing this."

"Whore's Gallows?" Blake asked, their voice even as they stopped beside Conrad. They looked back and forth between him and Nic before stopping on the latter.

"A serial killer in Ashview liked to torture prostitutes then hang them up for people to find," Nic answered, not looking away from the body staring down at us. "The killer didn't manage to string me up, but they left me for dead. Then Maeve found me."

Blake didn't react, like that was a normal thing to say, and maybe for them it was, but Wrenn paled, looking away from her ex-girlfriend.

"That's why you disappeared," Rhodes commented gruffly, and Nic nodded.

"I'm surprised you came here. I figured we'd get some vague message that you left without us to go to Millfield and we could just catch up." Nicholette grinned in response, though it was brittle, which did nothing to soothe the insistent feeling that something was wrong.

"I thought about it, but I decided to give you a little bit of a break since I made you chase me for a month. Old age and all that." She laughed when I grabbed her, squeezing her tightly to me. If it was slightly harder than necessary to get her back for the age comment, well, she liked a little bit of pain.

"You are pushing your luck lately, little whore. Pregnant or not, I'll make you pay for that."

"You say the sweetest things." She preened, wrapping her arms around me and tucking herself into my side. God, she'd only been gone a month, but it had felt like my entire world had ended when she left. Everything felt off, vacant, and now with her beside me like this I felt complete again.

"Should we call your detective friend?" Vas asked, shifting closer to us to brush a hand along Nic's arm.

Nicholette thought about it before replying "Yes. Allen should know about this. I'm sure that means we'll get questioned."

"Good thing I'm here already," a new voice said. I looked over to find Ansel Förstner and a guy I hadn't met before standing there.

"Roderick." Blake tipped their chin, an odd expression flickering across their face before focusing on Nic again. "How convenient you were close by."

"Full-service lawyer, Blake," Roderick deadpanned.

Ansel walked over to join Rhodes and stared at him with a bland expression that made me shiver. "Gasoline was definitely used for some of the buildings, but not all of them."

"What did they use?"

"IEDs," Ansel stated grimly. "Filled with chemicals to cause a huge fire. I wouldn't be surprised if they found shrapnel in the women that didn't make it out of here. It's one of the reasons this building was so badly burned compared to the others."

"So they set the fires in other buildings to mask the explosion or explosions in this building?" Nic asked, thinking it over aloud. "Did you hear anything explode, Wrenn?"

Wrenn shook her. "No. But I was outside when it happened. I rushed in to help people get out, but I wasn't inside when it happened. Why the women's quarters?"

Ansel answered in a calm voice. "Because the merchandise was here. A warning and profit all rolled into one."

Nic nodded a few times, and I could practically feel her brain turning it all over. "Is all the security footage lost then?"

"Yes." Rhodes kicked a piece of debris. "Everything was destroyed. Maksim isn't going to be pleased about getting a whole new setup."

"IEDs aren't hard to get a hold of, so that doesn't narrow anything down." Nicholette sighed. "Where are the others?"

"Our place and the warehouse. They decided to split up and get it all over with," I answered. "How did your meeting go?"

Nic shook her head, not answering my question. "Call Allen. We need to get to Millfield. And that's a statement I never thought I'd make. There's something I need to do before we go."

"Want company?" Wrenn asked as Nic pulled away. She turned to stare at the other woman, her eyes narrowed, before she gestured for Wrenn to follow her.

With that, they walked out without a word, and no one broke the silence until they were out of the building. Blake let out a sharp laugh and combed their fingers through their short hair. "So that's her ex? She definitely has a type when it comes to women."

Vas grunted, but I had to admit they were right. Wrenn and Maeve looked very similar—blonde, similar body types, and I bet once she was very comfortable around us, her sharp mind would come to the forefront. Another player to be added to our little mess of a group? *How the hell did I get stuck in a potential nine-person circus of a relationship?* Of course I was only with two people, Bodhi and Nicholette, but we still had to get alone and work together with everyone in some way. Fucking chaos.

"They're both from the same hometown?" one of Blake's guys said suddenly, the older one with dark hair, his eyes still trained on the doorway the two women had walked out of.

"Yes," Blake answered, looking at the guy with a confused glance.

"She's going to leave with Wrenn, isn't she?"

The younger guy with Blake smirked, and that's when we heard a car start.

Son of a bitch.

I patted my clothes and realized she had taken my keys.

I'm going to fucking throttle her.

Nicholette
Tuesday

I COULD PRACTICALLY FEEL Sacha's anger as Wrenn and I pulled away from the compound in his car. Wrenn was staring out the window while I hit the gas, getting us away from the burned down compound and Ashview as soon as possible. We didn't talk until I had gotten out of the city limits, heading north toward Vermont. It would take about three or so hours to get there depending on how fast I drove. If it was too fast, Sacha would kill me for messing up his baby. *The only thing he probably loves more than this car is that damn coffee machine.*

Taking Sacha's car keys had been a spontaneous urge that I couldn't resist. I hadn't planned on leaving them behind to go to Milltown on my own, not until I was at the car with Wrenn beside me. Looking up at yet another woman who'd been tortured and done up to look like me... All the revelations from Maeve and her death... I needed time to get my mind wrapped around this shit. *Apparently me processing just equals a lot of stupid decisions that are going to get my ass beat.* Emotions were stupid like that, but I needed to face some of the realities of my broken childhood on my own.

"Are you going to fill me in on what's going on, Nicholette?" Wrenn spoke first, not looking in my direction.

"Not everything," I told her honestly, ignoring my

phone buzzing with yet another call from Sacha. *He is going to be so fucking pissed when he sees me again.* "You'll need to be more specific about where you want me to start."

Wrenn snorted. "Always like you to split hairs." She sobered up then, shifting in her seat so she could look at me. "You have a stalker?"

I squeezed the steering wheel hard enough my knuckles went white, and with a deep breath, I answered her concisely, no details. That was more for my sake than hers if I was honest with myself. "I've had more than one, but this one has been consistent since I got to Ashview and started turning tricks. I got notes soon after."

"Notes?" she asked in a hesitant voice.

"I didn't live in a house or shelter," I told her matter of factly. "I lived under a tarp or cardboard box, if I was lucky, in an alleyway. So calling them *letters* isn't entirely accurate. Their content has run the full gamut of creepy—obsessive talk, photos of dead people, you name it. It's been... something."

"You don't have to talk so dismissively about it, you know," she admonished gently but firmly. "That's traumatic as fuck."

"I've had a lot of trauma in my life. They can take a number and wait their turn."

"It seems whoever this is is tired of waiting," Wrenn replied, and I snorted.

"You could say that."

"Your guys said they took Thomas," Wrenn ventured after a few moments of tense silence between us. "And that all this has something to do with a trafficking ring." Shock made me pause, and a creeping feeling of anger hit me. *Just how close did they get in my absence?* Just because we were starting to be friends didn't mean I was ready to do away with all boundaries.

I swallowed hard, thinking of the photos from my apartment. Dead lookalikes. A picture of a scared Thomas staring back at me. "Don't worry yourself about that. No need to get you in too deep, Wrenn. We aren't like that anymore. I told you that you didn't need to come with me... Hell, I told you that you *shouldn't* come with me, but you just flipped me off and got in the car. You are inserting yourself into a world that you don't understand."

"Nicholette—"

I shook my head to cut her off. "Leave it alone."

"What if I don't want to?" Wrenn whispered, her voice rough.

I quickly looked over to see her brown eyes shining with tears and filled with emotions that I hadn't seen in years. Cursing, I slammed a hand on the steering wheel. "Friends, Wrenn. That's what we are. Nothing more."

"I searched for you for an entire month, working with all of the men you're with—"

"And thank you for that," I shot back heatedly. "But that doesn't make you a fucking saint, Wrenn. I'm with a shit ton of people, and I don't have time for another person who's going to fuck with my emotions or expect me to be responsible for theirs."

"Are you really saying you have no feelings for me whatsoever?" Wrenn asked, her voice steady despite the tears starting to roll down her face.

"I'm not the girl you remember, Wrenn. She's died so many times over I don't think I could even picture her anymore. I can't be that person for you."

"Who says I even fucking want *her*?" Wrenn shot back. "Has it occurred to you that spending even that little bit of time with you made me start to like the person you are now?"

"And what does your girlfriend think about that?"

"I don't have one," Wrenn answered after taking a deep breath. "We split up. She was constantly jealous of my job, hanging out with you, everything. It wasn't working."

"I can't do this right now," I told her firmly, refusing to look her way. I squeezed the steering wheel hard enough I heard it creak under the pressure. "I have too much on my plate—"

"You can't do this right now with just me or everyone? I saw those new guys!"

"Wrenn," I warned, my chilly tone stopping the conversation in its tracks. "What I do with my life is none of your concern. We aren't together. We haven't been in five years. So don't you fucking dare judge me for how I put myself back together when you're one of the reasons I'm broken."

"I wasn't judging," Wrenn countered. "And in case you need a reminder that life isn't all about you, my life was shit too. I was too close to getting out to jeopardize it. I'm sorry that it was fucked up and that you had a bad hand, but so did I! Or did you forget that while you got all wrapped up in your shit? We were *kids*, Nicholette."

It was lucky for her that there wasn't much traffic. If we were at a standstill, or even moving slowly enough, I would have smacked her and kicked her out of the car. How dare she act like *I* was the fucking bitch in this situation?! As if I didn't know what had been going on in her life; she was the one that had no idea what happened in mine.

Not all of it.

No one had.

"I'm about to head back to a hometown that hated me.

To a place I was never truly welcome." We sat in tense silence for a while before I continued. "There are more bad memories there than good, so I appreciate you looking for me and coming along for the ride, but I can't offer you more than being friends. I love the men I'm with. I care about the friends I have. My life is going to get a whole lot more complicated than everyone realizes, and I can't drag you into that. More than that, I don't *want* to."

"You wouldn't have to drag me," Wrenn whispered brokenly. She turned away from me to face the window, but I saw the tears on her face in its reflection.

"There are too many things you don't know to bring you in without talking to other people. I don't know if I could even handle it because right now, my trauma is the deciding factor. My past, my boundaries, and my partners' boundaries are more important than you and your feelings. So get it together."

"Or what?"

"Or you'll be dead in a few seconds, and I'll only have to worry about disposing of your body."

"I hate you," Wrenn hiccuped, though a laugh broke through right after.

"You should join the club," I joked. "Although I think my stalker is the president, so maybe you can be vice president instead."

"That's a horrible joke." Wrenn wiped her face.

"But accurate," I shot back, and we shared small smiles, guarded and unsure of each other, as we stared at the road ahead.

Well, fuck, this wasn't exactly where I'd thought things were going, but I was going to do the best I could. I switched my phone to silent, letting the missed calls pile up, and turned on the radio. My heart was breaking and being pulled in so many directions.

Ansel.

Wrenn.

Maeve.

The babies.

The men I'd left behind. *Again*. Though just for a little while this time.

What would be left of me if I made it out of this alive?

I wasn't sure of that answer anymore.

Bodhi
Tuesday

"Son of a fucking bitch! I'm killing him!" Oli yelled from the other room, and something went crashing as my phone started to vibrate. "I just found another one."

"If you're going to start acting like Vas, we're going to need to get less expensive stuff around here for you guys to break," I told him, grabbing my phone out of my pocket. "Hey, Sacha. What's up?"

"Come to the compound," he ordered. There was an edge to his voice that told me he was pissed, but unlike the last month or so, he was actually remaining calm. At least for now. *I wonder what Nic did.*

"Why?" I furrowed my brow, confused by the deadly calm in his voice. "What happened?"

"Nic took my car and Wrenn," he growled out, his exasperation clear as I heard something crash on his end. *Guess calm is a relative term.* "The police will be here soon. There was another body."

"Oli isn't done here," I told him just as my other boyfriend walked into the room, his eyebrows raised in silent question. I waved him over, and he joined me on the couch, settling in close as I put the phone on speaker.

"I only got through three rooms. I'm tearing everything apart," Oli told him grimly, then he looked at me with a warning in his eyes. "I've already found five cameras, and my bet is there are plenty more."

Cursing filled the line, then Sacha switched to Russian, talking to whoever was around him. After a minute or two, he switched back to speaking to us in English. "A group of men will be coming to the apartment and warehouse in the next ten minutes. The Germans are going to tear everything apart and get it handled for us. Pick up Alexei and Maksim and meet us. We're following Nic up to Vermont, where we are going to have a *very* long conversation."

Click.

Oli whistled softly. "I'm so fucking glad I'm not her, but man, I wish I had been there to see his face when they realized Nic stole his keys."

"And she let Wrenn go with her." I chewed my bottom lip as I pulled up Alexei's contact info. "I'll let the others know."

Oli pressed a kiss to my cheek. "I'm going to grab a few things, then I'll be ready to go."

He got up and slipped away, probably to his room, just as Alexei picked up the call.

"Bodhi? What's going on?"

"I don't know if Sacha or Rhodes reached out, but the Germans are taking over the camera search. They'll be there in ten minutes."

"Why?" Maksim's hard voice yelled out in the background.

"What's going on?" Alexei followed up.

A small smile tugged at my lips. "Nic stole Sacha's car and is headed to Vermont with Wrenn."

There was dead silence before I heard Maksim burst out laughing, and even Alexei chuckled. I didn't think Sacha would appreciate this reaction, so it was a good thing we were getting it out of our systems now. But it *was* hilarious. Unlike last month, we knew where she was going, so there was less stress. I mean, deep down, was I happy that she had left without us? Fuck no. But Nic would come back, and I'd eventually need to talk with her to reconnect after her long absence.

"Need us to pick you two up?" Alexei finally managed to ask.

"That works for us. Oli is getting a few things together right now," I replied, looking back when I heard something fall. "I need to go check on him."

"I'll text when we're outside."

I wandered through the hallway to the bedroom Oli and I shared. The room was in complete disarray. My hands clenched, itching to reach out and start fixing it, but I restrained myself, barely, as I watched my boyfriend dig around under the bed and shove things into a bag.

"Oli?" I asked softly.

He didn't stop what he was doing, but he quickly looked over his shoulder. "Almost done. Sorry I dropped my laptop earlier."

"Are you okay?" I asked, curious what was going through his head. Sacha never pulled Oli off of a job once he started; usually, he would get defensive, saying he could handle it and no one could do it better than him. "It's been a lot with Nic coming back."

"I don't really know if we can count it as coming back if Sacha and Vas kidnapped her off the street to bring her back," Oli countered, but he sounded amused. He hummed quietly as if he were turning everything over in his mind. "We fought about it this morning. Some talking, mostly fucking. Not everything is okay, but... Fuck, even when I want to smack her, I want to kiss her. She's infuriating."

A faint chuckle escaped me as I walked over and sat down on the floor beside him. He was grabbing laptops and some weapons he had under the bed. Careful storage was not Oli's thing. "Nic is a force of nature. She likes the strong emotions she brings out in people."

Oli shot an arched look my way, and I had a feeling I knew what was coming. "You haven't been alone with her since she got back."

"She just got back yesterday," I deadpanned. "And there are a lot of us that want time with her. I'm not going to push my way past everyone."

"You were so set on her coming back, never faltering. I didn't think you'd hold back when she came home."

I didn't respond right away, his words opening up a question in my mind. *Was I holding back?* I was. I knew she'd come back, and that faith hadn't wavered once in the month of her absence, but the idea of her being pregnant and the reality were two very different things. I wasn't like everyone else in this group—violent, brash, and over-the-top protective. What could I provide for a baby, much less two? What if I ended up being like my mom or my aunt when it came to the kids? I'd never forgive myself. How could I do this? It wasn't that I wanted to avoid Nic, but she and the babies were a package deal now. I couldn't be around her, close to her, without thinking about what she was growing inside her.

"Bodhi..." Oli's hands on my face made me jerk, and he gently shushed me. "You are nothing like her. You are fucking amazing." My cheeks heated, and I looked away from him when I realized I had spoken aloud. "Don't look away from me," he urged me, forcing my chin up so I had to meet his gaze. The soft expression on his face showed me how much he loved me. "You are nothing like those cunts, and because of them, you're going to be amazing. Hell, you'll probably be the voice of reason, and god fucking knows those babies are going to need a softer presence than what the rest of us can offer, Nic included. You are going to be perfect."

"I didn't think this would ever happen," I told him softly, almost tripping over my words. "But what about you?"

"No, Bodhi." Oli shook his head at me, his mouth tightening. "My shit doesn't make yours unimportant. Don't change the subject. Right now, this is about you."

"I just don't know what I'm feeling or thinking when it comes to the pregnancy. There are enough hot heads in this group that I should get my mind wrapped around everything before I say something I'll regret," I told him, thinking over every word as I said them.

"Smart," Oli replied. "Likely for the best since all of us are probably having the same fight with her, over and over again, about her ghosting. As long as you're okay, though?"

I leaned forward and pressed my lips to his, losing myself in him for a minute. I needed him to know just how much he meant to me. The fact that he got me and the way my brain worked... I loved that about him. He kissed me back readily, his hand palming the back of my head as he pulled me close and took control of the kiss. His tongue flicked along my lips, and I opened up to him, letting him deepen the kiss even though we didn't move to take it any further than that. We had a girlfriend to chase down, and her stalker was losing control. There wasn't much time to waste if we wanted her to be safe.

He pulled back from me after a few minutes, resting his forehead against mine and closing his eyes. For the first time in a long time, he looked content, and that made me smile.

"Why are you smiling?" he asked without opening his eyes.

"Because this is one of the first times I've seen you completely happy and at ease in a long time," I told him softly. He opened his eyes, and I gently kissed him on the lips. "I like it."

"You and Nic make me happy," he said quietly, holding my stare. "This group, however crazy it has gotten, works, and I feel like I've found where I'm supposed to be. My past and everything... It's a lot. Most people would have walked away when they realized everything I lied about."

"You did lie," I responded slowly, pulling back so I could look him in the eye. He tried to avoid it, but I didn't let him. I lightly touched his chin, and that was all it took to have him looking at me again. It shook me to the core to see fear in his hazel eyes, like I had the power to completely destroy him right now. I wished we had talked about all of this before now, but our lives had been nothing but chaos lately. It was time we fixed that.

"But you had good reason to, and you don't remember most of it. Does that really count as lying? Everyone deals with trauma differently. I don't care what your name was before or what you want to call yourself tomorrow. You're mine, and I'm yours. As long as that stays true, everything else will work out."

Tears made Oli's eyes bright, then he crushed me in a hard hug, knocking the breath from my lungs. He buried his face in my neck, making me shiver when he kissed me there. "I don't deserve you."

"You do," I promised, rubbing his back. "You deserve every fucking good thing, Oli. I think I speak for myself *and* Nic when I say that you are amazing just the way you are."

My phone buzzed right then, and Oli grabbed it from my pocket while he released a shaky breath. "Alexei and Maksim are here."

I kissed him one more time then let go. He handed me back my phone and finished getting his stuff. A few minutes later, we were walking out. A group of men were standing in the hallway, and they explained that they were Emmerich's men. A few words were exchanged, and then we were in the elevator.

"I love you, Bodhi."

He wasn't looking at me and didn't glance over even as I twined our fingers together.

"I love you too, Oli."

"Now, let's go meet up with your other boyfriend, the others, and track down our loose cannon of a girlfriend before she burns her hometown to the ground."

"That would show a lot of restraint on her part," I murmured, recalling how Nic had broken down while talking about her parents and being kicked out at seventeen just because she was bisexual. Her parents were some of the top people in a trafficking ring that exploited children, but they had an issue with her liking more than just men?

Yeah, razing the town would be a huge sign of restraint, and from the maniacal gleam in Oli's eyes when he looked my way, he knew it too. We were both fucking excited to see what Nicholette had planned, and underneath their anger and frustration, I knew the other men were excited too.

A FEW HOURS LATER, we were pulling up to Millfield, and it wasn't anything like I had expected. Alexei parked at a gas station on the edge of town, and we got out, the others parking nearby. It was a small town, probably the smallest I'd ever seen—a gas station, about five stores in a row, a church, and a police station, then nothing. Just hills, woods, and country spread out for miles. *This is where Nic grew up?*

Rhodes got off his bike and lit a cigarette after taking off his helmet. Maksim did the same as he leaned against the car. Ansel and Blake shared a knowing look before Blake started quietly talking to their two men while their father went over to talk to Rhodes. Sacha and Vas strolled over toward us, my boyfriend wrapping an arm around my shoulder as Vas made a phone call, probably trying to reach Nic or Wrenn.

"Still no answer?" Oli asked, and Sacha shook his head.

"This isn't exactly what I picture when I think of Nicholette," I commented, still taking in our surroundings.

We all stood out, though some of us more than others. There was a church at the far end of the street, with a few people standing around watching us before running inside. How many people were at church on a Tuesday?

"No answer." Vas cursed. "And I don't see your car anywhere."

"We need an address." Sacha squeezed me tight, and I leaned into him.

"She never talked about here," Blake said, and their father confirmed as much with a shake of his head.

Commotion down the road caught my attention, and my eyes widened when the police station doors opened.

Out walked Wrenn. She wasn't in cuffs, and she didn't look concerned as she talked to one of the men in uniform. The guy started yelling, his hands gesturing wildly as if trying to prove a point, but Wrenn stared at him, unimpressed.

"Wrenn," Vas growled, but he stopped with a quick gesture from his brother.

"Let's see how this plays out. I think we'll draw enough attention without getting in the middle of things."

All of us stood there, some of us trying to look busy and others having their own quiet conversations. There wasn't much to do but watch this thing with Wrenn play out. They were far away, but I swore she seemed more amused than anything else by the guy's ranting. In my periphery, Ansel shifted, then his eyes narrowed, staring past Wrenn. I looked around to see what had caught his interest, but I couldn't make out anything important or unusual.

Before I could ask what he had seen, the cop started full-on yelling.

"Are you fucking kidding me, Wrenn?!" He threw his hands up in the air, stalking away from the blonde woman watching him. "No way." When he turned and caught sight of us, he paled. It would have been funny if he hadn't looked back at Wrenn before stalking toward us.

"Should we pull our guns?" Oli asked out of the corner of his mouth, getting close to my other side. I didn't know that I needed the protection, but I couldn't deny that I liked the feel of being surrounded by my boyfriends.

"Why would we want a gun if up close is way more fun?" Maksim answered. Alexei's long-suffering sigh told me he expected nothing less from his step-brother.

"Who the hell are all of you?" the cop asked sharply as he approached. He was young looking, maybe close to my age, with dirty blond hair and blue eyes. It was when Wrenn approached that it hit me. *They're related.*

"I don't know why you're getting so worked up about this," Wrenn said, seemingly continuing their conversation from before.

"I'm trying to work," he ground out, glaring at the woman beside him.

"No, you're avoiding the conversation," she pushed.

"You left here at eighteen, didn't fucking look back, and now you just waltz back years later without a fucking word."

"I've been here for a few hours, Ryan." She rolled her eyes. "I don't have to fucking check in with you."

"We had some crazy shit happen here recently, so excuse me that I want to make sure you're fucking safe. Besides, you came back here *alone*—" That caught my attention and Sacha's given the way he tensed beside me, but that was nothing compared to the Cheshire grin that overtook Wrenn's face when she replied.

"What makes you think I'm here alone?"

"You're here with these... *people?*" he replied, pulling a face. I didn't know what was more offensive—how he'd said it or the way Wrenn threw back her head in laughter.

"What? No. Men have never been my preference."

The cop started rubbing his forehead like he was getting a headache just talking to her. He took a deep breath. "Sis, can you just tell me what the fuck is going on?"

Right then, yelling came from the church, and Wrenn smirked, a bright gleam in her brown eyes. "Nic wanted a private moment with her mom. I think they finally noticed."

"Nicholette..." Her brother paled. "*Fuck.* Her mom is buried!"

"I know," Wrenn replied, glancing at us. "She wanted to pay her respects. I bet she's almost done by now."

Yelling turned to screams, and Wrenn's brother took off when another cop ran out of the station. Wrenn's expression smoothed out as she turned to Sacha. "For the record, I didn't think she was going to leave without the rest of you, but I figured going with me was better than her going off on her own."

"What happened?"

"She's destroying her headstone," Wrenn said softly. "My brother won't arrest her. Always had a soft spot for her, which I think will only get bigger when he sees her again. Let's go."

Not looking back to see if we were following, she started walking away. Sacha and Vas caught up, taking a spot on either side of her. Every step showed the controlled anger in both brothers as they headed for the graveyard.

"That will be explosive," Oli noted, grabbing my hand and pulling me along. "Don't want to miss anything!"

When we got to the graveyard, I didn't know what to concentrate on first—Nicholette standing there with a sledgehammer in hand, the headstone broken in jagged pieces, Wrenn's brother trying to pry the hammer from her grip, or the priest spouting biblical verses at our woman. "It's like some twisted joke gone wrong," I whispered, and Oli snorted.

The sound drew Nic's attention, her blue-green eyes bright with amusement as if she knew what I had said. Ryan took the opportunity to take the hammer from her then gently grabbed her arm to pull her away from the priest. He was whisper-yelling at her about destroying the headstone as he led the way to us.

"Why the hell would you do this? I swear, I don't want

to arrest you for destroying private property. You come here after all these years and just—"

"It's so good to see you too," Nic cut him off, not sounding the least bit sorry as she pulled her arm out of his grip. "I have things I need to attend to. Is the house still taped off?"

"How do you know about that?"

"Why didn't anyone in this bumfuck town think they should inform me?" Nic hissed, whirling around to face off with the man. She poked his chest and stepped into his personal space. "My brother is missing, and you all decided to just leave me the fuck out of it?"

"I did want to tell you!" he shot back. "But you were gone. Not a damn trace."

"That's a fucking lie," Nic threw back harshly. "If you ran my name through the police database, you'd have known exactly where to find me, Ryan. If you're going to lie, at least make it believable."

"I did! You didn't come up."

Nic stilled and tilted her head, studying him like a predator assessing its prey. "Show me."

"Excuse me?!"

"Show. Me. *Now.*" Nicholette raised an eyebrow, and the guy threw his hands up in the air, muttering about how she was still a pain in the ass before ordering us all to stay here.

The women watched him walk away, but as soon as he was inside, Sacha grabbed Nic and pulled her close. He fisted her hair, pulling hard enough that she was forced onto her tiptoes. Even though I'm sure it stung, she grinned up at him and leaned forward to brush her lips against his.

"You, whore, have a lot to answer for," he threatened her.

"I look forward to it, boss," she teased, running her hands over his chest.

"You have more to share with us," Vas rumbled from beside them, and Nic hummed as Sacha pulled her hair tighter before slamming his lips over hers. She wrapped her arms around his neck and fell into it. They broke apart soon after, both panting hard, and he drew her even closer, burying his face in her hair as she held him.

"Why are you getting him to look up your record?"

Nicholette shifted to look at Wrenn with a serious expression. "Because mine is about a mile fucking long, not including the open investigations. Him not being able to find me *at all* should be impossible."

"A mile long, huh?" Ryan said with some amusement, making us turn around to face him. "What exactly have you been up to?"

"Flipping tricks," she told him, not beating around the bush at all. "How do you think I met most of these people?"

"That's not how we met!" Oli protested, sounding offended. "We were roommates, Nic."

"And that's not how we met either," Sacha growled.

Nicholette rolled her eyes, but I could see the hint of a smile curling her lips. She purred as she pushed back against Sacha, pressing their bodies together, and he ran his hands down her body.

"Fine, a majority then," Nic sighed.

Ryan shook his head and held out a sheet of paper that Nicholette took before holding it up to Sacha. He raised his eyebrows and handed it over to Oli. Taking a peek, I saw that it had Nic's name and nothing else. No criminal record at all or even any kind of current address.

"How long is it supposed to be?"

"I think the last time it was pulled, it was around five or

seven pages." Nicholette shrugged lightly. "Either way, I need to see the house."

"It's a crime scene."

"From something that happened a month ago," Nic countered. "You can't tell me you're going to keep it taped off forever. I deserve to know what happened to Thomas."

"But not your parents?"

Nicholette's face flushed, but she met his stare with a hard one of her own. "I think they made it very clear what they thought of me the last time I was in this town. So no, I don't."

He sighed heavily then nodded a few times. "I'll escort you so there aren't any more situations to defuse."

"That would be for the best," Sacha muttered.

Nicholette tilted her head back, grinning at him, not the least bit sorry, and he melted, kissing her. I knew he'd have plenty to say to her later, but her being back was definitely more important than anything else. Damn, she had him wrapped around her finger. Of course, I thought it was safe to say she had us *all* wrapped around her fingers. I didn't miss the way Wrenn looked away, sadness in her eyes, like she couldn't stand to look at them.

"Stop making out in the street. Let's get going!" Ryan yelled out, and Nic broke free, threading a hand through Sacha's.

"He's so bossy. Some things don't change." Sacha let Nic lead him and the rest of us back to our cars.

"Where's my car, Nic?" Sacha asked.

"At the house. It's not far from here," Nicholette told him, then tipped her head toward the woods. "The gated neighborhood is that way, by the way. Maybe Ansel and Blake will have some luck checking it out while we're here."

Ansel spoke up. "Gated community?"

"One linked to the trafficking ring," Sacha said, not looking away from Nicholette. "No idea why, but every person we've found connected to the ring has ties to something that goes on there."

"We'll go," Blake volunteered, gesturing to their two men. "No use having too many people if you're trying to be discreet."

Blake smirked at their father's raised eyebrow and gave us all a two-finger wave, not waiting for a response before they walked away. The other two, Robin and Conrad, followed with no complaints about the constant change of plans.

"Did you go into the house already?" I asked Nicholette. She slowly shook her head, her face sober and empty when she looked at me.

"No. I never wanted to go back here or that house. Ever." Nic shuddered as she let go of Sacha's hand.

"How bad is this going to be?" I asked, and she gave me a sad smile.

"It's a normal house. Nothing too crazy, at least from what I remember. But I'd rather be back in that basement with Warren than go through the front door of my childhood home."

With that, she opened the car door and slid in. I remembered that basement—her tied up, bleeding, bruised, and half dead when we found her. Nic calling my name and her screams echoing through the walls. She would rather be tortured, raped, and drugged than go back into that house, yet she was going to do it anyway.

Cold pure fury filled me at the knowledge that someone would ever make her feel that way. I didn't let my anger get out of check often; in fact, it took a whole lot for that to happen. But I could feel it starting to wake up at her declaration. I hoped we would figure out who this stalker was and catch them before I lost it.

I didn't want to lose her or anyone else ever again because of it.

My sister had been enough.

Nicholette
Tuesday

It looked almost exactly how I remembered.

White, two-story house with faded blue shutters that were for decoration only. The front porch was clean of messes, holding just a few chairs and a table out front where my parents would sit and talk while I tried to stay out of Dad's way. The yard that was usually so well maintained was overgrown, and I could almost hear my parents yelling about it with disapproval while I cataloged every weed that had taken over the place. *Good.*

I clenched and unclenched my fists, fighting the urge to burn the place to the ground. The only good memories I had here were with Thomas, and even those didn't outweigh all the horrible things that had happened in this house—because that was what it was, a house. This structure was no *home.*

"Nic?" Vas' deep voice instantly tore me from my depressing thoughts. "Ready?"

"No." I tried to laugh, but it broke, betraying my nerves. "But let's get it over with."

Opening the door, I climbed out and joined the others

who were standing around, staring at the house, while Ryan got out of his cop car and gave us all a hard look.

"No destroying anything, Nicholette. Everything here is still evidence until we know who killed your mom and what happened to your dad and brother." He glared at me until I agreed.

"Fine," I answered blandly, feeling numb. I could barely tear my eyes away from the house. Wrenn shot me a concerned look, but I shook my head, not willing to lean on anyone right now. I couldn't have a breakdown here at this house; they, and it, had gotten enough of my tears. "Lead the way."

Ryan studied me and sighed before spinning on his heel and hurrying up the steps to the front door. I didn't look at anyone, worried it would keep me from moving forward, strode across the porch, and walked inside. It was mostly the same. The faded blue sofa was still in the living room, the TV set up in front of it, but now there was a Xbox sitting there as well. I could see the kitchen from here, and everything was clearly in its place, no mess made.

Except for the pool of blood staining the carpet by the front door.

"How did she die?" I asked Ryan as the others filed in behind me.

"Shot in the chest at close range." He paused for a second as if waiting for me to react, but I was so fucking numb I had nothing to give him. Roughly clearing his throat, he continued. "Then in the face when she was on the ground."

I nodded a few times as I silently and carefully walked through the living room to the stairs. The photos on the wall were mostly generic landscapes with a few family pictures mixed in—just my parents and Thomas. There was no evidence that I had ever lived here.

How cliché. The parents that weren't my parents had erased all signs of their false, unfavored child.

It was an odd thing to wrap my head around, so while I had tried to push it out of my mind since my meeting with Maeve, I couldn't do it now. Every part of this house was filled with memories, most awful, some not, but all of them were lies. I had always thought the snide comments and judgment were normal parent stuff, but the secrets I'd learned brought a startling and hard-to-swallow clarity to each of those interactions.

Blinking a few times, I stilled, realizing I had come to a stop in the middle of the hallway. I placed a hand over my abdomen as I looked around, as if that would protect my unborn babies from the memories echoing in the hallway.

"You stupid fucking slut!" My father's drunken voice yelled outside my door as he fumbled with the locked doorknob. I moved my dresser in front of the door, praying that it would hold him off. The dresser shook with each slam of his body, but that didn't deter him. "You fucking bitch, I'll make you wish you'd never been born."

Too late for that one.

He shoved the door open, his belt already in hand, and I scrambled back from him, but it was no use. He hit me with that fucking leather strap, over and over, until I was sobbing, begging him to stop.

The next morning, I could barely move, but my mother hauled me out of bed. There was no sympathy for my whimpers of pain, no application of medicine or even a bandage to make it the tiniest bit better. All I got was a rough grasp on my arm and an order to stop being lazy and get to school. I learned makeup early on to hide the bruises, not wanting others to know what was going on. To appear weak.

What would have happened if they had seen? If they had known?

I'll never know now.

That had been when I was younger, maybe twelve. It only got worse the older I got, but my defiance grew with every confrontation. My hatred of my "father" knew no bounds. And then Thomas came. Their miracle child. I had loved him with everything in me, so I protected him, acting out to steal away all violent attention. I'd never given him the chance to even *think* about hurting Thomas.

I hated it here.

The stairs creaked behind me, and I whirled around, instinctively moving into a protective stance, but it was just Rhodes standing there. He approached me slowly, his gaze flicking down to where my hand was. "Nic?"

I shook my head, fighting back tears as he reached for me, but I didn't turn away from the comfort he was offering. *I hate it here.* I never wanted to come back, and now that I had... I knew I'd be paying for it later. Trauma really was a bitch. Pulling me close to his chest, I breathed in deeply, savoring the smell of leather and cigarettes and finding comfort in the heat of him next to me. He ran his hands up and down my back, soothing me, as I buried my face in his chest, needing a minute. "Where are the others?"

"Downstairs and outside, looking around for anything useful." I felt the rumble of his voice in my ear. "What's wrong?"

"There are no good memories here." I shuddered, tightening my arms around his waist, and tilted my head back to look up at him. Whatever he saw there made anger spark in his gray eyes, but his touch was gentle when he rubbed a thumb over my cheek to wipe away the tears I hadn't realized were there. "I need to check out Thomas' room."

"I'll go with you," Rhodes promised before pressing a kiss to my forehead. "The photos on the wall confirm the boy taken was your brother, so at least we know with a hundred percent certainty that it's him."

Inhaling deeply, I led the way down the hall to the room at the end and pushed it open. My breath caught in my throat at how different it was. I remembered the little boy I had left behind, but Thomas had grown since then. Now, there were clothes everywhere, a messy bed, and a few different balls on the floor. Soccer. Basketball. Volleyball.

I tried to step forward, but my legs gave out. Luckily, Rhodes was right there, catching me and holding me close even as I silently berated myself for the show of weakness.

"Love…"

"See if you can find anything in here, hotshot," I ordered, the tremble in my voice revealing just how close to the edge I was. "Please."

Rhodes took a deep breath and carefully walked me over to sit on the bed. Once he made sure I was okay, he ran a hand over my hair then stepped away. He started digging around in the room, looking for anything of interest. I glanced around but didn't try to stand up, afraid that my legs would give out, causing every man here to rush over with worry. *No thank you.*

"What room was yours?" Rhodes asked.

"The second door on the left," I told him after clearing my throat. "It's smaller than this room though."

Rhodes paused and looked back at me with a confused crinkle to his brow. "There's only one room on the left."

"No, there isn't," I retorted as I forced myself up. After

taking a moment to make sure I could stand, I marched out of the room only to freeze. *What the fuck?!* There *was* only one door on the left. I slowly strode over to where I knew my room had been. Touching the wall, I turned to Rhodes and tapped the wall. "Here. This is where my room was."

Rhodes studied me for a minute then called out for Vas. I was surprised he didn't choose Maksim or Alexei, but I didn't have time to question him. Barely a second later, I heard pounding footsteps, then Vas joined us with Sacha not far behind.

"Nic says her bedroom is supposed to be where she's standing. I know how you like to kick down doors, Vas, so I figured you'd enjoy tearing into the wall." I huffed in laughter as Vas gave him an incredulous look.

"I can't just kick down a fucking *wall*, Rhodes."

"See if it's hollow, then you can punch through it." Rhodes shrugged, rubbing his fingers together as he came forward to stand beside me. I leaned into him, and he instantly wrapped an arm around me. "I'm too old for that shit."

"I'm sure there are tools around here somewhere," I told them with some amusement. "No need to hurt yourselves trying to tear into the wall. Plus, Ryan said not to damage anything."

"The crime scene is downstairs," Rhodes said as Vas rolled his eyes.

Sacha nodded at me as Rhodes and Vas started pounding on the walls to check if any parts were hollow. At least they were smart enough to be mindful of hitting any studs in the walls. Hurrying through the house, I went down to the porch. Ryan was over with Oli and Maksim, the three of them poking around by the garage. They seemed to be getting along. That, or Ryan was just trying to keep a close eye on Maks, which was probably for the best. Hopefully, he kept a close eye on Oli too. He was the one who would sneak off to do something; Maks would just do it right in front of your face while daring you to try to stop him.

"Nic?" Wrenn's voice was soft, and I looked over, realizing she was on the porch as well. A breeze blew through, stirring her blonde hair around her face. Her light brown eyes were cautious as she took a step toward me. "What's wrong?"

"My room is missing."

"What?! How can an entire room be missing?"

"I have no idea, but Vas is going to break down the wall. I need to see if there's a hammer or something." I gestured to the garage where Dad had kept his tools.

"Nic..." Wrenn reached out, but she stopped just short of touching me. I turned to face her, and she swallowed hard but made herself meet my stare. "About earlier—"

"Nic! Come here," Oli yelled out, and we both looked over toward the sound of his voice. "Now!"

"What's going on?" I asked, starting down the stairs with Wrenn right behind me. I had never been so glad to be interrupted. I wasn't sure what Wrenn was going to say, but I did know that I wasn't ready to hear it. There was way too much on my plate right now, and revisiting old flames was not on my fucking list.

Ansel strode out from around the back of the garage, and the cold glint in his gaze made my heart race. He crooked a finger for me to come with him. Oli and Maksim had gone around the side with Ryan, so I went to Ansel, curious to see what he had found.

"Your parents were leaders of the ring, yes?" Ansel asked when I got close. I tilted my chin in quiet confirmation, and with a quick glance toward Wrenn, he grabbed my arm and pulled me along to the back. "I think your cop friend is going to realize this very soon or at least understand their general involvement."

"Why do you say that? What the hell is in the garage?"

"Nic! Get over here, now," Maks ordered. The steel in his voice made the hair on the back of my neck stand on end, but not in fear.

"Guess I get to find out."

"It's not good," Ansel warned. Something dangerous took over his expression before it smoothed out. "Let's go."

He grabbed my hand, guiding me around the garage to find the other men waiting by an open door. Wrenn followed behind us, though she stopped next to her brother who was glancing inside, his face pale. He looked like was going to be sick, and Oli didn't look any better, even with Bodhi beside him. Maks lit a cigarette and trained his eyes on me as we came into view.

"What's going on?" I asked, my stare bouncing between everyone until I chose to stop on Maks. He appeared the most put together, so I figured I might get an answer from him.

Instead of making things easy on me, Maksim answered my question with one of his own. "Where are the others?"

"Vas is about to tear down a wall," I told him, ignoring how Ryan snapped to attention at that. "They boarded up my old bedroom."

"What?!" Ryan asked, the pitch of his voice rising.

Maksim slowly exhaled a bunch of smoke, but he otherwise showed no reaction. Alexei walked out of the garage, a grimace twisting his lips, and came to stand next to Maks. They shared a long look before Alexei released a shaky breath. "This is where he kept the kids."

"What?" I breathed, coldness filling me as shock hit. He'd kept kids *here*? How did I never notice? My lips parted as I tried to comprehend what he was saying.

"Your dad." Maks inclined his head toward the garage. "The stench is enough to say they were kept here for quite a while. And there are bodies in cages. Probably about a month old from the looks of things."

Ansel shifted until he was standing behind me, his hands on my shoulders as clarity and numbness took over. I could work with this. I had a job to do. I felt myself hum in acknowledgment.

While I was processing, Oli backed away from the garage, though he didn't run. I didn't need to see the inside to know Alexei was speaking the truth. I could almost picture what had happened here from what Ryan had told me. Mom was shot in the chest trying to protect Thomas, but Dad... He had run, unless he was in league with my stalker.

After Thomas was gone, the odds were that he knew my stalker, so he knew what could happen once shit hit the fan. He would have come to the garage and killed his merchandise, the kids he'd kept and abused here, mere yards from the house.

"What the hell is going on here? You're not reacting at all, Nicholette, and these guys know those kids have been dead for a month by just *looking* at them? Who are all of you?" Ryan asked, panic making the pitch of his voice rise with every question.

"That's not important right now—" I argued, trying to calm him down, but Ryan wasn't having any of it.

"You all know things, too many things that you shouldn't," Ryan stubbornly refuted, trying to regain control of himself. "It's obvious you're involved in things that aren't legal."

"Are you trying to insinuate something?" Ansel drawled from behind me, and Ryan's gaze flickered to him before fixing on me again.

"You can't leave. I need to bring the others here and show him the new evidence."

"That's not going to happen," I purred, reaching back for the gun I knew Ansel kept on a shoulder holster. Aiming and taking off the safety, I held it steady as every person around me froze.

Bodhi held Oli close, shifting their position so they were closer to the brothers and farther from where Ryan and Wrenn were standing. I arched an eyebrow at him as I stared down a man I had known for most of my life, knowing that if I had to pull the trigger to protect myself and my men, I would without hesitation.

"What are you doing, Nic? Pulling a gun on an officer—"

"Is the least of my problems," I finished for him. "Now, I'm going to ask you again. What are you going to do, Ryan? Are you going to cooperate with us? Obviously some on the force are corrupt since my record is squeaky fucking clean. Are you one of them, or are you just a damn problem I need to dispose of?"

"I'm not corrupt! No one here is!" Ryan countered indignantly. "If you hurt me, they'll find me and you."

I burst out laughing, though the sound was definitely not amused. "Darling, there would need to be a body left over, and I guarantee there won't be. So, choose a side. Mine or death."

"I won't help you." Ryan glared at me in defiance and opened his mouth to say something else, but it was too late.

His head exploded, brain and blood splattering Wrenn as she screamed, watching her brother crumple to the ground. I whirled around and backhanded Wrenn, snarling at her to shut up. She silently held a hand to her face, staring at me as if I were a monster.

It was about time she realized how much I had changed.

I am *a monster*.

Too many emotions, revelations, and secrets revealed back-to-back today. Emotional whiplash made me numb and even more practical than ever. My grip on sanity was slipping, I distantly realized, as I stared down my ex covered in her brother's blood and brains. Too bad there wasn't anything I could do to take it back... but there was also the small fact that I wouldn't even if I could. Petty was a good fucking color on me.

"Take care of him for me, Maksim," I ordered blandly, holding out the gun to Ansel. "Do whatever you want with him as long as he's gone before we leave. Ansel, come with me."

Maks and Alexei started to move as I turned on my heel and headed back for the house. The tools weren't important now. I heard three sets of footsteps fall in step with me then someone running to catch up. Wrenn hurried to get in front of us, making me stop. She was covered in blood and brain as she faced off with me, anger and pain warring on her face.

"You bitch!"

"He was in the way," I countered, cocking my head as I considered her. "And right now, so are you. Move."

"He was my brother! How could you?! You monster."

"Yes," I hissed, stepping toward her. "I warned you, Wrenn. Told you multiple fucking times that I had changed from the girl you knew, but you were *so* convinced that it was fine. I *am* a monster, and I won't make an apologies for what I became to survive the hand life dealt me. You want to hate what I've become? Look in the fucking mirror, Wrenn. You helped create this."

"It was years ago!" Wrenn screamed back. Behind her, the door to the house opened, and I saw the other guys join us outside. They seemed cautious, and even Sacha and Vas looked concerned once they realized what was happening. *Or at least some of it.* "Get over it."

"Get over it?" I repeated. "I lived on the streets for years selling the only thing I had, my fucking body, to make it. Every day could have been my last; every john I fucked could have killed me. We were kids, sure, but you fucking broke me, and age won't change that. So I guess we can call it even now. You broke me, and I broke you. Why don't you try to put yourself back together and tell me just how easy it is?"

Wrenn pulled out a gun she had hidden somewhere on herself. Time slowed down as she held it up, her hands shaking when she tried to aim with a finger on the trigger. I laughed, the unhinged sound filling the air as she hesitated, and then Ansel was standing in front of me, shielding me in case Wrenn actually took the shot.

"I might be a monster, but you aren't, Wrenn. How disappointing. But we can't have you messing up what we are doing either." I tsked, walking around Ansel and grabbing the gun from Wrenn who had collapsed onto the ground, silently crying.

Glock 22, probably Ryan's. I clicked my tongue and held onto it as I turned to face my men. The rustling behind me hinted at movement, and before Wrenn could do whatever she was thinking of, I spun around and shot her. The bullet hit her in the stomach, a shitty shot, but a painful one. I was losing control. Wrenn fell back on her knees, grabbing at her stomach. It wasn't a kill shot, but she'd bleed out soon enough. She started cursing me, so I slammed the butt of the gun on her head, feeling satisfied when she slumped over, blessedly silent.

When I turned around again, Ansel appeared the most neutral, his expression showing nothing but his patience and lack of surprise. The others... Their expressions varied from shocked to concerned, though Bodhi looked surprisingly understanding.

"Sorry, Bodhi." I half-smiled. "This might have been more violent than my reunion with Wrenn."

Bodhi chuckled, making Oli smirk. "Just a little bit."

"What the hell happened out here?"

"I killed her brother, and I think she had some issues with it," I answered Sacha's question. "He was in the way."

"Where are Alexei and Maksim?" Rhodes asked as Sacha rubbed his face.

"Dealing with Ryan's body."

"There are a bunch of dead kids in the garage," Oli said, his voice cracking before he took a shaky breath. "Did you break down the wall yet?"

"Yes," Vas rumbled, but he didn't elaborate.

Sacha pinned me with a hard stare. "I think it's time we put everything on the table. We need a game plan to get your brother back, Nic. Get inside so we can figure this out before we leave this house."

"What are you going to do with Wrenn?" Bodhi asked, staring down at my ex.

I nudged her with my foot, but she was out cold. "She'll be dead soon enough. Call me vindictive, but I don't feel inclined to let her die quickly. A secure place for her to slowly bleed out works for me. "

"I can help with that," Ansel volunteered.

"There's something else I want you to do instead," I told him, brushing past him to go up the porch stairs and back into the house. Heading straight for the wall, I grabbed one of the pictures and smashed it against a table. Ignoring the glass shards, I slipped the picture out of the frame and held it out to the man that had followed me. "Find him and bring him to me. Alive. I have some questions for my dear old *dad*."

Ansel's gray eyes never left mine as he reached for my hand and tugged me close. "I'll find him for you, Liebling, but there's a price."

"What price?" I asked, not breaking the hold he had on me. Instead, I stepped closer into his personal space.

"We are going to have a conversation when I get back, Nicholette, about us not being friends anymore. You let two others mark you, and you'll have mine to add to your body as well."

I shivered, feeling the weight of the others around us, knowing they'd heard everything he'd said. *I do not have the fucking time or emotional capacity to deal with this right now. Why is it always so complicated?* Vas grumbled something unintelligible under his breath as Sacha sighed. "Deal, but a conversation isn't a promise," I warned.

"When it comes to you, it is." Ansel released me. "I'll let Blake know what's going on." Then he was gone.

The house was so silent you could have heard a pin drop until Oli broke it. "I see we weren't enough dick for you, so you officially added someone else."

"I'm not adding anyone—"

"You're the only person in denial about this, love," Rhodes cut me off as Oli gave me an 'are you kidding me' look. "I told Alexei to take care of Wrenn. I figured he would be better than Maksim."

"Good call," Sacha said. "Let's start with the room we found and wait for the others to get back here. Then we are spilling everything. *Everything*, Nic."

"Yes, boss," I replied, my detachment fading at the mention of my bedroom. What the hell had they found up there? Why had they sealed it off?

Sacha motioned for me to follow him, and I did, going up the stairs. The drywall had, indeed, been hollow. Stepping forward, I looked through the hole, and my stomach dropped. Bile surged in my gut, threatening to come up, and Sacha grabbed me, holding me tight as I began to shake.

What fresh hell is this?

Oliver
Tuesday

What the fuck just happened?

Nicholette showed back up, and life decided to go into hyper-drive. Everything was coming together, falling apart, and piecing itself back together so fast that I thought my mind was going to explode.

She'd killed Wrenn's brother and probably Wrenn too... It was so jarring that the woman who had slowly opened up and became friends with her ex-girlfriend had shot her in cold blood. No, *torture* her. I had recognized that evil glint in her eyes when she stared Wrenn down to get what she wanted. *Is Nic spiraling out of control?* I was all for some murder and mayhem, but there were boundaries that needed to be drawn amongst allies, and I was thinking that Nic might have just obliterated a few.

I could tell the others were taken aback by her actions as well, but even though I didn't quite agree with them, I could understand what had driven her.

She'd come back to her hometown, a place she never wanted to come back to, and the trauma of her past and present were colliding.

Bodhi was a surprise though. He hadn't flinched back from what she'd with Wrenn or their argument beforehand. No, Bodhi seemed calm, almost detached, like Nic, which was concerning. He *never* lost control or went off, but under his vulnerability, Bodhi hid a temper that would rival anyone's. Honestly, it might even put Vas to shame, and the things that heated him up... Well, there was a reason he kept that part of himself in check so often. It seemed that it was slipping through the cracks now, and I just hoped everything would be okay after he lost it.

Nic's gasp pulled me back to the moment, though I instantly wished it hadn't. Vas, Sacha, and Rhodes had taken down the wall where Nic swore her room had been... and she was right. There was a space behind the drywall, but it no longer resembled whatever Nic's bedroom had looked like.

Behind the walls, they had set up cages, using the space as a place to keep people hidden. There were no windows of any kind to bring in light, and the smell of human waste made my eyes water. Apparently, Joe and Miranda Graves liked to keep their playthings close by.

Sacha was holding Nicholette, her face paled, and I worried she would throw up. He must have had the same thought because he scooped Nic up and carried her back downstairs. I followed behind, not willing to look into the room. Memories were teasing the edge of my mind, and I wanted no encouragement to relive them. He sat on the couch with her in his lap, rubbing her back as she took slow, measured breaths. Cautiously, I grabbed a seat beside them. Bodhi settled on the other side of me, both of us watching our girl closely. The others joined us soon after, Vas and Rhodes talking about the contents of the room when Maksim and Alexei rejoined us.

"Took care of the officer and Alexei took care of Wrenn, though we might need to move her before we leave if she's still alive. Better to cover our tracks," Maksim said as he leaned against the far wall, his step-brother resting beside him. "But she's good for now. Quite a show out there, killing an innocent man, a cop at that."

"He was going to get in the way," Nicholette replied as she shifted around to face the room. Her expression was calculating and challenging, lacking any remorse, and she looked over us all like she was expecting some kind of scolding for what she had done. "I took care of it. He isn't the first innocent man I've killed, and he won't be the last."

"Yeah, but this one was Wrenn's *brother*."

"Every man is someone's father, brother, son, friend... Why should he get some kind of special treatment?" Nic shrugged dismissively. "Now, you wanted to talk, boss. Let's talk."

Sacha threaded a hand through Nicholette's hair, but then he surprised me. He pulled her off his lap, forcing her down to her knees on the floor by his feet. His grip in her hair stayed steady as he leaned down toward her. "Now that you're in a better frame of mind, little whore, it's time to tell us everything. And if you try to get off your knees, I'll get my belt and beat you black and blue. I don't care that we're at your childhood home or that you're pregnant. You seem to have forgotten how this works here."

Nic lifted her chin in challenge, but I swore I saw something close to relief in her eyes and her posture softened after they had a stare-off. She melted just enough that she leaned against Sacha's leg, letting him support her just a little, and without looking, I knew my friend had a small smile on his face.

"What happened when you went to talk to Roderick?" Vas asked from the other side of the room.

"Maeve is dead," Nicholette announced, and everyone in the room stilled. I didn't think one person was breathing. Nic's eyes filled with tears, the cracks in her defenses shining through before she squeezed them shut. "I'm sure it's on the news by now. But she found out information about my parents and left it for me..."

"What did she find?" Sacha asked her gently, reaching out to wipe away the escaped tears that were slipping down her cheeks.

She opened her eyes slowly, turning as much as she could to stare at me, which wasn't a shock. I had reacted the worst when she revealed her parents were two of the leaders for the trafficking ring that had made my life a living hell.

"Joe and Miranda Graves adopted me after years of failed attempts to get pregnant." Her voice was husky, strained, and she continued to ignore everyone else in favor of looking at me. "She was digging into the agency, and when she died, she was still looking for the end of the trail of associated shell companies and LLCs."

"What does that mean, exactly? I can tell you're hinting at something, love. Say it."

"The agency is a front for the trafficking ring. It's how they move the kids. Maeve was able to find that out for sure, but she was still digging for names." I could hear my heartbeat ringing in my ears as I just looked at her, my mind unwilling to put everything together. Almost like she knew that, she pushed through the rest of her explanation. "This means I was also trafficked, and there was no trace of me before the Graves adopted me."

My mind was racing, clinging to consciousness even though I was lightheaded. I couldn't move. My heart was breaking, pain and rage taking the place of everything else. There were just too many questions. What had happened to Nic that she hadn't mentioned to us? Did she even remember that deep into her past? My stomach rolled, and the press of Bodhi's slender hand on my arm made me jump.

"You were—" I started, but I had to cut myself off.

She nodded, her expression serious as she watched me. "From what I remember, things were fine for a while. Until they got pregnant with Thomas, their miracle baby. Guess they didn't need to play pretend with me anymore. There were things before that that weren't all bright and sunny, but it's all fuzzy. I just know it got worse after Thomas was born."

"I see why you destroyed her headstone then," Bodhi stated softly, but an underlying cruelty curled along the words, and Nic flicked her attention to him. A hint of smile tugged at her face, and Sacha loosened the hold he had in her hair. He began petting her, and Nicholette fully leaned into him, accepting the comfort that he was offering.

"If Maeve is dead, that complicates things," Vas rumbled. "She might have been a bitch, but she had a lot of connections."

"Wonder who's taking over?"

Nic opened her mouth to respond right as her phone started to ring. She shifted and got it out before she wrapped an arm around one of Sacha's legs and answered the call on speakerphone.

"Hey, Em."

"Don't 'hey, Em' me, Nicholette," Emmerich bitched, and his accent only became thicker once he started to curse at someone in the background. "Where the hell is everyone? I get back from the airport, and everyone is MIA, my men are tearing apart buildings, neither Blake or Ansel are answering their phones, and the MC compound is crawling with more police... What did you do?"

"I've done a lot of things, Em." Nic sounded amused.

"I'm not in the mood for word games, Nicholette. These are *my* people—"

"They are," Nicholette interrupted. "We needed to go for a little road trip. As for the police, there was a present left in the building for us. Another body made up to look like me."

"Yeah, that's not the only body to show up today," Emmerich said grimly. "Maeve Cabbot's body has been found, and the same thing was done to her."

Nicholette's eyes narrowed, and she clicked her tongue. Surprise made me still. Maeve being dead was one thing. Having her body show up looking like her ex-lover was a whole other level of creepy. *Did the stalker get ahold of her too?* "Is that so?"

"The wicked witch is dead. Who's taking her place? That's the question. With all of this turnover and the Lords' place burning down, we will have people coming here thinking they can dispute our hold."

"That won't be a problem." Nicholette chuckled. "You're talking to the new Madame, Emmerich, so play nice."

"*You?!*" Emmerich choked, and Rhodes did the same thing across the room.

"Me," Nicholette purred. "But don't worry, this job is personal still, though don't expect every interaction after this to stay that way. Gotta be professional and all of that. Cosimo is with you?"

Silence. "No. He got tied up with some Family bullshit, so his trip here is delayed."

"Good, no distractions then. I'm going to text you a few things I need you to look into before we get back to Ashview. We might have to come back here later, but for now there are some other answers we need first."

"Back to Ansel's place?" Emmerich asked.

"Of course. See you there."

Click.

"You're the new Madame?" Vas asked her.

"Yes," Nicholette answered, leaning her head against the couch. "That's what Roderick needed to tell me this morning."

"Is there anything else we need to know before we go back?" Sacha pointedly asked as Nic typed a long message on her phone, presumably to Emmerich.

She shook her head, and it seemed like every man in the room let out a shaky breath. Nic really knew how to pack a punch, so I thought we were all glad that we would get at least a little bit of a break after these last two hits. Sacha looked toward me then leaned down to whisper something to Nic before he extracted himself from her and got up to talk to the others. Bodhi went with him, leaving Nic and me on the couch with the illusion of privacy.

Nic turned to me, staying on her knees as she searched my face. I didn't know what she was looking for, but a few seconds later, she scooted over and leaned against my leg. My hand was shaking as I petted her black hair, playing with the long strands.

"I'm still mad at you."

Nic snorted softly. "Everyone here is still mad at me."

"Wrenn might take the cake after today. You could have just knocked him out." I kept my voice gentle, as if that might keep her from going off on me.

I could hear her swallow hard, and her voice cracked as

she replied, "I know. Maybe I wanted to take the opportunity to lash out after all these years. Or it could have been the final fucking straw. All I want is my stalker to be gone and my brother to be safe, that's it, and now it's so much more complicated."

I couldn't not touch her at that point, so I bent down and scooped her up, setting her on my lap. She wrapped her arms around my neck and snuggled close, seeking physical comfort. Honestly, I wanted the same. Burying my head in her neck, I breathed her in, thankful that we had found each other and sad that we shared a history I wouldn't wish on anyone. None of us would blame her for cracking. Everyone here knew what it was like to be pushed to the limit and then beyond it. Hell, that was where we'd been for the last month with her gone; we'd done way worse things than putting a bullet in someone.

Now, I was just left wondering how the hell we were going to deal with everything else while tracking down her stalker. When I thought of the softening curves of her body, the babies growing inside of her, and my boyfriend who seemed on the verge of tumbling into his anger, I knew we had to get those answers fast.

Pressing a kiss to the top of Nic's head, I looked up and met Sacha's gaze. I knew he was thinking the same thing I was.

It was time to go underground again.

Nicholette
Tuesday

The ride back to Ansel's place was quick, probably because I fell asleep. The stress of everything, especially the pregnancy, was all taking its toll. I woke up to Sacha unbuckling me and picking me up out of the seat. I started to protest, but he gave me a hard look that cut off any words. Guess my nap meant I was ready for his lecture about stealing his car. *Well, okay, I earned that one.*

Emmerich was waiting at the front door, but I didn't have time to say hello to him since Sacha kept walking, going straight for the stairs. I could tell he had a lot on his mind because he headed straight for a bedroom and into the attached bathroom. Setting me on the counter, he gave me a soft order to stay there. He started running water for a bath while I fought the urge to let him care for me.

"Sacha—"

"No. No talking, Nic. You can follow my directions, or I'll remove the choice for you."

"With more duct tape?" I asked, unable to keep myself from alluding to Vas' use of it when they grabbed me off the street.

"I'll get creative," he threatened, finally turning around to face me. He stepped into my personal space, long fingers skimming up my legs to the hem of my shirt. Slowly, he pulled it over my head, and I stayed silent, waiting for whatever he had planned. He placed the shirt on the counter, eyeing my naked chest since I didn't have a bra on at the moment. I thought he would have reached for me then, cupping my breasts and teasing me, but Sacha surprised me. He simply moved on, pulling my leggings and underwear down so that I was sitting there naked while he remained completely clothed.

Tilting my head back, I stared at him, wondering what he was thinking. He was just standing there, looking me over from head to toe and back again, not touching me. His gaze lingered where Vas and now Maks had carved their names on my body, but besides a slight arching of an eyebrow, he didn't react. I bit my lip, keeping myself from asking what he was doing. Everything had spiraled out of control today... Maeve, Wrenn, Ryan... It was nice to let him take over for a little while. As if he could sense the direction of my thoughts, he grabbed my chin hard enough that I hissed, firmly putting me in a space where he was in charge. *God, I missed this.*

"In this room, tonight, you'll do everything I tell you to do. No questions, no smartass mouth. You're going to feel every ounce of emotion and pain you put me through when you disappeared and since you've been back. I'm going to hurt you. I'm going to make you beg. But I'll fucking worship every last inch of you, Nic. And at the end of it, you're going to know you'll never walk away from me again, little whore. *Never.*"

My throat was thick, emotion making my chest feel tight. My lips parted as if I were going to respond, but Sacha saved me from myself, slanting his mouth over mine to kiss me so thoroughly I felt dizzy. I threw myself into the kiss, willing to drown myself in him and his promises. Tugging at his clothes, I urged him to undress, pushing his suit jacket off his shoulders and working on the buttons of his shirt until he growled in frustration. He ripped it off his body so we could be skin to skin then made quick work of his slacks and his dress shoes. Once he was finally naked, he broke away from me, ignoring my attempts to keep kissing him.

We panted heavily, staring at each other, our cheeks flushed from arousal and steam. *Shit, the tub.* He turned around, twisting the knob so the water stopped, and luckily it hadn't overflowed. Ansel would have been pissed if we damaged his house.

"Get in."

"Join me?" I asked, knowing I needed him as close as possible. A hint of softness entered his brown eyes as he reached up and let his hair loose, those curls of his falling down around his face. He got into the tub and held out a hand to help me in. It was a tight fit, squeezing both of us in there, but once I was comfortably snuggled into his chest, I had no regrets about asking him to join me. Getting close to him was more important than being fully clean right now.

I knew how much I'd missed their company before, but with the feel of him against me, nothing between us, I realized just how much I missed *him*. Sacha was my anchor in so many ways, and to be with him now... It was almost dizzying.

I ran my hand over his chest, humming in contentment, as I thought of what to say. He didn't want to hear me talk tonight, I knew that, but there were things I needed him to know before any kind of worst-case scenario could happen.

"Do you know why I like baths so much, boss? Why

they became a whole thing for me? Salts, oils, bubbles, you name it." I drew shapes on his arms, loving the feel of him under my fingertips and against my back.

"No," Sacha replied, running his fingers through my hair, carefully pulling at tangles so he didn't hurt me. It seemed he was on board with a calm intimate moment between us before he made good on what he'd promised. Maybe he could sense my intention, that I'd be letting down my walls. Sacha always got me like that. "Tell me."

"I didn't start taking them until after I began to work for Maeve," I told him softly, tracking my fingers' journey on his skin so I didn't have to look up at him. "The first apartment I got for myself, not somewhere Maeve put me up in, I bought every bath thing imaginable. Loofahs, bubbles, a fuzzy robe, face mask... Most of it was ridiculous." I laughed breathily, shaking my head at my younger self. A lot had happened in two years. "But I used everything I got in a week. I could bathe in a place I paid for, a place no one had access to but me. I was *safe* and could let my guards down. It was a feeling I'd never had before then—not growing up in that house or on the streets. I'd earned every bit of those nice things I had bought for pure self-indulgence. They weren't to keep me fed or clothed; they weren't something I had to have on hand to trade for safety or protection. They were just for me, just because. The fact that the baths helped with bruising was just a bonus."

I exhaled a shaky breath, not fully understanding where I was going with this or if he would get it, but I'd already started, so I was going to finish it.

"Eventually, I figured out things I liked and others I didn't. The baths became something I did for me. No one else knew *me*, not really. People I slept with called out my professional name when they fucked me. Until I moved in with Oli, no one called me Nicholette or Nic, except Maeve sometimes." A sad smile curled my lips, and I slowly looked up to meet his intense gaze. He'd been silently listening as I opened up to him, playing with my now untangled hair.

"I haven't taken a bath in a month, boss. Not since I left Ashview. Even when I was hiding away at a friend's place, I didn't feel safe without you all there. Then Rhodes said everything was taken... all over again..." I shook my head, tears stinging my eyes. *Damn hormones.* It was somehow more violating to have those things taken away than my clothes. Clothes, I could replace. The bath stuff though... While it could be replaced, it was really the only part of my daily life that was exclusively for my comfort and pleasure. It was the principle of them being taken away that hurt the most... well, except for one thing. *The oil from Vas would be gone too.*

"Nicholette," Sacha murmured huskily, gently wiping away the tears.

"I left because I had to. I needed to protect everyone who ever made me feel like I was home." My voice cracked on the word *home* because that was a feeling I never thought I'd ever truly have. "I'd bury Ashview in bodies if it meant all of us were standing together on the other side. You would do the same, boss, all of you, and I can't give you anything less than that."

Sacha pulled me up, slowly and deeply kissing me despite the tears sliding down my cheeks. This whole speech of mine felt like such an elaborate way to say I love you, but those three little words didn't seem like enough. When he pulled away, he didn't go far, resting his forehead against mine with his eyes closed.

"Even if I understand why you did it, I'm still mad you left."

"I know, and I don't expect you all to be happy about what I did, but I do think you can all understand what my mind went through," I told him, gently but firmly. "Besides, you assholes are overachievers. Not even the IUD could keep you all out. So now we have twins to worry about as well."

Sacha groaned, but when he opened his eyes, I was humbled to see the love there along with a hint of fear. He rested a hand on my stomach while I pressed a kiss to my shoulder.

"Not one of us is qualified to do this."

"Nope," I quipped, "yet here we are. And much further along than I thought. At least the meds work, so I'm not getting sick morning, noon, and night. But hey, at least there are enough of us that we can get some sleep by taking turns."

Sacha chuckled, a grin tugging at his lips before he kissed me one more time. "I love you."

"I love you too, boss," I whispered against his lips, then I moved back just enough to give us a little distance. "So are you going to make good on your promise now, boss man? I need you to help me let go... or are you not man enough for it?"

"There's that smartass mouth," he taunted, though there was no menace behind it, at least not yet. "I'll remember that for later, little whore, but right now, I have something better to do."

He proceeded to wash every inch of me, and anytime I tried to help, he forced me to stop, leaving me completely reliant on him. Starting with my hair, he shampooed and conditioned, then he moved on to washing my body. His touch worked me up as he thoroughly cleaned me off, avoiding my breasts and pussy until the very end.

When he palmed my sensitive breasts, I whimpered as he bit my neck. "I see you have a new mark on your thigh. I'll leave that to Vas, but I'll give you one of my own before the night is through."

"Sacha," I moaned, my head falling to the side. He kneaded one breast, then the other, before his hand slid down my softening stomach and between my thighs.

"Even in the tub you're fucking soaked, so damn easy." He smiled against my skin and slipped one finger inside of me, causing my hips to jerk. "Does that thought excite you, whore? What if you got markings from all of us? Two down... six to go."

"Six?" The addition of a second finger pulled a gasp from my lips.

"Rhodes is right. The only ones in denial about Ansel are the two of you, and it looks like Ansel is coming to terms with wanting you."

"I don't—" I groaned. "I don't want to hurt you all again. Like with the others."

"Do you want him, Nic? Not in just a 'we fuck' kind of way." Sacha's voice was serious, and he stilled his movements with his fingers deep inside of me. "Do you feel safe around him? Do you want to tease him until he snaps or joke with him like you do all of us? Does Ansel give you something you *need*?"

I panted, thoughts warring inside of me as I pictured what life could be like—Ansel listening to me bitch about Sacha and his stupid coffee machine that was way too complicated. Would he agree with Sacha or get me Dunkin because he knew I loved it? I thought of the few times we'd seen each other that weren't strictly about sex. We'd watch horror movies, critiquing the killer's techniques and deaths. Oli would lose his mind, and the others would probably join in. Ansel would fit with not just me, but all of us. Would Vas like it? No. But I knew he loved me more than he hated other people... I mean, if he could put up with Maks, I thought he could deal with almost anything.

At least I hoped so.

"What's going through that brilliant mind of yours?"

"Vas..." I worried my bottom lip. "He doesn't... I don't know how he feels about this."

"You could always just ask him," Sacha replied darkly. "He's listening already." I jerked in place, glancing around for him, but Sacha refused to let me move any more than that. "Brother? I think Nic is worried about your delicate feelings."

A snort escaped before I full-on started laughing when Vas grumbled something from the other room. A moment later, the bathroom door flung open. Vas' large frame filled the doorway, his heated gaze drinking in my naked body. "Fuck you, Sacha. Are you really sure you need my brother, Nic? At this point, I'm not sure you do."

"Just try it, *little* brother," Sacha warned, then he started to play with me again, his hand kneading my breast while his fingers pumped in and out of my pussy. "I'll remind you why I'm in charge here."

"Kinky," I commented huskily, making Vas roll his eyes, and Sacha pulled away from me, leaving me feeling needy and achy. I really had no self-restraint.

"Out of the bath, then crawl onto the end of the bed. Stay on your fucking knees, little whore, and don't even think about looking up. If you try to walk, I'll beat your ass black and blue then make you do it all over again before we only fuck you in the ass tonight," Sacha crooned in my ear like the twisted lover he was. "Go on, little whore. We have a lot of things to work through with you before the night is over."

Vas helped me out of the tub and quickly and efficiently dried me off before he gestured for me to lead the way into the bedroom. Carefully, I got onto my knees and followed Sacha's directions. It reminded me of the first night they'd shared me—a date with Ben Wa balls in my pussy all night before they fucked me, ruining my orgasms before coming all over me. I could feel the arousal on my thighs from just the memory of that night, and my nipples were hard. The anticipation itself was threatening to push me over the edge. Who would touch me first? Would it be nothing but pleasure, or would it have a stinging edge to it that would make me grateful I was already on my knees?

I needed the pain, the pleasure, *anything* they were willing to give me tonight. I didn't want to be the Madame or the girl whose brother was missing. I wanted to be Nic, their whore, their slut. I wanted to let them take over and consume me until there was nothing left. Them owning me was exactly what I needed.

Good thing that was precisely what they had in mind.

Eventually.

Vas
Tuesday

I COULD SEE where pregnancy was changing her body. The softness around her waist and hips, her breasts becoming fuller... She was fucking gorgeous and even more attractive to me than before.

Sacha got out of the tub and dried off beside me, giving me a chance to reply to his not-so-subtle jab. "Little brother?"

"I *am* the oldest." He chuckled and dodged the playful punch I threw his way. "Is there a reason you came in here earlier, besides joining tonight?"

"Tomorrow, we should tell her about Gabriel and the job Maeve gave us. Since she inherited Maeve's business," I told him, taking a peek at our woman waiting for us. "She needs to know. Plus, she can make the call if we need to keep looking for him since it fell to the wayside once she came back."

My brother ran a hand over his beard, grimacing at the unkempt hair on his neck. *Bet he'll be shaving tomorrow.* "Tomorrow. Tonight, we need to remind her of her place with us."

"Good thing I'm here then. Too bad chasing her down isn't in the cards." I sighed, catching the way Nic rubbed her thighs together when I said that. *Noting that for a later date because I miss chasing her.*

"I'm sure we can think of plenty of other things to keep her mind occupied." Sacha grinned, a sinister light gleaming in his gaze as he approached the bed. I took that as my cue to undress and lock the door so I could join the fun. It was always good to have a brother that could share because damn, Nic was by far my favorite toy, and making her take both of us, pushing her body to its limits, was so fucking delicious.

"Are you going to be a good girl for us?" Sacha purred, trailing his hands down Nic's arms. "Tell me how much you want the pain we're going to give you tonight."

"You said I shouldn't talk, boss, so that's a bit contradictory if you ask me. Maybe you're just all talk," she sassed back, and I grinned at the sound of Sacha's growl. *Fuck, she's perfect.* He fisted her hair and forced her head back.

I walked over in time to see a cruel grin fill my brother's face before he looked up at me. That glance was the only signal I needed; I knew what he wanted to do to her. He walked around to the side of the bed, dragging Nic by her hair, and sat down, forcing her to sprawl across his lap.

"Vas, I'll warm her up. You can handle the second part," Sacha ordered, then he raised a hand and brought it down on her ass. Nic moaned and raised her ass up, silently asking for more, and Sacha began to really spank her.

Turning to the bedroom's closet, I was glad to see random clothes inside—a bit showy for my taste, but I knew Sacha would love it. Looking through everything, I found a belt. All it needed was a simple fold. I snapped it a few times to test its weight and hear that beautiful sound. *Perfect.*

Joining them again, I saw Nic's ass was pink, slowly becoming red thanks to my brother's attentions. Nic's ass jiggled with every hit, and her hips rocked back, pleading for another hit. Her breasts were swinging with every moment of contact, her nipples erect, and from here I could see her inner thighs were fucking soaked. God, I had missed her.

"I'd spank that cunt too," I drawled, ambling over to the end of the bed. Reaching over, I widened her legs until she whimpered. Her pussy was pink, wet, and fucking dripping. Sacha dipped his fingers down to play with her. "She likes to think with it too often for my liking."

Sacha laughed roughly and landed a loud hit on her pussy that made Nic cry out. I could tell he wasn't hitting her as hard as he would have before; the hits were mostly for the auditory effect more than the force behind it. He was being careful of the babies inside of her. We wanted to push her, but we didn't want to cross the line of too much. Good thing we were just the men to give her the balance she needed.

Sacha spanked her for a while longer, alternating between her cunt and her ass until she was a nice shade of red all over. Nic was so fucking turned on I could hear the wetness of her arousal with every hit to that pussy of hers. She'd gotten desperate enough to hump Sacha's leg, searching for some kind of relief for the lust building inside her.

"Enough," I rumbled, my voice deeper than normal. I pumped my hard cock a few times, willing my control to last. "It's my turn."

Sacha landed one more hit on her ass that dragged a choked cry from Nic's throat, making my brother chuckle. He rubbed his hands over her ass to soothe the sting a bit before he urged her onto the bed.

Nic sprawled out on her stomach, the delicious red of her ass about to be turned into bruises. I shifted the belt in my hand, and she looked over her shoulder at me, a challenge sparkling in her eyes. Somehow, she managed to hold her tongue. *Probably for the best.*

"You remember your safeword?"

"Yes," Nic whispered.

The crack of her voice and the healthy dose of nerves in that single word brought a smile to my face. Raising the belt, I brought it down on her ass, lust and power filling me with each of her cries. Over and over again, I whipped her ass and upper thighs until tears ran down her face. By the time she was sobbing, Sacha had her hands tightly in his grasp, keeping her from trying to get away.

I dropped the belt to the floor without a care, climbed onto the bed between her spread legs, and adjusted her hips so she was at the perfect angle for me to slam home. She screamed, her hands scrambling on the bed, and her pussy clenched my cock so tightly I knew she was coming. Firmly holding her waist, I fucked her with every ounce of anger and pain that had built up inside of me. Sure, we'd talked a bit since she got back, but this... This would always be where our connection started. I chased my orgasm, and it didn't take long.

I growled her name then yanked her up to bite down on her neck. Her hands came up, digging into my forearm, and her orgasm made her yell out my name. Sacha eagerly watched, his cheeks flushed, and slowly pumped his dick. Nic writhed until I pulled out, then she slumped down on the bed.

"Fuck," Nic sighed, and a fine tremble traveled through her body. "I missed this." If that didn't fill me with pride, nothing would.

"You're not done yet, little whore," Sacha rasped. I backed away, and he slid closer. "Come here."

Nic groaned as if she were complaining, but when she pushed herself up on the bed, I caught a half grin on her face. Sacha grabbed her by the throat and captured her lips in a kiss, yanking her closer so he could squeeze her bruised ass. A masculine chuckle escaped when she hissed, jerking at the rough treatment.

"I don't want to hurt you," Sacha said after he broke away from her.

"I won't let you, boss," Nic reassured him. "If it's anywhere close to too much, I'll stop you. I promise."

My brother studied her face, weighing her words, before he flipped onto his back with Nic on top of him.

"Ride me. I want to see you fuck yourself on my cock and lose yourself to everything else. Every plot and plan you have up there is going to disappear when I make you ride me until you're crying for me to let you off."

Sascha held his dick for her while Nic shivered at the threat, then she positioned herself over him and sank down. Her head thrown back, Nic set to work, riding Sacha like her life depended on it, grinding her hips as her breasts swayed. Her rhythm faltered when Sacha hit one breast then the other. Her movements became desperate until he shifted forward and started to suck on one of her nipples.

Her body jolted as if she had been hit by lightning, and Sacha still made her ride, his firm hands on her hips, forcing her to work through one orgasm and straight into another. He moved to her other breast as she started to sob, and he delivered a warning smack to her ass when one of her hands came up as if to stop him.

Fuck. It was hot.

After Nic had her fourth orgasm, he flipped them both, his hand shifting to her throat as he started pounding into her. He wasn't choking her, just pinning her in place.

"Sacha!" Nic gasped his name, tears in her eyes. "Fuck, please."

"Please what, whore? What do you need?" Sacha taunted her.

"I need— Fuck, boss, please!"

"You're done when I say you're done," he growled menacingly enough that the hair on the back of my neck stood up. "Did you see her new marking, brother? Maksim left one right next to yours."

"I saw it in the video and the way our slut came after he did it," I deadpanned, fire burning through me. *Fucking Maksim.*

"Seems only fair she gets something from all of us eventually. Give me your knife."

I arched an eyebrow at his gruff command but did as he asked. Reaching down to the clothes I had discarded, I grabbed one of the knives I always carried with me and held it out for Sacha. He took it without breaking eye contact with Nic. He stopped fucking her, though he stayed balls deep inside of her, and teased the blade's edge along her skin.

"But where to mark you since they took your inner thighs..." he thought out loud. Nic watched him, her gaze careful but excited, and Sacha studied her like she was a fucking toy he wanted to lay claim to. "I know just the place."

Right over her heart, he carved his name into her. Every movement of the knife was precise, and when he was done, her breast heaving, he leaned down and lapped up her blood like it was a fucking delicacy. She came then, her body tense and her voice hoarse, as he growled out her name at the same time.

Sacha didn't pull out of her until he had licked up all the blood, and when he did, she just laid there in a daze. He settled on his side, looking down at her with a soft expression I had never seen before. There was a warmth there that not even Ava had managed to get out of him, and I got it. Nicholette fit us, *all* of us. She didn't want to change us; if anything, I had a feeling we'd always be chasing each other further into the dark while also pulling the other out if we strayed too far.

I gently pulled at the covers, and Sacha shifted himself and Nic so I could get them loose. Settling them over us, I laid down on Nic's other side.

"Think we took it too far?" I asked with some amusement.

Nic shook her head, stretching slightly before letting out a hiss of pain. Whether it was from Sacha's cutting or the bruises on her backside was anyone's guess.

Sacha laughed darkly. "No, I think it was just what she needed and what she could take given the babies. If she wasn't pregnant, it would have been a lot more intense."

Nicholette sighed, resting a hand on her abdomen. "True. But now I'm hungry." She turned wide eyes to Sacha, receiving a narrow-eyed glare in return.

"When was the last time you ate?"

Nic bit her lip, breaking Sacha's stare to look around the room as if that was going to save her right now. "Lunch when I first got to Millfield?"

Sacha clicked his tongue in annoyance. "Why does that sound like a question, Nic?"

"It isn't?" she replied with a wide grin, and I started to laugh. Some things never changed. "In my defense, I don't cook, and there weren't many places to stop at on the way up there."

"For three hours?" Sacha asked incredulously.

"If I did, I would have been eating in your precious car," she shot back, making Sacha roll his eyes.

"It's been covered in blood before. The food clean-up would have been a good change of pace for the detailer." With a sigh, he forced himself to stand up and started for the bathroom for clothes.

He quickly got dressed and had started to leave when I spoke up. "Are you bringing food for all three of us?" He shot me an annoyed glare and left without responding while Nic chuckled, turned over, and snuggled into my side.

"Do you want to know a secret, big guy?"

"Oh god," I muttered, not sure what the hell she was about to say. "Do I want to know, slut?"

"I was the one who hired you all to look for Gabriel after he went missing. He's the one who hid me in Ashview along with a cabin on the outskirts of the city for obvious reasons," Nic purred, a cat-who-got-the-canary smile taking over. *She what?! How the hell did she pull that off?* I knew I shouldn't be surprised by her capabilities anymore, but this one... This one got me. "A program on my phone changed my voice, and we all know I was around Maeve enough to speak like her. I need an update. Soon."

"You—" I recalled mentioning to Sacha that we should bring this up with Nic tomorrow. *Guess she overheard me.*

"So, big guy, what progress did you make on finding my friend before all hell broke loose?"

I ran my hands along her sides, loving the way she shivered when I dug in just enough to give her a hint of my strength. "We don't have much. Just the hand that was delivered to the Lords' compound on Sunday, which we already told you about."

She hummed thoughtfully, lightly running her fingers through my chest hair and scratching me with her nails. "He'll wish he was dead if they did that. He used to work for Maeve before she turned him into an informant for her network. I don't know everyone she had under her, but he was a trusted person she introduced me to. He retired from turning tricks to do that, then opened Olive & Grove so he could rub elbows with the rich and privileged of Ashview." She was quiet for a moment before she asked in a tentative voice, "Are you sure it wasn't a boy's hand?"

"It was too big to be your brother's," I told her with a shake of my head. "It was the first thing we thought of when we got it. Then another dead body showed up. Not sure if the timing between those two things was a coincidence or not, but it certainly raises the question of whether your stalker could have had Gabriel."

"Possibly." She tilted her head back to look up at me, calculation and curiosity in her eyes. "But that means this person has two hostages, one of whom is skilled at getting out. So either my stalker is working with someone else—"

"Or someone else in the trafficking ring has Gabriel?" I finished for her.

I could almost see the gears turning, the jumps she was making with that little bit of information. It was intoxicating to see her mind at work.

"Vas, can you get my phone? It should be in the bathroom with my clothes."

I grabbed the phone, handed it to her, and climbed back into bed, wanting to keep her close. She unlocked it and selected a contact just as Sacha opened the door. I lifted my eyebrow at his tray of soup and bread, and he looked at both of us with a questioning glance.

"What's going on?"

Nicholette waved at him to come in and hit the speakerphone button so we could all hear the phone ring. Just as he closed the door. Ansel's smooth voice answered.

"Liebling, I'm good, but I'm not *that* good."

Nicholette chuckled, and Sacha put the food down on the dresser and sat down on Nic's other side.

"I had a thought that could be useful," Nic replied. "I sent a friend into the trafficking ring to ferret out information on my stalker and my brother. He went missing. There's a good chance one of his hands was delivered to the Lords' compound right after a dead look alike was dropped off. My stalker could have him, but that gives them two hostages to contain."

"Which would be hard... So instead, you think your father could have Gabriel?" Ansel asked, easily following her thought process. My brows raised in surprise, and Sacha clicked his tongue, looking thoughtful.

"The box with the hand was addressed to all of us," Sacha speculated, "not just Rhodes even though we were at his compound."

If it threw Ansel that other people were with her, he didn't show it. I heard an engine rev in the background as though he hadn't skipped a beat. "It could also just be someone else in the trafficking ring, Nicholette. But he could have your friend considering your stalker is interfering with his business. When was the last contact you had with Gabriel?"

"Two weeks ago. He was supposed to check in and missed the time. I figured something happened to delay him, but we had a back-up plan. He also missed that time as well, so I called the guys to look into it."

"But then you waltzed back into Ashview soon after," I told her dryly. "So there hasn't been much digging since things have been nonstop with you back."

Ansel chuckled roughly as Nic winked at me. "Sounds about right. I'll look into it. It could be a lead to finding Joe and dragging him back. There's someone I'm meeting with who might be able to help me find him sooner than I expected."

"Who?" Nic asked.

"It's always good to have friends on the inside, Liebling. I'll let you know when I have more."

Click.

Nic rolled her eyes at the abrupt ending, but she didn't look surprised. Instead, she tossed the phone onto the bedside table on Sacha's side, then she eyed the food across the room on the dresser.

"Soup?"

"I had other things on my mind than cooking," Sacha told her honestly.

"And I see three bowls," I told him with a cocky grin which made him flip me off. "I didn't even have to throw my shoe this time."

Nic threw back her head and laughed while my brother glared at me. I knew he was always annoyed when I did it, but that was what made it fun. He grabbed the food and brought it over, basically feeding Nic until she was halfway through with her bowl before digging in himself. Always the provider and protector, I could tell he enjoyed the fact that Nic needed him right now. She had wanted us before, but for at least a little while, she was going to *need* us, and that was a fucking heady realization.

She ate everything before looking at both of us like she was still hungry. Without hesitation, I held out my bread to her, and she took it with a big grin on her face.

Not long after that, she was asleep, snuggled between the two of us, lightly snoring. I was surprised Sacha didn't bother to take the dirty dishes downstairs since messes were something that always got on his nerves. But as we turned off the lights and he breathed her in, I knew why.

Every second we got with her wouldn't make up for the month she was gone. We'd never get that time back.

Dirty dishes would be there tomorrow.

We'd learned that Nicholette might not always be.

Unknown
Thursday

S he was gone.
Gone!

I screamed in frustration, kicking at one of the cages near me. The clanking metal just angered me even more. The sound was far too jarring in the silence of the early morning. My Nicholette had come to Millfield like a whirlwind, but she'd disappeared in less than a day. She had found Joe's hidden room and the garage from the looks of things.

Business had kept me away from following her up here Tuesday, and then there were even more obligations to keep up appearances, so I'd completely missed her. The opportunity to take her had slipped through my fingers. I had a feeling I knew exactly where she was, but it was only a matter of time now. I spent yesterday getting her room ready for her—clothes, bath things, lingerie. Everything would be as it was back in *their* apartment. She would want for nothing and have no reason to even think about that shithole they'd deluded her into thinking was her home. She was going to be the star of my every fucking fantasy, and if she cooperated, her brother would see the light of day.

He was my guarantee that she would do anything I said. Hell, I could punish him every time she did something wrong. Her mistakes would become his pain, and I'd make her watch. I knew she liked to do that. Or I could make Thomas watch, telling her it was all her fault, while I made her scream.

I released a shaky breath, my cock hard from just imagining it.

Soon, Nicholette, you'll be right where you belong.

Now I just needed to get those fucking Russians and their friends out of the way.

If she thought they would protect her from me, she had no idea just how far I would go to get her.

Uncertain steps made me spin around, and I stilled, startled by the familiar face staring at me. Wide brown eyes, messy blonde hair, blood all over her clothes, and a bruise on her face. Wrenn, Nic's ex, stood at the garage door, still and uncertain.

"Wrenn!" I exclaimed, acting like I was concerned. No need to let her know all the ideas running through my mind at the sight of her. How lucky for me and unfortunate for her that our paths had crossed. "What happened?"

"Nic," Wrenn started, but her voice broke. Tears filled her eyes. She rubbed at her wrists, and I saw bruising on one, noticed blood dripping down her hands as she stumbled inside. *So fucking trusting.* "She killed my brother. Right beside me. She shot me too and knocked me out. Then someone cuffed me inside of the house, but I—I managed to escape."

She sounded haunted, broken.

Perfect.

"I can get you back to Ashview," I told her consolingly. I reached out for her, but she stumbled back. "To a hospital. You need to get checked out."

"No. No, I'm not going back to that place. Not with *her* there."

"One person in an entire city? You can't let her take away your home and work."

"She fucks my bosses and their uncle, which you very well know." She shot me a heated look, completely pissed off. If I had met her first, maybe she would have been my obsession. When she glared at me, I could see the steel she had hidden. "At this point, Nic can rot in hell for all I care."

"I need to head out," I told her, nodding to the doorway she was still standing in. "I can give you a ride somewhere, any hospital at all. It doesn't have to be in Ashview."

Wrenn winced as she stepped back to let me exit the garage. "That would be great. Thanks."

"Don't mention it." Putting a hand on her back, I guided her to my car in the early morning light. I helped her into the backseat and buckled her in before getting in the driver's side. Backing out of the driveway, I made my way through Millfield.

"If you let me out here, the town doctor is here." Wrenn gestured to the small downtown, but I ignored her. When I kept driving, she turned to me with a furrowed brow. It didn't take long for her to put the pieces together. I knew the exact moment the last piece fell into place. Her face paled, and I could almost taste her fear in the air. "You..."

She reached for the door, desperately and ineffectively trying to escape the car. I chuckled, amused by how she'd just walked into my grasp. "So fucking easy. And you wonder why Nic doesn't bother with you now. As if you could have survived in a world like this. Pathetic."

"What makes you think someone won't look for me? I know more people than just Nic and her guys."

Genuinely amused by her bluff, I stared at her, loving how she shrank back from me. "I hope they do. After all, Thomas is getting lonely without any visitors. If Nic killed your brother, maybe you'll find the guts to kill him as fair repayment. An eye for an eye." Wrenn didn't reply to that; she sat there quietly, curled into a ball. I kept seeing her eyeing the doors like she was going to try to throw herself out. "Don't get any crazy ideas, Wrenn. I have plans for you."

Even if Wrenn hated Nic, I knew that Thomas and Wrenn would be the perfect bait to get my wayward woman under control. Because even after all their years apart and the trauma of their fallout, Nic still thought about her. And if that wasn't love... what was?

Nicholette
Friday

It had been days, yet there was no word from Ansel. He had made no contact at all with me, Blake, or Em. Guess this was just a hint of karma coming for me. The biggest surprise was the fact that no one from Millfield came looking for me. It would have been easy to put the pieces together. I had come back to town, one of their cops disappeared... Yeah, I knew it didn't look good, but apparently no one was questioning it.

Wrenn's angry, shocked face flashed across my mind, but I pushed it aside. Alexei never said where he had put Wrenn or what he had done with her, and I didn't care enough to ask right now. Her inability to move on and cut ties didn't mean that I couldn't. I was trying to figure out all this pregnancy bullshit and spend some well-earned time with my guys; *that* was priority, not raking myself over hot coals about the past and what both of us could have, would have, should have been in another life.

Blake and their guys had gotten into the exclusive neighborhood near Millfield, but all the houses looked abandoned. They hadn't had enough time to search them all before they had to leave. Would it be worth it to ask them to go back? But they had been busy helping Emmerich with his own Family issues, so I hadn't seen much of them or their guys recently.

Sacha, Vas, and Bodhi were busy looking for information on Gabriel. Rhodes and Maksim were dealing with club business. They were trying to sort out what had happened at the compound and figure out the Lords' next steps now that their base of operations and living quarters were gone. Alexei was stuck dealing with the clubs, and I'd been told in no uncertain terms that leaving Ansel's house wasn't in the cards right now. At all.

"Nic?" Oli's voice made me jerk. I looked up to find him standing in the entryway of the living room, looking at me curiously. "What are you thinking about?"

"That I hate this," I told him honestly, and a hint of smile tugged at my lips before it fell away. "And I'd much rather be arguing with you about what horror movie to watch than sitting here alone."

Oli snorted. "I'm not watching a horror movie."

"Chicken," I teased lightly. I studied him, knowing he wasn't down here just to talk to me. He'd been holed up in his room for days, looking at computer shit, taking no meal breaks. I was pretty sure he wouldn't have eaten if Bodhi hadn't been delivering plates to his room. "Did you find something?"

"No, but I have an idea of where to look." Oli walked over and sat down next to me, grabbing my hands. "I don't know how long it's going to take me to get inside though."

"You're going to leave?" I asked.

He nodded, his determination unflinching. "I need to go underground. Nothing can be traced back to any of us for this."

I didn't respond right away, letting my mind race through everything as I squeezed his hands. When it came to computer stuff, I didn't know much, not about hacking or anything like that, but I knew someone who did. "Would it be faster if you had someone else? Someone who knew what they were doing? Don't worry, I know that's not me."

"I don't think Rhodes can let Maksim disappear with everything going on right now..." Oli started, but I stood up, cutting him off.

"Come with me." I tugged at his hand, leading him upstairs and down the hallway toward Ansel's office where Blake and Emmerich had hidden away today. They weren't staying here, with Blake and Emmerich needing to travel back and forth to Boston, so my guys and I had plenty of time alone.

With a quick knock, I shoved the door open. Emmerich was behind his father's desk, his eyes trained on me with an annoyed expression. Blake was in the process of turning around to face the door, their amusement clear.

"Yes, why don't you come in, Nic. It's not as if we're discussing anything important and private," Emmerich drawled as he leaned back in his seat. The tic in his jaw showed that he was truly annoyed at me for bursting in. The tic might be concerning for some, but I was familiar enough with Em to know that you needed to worry when he *didn't* have a reaction. *Maybe he should have locked the door then.* "What can I do for you?"

"You can't," I replied, looking at Blake. "I need to talk to *you*. About Atlas."

Blake stiffened, their narrowed eyes studying me. I wasn't facing my friend; I was facing a killer and the lover of the man I needed help from. Whose lover had conspicuously gone MIA ever since my men had shown up. "What about Atlas?"

"He's a hacker, and Oli needs help digging things up. It will make it go by faster if they work together."

Emmerich sobered a bit, his gaze flicking between his sibling and me before stopping on Oli with a carefully blank expression. Blake broke my stare in favor of looking over the man beside me, and I prayed that Oli wouldn't say anything stupid. Honestly, I should have known better.

Oli broke the tense silence, of course, with his usual lack of tact. "Look, I don't need help from someone who doesn't know what they're doing. So he can work with traffic cameras, that's fucking nothing. I can do this on my own."

"Traffic cameras?" I turned to him with a furrowed brow.

"Emmerich here called Atlas to help find you when Warren took you. He did that, then he harassed Blake until they woke up to ask them questions," Oli informed me. "I appreciate you wanting to help, but I'll be fine."

"Are you sure about that given what you'll be pulling up?" I asked softly, unwilling to pull punches when it came to this.

"Tell me, *Oli*," Blake cut in before he could respond, drawing our attention. "What's your story?"

"Excuse me?"

"You're mighty invested in all of this." Blake waved a hand to vaguely indicate what was going on. "More than just it being about Nic. Why?"

Oli's upper lip curled in a snarl. "I don't give a fuck who you are. I don't owe you shit."

"Watch your tone, Oliver," Emmerich threatened quietly. Oli stepped toward Blake, ignoring the warning in their brother's voice, drawn in by the blank expression

Blake had fixed on their face. A predator dropping morsels to lure their prey exactly where they wanted them.

"You know something, Blake," I said, calling them out. "What is it?"

Blake slowly blinked, shifting their attention to me, and I felt a finger of coldness run down my spine just as a knock sounded on the door. Without waiting for an answer, it opened. I pulled Oli to the side so we weren't in the way, and in walked none other than Atlas with the rest of Blake's men behind him.

"Blake, we found something..." Atlas trailed off when he realized other people were in the room. Oli's hand tensed in mine, and I looked over at him. His face was pale as he stared at Atlas with wide eyes. "We can come back—" He cut himself off once he glanced sideways at us, but he completely froze when he spotted Oli.

It was as if time had slowed. Oli squeezed my hand so hard I could feel my bones starting to grind together. How did I not notice the similarities before? Similar dirty blond hair, builds, and there was just something I couldn't put my finger on that reminded me of the other man when I looked at each of them. I had thought Atlas seemed familiar when I saw him at the Förstner house, and now, with him and Oli in the same room, I realized why...

Atlas, his face equally pale, started to open his mouth, but Blake beat him to it. "Do you remember, Oli? Where you were taken from?"

"Who—" Oli roughly cleared his throat. "Who said I was taken?"

"We're in the business, Oliver," Emmerich chided him. "We know."

Oliver's hand spasmed in mine, and I repositioned myself, putting my body between him and the rest of the room. "Do you want to leave, Oli? This was *not* part of my plan, I swear. You say it, and we're out. Or I can call Bodhi?"

Oli looked at me, swallowing hard, and without looking away from me, he answered Blake's question. "I don't remember."

Lie.

"But you were taken?" Blake asked, their voice uncharacteristically gentle. I stepped into Oli, gently wrapping my arms around him to comfort him. He wrapped an arm around me in return, and I snuggled into him while checking out the others. Atlas looked sick to his stomach, and when Robin reached out to place a hand on his shoulder, he flinched before directing an apologetic smile at the older man.

"Yes," Oli replied, his voice cracking. "I got away when I was older. Why are you asking me this?"

"Because I have a younger brother," Atlas said, his voice empty of any emotion. "He was taken, but I was never able to find him."

Please don't say the name. I knew Oli didn't remember his birth name. His confession after Matthew Hughes had outed his past was still vivid in my mind. A small bit of his history pulled from him against his will, another violation to add to his litany of scars. If Atlas said a name and it wasn't Oliver, I didn't know how Oli would react. Would another illusion of security and sense of self be ripped away?

"That doesn't mean anything," Oli replied harshly. He shook his head as though the extra layer of denial would make Atlas' words less true. "Kids are taken all the time. I'm not special."

"Well..." Blake drawled, then an envelope hit the desk,

its thud loud in the tense silence of the room. "I have the answers you want right here."

"What did you do?" Atlas asked suspiciously, narrowing his eyes at his lover.

Blake slid it to the edge of the desk, moving it away from them and Em. "The moment I saw you and Oli in the same room, I suspected. I could tell Ansel did as well, or maybe he knew for sure? We'll never know. But this moment was inevitable, so *I* needed to be sure."

"Sure of what?" Oli asked them.

"You did a DNA test?" I guessed. Atlas' head whipped around to me as Oli stopped breathing. "To see if they were brothers or not. Are you fucking kidding me right now, Blake?!"

"Yes," Blake answered, their voice and expression carefully blank. "I didn't open it, by the way, but it's here for you both."

"I'm honestly surprised you didn't look," Emmerich commented dryly. "We should all go so you can figure this out."

Atlas and Oli shared a glance, probably considering whether they wanted to open the envelope or not, and that's when my phone started to ring. Oli muttered *thank god* under his breath as I answered the call.

"Nicholette." Roderick's voice surprised me. I hadn't been expecting him to reach out to me, not so soon anyway. "Are you still at Ansel's?"

"Yes," I answered slowly, drawing out the word. "Why?"

"There are some things I need you to handle and take over for Maeve's estate," Roderick replied, and papers rustled on the other end of the phone. "I'll be there this afternoon. Also, I was contacted by Allen. He needs to continue his interview with you as soon as possible. I can arrange for that to be done at the house as well."

"Just give me a heads up if that's also arranged for this afternoon, and I'll make sure I'm ready," I told him smoothly. "When should I expect you?"

"Two hours?" he asked after a brief pause as if he'd checked his schedule.

"Sounds good. Do I get any idea of what you're throwing in my lap?"

"Some things are better discussed in person. I'll see you soon."

Click.

Everything was a damn secret right now... as if I needed more of those in my life. Oli rested his chin on my shoulder and held me closer, ignoring the others for a moment to ask if everything was okay.

"Yes." I let out a long sigh. "No. I don't know. Guess I'll find out in about two hours when he gets here. But that's not important right now. What do you want to do?"

I shifted back enough to look him in the eyes. He was conflicted, his gaze shifting from me to Atlas to the others in the room. Reaching up, I cupped his face, hoping my expression told him that he didn't have to do anything he didn't want to. If he wasn't ready to open that envelope, I'd get him out of this room, no questions asked. This wasn't why I brought him up here, and I hoped he believed that.

As if he could read my mind, he turned his face to kiss the palm of my hand. "I should get going. I have a place in mind, and it's going to take a bit to get to."

I nodded slowly, sad that he was going to leave even though I understood why he wasn't going to linger. He wasn't ready to know. He might never be ready to open that envelope, but that wasn't my choice to make.

Oli pulled away. Without looking at anyone, he walked out, brushing past Conrad in an effort to avoid getting anywhere near Atlas. His maybe-brother didn't move, not toward Oli or the envelope that Blake had offered.

"Where is he going?" Atlas asked.

"I don't know. He said he needs to go off the grid to do the digging he needs to. Something about leaving no traces back to us. I came here to see if you could help, then Blake dropped this bombshell on us."

"Not a fan when you're not the one dropping them, Nic?" Blake taunted.

"No," I snapped, more than a little annoyed at their attitude. Oli retreating worried me. Without Bodhi here to help reach out to him, I wasn't sure what he would be like when he came back. "It's much more fun on the other side of things. Now, if you'll excuse me, I need to call Bodhi before Oli leaves. He'll want to know what's going on."

I slipped past them and hurried down the hallway. No Oli in sight. *Shit.* That wasn't how I'd seen that going down at all, and I had no idea how Blake had gotten samples for a DNA test. Grabbing my phone, I hit Bodhi's name and started a text.

Nicholette: Oli's leaving

Bodhi: Going underground already? Alone?

Nicholette: I tried to see if Atlas would go with him... Then Blake happened.

Nicholette: Either way, I told someone, so now I'm not responsible for being left alone.

Bodhi: You messaged me so I could tell Sacha and Vas, didn't you?

Bodhi: Why not the group chat?

Nicholette: Well... you're dating Sacha too. He might take it better from you.

Plus, this has been the only way we've really talked since I got back. A frustrated sigh fell from my lips as I kept that thought to myself instead of texting it. Oli said Bodhi had kept insisting I'd come back, but after I did...nothing. He wasn't avoiding me like when we first met, but he was somehow always busy.

I shoved all that aside for now. I needed to figure out what the hell Roderick was bringing my way. Walking into the bedroom I had claimed as my own, I pulled off my shirt only to realize I wasn't alone. Ansel was sitting on the bed, his sharp gray gaze intent on my shirt's descent to the floor beside me.

"I didn't realize you were back."

"I found Joe," he replied, his hands loose on his lap. My lips parted in shock as my breath was knocked out of me. Shock made my hands feel numb, and Ansel's brow furrowed with concern.

"Where?" I finally managed to ask as I bent down for my shirt, ready to confront that asshole. I had so many fucking questions.

"No," Ansel ordered harshly. "Nicholette, come here. Now."

I swallowed hard, slowly standing up straight as I recalled the price for his help in finding my dad. Us. Talking. *About feelings.* Couldn't I just murder or fuck someone instead? I was much better at those two things than what he wanted from me. Too bad he wouldn't be interested in either option, at least not right now. I could tell from the stern set of his face that he wouldn't let me run from this conversation; I wished that I could pull an Oli and just leave. Ansel would chase me down though, and I knew what it was like to be chased by him.

Relentless.

He'd stop at nothing until I was his, and he'd opened the door to move that from the physical department into the emotional one. I stood no chance at all when he beckoned me to join him on the bed. Haltingly, I went to him, trying to sit beside him, but I should have known better. He grabbed my waist and tugged me until I straddled him, forcing me to look him in the eye.

"We need to have a long overdue conversation, Nicholette, and you aren't escaping it because I won't give you what you want until you do. Just so we're clear, I'll know if you lie." He breathed that last bit to me as he ran a hand through my hair, using it to pull me closer, and I shuddered at the threat.

"Truth is a two-way street, Ansel. I'll give you what you give me," I challenged.

We were locked together, sizing up the other person as we tried to figure out where to start. But if he thought I was going to talk first, he didn't know me as well as he thought he did.

Oliver
Friday

"OLIVER!"

My footsteps faltered on the steps outside the house. *Guess getting away without any confrontations just went out the window.* I remained where I was, listening to his approach until he stood a step or two away from me.

"Do you still need help? With the hacking, I mean."

I gave in and glanced over. Atlas was standing there with a neutral expression, and I took that opportunity to inspect him. Shoulder-length blond hair hung loose around his face, and careful blue eyes were fixed on me as he waited for my answer. He was in a loose white t-shirt and ripped jeans, with no shoes. If I had to describe him, I'd say he looked like a surfer. He seemed like he would usually be laid back even though he didn't appear that way right now.

"This is going to take more than just the skill to hack traffic cams," I said, trying to brush him off. Was I being just a tiny bit of a brat? Maybe. But if there was ever a time where a little brattiness was warranted, it was definitely when you were unexpectedly confronted with a DNA test you didn't consent to while your possible brother watched it all play out.

Atlas laughed, the sound light, as he confidently smirked at me, not the least bit put off. "I can do more than hack traffic cams. Making fake documents and hacking are the areas of expertise that I gained after... after things happened in my life. I have my own computers and can pull my weight."

I fully turned around then, scrutinizing him and his offer. "I don't want to talk about the shit from the office. This is about getting information regarding the trafficking ring and anything else related to Nic. That's it."

"Sounds fair." He licked his lips. "And just for the record, I didn't take the envelope either. Blake means well, but they are about as subtle as a wrecking ball."

"Well, Blake and Nic have that in common," I said dryly, smiling despite myself. "Alright, if you're coming, we need to go now. But if you bring up any of that... brother shit... I can't promise I'll react well."

A wide grin filled his face, making his eyes dance with amusement. "I can work with that. We can take my van. It already has everything I need in it."

"Always ready to leave at the drop of a hat?" I joked, gesturing for him to lead the way.

"Sometimes I need space when my past and present start to blur," Altas replied offhandedly, but I could feel the seriousness beneath his flippant tone. Then his statement really hit me... I could relate to that sentiment. What the hell had happened to him? Despite not wanting to get into the possibility of him being my brother, I was itching with questions. But as much as I related to what he'd said, I also knew that tone... He wasn't going to share, and asking would seem a bit of a pot-and-kettle situation, so I left it alone.

He led the way toward a parked van hidden by the trees. It definitely looked like it had seen better days, and when I pulled open the passenger door, I saw the interior was littered with trash, guns, and papers. In the back were a shit ton of computer bags, a sleeping bag, and some other things I wasn't sure I wanted to ask about yet. The passenger seat looked like it was held together by more duct tape than fabric, and Atlas was tossing takeout bags and coffee cups into the back with abandon.

"I know she looks a bit rough, but she'll get us where we need to go."

"She's awesome," I told him with a grin. "Even if I now know what you've had to eat for the last two weeks."

Atlas laughed, smiling at me. "At least you get it. Wulfric won't come near my van at all."

"Which one is Wulfric?" I asked, shutting the door and buckling myself in.

"The older one who looks like he'd kill you just for

irritating him."

"Ah, the suit guy." I nodded. "He and Sacha could take notes. I swear I've never understood the appeal."

"People are fucking lucky I wear clothes most of the time," Atlas agreed. "Though it does make them more comfortable if I have something on. At least usually."

"Because they don't want to see your dick just hanging there?" I quipped.

"That, and other reasons," he replied cryptically. "Now, where are we going?"

He started up the van, and we began going down the driveway. My cell phone vibrated in my pocket a few times, so I took it out.

Bodhi: Nic said you were going.
Bodhi: Be safe and hurry back.
Bodhi: Love you.
Oliver: Love you too.

Then I turned off the cell phone and slipped it into the backpack at my feet.

"It's not on a map or in a town. I'll direct you as we go."

Atlas switched on the radio. Guess he was happy to let me give him directions as needed. Classic rock filled the van, doing little to stem the underlying awkwardness between us. He was pleasant enough, *this* was pleasant enough, but it was odd sitting in a van with someone who may or may not be my brother. The possibility was crazy to me. I couldn't even recall my brother's face, his name, or mine. No matter what Blake did, a DNA test wouldn't make him my brother.

Blood only got you so far.

Ansel
Friday

Joe had gone into hiding after his wife was killed and his son was taken away. But after meeting up with my contact and getting Christopher's assistance, I was able to track him down fairly quickly. That was a good thing because my mind was whirling with everything Nicholette right now like her revelation that I called her for sex on the anniversary of my wife's murder and the fact that despite everything, like her pregnancy and the fucking harem of men that coveted her, I was still interested in being with her. I wouldn't say I loved her because I didn't, not right now, but it was disturbing to think that I eventually could.

Nicholette sat on my lap, her blue-green eyes calm and steady. She was waiting for me to talk first, trying to exert her control over the situation without even saying a word. She wasn't anything like Iris. Iris had been strong in her own way, quiet, reserved, and submissive. The moment I saw her as a young teen, I knew I wouldn't ever let her go, and I'd apologized to her for it every time I saw her. Every moment of pain I put her through. The apologies ran out when I fully claimed her as my own and later married her.

She only ever argued or stood up to me when it came to the kids, asking me to wait, not to train them like I had been trained, at least not yet. She knew as well as I did that there was no escaping the Family obligations they'd inherited, but it had been a dream of hers that they manage to have some kind of childhood.

I had loved her. I *still* loved her. My body and soul ached with missing her even though I knew she was probably happier without me beside her. Loving her had been easy on my part, though I doubted whether she'd ever really loved me.

No one could love a monster, and that was exactly what I was.

But then along came Nicholette.

Fearless.

Reckless.

Broken.

She was a breath of fresh air, this woman who never flinched away from me when I showed up with blood on my hands. She only asked for more details or for more pain. She craved the demon inside of me, basked in the darkness of my soul, and accepted me in a way no one ever had before. It was terrifying.

"I didn't realize," I said softly, forcing myself to focus my scattered thoughts.

"Realize what?" she asked, her hands coming to rest on my shoulders as she shifted, getting comfortable.

My hands ran up her hips to her sides, loving the feel of her warm flesh against my rough hands. "That I always called you on the anniversary of my wife's death."

Nicholette shrugged after a beat of silence. "That's not the only time you would reach out, but you did reach out at that time every year without fail, which makes sense.

Sometimes pain is easier to bear when you share some of it with someone else."

I reached up and cupped her face with one hand, forcing her to look at me while I said this next part. "You did wonderfully, no matter when I called you. Most people wouldn't have kept in touch or asked for me, yet you always did. It never made sense to me why you would be interested in someone like me. Outside of the money, obviously."

Nicholette hummed, a spark of amusement in her eyes and her smile. "The person closest to my age is probably Oli or Bodhi. Everyone else in this arrangement is older than me by a lot, though don't tell Sacha that. He gets a little prickly about the old man jokes." Her good humor faded a bit as a more serious expression took over her face. "But age is just a number, Ansel, and it's not really that important. Not for people like us."

"Then what is?" I asked. She reached up and started to run her fingers over my short beard, looking contemplative.

"Pain. Trauma. All that fun bullshit that made us bend and break, forcing us to put ourselves back together into the people we are now. Anyone else would look at my past and try to *save* me. As if I need their pity or saving." She rolled her eyes at that. "We don't want to be saved, Ansel. Both of us embraced the darkness when life threw us into it, and we aren't afraid to run into it when it's necessary. Everyone I'm with... We are all like that."

"You don't want to change me? Make me a better man?" I asked, half joking. But in truth, I needed to hear her say it, to know beyond a shadow of a doubt that it was *me* she wanted, not some twisted fantasy I'd never be able to fulfill.

Nicholette didn't laugh. She just tilted her head before trailing her hand down my neck to my chest. "Why would I want to save you, Ansel? I like the man you are and the killer you were made to be. I have no use for good men because I have no intention of being a good woman."

I didn't have a response for that. Not many people could make me feel this way, but Nicholette did. Usually, I knew exactly what to say and what others were thinking, but right now, as I studied her, I wasn't sure, and I'd be damned if that wasn't intriguing.

"You always manage to keep me guessing, Liebling."

"I'd hate to be boring," she quipped. "But there's also something I don't understand. Why me? I've been with... Well, it's not an exaggeration to say I've fucked most of the people in your family. I'm dating seven other men, including one of your good friends. You're still in love with your dead wife. Why are you pushing this with me?"

Straight for the jugular.

"I loved Iris, and I still love her. She was my wife and the mother of my children," I replied, my voice rough with the grief that had never faded. "That won't ever change for me. I don't know if I could love anyone else like that, but you make me feel again. When she died, she took part of me with her and I've never been the same. I'm sure Blake and Emmerich would agree with that assessment. I was more than broken... *I shattered.*"

Nicholette didn't say anything, but when I searched her face, she had no pity in her gaze, just patience as if she knew I had more to say. I traced random designs on her skin, loving the way her muscles tensed and relaxed in reaction to my touch.

"But when I'm around you... You don't look at me like you're afraid of what I'll do. You're not scared when I walk into a room or go on the defensive, bracing yourself as if I'm the villain in your story. And when you call me to bitch about killers in horror movies, I actually relax as I listen to your critiques. You make me *laugh*, Liebling. I haven't laughed in a very long time."

"That's because the screenwriters don't know what they're doing," she joked, a small smile on her face. She loosely wrapped her arms around my neck, her black hair falling around us. Her gaze was serious as she studied me, turning over my confessions. It wasn't everything that needed to be said, but it was a start. "So, you want to be with me, in this insane arrangement, with no promises of love between us?"

"You sound so hopeful." A smile tugged at my lips as I closed the space between us, unable to keep away from the soft skin so close to me. I brushed my lips across the top of her breasts, envious of the lace that kept her from fully being on display for me. I stopped when I felt something rough and leaned back just enough to realize that Sacha's name was now carved into her skin. Selfishly, I wished I had my own claim to her body, but that was jumping the gun way too fast. But, hell, even the passing thought was intoxicating, stirring my darker desires. "Most people want love."

"Love is not a requirement to be with me," she gasped, her back arching into my touch when I started to trace the other man's name with my tongue. "I'm not perfect. I can't even *see* perfect from where I'm standing. But you have to get along with the others, at least somewhat, and there has to be trust. It's not just about me anymore though, so maybe I'll need more in the future... for them."

"Twins," I breathed, and my dick, which was already hard thanks to her proximity, throbbed at the mental image of her swollen belly. "You're going to be fucking gorgeous."

"I'm going to look like a beached whale," she complained with a heavy sigh. "And don't think I didn't notice that you liked that thought. I swear, if you and Maks both threaten to keep me pregnant for all the extra curves, I'll lose my mind and you'll lose your dicks."

The mention of the other man should have stirred jealousy in me, I expected it to, but I laughed instead. "I'll help him tamper with your birth control so we can pump you full of cum at every opportunity, Liebling. Breasts full and heavy, softness in every damn curve. I'll make you beg for me to fill you up before I let you come on my cock. And don't try to deny it because we both know if I checked right now, I'd find your pussy wet as hell."

"Maybe you should check just in case you're wrong," she taunted even as her hips ground against my cock through my slacks.

"You want sex? Tell me what you're thinking. No questions or redirections." I reached around and unsnapped her bra, my mouth watering when her breasts spilled free. "You can choose to let me past your walls, or I'll tear them apart for the fun of it, Liebling. So what will it be? We both know I love tearing people apart piece by piece."

"Do your worst, old man."

God, she's perfect.

Nicholette
Friday

THE EXCITEMENT in his eyes was enough to tell me he didn't mind the nickname that had slipped out or the challenge I'd given him. But if he wanted me to come out from behind my walls and open up, he could fucking earn it. Declarations were nice, but we both worked better with pain, and I'd need it to cling to if he wanted me to open up. Emotions weren't my friend, and even for Ansel, who I'd known for years, I wasn't going to give in without a fight. Hell, I knew he'd be disappointed if I did.

With a glint of sadistic glee, he held me tight and twisted us so I was flat on my back with him hovering above me. A calloused hand wrapped around my throat, squeezing just tightly enough that I could feel his strength, then he trailed his fingers down my chest and between my breasts, heading for my leggings. He quickly pulled them off of me, followed by my bra, and then I was completely naked beneath his fully clothed body.

"Talk to me, Liebling. This isn't a one-way attraction, or you would have told me off long before now. *You* reached out to *me* to relax, not just for profit or sex."

He carefully ran his hands all over my body, up my legs, my stomach, arms... none of the places I really wanted him to touch. This soft torture was out of character for him, and right now it was so fucking cruel considering how turned on I was. Trying to get him to touch me where I wanted him, I shifted my hips, chasing his touch, but he immediately pinned my pelvis to the mattress, his grip so tight I moaned with pleasure. Fuck, I loved the brutal handling.

"You take what I give you, Nicholette," he warned, "or I'll get the ropes and tie you in place until I'm done with you. Every person in this house will hear you scream and cry out for mercy until you don't have a voice anymore. Unlike most of the men you're with, I know *exactly* how far I can push your body right now."

"Ansel..." I whispered, my voice cracking as I searched his expression.

"Talk. To. Me," he ordered, his hard tone leaving no room for argument.

"I don't know what you want me to say," I rasped.

"The truth," he told me, his voice so fucking gentle. Tears burned my eyes, making me squeeze them shut. I wanted to blame the babies and the pregnancy hormones, but this was all me. And him. I loved his brutality and all of his sharp edges, but that soft voice was somehow undoing me. I didn't want him to change himself, to become *less than* who he was now, but hearing this other side to him that was currently reserved for just me... It was something special that I couldn't fight even if I was struggling to put that into words outside of my mind and body. "You wanted honesty from me, and I expect it back."

"I don't know," I rasped, my muscles tensing and relaxing as he continued to stroke my body, fanning the flames inside of me. "There's just something... something I've always been drawn to when it comes to you. You didn't care how far you pushed me when we were together. There was no restraint and no hesitation when you ordered me around, degraded me. So fucking confident in what you were capable of and what I could handle."

I swallowed hard when he patiently waited as if he could see my mind trying to form the words for what I wanted to describe. But how could I describe how I felt about him when I was still trying to figure it out for myself? The others... They talked as if this was inevitable, but my heart had already been torn into smithereens. Did I have enough to piece together to give it to someone else? Cold gray eyes met mine, and something inside me just knew that it was a stupid question because even without me consciously choosing him, he already had a part of me.

Ansel Förstner was a force of nature, a boogeyman that scared grown men even in broad daylight, but to me, he felt like a protector. He didn't hide who he was from me; every ugly scar and painful memory was laid bare when we were together. I didn't want him whole. I wanted his pain, his rage, and his detachment to play in. When I was with him, I felt like I was protected from everyone in the world except for him. He was my monster, and he had more limits than I think he credited himself with.

Just as I opened my mouth, he leaned down and took one of my nipples in his. I whimpered; the hot heat and wetness of his tongue swirling around the peak made me lose my train of thought. He sucked harder and harder before he suddenly pulled away with a loud pop and did the same to my other breast. He took his time, his lips, teeth, and tongue playing with me until I was a whining mess under him.

"Ansel, please, god, please," I begged, my head tossing and turning. I tried to find some relief, but there was no mercy in the grinning older man above me.

"You think your breasts are tender now, just wait until they're heavy and full of milk. So fucking sensitive that you'll be crying for some relief from the building pressure." He scraped his teeth over one of the hard peaks, making me hoarsely cry out his name. "You still have more to say. Concentrate and get through this, Liebling, and I'll give you what you need."

"When we met, I was... I was a mess. I'd been on my own for a while, and I'd run into Frederick... Well, that doesn't matter." I shook my head and took a few deep breaths to focus my erratic thoughts in spite of his continued teasing. "Maksim had broken me. He had helped me tear down the last bit of who I was before I got to Ashview, and you helped me put the last pieces of myself fully back together in a new way. I saw the darkness inside me reflected back at me in your eyes."

Ansel pushed himself off of me, and I started to panic until I realized he was taking off his clothes and tossing them aside before he settled over me again. I moaned at the feel of his naked body against my own. *God, he feels fantastic.* He spread my legs, and I felt the hardness of him at my entrance, waiting.

"You were one of the first people that made me feel like it was okay to just be me. Ansel, you were like coming home for the first time. I felt welcomed and safe; every hit and drop of blood you wrung from me was a baptism into my new life. It felt like the only person who could hold me steady was you. I don't care about the age difference between us or the fact that I've been with other people in your family." He thrust inside of me, slowly, deliciously stretching me. "But... I resent that you did that for me. I hate that you make me feel things. I hate that you never had to tear my walls down because you've always been inside of them. I hate that I didn't stand a chance against your fucking relentlessness. And most of all... Most of all, I hate that you're such a part of me when I'll never be that for you."

That was it. That was what kept me from opening up to him or letting myself accept how I felt about him. The other guys might have thought I had feelings for Ansel, but I didn't think they had any inkling just how deep those feelings ran or at least that's what I'd like to think. I sure as fuck hadn't known until everything spilled out of me.

I turned my face away from him, or at least I tried to, but he grabbed me, his hands rough. He forced me to meet his eyes as he bottomed out inside of me. A cry fell from my lips as he stretched me, and I thought he would kiss me, capturing the sounds he was wringing from me, but he studied my face as I tried to become accustomed to his cock inside of me. He fucked me slowly, and I started to close my eyes only for him to shake my face, snapping an order to look at him.

Ansel leaned forward, licking up my tears with long slow swipes of his tongue. He murmured how fucking good I felt around his cock, how I was such a good fucking girl. His pace increased until he was fucking me so fast and hard that my breasts jolted harshly with every slap of flesh on flesh.

"Please," I begged, not sure whether I was asking for more pleasure or for him to let me go.

"Shhh," he whispered before slanting his lips over mine. I could taste the salt of my tears on his tongue, and he finally released my face. His fingers ran down my side, then he reached between us, teasing my clit until I screamed into our kiss. He grunted soon after, filling me up with hot cum while he fucked me hard enough that I saw fucking stars.

He kept kissing me, his tongue sliding along mine, urging me to get my brain back online. I wished he hadn't. I didn't want to face what I had told him. No part of me wanted to face Ansel right now.

When he finally broke the kiss, I shifted away, sliding over to try to get out of the bed, but a hard yank stopped me. Ansel had grabbed a handful of my hair to trap me in place.

"Nicholette—"

"I need to get ready, Ansel," I replied, refusing to look at him. "Roderick is coming. Something about Maeve…"

"Liebling," he rumbled, yanking me backward into his body. "What you said—"

"Don't, Ansel," I rasped, my throat thick with emotion. "I don't want you to lie or make promises."

"Do I seem like someone who would lie to you, Nicholette?" he growled, making me shudder. He pulled my hair until I was forced to look up at him. His gray eyes glittered with emotion, and I licked my lips.

"Ansel..."

"You make me *feel*, Liebling. You make every ounce of my self-control threaten to leave me at the drop of a hat. I will always love my late wife—"

"I would never ask you to not love her, Ansel," I interrupted softly, my heart pounding in my chest. What was he going to say?

A hint of warmth softened his expression before it faded. "I know, and that makes you special. Most wouldn't want to hear about her or anything... They want to act like they're the only ones to have ever been in my life. I *could* love you, Nicholette, despite every reason running through my mind that says I shouldn't or can't. You were with my brother. Hell, you've been with my *kids*..."

"Not in a relationship," I pointed out, unsure if that would help or hurt at this point. He tugged my hair hard enough that I hissed, but he chuckled at the same time.

"You are beautiful, inside and out, Nicholette. Every damn part of you entices me to dive into you even while knowing I'll never get back out again. But I'm an old man in a line of business that's made for the young. My time is limited... Is that really something you want to deal with?"

My heart was in my throat. The seriousness of this conversation had taken a turn I never thought it would. When I turned to face him, he relaxed the hand in my hair, and I decided to answer without words. Not caring that Roderick was probably going to be here soon or that any one of his family or my guys could be outside the door, I kissed him. Cupping his face in my hands, I lost myself in the feel of him—his short beard that needed to be cleaned up, the hard muscles that he usually hid under suits and nice clothes. I ran my hands down and across his back, touching every scar and burn on his body that I knew very few people had ever seen. It wasn't that Ansel cared, but I had a feeling he didn't want to relive the stories of how he'd gotten them so he kept them covered.

I didn't care how old Ansel was, but the idea of him not being around made my stomach turn. He was formidable in a way that made him seem invincible, like even time couldn't touch him. When my hands came around to his new wound, he jerked and pulled away.

He moved his lips down to my throat as he pulled me toward him, positioning me to straddle his lap so I could feel the hardness of him against my sensitive pussy. Reaching down, I held him in place. I wanted to take him inside of me while he scattered kisses along my collarbone and back up my throat to my lips.

"If you want me, Ansel," I whispered, rocking my hips to start riding him, "have me for however long we've got left. We both know it doesn't matter how old someone is in this life; death could be around the next corner. So... stay. Stay with me for however long we've got, and we can deal with the damage later."

If I was going to go all in, I might as well jump right into the deep end, and Ansel must have agreed. With a low growl, he kissed me again. The possessiveness in that contact made me shiver, and he urged me to ride him. We lost ourselves in each other, forging a give and take that neither one of us had expected when we first met. Wrenn had claimed I was a monster, and maybe I was, but I had found a home among them, and I had no regrets.

Another climax, then we fell back together on the bed. The only sound in the room was our breathing until Ansel shifted. "Why is Rorik coming here?"

"Something about what Maeve left me," I told him with a shrug. "I don't know when the others are getting back, but Oli just left, and I have no idea when he's coming home. I just want this stalker taken care of and my brother home. Where is Joe? I need to deal with him–"

"Joe will keep until tonight or tomorrow. He won't be going anywhere," Ansel promised. He reached over, tracing the names on my inner thighs then moving up to Sacha's. "They're all marking you."

"Possessive men," I teased, reminding myself that I couldn't fuck him again. "They all wanted to remind me of who I belong to. Are you planning to play along with their games, old man?"

"Is that really the nickname you're going with?" he asked, arching an eyebrow.

"Do you have another one I should use instead?" I asked tartly, not bothering to suppress my growing smirk.

"I hope you remember who you're dealing with, Liebling. I won't bother carving my name into your skin... I'll burn it into you."

"I look forward to it," I told him as I slowly sat up. "But I do need to clean up before Roderick gets here, or I'll be meeting him naked. Which doesn't bother me, but you all tend to get a bit jealous, and I'm not sure Roderick would be a fan."

Ansel laughed and stood up. "He probably wouldn't even bat an eye, Liebling. You're not his type."

Ah. Well, that made sense. I thought over a few odd reactions on his end and shook my head. I had enough on my plate that I wasn't going to try to figure out another man I wasn't even in a relationship with. Really, how the hell I'd ended up with so many men, I'd never know.

Ansel started the shower and pulled me in after him,

ignoring my protests when he started to clean me up. Taking his time, he carefully washed me, his beard rubbing against my skin, before I took the opportunity to do the same to him.

I kept sneaking peeks at his face to make sure I didn't cross some boundary I wasn't aware of. The way he slowly relaxed under my attention told me not many people had taken care of him, and that knowledge made my chest ache. The broken really were attracted to each other, weren't we?

We needed people who understood us and others who wouldn't be afraid to break themselves just a bit more to be with us.

Alexei
Friday

A tired sigh fell from my lips as I ran a hand over my face. I was fucking exhausted. Maksim had been gone with Rhodes for the last few days, helping figure out shit with the Lords of Chaos, which meant I was burning the candle at both ends trying to run all three clubs. Wrenn, who we had started to count on, was gone, and part of me felt bad about just leaving her to bleed out and die beside her brother, but we had more important things to deal with. People like Wrenn could be replaced even if it took time for a newcomer to earn our trust.

The clubs had been thoroughly searched while we were all taking care of Nic and everything having to do with her stalker. There had been cameras all over. Offices, storerooms, the bar, the dance floor, bathrooms... They hadn't let a single square inch of this place go unwatched. *How the fuck did this asshole get into all these places?* I didn't know the answer to that, but the fact that they'd gotten into so many private areas of our businesses and homes had me worried. What had this person found out about our operations, my cousins' business, or the MC's deals? What the fuck had this person *seen*?

When Nic left, we had all been left reeling, lost in our own feelings of frustration and abandonment, while trying to figure out how to track her down. Rhodes had turned to drinking, and I... I had turned to Maksim. I'd drowned myself in the dominance he offered and the softness that had recently started to creep into his touch. At work, the compound, his place—it didn't matter. Maksim never refused me, which meant that Nic's stalker absolutely knew about us, and a part of me was worried about what this person would do about that.

I wasn't ready to just come out and tell people we were together, I was too caught up in my head for that, but I was tired of denying what was between us when we were among the people I'd started thinking of as some warped kind of family. *God, I'm so fucking selfish.*

A beeping sounded near me, and I answered my phone without looking at the caller ID.

"What?" I could hear just how exhausted I felt in that one word, and there was a long pause before Maksim's voice filled the line.

"Going that well, huh?"

I laughed before sighing, some tension draining out of me. With everything going on right now, just the sound of his dry voice comforted me. Part of me swore I could smell a hint of smoke from his preferred brand of cigarettes. God, I was fucking hopeless. "It's been a long few days, and now that it's the weekend, it's only going to get crazier."

Gravel crunched on the other side of the phone, telling me he was walking around, then came the deep inhale that meant he was smoking. *No surprise there.* "The Lords are settling things for now, but there's still a lot more to figure out. Rhodes is wrapping some shit up with Razor's help, then I can come help with the businesses after that."

"Did he find a new place for operations?"

"No." He blew out a long breath. "Shit has gotten complicated. Ansel reached out and said he found Nic's father. Looks like we all need to get back to his place soon, though from what Ansel was hinting at, the questioning wouldn't be happening until tomorrow."

"Confronting Nic?" I laughed, imagining how that was going to go down. "Good luck to him."

"Not her?" Maksim sounded slightly amused, and in the background, I heard a door open then clatter shut.

"Remember our conversation with her about us?" Nic had orchestrated me breaking down and spilling my guts to Maksim, making us confront my insecurities. The fight sparked by her shit talking had riled me up so much that I'd smacked her. The puppeteer, the mastermind... She'd do well as Maeve's replacement that's for sure, and that certainly meant she could handle one man.

"Yes," Maksim replied dryly. "I remember. But this is *Ansel* we are talking about. Either way, that means we have time."

"Time? What are you talking about?" I asked when my door suddenly opened. Maksim stood in the doorway, a cigarette between his lips as he stared me down. "What the fuck?! Maksim?"

He ended the call and slammed the office door shut with his boot. With a deep inhale of his cigarette, he sauntered up to the chair across from me and flopped down. "Rhodes didn't want to waste time, so he decided to go back to Ansel's house after he and Razor finished up. He didn't want to miss anything, and I think he needs some time with our girl. I got sent here to talk with the police since one of them said something about following up."

"Want me to come with you?" I guessed, knowing that peopling was *not* his thing.

He nodded, putting out the cigarette on the ashtray I kept on my desk for him. "Anything on her stalker?"

I shook my head, frustrated. "Nothing. Sacha and the others haven't found anything. At least that's what he said the last time I talked to him."

Right then, my phone beeped with a message from the man himself.

Sacha: Oliver has gone underground for his own search into the trafficking ring. No idea when he'll be back.
Sacha: Which means Maksim is our go-to for anything computer related until he resurfaces.
Alexei: What about Blake's guy? Atlas?
Sacha: He went with him.
Sacha: So tell your brother he has to be a team player until Oli gets back.

Well then.

I looked to find Maksim staring at his phone too.

"Sacha?" I asked, wondering if he had messaged him the same thing.

He clicked his tongue in annoyance. "Hopefully nothing comes up because I don't feel like being people's fucking errand boy."

I barely suppressed a smirk, but given the glare Maksim threw my way, he'd caught my amusement. But I couldn't find it in me to care. It was crazy how much more relaxed I felt with him nearby. "Did you all have any luck reaching out about the kids after the fire? Were they actually taken by the CPS, or the trafficking ring?" Rhodes had been turning over that thought ever since the Förstners had brought it up. After what had happened to Alicia, Razor's girl who'd been pregnant when she was murdered, he was always on the lookout to keep our girls' kids safe.

Maksim scratched his beard as he nodded. "Yeah. Razor tracked them all down and told the CPS rep that he'd be keeping tabs on everyone to make sure no one disappeared. Everything was legit from what he saw and what I found on my end."

"So strange they didn't try to take them."

Maksim shrugged. "Maybe it was all about Nic? Otherwise, they *would* have taken them. There weren't a lot of kids, but it's not like the trade is fucking cheap, so that's just profit running through their fingers."

"Or the stalker is losing it, spiraling because they haven't gotten their hands on Nic yet," I murmured. When Maksim didn't say anything, I pushed myself out of my chair. "When are we supposed to talk to the police, and where are we meeting them?"

Maksim didn't say anything right away. He stared up at me with a bland expression, his blue-gray eyes looking me over from head to toe and back up before he spoke.

"Knees." My mouth went dry as I looked over his shoulder to the door, but Maksim wasn't having any of that. "On your fucking knees, brother, or you can lean over the desk so I can beat your ass before I play with you. Either way, I can feel the tension in you, and it's making me antsy."

I licked my lips and took a few steps around my desk to slowly sink down to my knees in front of him. My cock was already throbbing and hard in my slacks from his simple command, and the glint of amusement in his dark eyes said he'd caught it all. His domination of me made me start to loosen up. A fuzzy feeling in my mind was taking over at the hint of pleasure and violence he was promising.

"Good boy." He leaned forward and grabbed my chin in a steely grip, forcing me to meet his gaze. He slanted his lips over mine, possessively kissing me, his tongue sliding along mine as our beards rubbed together. I sighed into the kiss, and more of the stress that had been building inside of me faded away as he took command of me. Being in control and in charge was something I loved, in and out of the bedroom, but it was nice to give all that up and fall into Maksim, trusting him to give me what I needed to get a break from it all. He'd been my safe haven for years, even before we'd become what we were now.

"I missed you," I whispered against his lips when he slowed the kiss a few minutes later. My cheeks were flushed with embarrassment, and I wished I could take back those simple words even though they were a vast understatement.

"Ever since Nicholette came back, you haven't slept with me, besides that one night we shared her." Maksim tilted his head. "After you spent almost an entire *month* in my bed, Alexei." My lips parted, but I shut them again, not sure how to respond. He didn't need me to actually say anything; he knew me better than anyone. *Ten years together will do that.* "I'm not hiding anymore, Alexei. You want to use me, lose yourself on my cock, then you're going to own up to it."

"Maksim—"

"Remember that night, fight and fuck it out with Nic?" he said softly. "No more hiding. She's back, and if I have to thrust you into the fucking spotlight as you ride my dick, then I will."

I laughed despite myself and swore I saw a hint of a

smile at the corner of his lips, though it was gone in the blink of an eye. "In my defense, we've been all over the place, and you've been gone for the past few days. Not exactly a ton of time to be with you for sleeping, fucking, or anything else. I might not be ready to just say it outright, but I'm not avoiding you."

"You're in my bed tonight, Alexei," he ordered, leaning forward again to tease his lips against mine. He laughed when I chased the taste of him. "Because it's been days since I've been inside of you, and that's going to change. I want to be so far inside of you that you'll feel me for days."

"Fuck," I ground out. My cock twitched as I visualized what he had planned, and I could feel him grin as he reached down and unzipped my pants, dipping his hand inside to palm my hard dick. A whimper fell from my lips before I could stop it, my hips beginning to jerk as he slowly pumped me.

"You were telling the truth. You *did* miss me," he teased, his voice deep and raspy. I knew better than to try to push his hand away, Maksim's need for control was absolute, and when we were together, my dom side fell beneath the submission he brought out of me. "Should I leave you like this until tonight? We do have to go to the police station."

My hips flexed, needing more friction, but he pulled back to lazily play with my tip until I felt precum dripping down my cock. I whimpered, and he laughed tauntingly.

"Please, fuck... please."

"We might have to go back to join the others tomorrow. Before we do, I want to hear you scream and beg until you lose your voice, brother. I want to watch you fucking fall apart for me. And only when you're completely fucking spent and helpless will I even begin to consider fucking you."

I groaned, imagining exactly what he was saying. I knew he would do it, too. He'd play with me until my body was covered in sweat, blood, bruises, and his cum... That was when he'd say he was done with foreplay. He knew that was exactly what I needed from him right now—brutal and intense. I needed him to fucking take over every inch of me so I could drown myself in him, pushing me until I was putty in his hands.

"But I guess I can be merciful since you didn't fight about tonight." *I really fucking doubt it.* "Fuck yourself into my fist and get off, Alexei, but when you come, you better cry out my fucking name. Then I'm going to make you lick your cum off my hand and the floor, so get to humping like the bitch in heat that you are. We don't have all day."

It shouldn't turn me on that he talked to me like that, a part of me recognizing it was degrading as all hell, but it did every damn time. My cock was thrusting in and out of his fist before I even realized I had started moving. His other hand came up to cup my face, making sure I didn't look away from him, and when he rubbed his thumb across my bottom lip, I opened up. I sucked his thumb into my mouth and swirled my tongue around it, acting like I was sucking his cock. His irises grew bigger, and a flush filled his cheeks as he started pushing his thumb in and out.

Being on my knees in front of Maksim was a terrifying and safe place to be. He was like no one else I had ever met. Our attraction to each other had been unexpected, unwelcome, but it was still so damn consuming even after all this time together.

Suddenly, he pushed his thumb deeper, making me gag until he pulled back slightly. "You're thinking too much for someone so determined to get off before we have to leave.

Let me help you with that, brother. Don't say I'm not the giving type."

Oh no.

Maksim tugged me up by my cock, making me shudder, before letting go of me completely. "Stay."

He walked out of the office, leaving my throbbing cock out and pants falling to my ankles, and I was grateful he closed the door behind him. He shut and locked the door behind him before he looked me up and down with a critical glance. *What is he doing?* I didn't have to wait long to find out. Stalking across the room, he lightly swung a duffle bag in one hand while holding some kind of toy in the other. "Strip."

Fuck, his one-word orders were going to be the death of me.

I did as he instructed, my hands only stuttering once when I saw what he had brought in—a thick-as-fuck dildo that looked to be about six inches, give or take, with bumps on the end that I knew were going to feel amazing and torturous inside of me. He lubed it up with a bottle he'd pulled from the duffle bag then pushed my papers off the desk, not caring where they fell, and stuck it on top.

"You need to lose yourself, Alexei," he rasped, his arousal clear as he crowded close to me, forcing me back toward the desk. The rough material of his jeans and the smoky smell of cigarettes on his breath made me groan. He was just fucking perfect. "So much stress. The clubs, Nic, the babies, us... I can tell how tightly wound you are, and you need to let go. Let me help you with that. I was going to wait until tonight for more, but I can tell you can't wait that long."

"But the police—"

"We can deal with them after. Even if you need some

time to recover, I know you'll handle it fine. Besides, you need this more than I hate talking to people," he replied softly, his rough hands running down my tattooed arms.

My eyes snapped to his, and his face was serious. Maybe that offer was a small thing for other people, but for Maksim, it wasn't. He didn't do well with other people and managing their hang-ups. He wasn't great at reading emotions or knowing what people needed... but he had made the effort to figure me out. Even if he handled some things the wrong way, he understood me, at least partly. My lips parted to speak, but he stopped me by pressing his lips to mine, kissing me so I'd forget everything I was about to say. His hands teased my body, running down my muscular chest to play with my cock.

"Maksim... Sir, what do you want me to do?" I whispered, desperate to please him. Giving him my obedience, my submission, was the only thank you he'd accept.

He smiled against my lips. "You're going to fuck yourself on that dildo while I watch. No coming until I give you permission. It's a good thing you thought to soundproof the offices. I'd hate to have to kill someone for seeing you like this. Besides Nic, of course, but she's not here right now."

"You like to fuck Nic in public," I ground out, trying to think of anything besides his lean, strong body near mine as he pressed closer. There was no way I was going to come before we even got started.

"Yes," he breathed, then he grabbed my ass and pulled my cheeks apart, maneuvering my body until the dildo's head was lined up to my asshole. He slowly pushed me down, steadily forcing my body to accommodate the toy. I groaned, my cock twitching, as I threw my head back, attempting to focus on anything but the dildo sliding inside of me. His rough grip on my ass and the pulsing need in my chest were making me feel lightheaded.

"But she likes to be on fucking display. I could fuck her in front of the entire club, and she'd come from people watching her alone. But you... You want to be degraded and humiliated in private. My private bitch and cum slut. You take that almost as well as you take my cock, Alexei. You were fucking made for this. Fuck yes, you like that."

I *did*.

I more than liked it. I *loved* it. Everything he'd said was true. I liked being in charge with Nic, ordering her every move, but I also liked getting that from Maksim. He overwhelmed me in the best possible ways until I could just fucking let go. Maybe that was how Maksim felt most of the time, not caring about most people's bullshit. *Lucky*.

My body was shaking by the time the dildo bottomed out in me, my ass hitting the cold desk. Chest heaving, hands trembling, I watched Maksim take a step back from me, his heated gaze sweeping from the top of my head to my toes and back up again. At this moment, smirking back at me from a few steps away, he felt larger than life, bigger than his six-foot-two slender frame.

"Get moving, brother. I want to see you slam those swollen balls on the desk with every fucking movement. I was generous enough to let you do it on top of the desk instead of on your hands and knees on the floor."

Fucking myself would have been easier on the floor, but we both knew I didn't want easier. I shifted, leaning back to get the leverage I needed, planted my hands on the desk, and started to move up and down, cursing when the bumps hit sensitive spots inside of me. My cock bounced, hitting my stomach with every movement, ensuring I was aware of just how hard I was from his little games. Maksim settled down into the chair again, content to watch me. He unashamedly adjusted himself, not hiding his building arousal.

He watched me like I was his favorite show, ordering me to spread my legs wider, move slower, move faster, every small change driving my pleasure higher and higher. I begged for release, but he just smiled and told me no. I didn't know how long I fucked myself on that silicone cock before he ordered me to stop and stand up. I groaned when I pulled myself off the dildo, feeling achingly empty without it inside me. He reached down for the bag at his feet as I wobbled, trying to get blood to flow somewhere besides my cock, and searched for whatever it was he wanted.

My dick twitched, desperately needing just a small touch. A simple graze of his fingertips would be enough to send me over the edge, but that wasn't the game he wanted to play. He pulled out a cock sleeve, a bottle of lube, and something else I didn't see. *Oh fuck yes.*

"Please."

I wasn't aware I had uttered it aloud until he looked over at me, and my gaze fixed on his now exposed thick cock that made the dildo jutting lewdly from the top of the desk seem small. He smirked and grabbed his hard dick. "See something you want? You want a taste, cum slut?"

"Yes." I licked my lips as I fell to my knees, needing him more than I needed my pride.

He walked over, and I didn't wait for instructions, taking him deep into my throat without hesitation. Maksim was large, but I'd had a lot of practice, and the taste of him on my tongue made my eyes roll back in my head. There wasn't one thing about him that I didn't crave, and I wanted to let him know that in whatever way I could. When it came to him, my silver tongue always faltered so I needed a way to show him how I felt without words.

I worshiped him—every swirl of my tongue or graze of my teeth was my way of telling him how I felt without saying a single word. I took my time and didn't stop until wiry hair hit my nose. Maksim grunted, and I looked up to find his head thrown back, the muscles in his neck standing out as he tried to control himself.

"Enough," he said gruffly, pushing at my head to shove me off of him. He gestured for me to get up, so I did. I was roughly spun around and shoved against the desk before I finished my next breath. Maksim lined himself up to my asshole then slammed home, his balls hitting my ass as I cried out. He fucked me a few times before he reached over for the cock sleeve he'd grabbed earlier. "Let's see how you like this."

He thoroughly lubed up my hard cock, absolutely drenching every inch of me. I thrust into his fist, and he chuckled mockingly in my ear as he pressed an open-mouthed kiss to my back. Maksim wiped the gel on his hand onto my hip then grabbed the sleeve, easily sliding it onto my hard dick. I whimpered, distracted by the sensation of tightness, before I realized I was feeling something else. *Wires?* I could feel them brushing against my leg, and I tensed when he rested a box on my back.

"Maksim..."

"Did you figure it out, bitch? God, you're trying to strangle my cock... I can't wait to see what you do when I turn it on."

A fucking cock sleeve with electro shocks... Where the hell did he find shit like this? Why did it turn me on even more? I rocked back, fucking myself on him as he threaded a hand through my hair and started to fuck me viciously. The loud slapping of flesh against flesh filled the room, followed by my moans and pleas—for more, for mercy, to fucking come. I told him I'd do anything. The earlier teasing and the threat of the electro shock cock sleeve were enough to make me desperate to come.

His balls swung into mine, our hips slamming together, as he squeezed my hand. He easily kept a steady and brutal pace as he claimed me, silencing the anxiety that had been building up for what seemed like far too long.

"Maksim, fuck, please," I keened just as a cell phone started to ring. I froze, but he kept fucking me as he leaned over and grabbed my vibrating cellphone. "What the hell are you doing?"

"Better keep quiet, brother, or they'll hear you getting railed on your desk by your step-brother," he threatened before answering the call.

I'm going to kill him.

Maksim

Friday

GOD, he was pissed, but that just made me even more turned on.

"Detective," I greeted the man on the other end of the phone, silently laughing when I felt Alexei tense under me. I continued to fuck him, not losing my pace or slowing down at all. I thought of turning on the sleeve but decided to wait. He was being so good for me, and I knew that he'd end up reveling in the humiliation in the moment, but I didn't want to stress him out so much that all my hard work was undone the moment I pulled my dick free from his grasping hole.

The officer on the other end of the line started explaining that they didn't have any leads on who'd started the fire, but they were finally going to release the property back to Rhodes. This wasn't the call I had expected, but I'd take it. I hummed, agreeing at the right times, all while keeping my full attention on fucking Alexei. A few grunts slipped out, some whispered moans, but he was otherwise keeping it together very well. *Too well.*

I wanted him to be a fucking mess. To cry as I fucked him and filled him with my cum. I needed to break that control he held onto so tightly.

The detective said a few more things I ignored, then he hung up, but I didn't let Alexei know that. No, I had a much better idea. After catching Bodhi and Oliver in my office, I'd heard what they'd said about me. I wasn't interested in them, but the idea of sharing for just sex... that I could get behind.

Switching to another app, I hit record, then I pulled back until just the head of my cock was inside of him. I didn't thrust back into him until I turned on the electro shock. Alexei cried out, his body tensing as the shocks on his dick teased him. I had turned it on medium, not wanting to ease him into it or throw him into the deep end right off the bat. *Not everyone is Nic.*

"Fuck!"

"Oh hell yes," I ground out, running my hands over his muscular back. "Just like that, cum slut. Don't hold back now."

"Maksim!" Lust made his deep voice crack when he called out my name.

"Do you want to call me that while I'm balls deep inside of you?" I teased him darkly, reaching around to grab the cock sleeve and jack him off, forcing the shocks to hit every part of him. "I think you can do better than just my name."

"The phone—"

"Let me worry about the phone," I scolded him. "If you don't want to pick a good name, I'll pick one for you to call me, and I won't accept another one. Any ideas?"

"Oh hell," he hissed, his jerking hips fucking himself back onto my dick then forward into the shocks. "Sir..."

"I'll take that," I praised him. "Tell me you're mine. Tell me I own every fucking inch of you, bitch."

"Yours. Always. Please, sir, can I come? Please!"

"Not yet," I told him grimly. "I want to watch you. Hold it off for me."

I didn't make it easy on him, pounding into his body while I built up the pain and pleasure by toying with him. When he was ready to break, I abruptly pulled him off of me, manhandling him until I had him poised above the dildo again. I shoved him on top of it, violently forcing his body to take it as quickly as he'd been taking my cock. He shouted out, his back arching, and that was when I turned up the power on the cock sleeve. His body twitched, and I leaned over to whisper into his ear.

"Come, Alexei."

He growled my name as his body obeyed my command, and he grabbed the back of my head, pulling me into a kiss that I easily accepted. Our tongues tangled while I played with his balls to add even more sensation as he rode out his orgasm. His groans and whimpers of protest were so goddamn enticing, I kept at it, stroking his overly sensitive balls before moving to the cock sleeve, jacking off his overstimulated dick until he pulled back with tears in his eyes, begging me to stop.

Fucking perfection.

I ripped the cock sleeve off and let him sit there, dazed and impaled on the dildo, as I stepped back and jacked off until I came all over him. Ropes of cum hit his softening cock and chest, marking him. I grabbed his phone off the desk and ended the recording so I could take a picture of him like that—covered in my cum, twitching, and owned by a dildo. He looked blissed out, relaxed, and fucking *mine*.

I peppered him with kisses when his body kept twitching, slowly adjusting to the lack of stimuli. Carefully, I pulled him off the dildo and into my arms, reaching down to scoop up my cum and feed it to him. He licked my fingers clean so I could come back with more, my perfect cum slut. If Nic had been here too, I bet she would have loved to lick it off of Alexei, her juices covering her inner thighs. Fuck, they were just perfect for me.

"You were amazing," I praised him gruffly. "You took that so well. Fucking perfect." He turned and looked at me, his eyes bright with emotion, and I felt my throat thicken. He opened his mouth, but I stopped him with a finger against his lips. I wasn't normally one for words, preferring to let my actions express the few emotions that readily came to me, but I could give this to him. I *wanted* to give this to him. "I know, Alexei. I love you too. And for the record, that is going to be one hell of an audio to listen to and enjoy later. Next time, I'm getting a camera set up because I want to make you watch it the next time you want to get off."

Alexei rolled his eyes as he kissed my throat. He didn't push for more, and I was glad that he left it at that. I didn't usually say all that bullshit out loud when it came to how I felt about him. I was glad he was one of the few people who *saw* when I pushed myself out of my comfort zone and fucking appreciated it.

"Who called?" Alexei asked softly after we sat there in silence for a few minutes.

"A detective about the compound. We still need to go to the station though."

"When?"

I grabbed his phone and checked the time. "Five minutes."

"Let's get this over with," Alexei groaned, rolling away from me to get his clothes. Grabbing mine, I got presentable, well, as presentable as I ever got. I slid on my club jacket last and took out my pack of cigarettes, lighting one up as we strolled out of the office toward his car. Inhaling deeply, I savored the nicotine filling my veins while I looked over at my lover.

Alexei seemed at ease now, the lines of tension in his body and around his eyes gone. I would ask him about what was going on with the clubs later. We needed to sort out who would be taking over so we could be there for Nic. Something in my gut told me that shit was about to hit the fan big time.

The storm had just started, and her stalker was still hiding, waiting to come out.

Nicholette
Friday

"One day, I'm going to have to go shopping. I can't keep wearing clothes from all of you." I commented as Ansel threw me one of his button-ups. Blake had gone out and bought me some underwear, two bras, and a few leggings, but I had mostly been wearing my boyfriends' clothing.

Ansel ignored my complaint, so I let out an exaggerated sigh and slipped on the shirt. I didn't bother to button it up before grabbing my cell phone and walking out of the room. Hurrying downstairs and into the kitchen, I found some leftover Chinese food and heated it up, digging in just as knocking came from the front door.

It was like people didn't realize I was growing fucking human beings. I ignored it and kept eating, determined to use the excuse of being pregnant if anyone complained. A few more knocks, then I heard Ansel's measured pace before the door opened.

Roderick's even voice hit my ears, the familiar sound accompanied by a surprise—Allen. I shoved a few more forkfuls of noodles into my mouth before they got to the kitchen. Roderick looked like his normal put-together self, but Allen seemed worn out. Exhaustion lined his face, and real concern filled me as I inspected him.

"What's going on?" I asked after swallowing down the food.

"If you could get dressed..." Allen waved at the still open shirt, being totally ungrateful that I had a bra on underneath.

"This *is* dressed," I huffed in mock annoyance as I did up a few buttons then propped my elbow on the counter. I looked between the two men as Ansel came to stand beside me, his hand brushing my side. "Are you two here for the same thing or different things?"

"Different," Roderick answered, not the least bit ruffled by my direct demeanor or lack of clothing. "Allen, you go first."

"Fine, I'm sure you already know that Maeve is dead." I tilted my chin in agreement, keeping my expression carefully blank. Allen took a deep breath before he continued on. "Her status in Ashview means there's a lot of pressure on us to figure out what happened to her... from legitimate *and* not-so-legitimate sources. There are a lot of people speculating about who's going to fill the void with her gone."

"Meaning you need me to come back in?" I asked, my mind racing. Why was he coming to me right now? Then I remembered that the body had been done up to look like me...

"Sooner rather than later would be good," Allen replied honestly, running a hand through his gray hair. "We need answers. Even if it's off the record, we need *something*."

"I have no idea who is behind this," I slowly replied after a beat of silence. "But we might have answers tomorrow, no guarantees though. Anything else about the other case?"

"Unfortunately." Allen grimaced. "Lewis is taking over your assault-turned-murder case. Despite your complaint and everything else against him, he was put back on the team. I might be able to join him when he questions you, given the history between you two, but they put him in charge of it again."

A long sigh escaped me as I shifted in my seat, brushing against Ansel's side in the process. He wrapped an arm around my shoulder and pulled me against him. Humming, I leaned into it, snuggling against him. The thought of dealing with Lewis again was making my skin crawl, so I'd take any comfort I could get. If the two men had opinions about our familiarity, they kept them to themselves. I snagged the leftovers and took another bite as Allen spoke up again.

"I'm also looking for Emmerich. Is he here?"

A door somewhere in the house slammed open right then, and I smiled. "Ask and you shall receive, Detective." The only other person who exited and entered rooms like that was Oli, and he wasn't here.

Shouting started, and my eyebrows rose as Emmerich entered the kitchen, oblivious to our presence, arguing with whoever was on the other end of the phone. I couldn't tell who he was talking to or what they were talking about until it registered that he was speaking Italian. *When did Em learn Italian?!* The person on the other end of the phone started cursing loudly, cutting off Em's tirade. *Oh man... I bet I know who this is.*

"A lovers' spat already?" I asked sassily, not missing the way Roderick stilled at my teasing before he masked it. *Interesting.*

"Shut up, Nic," Emmerich growled, throwing a glare in my direction before finally getting a word in edgewise.

I laughed at his irritation, not the least bit put off by his attitude. "Fight and fuck it out, Em, but you have a visitor first."

"Can we please not talk about fucking people?" Allen implored as I fought not to smile. "I know more about your sex lives than I ever wanted to know."

"Yeah, no shit," Em grumbled. "Nic fucking my dad is the fucking cherry on top."

"I mean, I was fucking him *before* this," I pointed out helpfully, but given the startled look from Allen and the sigh from Ansel, they didn't agree with my problem-solving skills. "What? I was!"

"Nic—"

"Let's not talk about all the people in your family I've fucked?" I guessed innocently, trying and failing to hide my smirk.

"I swear to god, Nic, someone needs to beat your ass." Em muttered as he ended the call, though it was anyone's guess whether the conversation had actually finished or if he'd just given up and hung up.

"I have a lot of people who do that on a regular basis for the fun of it. They don't need a reason, but you're welcome to share this incident with them."

"Can you please just stop being a smartass for a fucking second?" Em pinched the bridge of his nose. Ansel wisely stayed silent, but I saw a sparkle of humor in his gray eyes.

"I can already tell you the answer to that is no." Blake chuckled as they walked into the room, Conrad and Wulfric following behind.

"No one asked you, Blake," Emmerich shot back, though there was no real heat behind it.

"You were saying that you needed to talk to him alone, Allen?" Ansel drawled, trying to get the conversation back on track.

"Who needs to talk to me?" Emmerich looked around then, suddenly becoming serious when his eyes spotted Allen. After a few beats of silent conversation between them, Em nodded. "Let's go to my office. Blake, join us."

Blake followed behind their brother while gesturing for Wulfric and Conrad to stay with the rest of us. Roderick watched the group leave, a tic in his jaw betraying some kind of frustration. He exhaled, a quiet, measured breath, but that did nothing to conceal his feelings.

"So, Roderick, you said it was important, something to do with Maeve, and we could only talk about it in person. What's going on?"

Roderick dove right in, his tone hard, as he stepped forward and settled on the chair beside me. "There are contacts that want to speak with you now that you are taking over as the Madame, which means a trip to Ashview as soon as possible. They won't like being kept waiting for long."

"I have shit going on—"

"They don't care," Roderick replied curtly. "That's not their problem."

"Well, I'm not fucking Maeve," I told him with venom dripping from every word. He stilled as I brushed my hair over my shoulder. "They get to wait for me, not the other way around. Now, is that all?"

"No," he said as he shook his head. "I need you to sign some things, and I have paperwork you'll need to look over. I can answer any questions you have about all of it."

I slipped off the chair and gestured for him to come with

me. "Let's find an office then. We can get that all taken care of."

Roderick caught up with me and took the lead, bringing me to an office I hadn't been to before. He let me go in first, shutting the door as I sat down behind the desk, running my hands over the dark wood. There were some papers sitting around, two cigars set to the side, and a few books stacked on the side. No computer or phone anywhere in sight. It must be Ansel's office since he wasn't a fan of technology.

"We won't be disturbed here, and I know he soundproofed this room," Roderick mentioned as he pulled papers out of his bag and laid them in front of me. Just glancing over them, I knew they weren't documents related to Maeve's stuff. "This is the will that you wanted me to draw up. I know that I had it all done up before, but with your new position, there were more things that I needed to include in the document. Look over everything and make sure it's all set how you want it. Sacha was named the guardian of the children if something happens to you. I'll be your executor, handling the money for you. Do you have that information for me?"

I grabbed my cell and pulled up the information, giving him everything he needed. He filled out a few things then had me check it all over before signing. It felt odd to be signing paperwork about what would happen if I died or was seriously injured. I was twenty-two fucking years old. This wasn't what I should be worrying about.

"Nic?" His gentle tone had me jerking in my seat, making me realize I had been staring off into space.

"Sorry," I said, trying to play it off. "Just lost in thought. Do you know who wants to meet with me?"

Roderick didn't say anything at first, his dark eyes studying me before he leaned back. "A very powerful group of men who are also part of a huge network... I don't want to say more. It's not really an organization that you talk about, even behind closed doors. They have eyes and ears everywhere."

My lips curled, my mind already guessing who he was talking about. After all, there were only a few people who would fit that vague but powerful description. "Time to find religion then, Roderick? I haven't been to church in a long time, but I have plenty of sins I could repent for if I felt so inclined." The blood drained from Roderick's face, and I smirked cockily. "Not a religious man?"

"How?"

"The real question is whether you really want to know the answer to that question." I hummed. "I was picked to be her successor for a reason, Roderick, and while I might be young, do not mistake that for me being inexperienced. I made more connections than even Maeve realized."

"Duly noted," Roderick choked out before roughly clearing his throat.

"My brother takes precedence over fragile male egos," I told him coldly. "And I won't be starting my role as Madame by dancing to their tune, or anyone else's for that matter. Maeve had something to prove, but I don't, not anymore. If they reach out to you again before I'm ready, tell them to wait."

"You have a death wish," he replied softly, but there was respect glowing in his eyes.

"Says the man who's interested in the new head of the Förstner Family." I chuckled, continuing on in spite of the shock in his eyes. I liked Roderick, but this man had to get a better poker face. "But I think we are both people that are good at taking secrets to the grave. Is there anything else?"

Roderick studied me for a moment, weighing my words,

then he grabbed a folder from his bag. "Here's all the property information on what Maeve left you. I'll make sure to schedule time with Allen before we leave."

"Not tomorrow," I told him softly. "The day after will be the soonest I'm available. Probably."

"I'll keep that in mind."

Roderick stood up, gathered his things, and walked out. I remained curled up in Ansel's chair, opening the papers and skimming through everything. There were multiple homes as well as a large estate that was surprisingly close to here. Security, privacy, it would be perfect for a fresh start.

Rhodes
Friday

RODERICK'S CAR was pulling out as I approached Ansel's home, speeding up the driveway to get to Nic. I'd only been gone a few days on club business, but I *needed* to be with her. Ansel had found her father, and that meant she was going to confront the asshole soon. I knew we would all be there when she did. She would take the lead, but we'd be there to provide whatever kind of support she needed.

The compound was a complete loss, and I had no idea where we were going to go now. Business still needed to be conducted, and deals had to be made. Luckily, we had just moved our last big deal a few days before the fire, so our loss on that front was minimal, but I had to figure out everything ASAP. Thankfully, Razor had no problem stepping up, and I was seriously considering moving him up in the ranks. Maksim would always be my right-hand man, but Razor was proving his loyalty over and over again lately, especially considering he always asked after Nic. That kind of care for family wasn't something you could teach.

The house was silent when I walked in, but it wasn't empty. Emmerich, Blake, and Ansel were all sitting in the living room, along with Wulfric and the younger man, Conrad. They all looked in my direction as I came in, but it was Ansel who spoke first.

"She's in my office."

"Why was Roderick here?" I asked, shutting the door behind me.

"Paperwork shit from Maeve," Emmerich answered. "She's been looking it over for the past hour or so."

I didn't bother to figure out what they were doing, immediately heading to the office where Nic was hiding away. Ansel had gotten this house a while ago, needing distance from Frederick, and he wanted to give Emmerich space to grow into his role in the Family, which he felt like his son wouldn't fully do if he were there. Ansel was a hard man in many ways, but he loved his children even though he hadn't always had the best way of showing that affection.

Nerves hit me harder the closer I got to Ansel's study—about Ansel with my woman, the children Nic was pregnant with, the memory of Lia dying because of complications, all the complicated shit with the club.

Not bothering to knock, I opened the door. Nic was sitting behind the desk, looking at the papers in her hand. As I entered, she spun around to face me with a growing smile on her face. The happiness in her blue-green eyes made my heart race and warmth fill me. Her being happy the moment I walked into the room was a powerful feeling. The fact that I made her look like that with just my presence... She was amazing.

"What's wrong, hotshot?" Nicholette asked, worry

making her brow furrow. I sighed, realizing I had been standing there without saying a word.

I shut the door behind me and made sure it was locked before I walked over to her. With no questions asked, she was scooped into my lap while I claimed the chair. Nic cuddled into my chest after shifting around to get comfortable. She placed a hand atop the center of my chest, tilting her head back to stare at my face. I knew she was waiting for an answer, but where did I start?

"Everything, love." I clenched my jaw before letting out a long breath and closing my eyes to work on relaxing now that I was with her. "I have no idea where the club is going to set up shop now. Your stalker. The pregnancy... You think you can slow down a bit after all of this? I'm feeling every day of my fifty years lately."

Nic chuckled as she snuggled closer to me. "I hope so. Given the possibilities for fathers, we should start concerning ourselves with the mischief these hellions are going to create when they get here." A lump in my throat made it impossible to respond, and of course she noticed. "Rhodes?"

"It's nothing."

"It doesn't seem like nothing," she replied carefully.

I shook my head, my fingers twitching with the wish for a cigarette. It would give me time to think before I responded to her, a few moments of nicotine bravery and calmness to remember Lia. After a few moments of strained silence, Nic actually let it go.

"I have something for you, hotshot." I raised my brows, wanting to see where this was going. She leaned away from me and flipped through the papers on the desk before she grabbed a set and offered it to me.

With a curious look, I grabbed the papers and started to

look through them. My eyes widened when I realized what she was showing me. It was a sprawling estate down the road from Ansel's. Close to Ashview and Boston, yet part of neither, it was nestled in the protection of Shadowglen Estates. It was impressive, with lots of bedrooms, offices, a huge garage, and a few other buildings scattered throughout the twenty-some-acre property. *But why is she showing me this?*

"My stalker destroyed your compound, President," Nic murmured, her voice velvet steel. "This was left to me by Maeve, and I'm gifting it to you. It's not the same as what you had, and maybe the location isn't the best for what you need, but it can be a starting point at least. No scrambling or worrying about future fires considering where we are." My lips parted in shock, and I didn't realize my hands were trembling until her soft fingers curled around mine, steadying them. "I came back into your life and caused nothing but chaos. Let me make it right, hotshot. The Lords are your family, your friends. Let me help you take care of them."

"Trying to get old lady status, Nic?" I joked, unable to really process what she was offering me right now.

"I'm your partner, Rhodes, your equal, and I'll accept nothing less. You can rule the Lords of Chaos, and I'll sit pretty as the Madame, pulling strings to make people dance to my tune, both of us savoring the violent delights like a fine wine," she breathed, her heat and vulnerability a heady mix as she stared up at me.

I pushed her off my lap and tossed the papers on the desk before standing up and pulling her lips to mine. There were no words I could utter that would express how much she meant to me. Her power, humor, and sharp edges mixed together into a woman who was my dream in every way that mattered. I never imagined the woman I loved would be someone I'd have to share, but as she flicked her tongue against mine, I couldn't find it in me to care.

The study was small—a desk, two chairs, and a small sofa off to the side. Ansel liked quality over quantity, and it showed. Backing her up, I led her to the couch and wasted no time pulling at her clothes until she was naked in front of me. There were names carved into her thighs and another over her heart, taunting me to make my own mark. *Soon, but not right now.* Her soft hands tugged at my jacket, urging me to join her, and I did.

Jacket, shirt, and jeans hit the floor, then we were kissing again. We fell onto the couch, a tangle of limbs and reassuring touches as we lost ourselves in each other. Nic was intoxicating and gorgeous. I let her straddle my lap, riding my dick while she screamed my name, her pussy milking my cock until I spilled inside of her, marking her.

"I need you tonight," I admitted, pressing a small kiss to her shoulder.

"Can you share with Ansel?" she asked after a slight hesitation. "He already—"

"I can do that." I released a put-out sigh. "Guess he and I are about to get closer than we ever thought."

Nicholette chuckled. "You can focus your attention on me, hotshot. I'm even more needy now that I'm pregnant."

She was going to be the death of me, but what a way to go.

Bodhi
Friday

We had found nothing on Gabriel. No trace of the man or any information in his home or shop, Olive & Grove. Everything was clean, neat, and so organized I felt instantly at ease in both places, though they didn't stay in that state for long.

We tore the places apart, exploring every nook and cranny to see if we could find anything useful. I sighed heavily and jumped up on the counter beside the register at the shop. Besides the expensive clothing that Nicholette would love, there was nothing here. No money in the register or traces of what Gabriel had done outside of running this business.

"Are we sure that hand was Gabriel's? Couldn't he have just run off?"

"That's a possibility," Vas answered after a frustrated curse from further in the store. "We just guessed whose hand it was."

"If it wasn't his, then whose could it be?" Sacha speculated from behind me, making me jerk in surprise. I turned to glare at him, but he was uncowed, humor dancing in his brown eyes.

"Who knows?" Vas shrugged nonchalantly as he ambled toward us. "Right now, we have nothing though, and Nic sent me an update. Ansel found Joe, but she's waiting until tomorrow to confront him. She wants us there."

"Did she actually say that?" I asked. *Nic doesn't like to say she* needs *anyone.*

"No, but I think her saying she's waiting until we are back means the same thing." Vas grinned, and Sacha laughed, the husky sound giving me a little chill. "Any updates on your end?"

My mind immediately went to the personal message Nic had sent me earlier. She had reached out to say that Oli was leaving instead of the group chat. There wasn't anything in what she said that was weird but there was just something about it that was off, an edge to her words that wasn't usually present. For me, at least. I hadn't really talked to her since even though I knew I should have. Every day that passed just made the distance between us seem wider and wider. Hopefully I'd get my shit together before it was too late.

I shook my head as Sacha did the same beside me.

"We should get going. We don't want her to get pissed off about something and miss out on the consequences," Vas muttered, glancing at the car outside.

"I'm going to grab some clothes for her." Sacha looked around with a critical eye. "Knowing her, she's probably complaining that she doesn't have any of her stuff."

"You do that," Vas said over his shoulder as he headed for the door. "I'm going to go grab some stuff. I'll meet you at the car in thirty."

Sacha and I agreed, but instead of heading for the racks like I expected, Sacha crowded me and brushed his lips against mine. "What's going on, Bodhi? I can feel the gears turning in that head of yours. What's wrong?"

"Why would something be wrong?" I asked breathlessly, loving his nearness. His beard brushed against my neck as he pressed kisses up my jaw.

"Oli being gone for a while without much of a goodbye?" he asked. "The fact that you're avoiding Nic like the plague after steadfastly refusing to think she wouldn't come back to us?" My body tensed, not expecting him to call me out. He noticed my reaction and braced his hands on either side of me, refusing to let me escape this confrontation. "Is it the babies?"

"What if I end up like my mom?" I managed, my voice cracking even though it was barely above a whisper. I had brought up this concern to Oli, but his reassurance didn't make my worry go away. "I wanted Nic back, but a baby? *Multiple* babies? I don't know how to wrap my head around that."

"She's still our Nic. In fact, I think we could argue that being pregnant has made her even more ruthless," Sacha gently replied, pulling back so he could cup my face and meet my gaze. "No one was expecting her to get pregnant, much less Nic, but she's ours. The babies are ours. We just need to hope we don't have a little Vas because he was a fucking handful. Plus, my brother won't ever let us live it down if he's the one who got past Nic's birth control."

I laughed despite myself, the image of Vas' boasting amusing me. His ego was already crazy; there was no way we could handle it getting any bigger. "I know it's dumb—"

"It's not dumb," he cut me off harshly. "You went through hell because of someone you should have been able to depend on without question. You aren't her, Bodhi, and none of us would let you end up that way."

"I just... Nic noticed. That I've been avoiding her, I mean." I swallowed hard. "She didn't come right out and say it, but I could tell."

"Talk to her, Bodhi. Before we deal with Joe tomorrow."

"Not tonight?" I asked gruffly, rubbing my face.

"No," Sacha replied softly, sounding uncharacteristically unsure. "Tonight, I need you. I'm tired of waiting and getting in my head. I just want it to be us, finally. Sleep with me tonight?"

My breath caught in my throat, my eyes shooting up to search his face, but he ignored the weight of my stare. He ran his hands up and down my thighs almost as if he were nervous. "Just sleeping?" I needed him to be very fucking clear about what was going to happen tonight. It felt like I'd waited forever for him to be ready.

He shook his head just a little bit. "I need you, Bodhi. I'm tired of imagining what you'll feel like against me and the sounds you'll make when I fuck you until you're crying for me to stop. I want to feel you milk my cock for every fucking drop of cum so I can finally mark you as mine. The taste of you, the smell of your skin when I wake up in the morning, I want that. Stay with me tonight?"

I didn't answer with words, hungry for everything he'd said. I slanted my mouth over his, diving into the kiss, and I began to whimper when he took over, tilting my head just right so he could plunder my mouth. He was sending a message loud and clear: I would not be hiding any part of myself from him. *The damn miracle will be making it to the house tonight.* His beard was soft against my face, and he tasted like the rich, bitter coffee he loved. I closed my eyes, moaning, as I instinctively pushed my body closer to his. God, I couldn't believe we were doing this.

He broke the kiss, leaving both of us panting as he rested his forehead against mine. "If we don't stop, I'll take you right here."

"I'm okay with that," I told him. My need for him was rising with every twitch of my dick.

"My brother is going to be back soon," Sacha said harshly, then he grabbed my wrists, stopping me from running my hands up his chest.

"Vas isn't an idiot. He won't come in for us," I breathed, needing Sacha more than I cared about any hint of modesty I might have left. Though given the fantasy I'd shared with Oli about Maksim watching and directing us, I didn't care about modesty as much as I'd once thought.

Sacha watched me, clearly at war between wanting me right now and whatever he was thinking for tonight. "Our first time together... I didn't picture it happening in an empty store."

My breath caught in my throat, and I licked my lips. The first time I had been with Oli hadn't been planned either. The tension between us had been building for days, and one night, after a job well done, he grabbed me, claiming a kiss and my heart in the process. We had fucked beside the man Oli had just tortured and killed, blood all over him, then me, as he violently fucked me against the cement floor.

The floor had been hard against my back, giving me bruises that lasted for a few days, but the ache of those marks was nothing compared to the violence with which Oli had fucked me. My body had slid in the blood until the dead man hung above us, his remaining blood dripping down on our bodies as Oli kissed me, our fingers laced together. Blood always made me think of Oliver and the wicked cruelty that he didn't bother to hide from the world.

Sacha was completely different. He wanted something special, or at least something more special than the shop counter for our first time. He'd planned something, which was so like him. Granted, this was his first time with a man, so it probably held a different weight than my and Oli's coming together.

"What were you thinking?"

"Stay with me in Ashview tonight. We'll leave early tomorrow morning to get back home," Sacha said seductively. "Let's have it be just us so I can show you what it means to be with me."

"And I'll show you what it's like to be with a man?" I asked teasingly. Heat curled in my stomach when he slowly nodded, his uncertainty making him break our stare to look behind me. *He thinks I'm going to turn him down.*

I rocked up, kissing him as I wrapped my arms around his neck, wordlessly telling him how excited I was by the idea of the two of us finally coming together. "Let's hurry up. I don't want to wait a minute longer than I have to before that happens."

Sacha growled, but he managed to contain himself and step back. "Stuff for Nic, then I'll tell Vas our new plans."

"What were you planning on getting her?"

Sacha roughly cleared his throat as he chuckled. "There are a few pieces that reminded me of our whore. Come with me."

I laced my fingers through his, jumped down off the counter, and let him lead me through the store. Carefully browsing, he grabbed a few dresses, all black but different styles. He passed them to me to hold as he flipped through the suits and grabbed navy blue slacks and a blazer with a white blouse. Of course he didn't miss the lingerie section either, snagging one of everything in a few sizes. I appreciated his attention to detail. Despite the pregnancy changing her body, he'd already noticed what sizes Nic would need and what would flatter her and make her feel comfortable.

And all that attention is going to be on me tonight.

I shivered at the thought of his intensity completely focused on me and my pleasure. *Fuck... Is it time to go yet?*

A loud banging made me jolt, and I whipped around to see Vas standing outside, gesturing to an imaginary watch on his wrist with an annoyed expression. Sacha muttered under his breath in Russian as he grabbed a few bags for us to throw the clothes in.

"With how long you two were taking, I thought you'd at least have been fucking," Vas said right when we stepped outside.

Sacha didn't say anything, but I coughed to cover up a laugh. He grabbed the bags and put them in the backseat before facing his brother. "Did you get what you needed?"

"It's in the car."

"Good." Sacha opened the door and gestured for me to get in the front passenger seat. I hesitated, looking at Vas. He always sat up front since it was the most comfortable for him when he wasn't driving. Sacha didn't let me stand there for long before he sharply gestured to the door again. "Get in, Bodhi."

"Are we going to get in a fight here on the sidewalk, brother?"

"Of course not," Sacha replied dryly as I slid into the front seat. "But Bodhi and I are going to be going to Ansel's in the morning instead of now. You can figure out a way back on your own, yes?"

"You wouldn't fucking dare," Vas shot back, but Sacha moved faster than I thought possible. He was around the car and inside before his brother could react. I slammed the door shut and was buckling up as he started the car and pulled out onto the street. A glance in the mirror told me Vas was standing on the sidewalk, laughing and yelling crude things as we drove off.

Sacha chuckled as I hastily took care of his seatbelt before a cop pulled us over. "I've dreamed of doing that for years. Vas is such a pain in the ass."

"He's going to get you back for that," I pointed out, but I couldn't keep the laughter from my voice.

"I can't wait to see it," Sacha replied gleefully, reaching out to place a hand on my knee. "Now, I have better things to think of than my brother."

"Oh yeah, what's that?" I joked.

"Me fucking you all night until we get back tomorrow and have to deal with Nic's father. I can't wait to see how she kills him."

I swallowed hard. That was certainly one way to look at it, and I couldn't fucking wait.

For tonight and tomorrow.

Sacha
Friday

I knew that Vas still had his bike at our apartment, so he'd get back to Nic and the others with no problem. Having alone time with Bodhi was rare. We always ended up getting interrupted for work, by Nic, by the others... Now that I'd decided to get out of my own way and take the next step with Bodhi, I didn't want anyone or anything to interrupt.

Nerves. I chuckled to myself. Who would have thought that I would be fucking nervous? I had a ton of experience, but this was different. It was Bodhi, and it was my first time with a man. I was already doing a shit job of getting out of my head.

"Sacha?" Bodhi called my name as I parked the car on the side of the street in front of a nondescript apartment building. "Where are we?"

"I have my own place. I've kept it so I can get away when I need it. Not even Vas has been here, though he knows I have it." When I looked at Bodhi, there was unfiltered astonishment on his face. "What?"

"I just... I didn't realize..." He bit his bottom lip, a blush heating his cheeks as embarrassment took over. "Nevermind."

"We all have demons, Bodhi," I told him with a rueful half smile. "I just deal with mine privately. Come upstairs with me."

After a brief pause, he unbuckled, and we got out of the car together. I sped up until I was beside him, grabbing his hand so I could lead the way to my apartment on the fourth floor. It was a simple studio apartment without much in the way of furnishing. A king-sized bed, a sofa, television, and coffee table. I didn't stay here for more than a day or two at a time, so I hadn't bothered to fix it up much.

Bodhi looked around with wide eyes when I let go of him to lock the door behind us. He glanced over his shoulder at me and licked his lips.

"This doesn't seem like your usual taste," he said carefully.

"This is where Vas and I lived years ago. After our grandmother died... After she was gone, we got this apartment with all the money we could scrape together," I told him softly, pushing away the memories that threatened to creep up on me. Now wasn't the time. "I kept it. When things get bad, I come back here to remember where we started and what we overcame to get where we are. Vas and I fit two doubles in this place with a sofa and a tiny TV. We worked measly jobs until we started getting really good and gained the attention of higher-ups in this city. We built everything from the ground up, and this... This was our start. It's not glamorous by any means, but it's humbling to come here and think of it again."

"I never look back at how I started," Bodhi said darkly, a shiver running through his body. "It was all about survival. I stole to live and found out I was really fucking good at it." I slowly approached him, already feeling a hint of guilt. Seeing him lost in the past hadn't been the point of bringing him here. Reaching out, I brushed my fingers along his arm, and he jumped before looking up at me with a self-deprecating smile on his face. "Sorry. I didn't mean to ruin the mood."

"You didn't," I reassured him, tugging on his shirt until he stood right in front of me. "But I'm tired of talking right now. We've talked enough. I'm done going slow."

Bodhi's lips parted, but I cut him off with a soft, thorough kiss, groaning when he wound his arms around my neck and pulled me flush against his body.

Soft fingers slid down my chest to the hem of my shirt, and we broke apart so he could pull mine over my head while I did the same to his. *I need the heat of his skin against mine.* We didn't stay separated for long, our lips crashing together and teeth nipping as I led him back to my bed. Clothes and shoes were tossed aside with abandon until he fell back onto the bed and I climbed over him.

Both of us were on the leaner side, but where my muscles were more defined, his body hinted at the strength I knew he possessed. Reaching down, I brushed a few long strands of hair out of his face, loving the shiver that ran through his body at my touch. His brown eyes stared up at me with a mix of wonder and anticipation that made me feel like a fucking god.

"If I do something you don't like or can't do—"

"I'll tell you," Bodhi reassured me. His long fingers ran through my hair, tugging just hard enough that I growled at him. "Show me, Sacha. Show me what it means to be yours."

I couldn't have stopped myself if I wanted to. Fisting a hand in his hair, I yanked him up and slanted my lips over his. This was everything I'd been waiting for. Giving him no mercy, I flicked my tongue along his, silently urging him to catch up. The way he groaned into the kiss had me smirking, but I was just starting. Pulling back, I trailed kisses down his throat, occasionally nipping just to hear his gasps and whimpers. His hips snapped up, his hard cock rubbing against mine, and I bit down extra hard right where his neck met his collarbone. *Fuck, he's fantastic.*

"Please," he cried, his hands scrambling along my back, nails digging in. I fucking loved every sting, everything sign that the contained man beneath me was coming undone. "Sacha, please!"

"What do you need, baby?" I whispered, loving the way he bit his lip at the nickname.

"You."

"You're getting me," I teased, moving my lips down his body. I flicked my tongue against each nipple before biting down. He hissed a string of curses as I moved lower, savoring each twitch of muscle when I got to his abs.

"Fuck," he cursed, his back bowing off the bed. Satisfaction grew as he writhed under me, already begging for more. All the anxiety I'd had building up inside of me was draining away now that I was finally with a man for the first time—not just a man, *Bodhi.* Thanks to the curses and gasps falling from his lips, he was making me feel like I was on cloud fucking nine and ten feet tall.

Passing by his hard dick and the shine of precum that made my mouth water, I kissed his inner thighs, then moved down his legs. My hands followed my lips with a firm grip. I massage each spot I'd kissed, savoring his gradual loss of control. At first, he was quiet, his rocking hips silently asking me to move to his cock, but when I lightly smacked his thighs and went back to what I was doing, he started to beg.

Bodhi brought out a protective side of me that I wasn't used to. Sure, I wanted to protect Nicholette, and I did, as much as she let me. But Bodhi... I wanted to fucking wrap him up and hold him close. I wanted to be softer with him, something I'd never felt before. When I leaned back to watch Bodhi, his cheeks were flushed, and sweat beaded on his forehead. His breathing came in short pants.

"Please fuck me. God, I can't do this," Bodhi pleaded, his eyes wide.

He tried to reach down for his cock, but I tsked him and carefully batted his hand away. "So damn needy. You take what I give you, baby. No complaints."

Bodhi whimpered, his cock twitching, and I couldn't help myself. I swiped a fingertip over the shiny head before slowly sliding the finger into my mouth. Bodhi cursed, his body tensing like he was fighting off an orgasm just from watching me taste him.

Stepping away, I ignored his immediate protests and crooked a finger at him. "I need to take the edge off before I fuck you, Bodhi. Come here and suck me off. I want this to last a long time." He scrambled up, almost falling over in his haste to get to me, which only made me smile despite his flushed cheeks. How fucking amazing was it to know someone wanted you so badly they were literally falling all over themselves to get to you?

A grunt fell from my lips when Bodhi took me in his mouth. Wet, hot... fuck. I wanted this to last, but I wasn't sure I could hold it together this time. Right now, with his hands grabbing my ass to pull me closer, I wasn't sure I'd be able to push it off.

God, he looked amazing on his knees with my cock

down his throat. He swirled his tongue around my length, but he must have sensed my attention because his eyelids suddenly fluttered, then he looked up at me. That was when I lost it.

Groaning his name, I came down his throat, fucking loving how he hummed and swallowed me down. He kept sucking on my cock until I stepped back, slightly unsteady on my feet. I had to put my hand out to stop him from following.

"Fuck, you're good at that," I commented gruffly, clearing my throat after I heard how scratching I sounded.

"Fuck me. Please, I need you inside of me," Bodhi asked softly, licking his lips.

"I need a minute," I responded, and he smiled, holding out a hand. I took it and let him pull me back to the bed.

Laying down, I enjoyed the way he curled himself into my side, one hand on my chest as he threw a leg over mine. His cock was still hard, but I appreciated the way he listened, waiting for me to be ready.

Combing my fingers through his hair, I pressed a quick kiss to the top of his head. I never thought I'd get here with him, and part of me wondered if we would have ever gotten here without Nic. Honestly, I didn't think so. She made Bodhi feel more comfortable in his skin and pushed him out of his comfort zone, willingly and unwillingly. I owed a lot to the whore that had waltzed into our lives with a cocky smirk on her face and a heart of fucking gold under her psychopathic hobbies.

"What are you thinking about?" Bodhi asked while tracing patterns on my stomach.

"That I wasn't sure this, us, would ever happen, but I'm fucking happy it did," I told him.

Bodhi chuckled breathlessly as he nodded. "I know

what you mean. I had no idea that you were even interested in me."

"But what does matter is that we're here," I told him as I gently put a finger under his chin and urged him to look up at me. "I'm not going anywhere. Just so we're clear, this isn't just me looking to hook up with a guy and then bail."

"Is that why you waited so long?" he asked, understanding dawning on his face. "To make sure I knew that this was more than just fucking. You didn't think I'd believe you?"

"Actions speak louder than words," I told him softly, feeling suddenly self-conscious. "I didn't want there to be any doubt in your mind about what I was doing with you. This isn't some game to me, not that I won't play some games with you. I have a lot of things in mind for future dates when we aren't on a time crunch."

"Like what?" he asked, his breath hitching through his parted lips. Fuck, he was so eager.

Brushing my lips against his, I grabbed his hips and maneuvered him so that he straddled me. He gasped and fell forward, catching himself on his hands as I pulled his ass cheeks apart, loving the way his breathing caught.

"Open yourself up for me, baby. One finger at a time," I urged him. I wanted, no *needed*, to see how much he wanted me. There was no way I was going to miss a single second of our first time together.

Bodhi sucked on his fingers before he reached back, hurriedly stretching himself out. I knew he was using more than one at a time, and while I couldn't blame him, that wasn't what I had instructed him to do—something to remember for next time. The next thing I felt was his hand on my cock, then he impaled himself on me.

He worked himself slowly up and down, trying to ease

my way inside him after not doing enough to stretch himself. Well, maybe he would learn something after this. I tightened my grip on his ass cheeks, keeping them apart, as I snapped my hips up to bottom out in him.

He cried out, his head thrown back, and his entire body trembled. He took deep breaths, trying to get himself under control, but that was too bad. I didn't want him to get his shit together while I felt like I was falling apart. Using my hold on him, I easily manhandled him, making him ride my cock as he gasped and whimpered for me to show some mercy.

"Maybe you should have listened when I said to prep yourself slowly," I taunted, loving the way he screamed when I slammed him down on me. "I told you I'm a man that likes control, and I especially like controlling *you*. Now you're going to ride my dick so I can watch you come apart for me. Keep your eyes on me."

"God," he whimpered, his cock twitching.

He started to take over, following the pace I set for him, so I loosened my hold on his hips. Wrapping a hand around his throbbing dick, I started to pump him slowly, teasing him.

"Sacha, I can't— Not with you touching me like that."

"Are you trying to tell me to stop?"

"No!" he shot back, a distinct whine in his voice that had me laughing at his desperation. "Please don't! Don't stop!"

"You beg so prettily," I praised, lightly trailing my fingers over his cock. "But it's my turn now."

"What?"

I flipped us over, and his legs instinctively wrapped around my hips, keeping us pressed together. I fucked him, every thrust hard enough that he started to sob. He begged me to go slowly, to fuck him harder, to come. He wanted it all, everything, and god did I want to be the one to give it to him.

"Can you come without touching yourself, baby?" I asked roughly, shifting my angle enough that he screamed the next time I thrust into him. *Fuck yes.*

"Yes," he keened.

"Perfect."

I grabbed his hands and pinned him to the bed before I completely let myself go. I pounded into him, and despite the force, he leaned up in a silent request for a kiss. We met in a battle of lips, tongue, and teeth until I lost my rhythm and filled him. When I felt ropes of cum hit my stomach, I smiled into our kiss. I was fucking proud that I was able to reduce him to the cum-covered mess below me.

As he caught his breath, I eased out of him, falling to his side so I could chase that fucking amazing taste. With long swipes of my tongue, I cleaned off his chest and stomach, making my way to his cock. I took him into my mouth, sucking him clean. Bodhi whimpered, and a trembling hand gripped my hair, but he didn't try to pull me off him. Instead, he flinched under the attention and let me have my way with him. *Such a good boy.*

When I finally pulled off of him, he urged me up and kissed me again. He didn't seem to mind the taste of himself on my lips because he kissed me languidly, savoring us coming together, until I pulled back when I became dizzy.

"Holy shit," he breathed. "Fuck."

"I take it I was good?"

"Fishing for compliments?" he teased, his eyes bright when he rolled his head over to look at me. I growled, and he burst out laughing at me, but the warmth in the sound made my mask crumble. "I was surprised..."

"Surprised?" I asked when he trailed off. I threw an arm over his stomach and pulled him closer, shifting him around until he was positioned how I wanted him, his back to my front so I could cuddle him close. Bodhi snuggled back into me as he rested an arm over my own.

"You were a lot less... sadistic than I thought you would be. Not that it's a complaint or anything—"

"I could be, you know," I said gruffly. "Sometimes I probably will be."

"Which isn't a problem," Bodhi rushed to reassure me as if I needed it. "It's just..."

"Just?"

"I don't want you to take this the wrong way," he said softly as if he was nervous.

"Well, now you have to tell me," I told him gruffly. My hands wandered down his body, teasing him, trying to show him that I wasn't pulling away from him. When he didn't immediately say something, I wrapped my hand around his dick. He jerked and tried to get away, probably because he was still sensitive from coming a few minutes ago, but I didn't let him out of my hold. It just took a few teasing strokes for him to start talking.

"You just come off as more of a Daddy than a sadist," he revealed. He tried to reach down and push my hand off his cock, but now it was time for my own fun.

"A Daddy, huh?" I rasped, running my tongue along the shell of his ear. "For you, I can work with that."

"Wait... what?"

I stroked his cock, loving the tortured little gasps escaping him as I continued to play with him. I didn't stop until he came again, gasping through the tears running down his face. His hips rocked, instinctively helping me pump the cum out of him. Praising him, I let go of his dick, loving that he immediately turned in my arms, tucking his face into my chest and cuddling into me.

I grabbed the sheets and pulled them over us, content in knowing that we were safe here for the time being. Bodhi tilted his head back to look at me with a sleepy, satisfied expression.

"If you tell Nic about this, I'll let you see my sadistic side, Bodhi. I'll even get Oliver to help me."

"Oli wouldn't let you live it down either," he replied, not the least bit intimidated. "But I'll remember that." There was a beat of silence, then he asked, "Should I call you Daddy then?"

"Shut up, Bodhi, and go to sleep," I grumbled, though I couldn't hide the warmth that filled me when he chuckled.

Before long, he passed out, completely wrapped around me. Absentmindedly, I ran my hands over his back, needing to touch him so I knew this wasn't some dream. I never thought I'd end up here, but now that I was, I wasn't going to give it up—my team, my family, my lovers. There was so much on the line now.

My dream life was in my hands, and no one was going to take that from me.

Nicholette
Saturday

I sat on the kitchen stool watching Ansel cook breakfast while Rhodes smoked his morning cigarette outside. My fingers traced the rim of the coffee mug in front of me as I let myself get lost in thoughts of tangled limbs, dirty talk, and the fucking stretch as they pushed me to my limits... Rhodes and Ansel sharing me last night and this morning was something that would stay in my mind for days to come.

"Liebling?"

"Hmm?" I asked, grabbing my mug and pulling it closer to me. Ansel was watching me with a bemused expression that I'd totally missed at first. "I can have this. One cup, Ansel. The doc said so."

"I was just asking if you wanted food yet," he replied with a quiet laugh. The sound of the glass door sliding open came next, then Rhodes rejoined us.

"What's so funny?"

"I think Liebling was too busy daydreaming about us fucking her six ways to Sunday to tell me if she's ready to eat or not," Ansel replied.

"I mean, you both were there. Can you blame me?" I

shrugged, not the least bit embarrassed to admit that was exactly what I was doing.

"Oh god, knowing you fucked my dad and Rhodes in theory was bad enough," Emmerich's voice rang out from behind me. "Please don't give more details. If this is how it's going to be from now on, I'm yelling out a warning before I get to the doorway."

"Solid yet dramatic solution," I deadpanned, and Em gave me a cocky, lazy smirk.

"Don't flirt with me, Nic." Emmerich waved a dismissive hand. "You have a full plate and then some. Plus, I don't want to see my dad's dick. Ever."

"Wondering how you'll measure up against him? I could make a comparison chart," I teased, and he flipped me off and grabbed the stool to my right while Rhodes settled down on my left.

"Shut up," Emmerich growled as Ansel tried and failed to cover a laugh by coughing. He jolted at the sound as if it was unfamiliar, but he focused on me instead of looking toward his dad. "So what's the plan for today?"

"Question, torture, and kill Joe," I told him with a sharp smile.

"Any plans on how that's going to happen?" Em asked, eagerly leaning forward.

"I know exactly how I'm going to kill him, and I'll need some help with it." I glanced in Rhodes' direction. "I need you to bring heavy-duty chains and motorcycles. But I need answers first."

"What the hell are you going to do? Drag his body behind the bike?" Emmerich asked. I just stared at him blankly, and he whistled. "Savage."

"Where he is right now... Will that work for privacy?" I

directed the question at Ansel who was currently placing a full plate in front of me.

"We'd need to find a good place for the motorcycle, but no one will bother us," he reassured me. "Eat."

Picking up the toast, I dug in, not about to fight with someone who willingly cooked me food. The men around me started talking about business I had no real interest in as I thought over the man I was about to see for the first time in five years.

I had thought he was my dad until just a few days ago. Now, he was just the bastard that had bought me, the head of the group of people who had kidnapped me as a child. Part of me wondered if I was broken because not one part of me wanted to know about the family I had been taken from. That life was so far away that there was no way I'd ever be that girl. I was a whore. A killer. It wasn't like I was great material for a long-lost daughter coming home.

Reaching for my coffee, I realized that I had finished it at some point and let out a long frustrated sigh.

"No more." I glared up at Ansel's firm statement, already thinking about stabbing him with the knife on my plate. "Go ahead and try."

I huffed. "It's not fun if you're expecting it."

"I can see last night was great bonding time," Em remarked sarcastically. "You might need to step up your game."

"What happened last night?" a deep, rumbling voice asked, then Vas was right behind me. I turned around to face him with a wide smirk. "No, wait, nope. Don't tell me."

"Aww, you're no fun."

"Not what you said last time I was balls deep inside of you," he shot right back at me.

"I don't really recall saying that..." I tapped a finger to

my chin as if I were trying to remember. "When did you get back, by the way?"

"Last night, late. Crashed right when I got back since Sacha and Bodhi are coming back this morning instead."

Happiness filled me at what Vas was implying, that Sacha and Bodhi were finally having sex, but at the same time, a pang of hurt churned in my gut. *Bodhi*. The one man I hadn't been able to reconnect with yet. I missed him, and it seemed like I would continue to do so because he was finding every possible way to avoid me.

"That's good for them then," I said, my voice slightly off.

The front door opened before Vas could reply, and I heard Blake and their guys talking as they came downstairs. It seemed breakfast was going to be a party, but Vas' pointed look told me he wasn't going to forget what we were talking about.

By the time Blake and their crew made it to us, Alexei and Maksim had wandered inside. They were talking quietly together when Sacha and Bodhi arrived. A hint of self-consciousness hit when Bodhi met my gaze then quickly looked away. I saw Sacha say something to him, but I slipped out when everyone started talking, making the excuse that I needed to go to the bathroom. Technically, it was true, but that wasn't the reason I needed to get out of there.

I felt their stares on me as I left, but no one moved to stop me. The bathroom was on the other side of the living room, and I made sure to lock the door behind me this time. Bracing my hands on the sink, I tried to remind myself that this was a lot for anyone to adjust to and that I hadn't expected anyone to take the news well. But my heart twisted at the thought that Bodhi might turn his back on me.

On us.

I pressed a hand to my abdomen as my stomach flipped. *Please don't get sick. Please don't get sick.* My mantra was interrupted by a light knock on the door.

"Nic?"

Oh fuck. It was Bodhi.

"Yes?"

There was a beat of silence. "Can we talk?"

I swallowed hard and checked the mirror, hoping I didn't look pale or teary eyed. Then I opened the door and pulled Bodhi into the bathroom with me, not wanting witnesses for this just in case. I didn't mind some humiliation when it came with a healthy serving of orgasms, but this was a whole different situation. He stumbled at my unexpected force but managed to keep himself upright. I locked the door then whirled around to face him, practically holding my breath.

I didn't know what to say, so I just stared, waiting to see what he wanted. I knew how to be ball-breaking, sometimes literally, Nic in just about any other scenario, but I couldn't summon that courage and sass when I was worried that one of the men I loved was about to tell me this was too much, that *I* was too much for him to handle. How would I deal with that? What would I do when I had to see him snuggle up with Oli or be held by Sacha when I could no longer have that with him?

Bodhi's hands shook as he deeply inhaled. "I know I haven't had time alone with you since you got back. A lot has been going on. The police, your stalker, Maeve, Ansel... everyone else." He waved a hand before letting out a rough laugh. "But I also needed time."

"I get that, Bodhi," I said softly, but he shook his head.

"You coming back was always something I knew would

happen. One way or another, I *knew* you'd come back to us. But the... pregnancy, *twins*. That's something I couldn't wrap my mind around."

"I know the feeling," I told him, cautiously taking a step toward him. "Every day I was gone, I missed you. All of you. It was a lot for me to take in too, and I know that me leaving without a trace wasn't easy. It felt like hell not being with all of you. I missed *you*, Bodhi. I get needing time to process shit."

"I hurt you," he replied, a slight crack in his voice.

"I've hurt you too," I retorted gently. The two of us stood closely enough now that I cupped his face. With only two inches on me, we were pretty much eye to eye when I got him to meet my stare. "I think we'll hurt each other plenty as long as we're together. We're human, Bodhi. But I'll take every cut if it means one more day with you. We'll figure this out together. Given the hell we both went through, I know we'll protect these babies from everything we can."

A tear broke free, and I reached up to wipe it away as Bodhi crushed me to him. I automatically moved my arms so I could hug him back. This was one of the more emotional homecomings, especially since it lacked the simmering anger that had marked almost all the others. Bodhi, the others, they had managed to do what no one else had... They were well past my walls, having laid claim to the real me that was hidden behind every mask. They'd poisoned my heart, and I knew I'd crave them forever.

"I wish I had time to say I missed you properly," I told him, grinning when that earned a real laugh. "But I do have a dad to torture and kill so I can find Thomas. If he saw my stalker, then we'll finally have a name."

"Sounds like the perfect foreplay to me."

I pressed a soft kiss to his lips, humming happily when he responded in kind. "I always loved that about you, pet. You know how to give a girl all kinds of ideas." Pulling back, I studied his face, and my smile grew. "So you and Sacha finally gave in, huh?"

Bodhi blushed, but he didn't look the least bit embarrassed when he answered me. "Yes. How the hell did you... No, I should know better than to question you about sex stuff."

"Are you happy?" I asked him seriously. Was he happy with me? With Sacha? Oli? With everything? *Such a fucking loaded question, Nic.*

"Yes," he answered firmly, no hesitation at all, then he rested his forehead against mine. "Very happy."

"Now to take care of a few loose ends, then we can go celebrate." I ran my hands along his ass suggestively. "I'm glad I'm back."

"Me too. And you stayed safe."

My throat thickened, recalling him asking me to stay safe around the time we had first gotten together. Warren had taken me then. This time, I had left but come back in one piece.

Safe.

I'd managed to do that this time, fighting like hell to get my life back together and reunite with my guys with information in hand. Tilting my head, I kissed him one more time before we had to leave the bathroom and get back to business. At least that was my intention until Bodhi slid a hand along my jaw, deepening the kiss. I moaned into the kiss, and I'd started trying to figure out whether we could fuck in here when there was a firm knock on the door.

Bodhi groaned in protest as he moved down my neck

with teasing kisses as I tried to form words. Sacha beat me to it.

"Ansel is getting Joe now, Nic, and I have something for you before you get started with him."

Bodhi muttered some not-so-nice things about his boyfriend that had me chuckling as we broke apart. I didn't try to straighten up because I knew that Sacha would love to see us like this, unlike his brother. Opening the door with an unrepentant grin, I found boss man standing there with a bag from Olive & Grove, Gabriel's store. His dark eyes scanned me, then Bodhi, and his amusement was overshadowed by the warm happiness there as he held up the bag.

My brow furrowed until I looked inside and saw the neatly folded clothes. Immediately, I knew Sacha had been the one to pick everything out. He understood that clothes could be both armor and a weapon when needed. Maeve had ingrained that in me, and I'd be damned if the thought of Sacha knowing me so well didn't make me tear up. *Fuck pregnancy hormones.*

Sacha didn't say anything, probably knowing that I didn't want to deal with it all right now. He just pressed a kiss to my forehead and told me to go get ready. I nodded and pressed a quick kiss to his lips before heading upstairs to take a quick shower. I used the time and space to push off all the emotional crap that had been happening lately. I needed to focus, to harness everything life had taught me to confront the man that had made my life hell for so many years.

I dried off and stepped into the room only to pause. Vas was sitting on the messy bed, waiting for me. He was holding a small brown bag, looking uncharacteristically unsure.

"Vas?"

"Come here, Nic." He spread his legs so I'd know where he wanted me.

Carefully watching him, I dropped the towel onto the floor and walked over. When I was close enough, he grabbed my ass, tugged me closer, and held up the bag.

"What's this?"

"Open it."

What was it with today? Both brothers were giving me gifts? Was I missing something? Sacha getting me clothes, I could understand, but Vas wasn't a gift kind of guy. Giving him a curious look, I opened the bag. Vas' rough hands ran up and down my back as he gave me a moment to get myself together.

Shaking hands pulled out the small glass bottle that was nestled inside, and I absently let the paper bag fall to the floor. I knew if I opened the bottle, it would smell the same as the one he had given me before. The familiar scents of coffee and vanilla hit me, followed by afternotes of oranges, pears, and jasmine. Tears filled my eyes at the sense of home that came over me.

"It's around the same time it was last year when I gave you the first bottle." Vas' deep gravelly voice broke the tense silence. "Since the stalker took everything, I figured you might want another bottle, but I would have found a reason to give you more anyway. This is something that's just for us, not because of what's going on right now."

Tears spilled over, and I swallowed hard a few times, damning Vas for tearing down what little walls I had managed to put back up. At the same time, though... he had remembered. Hell, even I barely remembered my birthday since I hadn't celebrated in so long. As soon as Thomas came, I never got parties or even a card from my family. My friends would sometimes get me stuff, usually something small enough that I could hide it, but that was it. Vas, though... The gruff, rumbly grizzly bear remembered my birthday.

Gently, he took the bottle from my hard grip and pulled me into his lap, holding me close as I wrapped my arms around him. Neither of us tried for more. My heart was simply happy with his closeness and the sensation of him against me. This was one of the few times in my life where my mind didn't jump to sex to avoid the emotions building inside me.

"Thank you," I choked out.

"Anything for you, Nic. Anything."

I buried my face in his neck, needing to breathe him in and ground myself in him as he possessively ran his hands along my skin. I felt at peace, with him and all the other people in my life. Was this happiness? Even with everything still up in the air, could I be happy? There was only one more thing that would help me today.

Breaking away from him, I leaned over and grabbed the bottle. "Help me get ready?"

Heat filled his gaze, and he nodded before he oh so carefully took his time covering my entire body with the oil. I centered myself with every inch of my body he claimed as his own, loving the way he kept this moment simple. After Vas was done, he stayed with me, watching me sort through what Sacha had given me.

Finally, something spoke to me—a short black dress with spaghetti straps. It hit mid-thigh and hugged every curve I had once I tugged it on. I brushed my hand down the dress to make sure there weren't any rolls or lines around the underwear I had slid on. Inside the bag, there was also a pair of flats and stilettos. Smiling, I braced a hand on Vas' shoulder and slid into the high heels, loving the way they made me feel. *Powerful.*

"Ready?"

I took a deep breath and let myself fully slip into that cold part of my brain that I would need to get through today.

"Yes. Let's go say hello to my dear old *dad.*"

Vas
Saturday

It was like I could see her slip on the mask of the manipulative bitch that had walked into Twelve Tables the night we met outside of our client-and-call-girl arrangement. This time, it wasn't aimed at me, which I was really happy with considering the sharpness of her smile when she grabbed the knife I'd given her so long ago from the bedside table. My arousal was a steady thrum from the moment her fingers grasped its hilt, and that only increased when she came over and held it out to me.

"Hold this for me, big guy? I might need it later, and it would ruin the look of my dress."

"It's my knife, slut," I reminded her.

"It *used* to be your knife," she retorted as she started for the door. "Not anymore."

This woman had stormed in and fucking wrecked my life, my head, and my heart, claiming not only me but seemingly every fucking guy that got close to her... and apparently my favorite fucking knife as well. But god, I loved her. I loved her more than I ever thought I could love anyone. It wasn't the time for those kinds of declarations though.

Without another word, she led the way downstairs, her heels clicking on the floor. It was almost like I could see her confidence building with each step, every movement filled with the promise of violence. She was my wet fucking dream come to life in that moment, and I knew the others felt the same. She entered the living room, and all the talking came to a complete stop.

"Damn, Nic. You really embraced Maeve's black widow status when you took over for her, huh?" Emmerich joked.

Nicholette didn't laugh, and I didn't have to see her face to know she'd probably given him a bland look and arched an eyebrow in response. When it wasn't broken, you didn't fix it. "Did Ansel say where he was bringing him?"

Blake's eyes slowly moved from head to toe, taking my woman in, obviously liking what they saw. Wulfric and Robin were more focused on Blake checking out Nic than Nic herself. Something flickered in Conrad's gaze as he studied Nic, but it was there and gone before I could completely process it. All I knew was he better stay the fuck over there with Blake because Ansel was my absolute fucking limit. From now on, I just might start stabbing any new people that came around just to get my fucking feelings across.

My brother and Bodhi made their way toward me, heated gazes trained on Nic, but I couldn't blame them. I didn't know how she'd cultivated it, or when, but she was a master of the power pose, commanding the weight of the room's attention. Sacha brushed his hand down her side but didn't say anything. Bodhi put his hands in his pockets, his cheeks flushed, and chewed his bottom lip. I couldn't tell if his reaction was because of something Sacha did or from

Nic. *Probably both, but it's his own fault if he's still feeling pent up.*

"Out front," Conrad replied, slowly standing up before grabbing a cigarette from his jacket pocket. "He should be ready by now."

"Let's start the party then, shall we?" Nic gestured for him to take the lead. I didn't see Rhodes, Alexei, or Maksim. Where the hell could they be? It didn't seem like them to miss our woman's grand entrance.

Nic fell into step beside Conrad, and they shared a look that had me questioning just how well they had gotten to know each other while I had been gone for the past few days. But then we were outside and other things grabbed my attention—a man was yelling, cursing, and threatening the people around him at the top of his lungs.

Joe Graves was big, though he wasn't nearly as big as me. He was taller and had more muscle than I had envisioned. He looked like he had played high school or college football, and he'd somehow kept that physique. Ansel had restrained him between two trees on the edge of the driveway. He was on his knees, arms strung up with ropes around his wrists that connected to tree branches on either side. *How had Ansel gotten him to stay on his knees?* If I were in this position, I'd be doing everything I could to get my feet under me, but Joe didn't even try to get off the ground.

I'd barely thought the question before the answer became apparent. The German was practically hovering next to him, carefully watching his gift to Nic with a steely look in his eyes that had probably been the last sight of many a dead man. Rhodes, Alexei, and Maksim were lurking nearby as well, which was overkill in my opinion, but hey, at least they were all working together.

I came to stand next to Rhodes, standing on the older man's unoccupied side. Maksim and Rhodes were smoking, their cold eyes fixed on Joe until Nic glided down the stairs with Conrad by her side. Blake stayed back with their other men, their brother by their side, keeping an eye on the situation from further back. The whole group tracked Conrad and Nic's movements, though the real source of their focus became clear when Conrad stepped away from my woman. Their eyes followed the young man's step away from Nic, and I didn't think I was imagining the hint of relaxation in Blake's stance when Conrad was back by their side.

I wanted to know what was up with that, the way they seemed to almost gravitate around him more than Blake, but right now I had to keep myself homed in on the reason we were all here—Nicholette.

She calmly and coolly sauntered up to the man who had raised her, and that fucking smile on her face... That alone was sharp enough to kill a man.

God, she was magnificent.

"Hello, *Dad*. So nice to see you again."

"You fucking bitch!" he spat at her, but his struggling against the ropes only resulted in hisses of pain. Ansel stood on Joe's other side with an expression I hoped to never see again. Scaring me wasn't easy, but the emptiness in his eyes as he stared down at the other man made my blood run cold. It was an expression I wasn't sure I ever wanted to see again, and I instinctively knew I was seeing only a small part of Das Gespent. A scary ass motherfucker... that's who he was.

"I can see you haven't changed much since you kicked me out." Nicholette rolled her eyes in mock disappointment as she pushed her hair over her shoulder. "I thought you'd have something more original to say after all this time."

"Let me go!"

"Now, why would I do that?" Nic asked as she arched an eyebrow. "After all the hard work that was done to get you here. That's just... ungrateful. And I know how much you hate it when people aren't grateful for the things that are done for them..."

Joe's expression changed then, smoothing out, though I could still see the anger and panic in his eyes. There wasn't any fear there... not yet, at least. He had a lot to learn, and he was going to understand that pretty quickly. The man looked around at everyone, and his lips curled up in disgust.

"I see you fixed yourself, found some dick that was enough to straighten you out." His attention jerked to Blake when they snorted, but he didn't add anything else.

"Money can do that to a girl," Nicholette drawled, stepping closer to him. "But I'll let you in on a little secret... I still like women. *A lot.* No money can change that. In fact, I'm sure you know who my last lover was before all this happened. I'd be more surprised if you didn't know her."

"You mean Maeve Cabbot? Your friend Gabriel told me all about her and you before I killed him. He was pretty fucking useless aside from that." Joe rolled his eyes. "And that haughty bitch got what was coming to her, thinking she could be in charge of anything. She needed to stick to what she knew best, and that was lying on her back to make money."

"She taught me almost everything I know, you're even more of a fucking idiot than I thought if you truly think Maeve was the one on her back. But that's really not the point since I'm with other people now."

She waved her hand to indicate all of us, and Joe followed the movement with his eyes. "So you're basically a whore? Twenty dicks is what it takes to satisfy you?"

"Not basically," she replied, a twinkle of cruel amusement in her eyes as she tapped a foot on the asphalt. "I *am* a whore and a damn good one. I make more money in one night than you did in months at your little mill job. Though I've recently learned about your side job selling children, so perhaps you're made of more money than I thought, Joe."

He froze. Hell, I couldn't even tell if he was breathing. Nicholette tilted her head, her smile firmly in place even though she wasn't amused. "What? Surprised I found out? Maybe we should start over and reintroduce ourselves. Hello, Mr. Graves. I'm the new Madame, and I have some questions that you're going to answer. Or I'm going to hurt you really fucking badly."

"You're going to hurt me anyway," Joe countered, but he finally looked nervous and unsure. *About damn time.*

"Maybe. But there's a difference in what kind of pain I'll put you through and just how long that pain will last. So tell me, what will it be? I have better things to do than waste my time talking to the likes of you."

"A waste, huh?" Joe asked, the slyness in his voice instantly putting me on high alert. "Considering the lengths you went to to get me, I must have something you want. Like the name of the man who took Thomas? Oh, did I hit the nail on the head? You and that boy."

"You know who took him then?" Nicholette asked, venom dripping from every word. "Because if *you* didn't, you wouldn't have said a name. And it's man... Good to know."

"I'm not telling you anything. I'd rather watch you fucking squirm and know you'll never find him."

"You'll let some monster have your own son just to fuck me over?"

"Yes." Joe started laughing, the sound harsh in the silence that had taken over while we all listened to their exchange.

Nicholette nodded a few times then turned to Ansel. "I need some tools and a few weapons. It seems I'll be getting my dress bloody after all. Good thing this is black."

"What tools do you need?" Ansel replied, cutting through Joe's laughter with cool precision.

She looked at the older man, thinking over the offer with the care it required. It wasn't like she could say bring me everything. A seasoned hitman like Ansel probably had *every damn thing* you could ever want for something like this. Nicholette walked over to him and whispered in his ear before he nodded and walked away.

Nicholette turned back to her father and clicked her tongue. "I would have hated to ruin the surprise for you. I know how much you love them."

What came next was one of the most brutal and wonderful torture sessions I'd ever seen. Nic used a sledgehammer to shatter Joe's legs without so much as a flinch when she repeatedly broke his bones into fucking pieces, including his foot, before moving to the other leg. Tears and snot ran down his face. His cheeks had long since been stained with the brutal shade of red that accompanied extreme pain, and the scent of piss hit us with every passing breeze.

I wrinkled my nose and looked around to see how the others were doing. Sacha's face was blank, but Bodhi seemed enraptured and turned on given the flush on his cheeks. If Oliver were here, they'd probably be messing around in the background. Rhodes, Alexei, and Maksim's expressions were all grim, though they didn't look disturbed by what was happening before them. Ansel watched Nic with hawk-like focus, his fingers sometimes twitching like he wanted to take the heavy hammer from her so that she didn't overexert herself.

Nic tossed it aside after she had smashed his second foot for the third time, seemingly happy with the damage she had caused so far. She wiped at the slight sheen of sweat on her brow as she came back around, high heels still on.

"So, let's try again. I'll even be nice and prompt you," Nic said condescendingly. "Who took Thomas?" Joe weakly shook his head in answer. "Do you really hate me that much? You paid for me, after all. Am I just a case of buyer's regret?"

He jerked at that, hissing and looking up at my woman with a death glare that had me stepping forward. Then he started laughing with an edge of hysteria taking over. "Buyer's regret? That's one way of putting it. You used to be this meek, submissive thing. You'd listen to whatever we said if it kept us happy. And then..."

"And then I started getting my own opinions?"

"No." Malice made Joe's face twist with a condescending smirk as he homed in on Nic, and I knew without a shadow of a doubt that whatever he was about to say was going to be big. "Then you became useless the moment you gave me what Miranda never could."

"What was that?"

"A son."

Oliver
Saturday

We had gotten to the cabin Friday night. The closest town was an hour away, so there were no people for miles. It was perfect for what we needed even though it wasn't much to look at—one large room with just a small bathroom. There was a tiny kitchen off along the wall, which was basically empty, two couches along the side, and the real prize was the giant table in the middle with a sheet draped on top of it.

Walking over, I pulled it off to reveal four computers, old notebooks, pens, and a bunch of other shit all tangled together.

"Nice." Atlas whistled as he walked up to the other side of the table. "Got any coffee, or are we starting tomorrow?"

"Coffee. I want to get back as soon as possible."

He didn't say anything for a minute, just staring at me. When I didn't say anything else, he turned toward the kitchen. "I'll go get it started then."

By now, we were on pot number three, and Friday had long ago turned to Saturday. Atlas had claimed one side of the table while I got the other, both of us getting to work without a fuss. Besides sharing information back and forth, we didn't really talk, just did our own thing... which was good and bad. It gave me way too much time alone with my thoughts, and I had plenty of them with everything that was going on.

Nic.

My past.

The man across from me who could be my brother...

What the fuck has my life turned into?!

Nicholette had been part of the same trafficking ring I had been in as a child. Thank god she'd only been bought once. And wasn't it sad that that was my measuring stick? Flashes of my past kept hitting me as I dug into the LLCs that were hidden behind the Sacred Heart Adoption Agency.

Being naked and chained up in a dark room. Bright spotlights showing me off, making it impossible to see anyone else. The vulnerability, fear, and humiliation as I heard numbers being called. That was the first time. After that, I was simply traded, sold through private deals in someone's home, given away to pay off a debt, or as a result of someone being bored. There was also the lovely explanation that I'd aged out of my owner's preferences.

Sick fucking bastards.

I had been called so many names that after I'd managed to get away from the last person, I picked a new one. I chose a name I'd never been called before, something that just felt right... Who knew if it was the one I'd been born with or not. *Why the hell am I thinking about all of this right now?!*

But I knew why. The answer was sitting across from me.

Atlas.

No last name or anything, just Atlas. Curly blond hair curtained his face as his serious blue eyes studied the screen. He was silently mouthing whatever he was reading, and I looked away before he noticed I was staring. I couldn't deny we looked similar, but that was it. The memory of my brother was fuzzy, barely more than a feeling by now. I couldn't recall a face or a single feature of the boy.

But Blake's words spun around in my head, and the envelope kept popping back to the front of my mind. How did they even get my DNA? At least Atlas had looked just as shocked by that as I did. Or maybe it was the idea that we could be related?

I had more questions than answers, and it was pissing me the fuck off. Part of me wished I had opened the envelope so I could confirm the answer was no and keep going forward with my life. Before we left, I had warned him not to bring up the brother thing, but here I was... thinking about it non-fucking-stop.

"You find anything?" Atlas' question made me jump and curse. A deep chuckle was his answer, then came the scraping of his chair along the wood floor. "Let me make another pot of coffee. I'm struggling too."

"They're good," I complained, rubbing my face as I leaned away from the computer screen. My eyes were dry, and exhaustion pulled at me, a reminder that I hadn't slept in almost twenty-four hours. "I can't go back without something. I need a location at least."

"A few of the shell companies have been in the same place, so I'm keeping track of everything that overlaps," Atlas replied as he dumped more coffee in the machine. "But they definitely created a huge web of shit for us to sort through."

"I wonder what the others are up to," I muttered,

wishing like hell I had Bodhi with me. Fuck, just recalling how he had sucked my dick the last time I was sitting at a desk was enough to make me horny as hell.

"I don't know Nic well enough to guess," Atlas replied with dry amusement. "But if they're anything like Blake, I'm betting it's bloody."

"How did you meet Nic?" I asked, both my curiosity and my need for a break getting the best of me.

The other man turned to face me, leaning back against the counter beside the coffee maker. His expression was careful and contemplative before he switched to looking at his bare feet.

"I met her through Blake. Nic needed some documents, and I set them up for her. I learned my skills as a forger before I figured out hacking."

"That's it?" I asked, unable to help myself.

"Meaning did I sleep with her?" Atlas asked with a hint of laughter in his voice. His blue eyes were practically twinkling. "No. My shit... it's complicated with stuff like that. Blake and Emmerich slept with her, not me or anyone else in our group in case you were curious."

"Not that it matters." I shrugged, trying to act nonchalant. I didn't care that she slept with other people, so why did the idea that he might have irritated me? I guess there was something different about her sleeping with strangers rather than her sleeping with my possible brother.

Now that Blake had put the question in my head, I wanted answers, but I hated that I wanted them.

"I can't stop thinking about it either," Atlas said into the silence. "The envelope Blake offered. The DNA test. I... I lost my brother a long time ago."

"What happened?" I asked quietly, not looking up at him.

He didn't say anything for a minute, then I heard the soft tread of feet and the slide of a zipper. Looking up, I caught him digging through his backpack before he turned to face me. My vision tunneled on the sight of the crinkled white envelope in his hands. It was still sealed, but it was here with us.

"I didn't open it. After you walked out of the office all kinds of pissed, I grabbed it from Blake and stuffed it in my pocket before following after you." Atlas took a deep breath. "I wondered for a really long time about my brother and what had happened to him, but this isn't just about me. It's about you possibly having answers too, so... I grabbed it and figured if you brought it up, we could decide whether to open it or destroy it together."

"Sometimes answers are more painful than wondering."

"But the pain will heal. The what ifs never go away," Atlas replied before walking over and placing the envelope on the table beside me. Distantly, I registered the beeping sound that meant the fresh coffee was ready but I couldn't look away from the envelope and the man in front of me.

"Why would they even test our DNA? *How* did they test it?!" I asked, trying to make light of this clusterfuck situation.

Atlas grinned, but it didn't reach his eyes. "Like I said before, Blake is a force of nature. I don't even *want* to know how they got a sample from you. They mean well, but sometimes they don't show it in the best ways."

"Sounds like an understatement considering..." I tipped my head toward the envelope. "Anyway, compared to my past, what's one involuntary medical test? At least it didn't hurt." Dark humor was something we apparently had in common because Atlas laughed then, a real laugh, though it was full of just as much pain as amusement.

"Think we should open it?" I asked when our laughter died down.

Atlas snagged a chair and sat down beside me. "What *do* you remember? I know you said nothing, but was that just because of what Blake did or because you actually don't recall?"

"Bright lights. A fair. Wondering where my brother was," I managed before having to clear my throat. "Then a lot of things I'd rather not remember at all but can't get out of my head. Eventually, I got away and fell in with that crazy lot. Then Nic showed up."

Silence.

I wasn't sure what I expected in response to my concise story, but silence wasn't it. Glancing over, I stilled at the expression on Atlas' face. He was pale now, and if he hadn't been sitting down, I would have worried he'd pass out.

"What?"

"A fair?" he choked out. "Are you sure?"

"Yeah," I answered slowly, knots twisting in my stomach. "Were you at one too?"

"I was at the fair with my younger brother when he went missing," Atlas said so softly I wouldn't have heard him if he hadn't been near me. "I turned away to get something, then... he was just gone. I spent the whole night looking for him until I got kicked out. I went back the next day to look again, and that's when I was taken."

"You?" I asked him, shocked.

Atlas nodded a few times, a solemn look on his face. "But not by this trafficking ring."

It was easy to read between the lines, but shock filled me nonetheless. "The Förstners?! They took you, yet you still work with them?"

"It's complicated." Atlas managed a weak half smile. "It's a long story that's hard to tell. But no matter how I got here, I *do* love Blake. Them and the others, they're all it for me."

"I couldn't—"

"I wasn't taken as young, and like I said, the things that happened to me are complicated. Blake is my nightmares and dreams come to life in so many ways, but there isn't one day I wouldn't fight to be right there with them. They fight the same things too."

"Apparently, we both have a thing for broken people. Makes us feel like a complete mess," I said, falling back on a weak attempt at humor, then I snagged the envelope off the table and held it out to him. "Together?"

Blood only got people so far, but there was something in my gut that told me I should open it. If we weren't brothers, then I could move on and so could Atlas. And if we were related... Well, at least I knew Atlas wouldn't push if I needed time—not more than I could handle anyway. I was sure Blake would be the one to watch out for on that front.

Atlas nodded, and neither of us commented on the other's shaky hands as we ripped it open and pulled out the papers. I skimmed the report and went for the letter of explanation. My hands went numb, and I heard my heart pounding in my ears.

'Based on the samples provided, I am one hundred percent confident in saying these two individuals are siblings.'

The silence in the cabin was deafening.

What should I say? What do I do?

The bravery I'd had just moments ago abandoned me in the face of the test results. Luckily, I was saved by dings on both our computers. Letting go of the paper, I whirled around to check the notification on my screen.

"What the fuck?!" I cursed, going up to my computer to check that all the information displayed was correct.

There's no way.

Oh, this is bad.

This is really, really fucking bad.

"What is it?"

"Check your computer," I told him curtly, not ready to look at him right now. *My brother. I really don't have time for this.* "What did you find?"

"Same thing you did," Atlas replied grimly, and that was when I looked up, knowing what thought would be reflected back at me. We needed to get back to Ansel's now.

"Dump the coffee or throw it in some cups. We need to leave."

"What about this place?" he asked, moving to do as I ordered while I memorized everything on the screen then shut it all down.

"I got that taken care of."

Without asking anything else, he poured the coffee in some cups. A few minutes later, we were out the door and on the road. I sipped my coffee, praying that adrenaline gave us enough juice to get back to the others.

There was no cell phone service out here, so there was no use in turning on my phone until we were a ways down the road. He better start driving faster because my entire fucking life is riding on the line here.

"Oli... the papers... You know what that means?" Atlas finally broached the subject, his eyes still on the road.

"Yeah," I replied seriously. "You're going to be an uncle."

Atlas somehow paled more than I thought humanly

possible, but I grinned, delighted that I could already fuck with him. I might not be ready to call him my brother yet, but I couldn't resist causing a little bit of mischief. I couldn't say it out loud, but I could practice saying it in my head. *What are little brothers for?*

Nicholette
Saturday

The only thing that kept me upright and not slack-jawed from shock was Maeve's teachings. My heart pounded in my ears, and my breathing sounded extra loud. The world seemed to slow down and speed up around me at the same time as I tilted my head at him. *Keep every emotion on lockdown. He'll just use them against you.*

"Miranda was never pregnant. Never could get that old cow to breed, but you... You had no problems at all. You were small and young, but that just meant your body bounced back quickly. Guess that worked in your favor given the job you got. That's all you've ever been good for."

"Who took him?" I asked, ignoring the taunts and the bombshell he'd dropped at my feet. *Concentrate. Concentrate on what needs to be taken care of then deal with the fallout afterward.*

"Our son? Find him yourself. Miranda died trying to protect him, you know. I saw her get shot in the face when she tried to reach for him. She might have hated you, but she never hated that boy."

"So just the monologue then?" I asked, my rage and

pain simmering under the surface. I stared down at the man who'd just admitted to raping me and forcing me to have his child when I was so fucking young I couldn't even think about it. "Rhodes, I need the four motorcycles and those chains I mentioned earlier."

"What do you have planned, Nic?" Sacha asked as he approached me. There was pure rage in his face, but his tone was nothing but caring. He stopped beside me and held out a hand, a casual and perfect way to give me control of my body after learning how little I'd had as a child. I took it and let him pull me close, taking a deep breath to help me keep it together until this was done. No way would Joe see me cry today. He'd been the cause of too many of my tears already.

"History was always one of my favorite subjects in school. There was one thing that always fascinated me, and I'm interested to see it in person." I ran my hands over his arms while directing my words at Rhodes and the others. "Quartering. Using four horses to pull a body in different directions until it was ripped into pieces. Motorcycles would be a good substitute for the modern era, don't you think so?"

"Holy shit." I couldn't tell who muttered it, but they sounded more impressed than appalled. These really were my people.

"So, hotshot, think you can handle that for me?"

"We need another bike," he rasped as he indicated himself, Maks, and Vas. "I'll call Razor."

"You can't do this!" Joe yelled out, and I savored the desperation in his voice, committing it to memory so I could replay it later when I was forced to face the feelings his confession had stirred in me. Rhodes pulled out his phone as he and Maks strode away. Alexei and Vas stayed behind, staring at Joe like they were trying to figure out just how whole he needed to be .

I pulled out of Sacha's arms and strode over to Joe. With a hard yank on his hair, I tugged him upward, knowing his broken bones would only shift and grind with the forced movement. "I can do anything I want with you. There's no one here who can stop me or would want to. In fact, they'd all help. If I had asked them to help me pull you apart in a game of fucking tug-of-war, they would have lined up. And I'm sure I can think of some ways to pass the time before our friend gets here. The only thing that matters is you're still alive so I can hear you scream when you die."

"That does leave a lot of leeway," Vas rumbled to the others. He was pissed, and when he cracked his knuckles, I knew his tool of choice would be his bare hands.

"I think we can think of some ways to keep him entertained," Ansel said softly, the promise of pain in his voice making me shiver in anticipation. "I'd hate to be considered rude to my guest."

"Have at him."

Vas pulled back and punched him in the face just as Ansel opened the box he had brought with him. It was filled with an array of small blades, their edges super thin and sharp. I knew from experience they would cut through skin like paper, leaving a trail of bright pain that made you breathless. As Ansel considered which one to start with, Alexei threw a punch at the restrained man, making Joe grunt. The contrast of pure physical brutality and the finesse of Ansel's skills made me appreciate them all the more.

The clearing of a throat caught my attention, and I looked over to see Bodhi standing there with a serious expression on his face. He kept me company, and I felt Sacha's nearness again when he came over to join us.

"I don't want to talk about it," I told them, my voice empty. "I can't even process the idea that I'm— that he's—"

"That's understandable," Bodhi reassured me firmly, cutting off my rambling.

"Anything you need, Nic. We're here," Emmerich called out, and I looked back. Em, Blake, and the others were all so fucking serious and angry on my behalf.

Before I could respond to his offer, a phone started to ring. Bodhi reached into his pants, and his eyebrows raised at whatever he saw on the screen.

"Oli?"

"Where the fuck is Nic?! I called her three damn times, and no one answered. Neither did Sacha for that matter." Oli was yelling loud enough for me to hear him without it being on speakerphone.

"Oli—" Bodhi started, but I shook my head, a hint of a smile tugging at my lips.

"We've been busy entertaining Joe," I drawled as Bodhi hit the speakerphone button so we could all hear. Just then, Joe screamed out thanks to Vas landing a solid punch in his stomach. "What did you find?"

"Sounds like you all are having fun without me. Fucking rude if you ask me."

"Oli," Sacha reprimanded, and Oli let out a loud sigh.

"Okay fine, focusing. I think I know who your stalker is," Oli replied grimly. I stilled, my anxiety rising and my stomach turning over. "We confirmed through multiple channels that there is only one person who has connections with the Ashview trafficking ring, the Förstners, *and* the Lords of Chaos. All with the influence and power to do all of this, plus, you already know him."

Ansel pulled away from Joe, as did Vas and Alexei. Everyone was staring at the phone Bodhi was holding.

"Who?" I asked, trying to brace myself for the answer.

Nothing could have prepared me though.

"Christopher. Over half the LLCs related to the trafficking ring lead back to him or his business. He's the one that ratted out William to Rhodes so it took the pressure off him—"

"And it meant he probably got insider updates of what we knew," Sacha cursed.

"Plus, he was a trusted member of the Förstner circle or at least trusted enough," I said gently, taking in Ansel's completely empty expression. That killing calm of his taking over. "And someone I trusted as well."

"Fuck," Vas muttered, shaking some blood from his hands.

"How far out are you?"

"A few hours," Atlas said from the background. "But we haven't slept since Thursday night."

"Then I suggest taking turns," I told him firmly. "We have a lot to do when you get back."

With that, we ended the call. All of us stood there, no one moving or speaking until Joe started to laugh hysterically.

"Of course you trusted him. He's always had a soft spot for you, Nicholette. So fucking easy from the beginning, and it seems you haven't changed a bit."

"The beginning?" I asked, unable to help myself.

"You think I was the only one interested in buying you?" Joe scoffed, cruelty dripping from every word. "He doesn't usually do young, but you... Nicholette, you have had him wrapped around your finger since you were a child."

"Vas."

"Yes?"

"Rip his tongue out."

"That will probably kill him," Sacha pointed out.

"Then cut it up using my knife." I gave Vas a cruel grin as he took out his old knife. "Over and over again until we can pull him apart completely. Just make sure he doesn't die while you play with him, big guy."

Vas grinned at me, too excited to care about the nickname, and asked his brother if he was joining him. Sacha pressed a kiss to the top of my head then rolled up his sleeves as he approached Joe and Vas. They got to work while Joe wasted his breath pleading for mercy that neither Russian had.

"Em. Blake. Find me Christopher. Kill anyone who gets in your way. No exceptions. I don't give a shit who you get rid of along the way."

"Nic..." Alexei finally spoke up as the two Germans replied that they were on it. "I'll update Rhodes and Maksim. Rhodes might have some more information too."

I nodded in acknowledgment then watched him stride away toward the others. Blake and Emmerich had left, following my orders, with their men in tow. Ansel had disappeared at some point, which left Bodhi and I essentially alone in our own little bubble.

"If this gets to be too much around me right now, I'll understand," I told him, fully expecting him to walk away, but he surprised me. There was a breath of silence between us, then he gently grasped my hand.

"Never too much," Bodhi corrected me, and I turned to look at him. His gaze was steady and unwavering. "*You're* never too much. I'm here for whatever you need."

I searched his face and saw what he was offering. He

was offering me control, someone to ground myself in while my life spiraled out of control. I knew they would wait for me before finishing off Joe, so taking Bodhi up on his offer wasn't something I could pass up right now. Plus, I missed him. I missed *us*, and I'd be damned if I didn't need him now more than ever. Leading the way, I pulled him inside, tugging him along until I got to the closest bathroom I could find. I slammed the door shut and wasted no time, crashing our lips against each other's. We were reconnecting after all this time apart.

Finally.

We came together in a brutal kiss, losing ourselves in each other as we pulled at our clothing. Bodhi's hands were firmer than normal as he tugged at my dress, and I ripped his shirt off, tossing it aside so I could feel his bare skin.

"Are you sure?" I asked, needing to make sure he was really okay with this.

"Use me, Nic. I trust you to not go too far."

Trust.

He trusted me even without Oli here to help balance things out and guide us so Bodhi didn't get triggered. The fact that he trusted me right now, even with everything pushing me over the edge, spoke volumes about how far we'd come.

Leaning forward, I gently kissed him. I cupped his face and moved him just how I wanted him while I deepened the kiss, loving how he moaned into it. My hands ran through his hair before they began their descent toward his jeans. I slowly undid them and pushed them to the ground, smiling against his lips when I felt his bare cock.

"Commando, pet? You really were excited for today." He blushed and muttered something about not having anything at Sacha's place. I couldn't resist the urge to tease him a little bit. "And Sacha didn't have anything you could have worn?"

Bodhi shrugged, his blush going down his neck now. "I'd rather just go without."

"Show me how much you missed me, Bodhi," I commanded, dropping the teasing. "No coming until I say you can."

He looked around the room like he was trying to figure out how to do what he wanted. "Wish this had been a bedroom."

"We could always find one," I told him with a smile. "I have no idea where one is, but I've never minded an audience."

He paused, then a light I'd never seen before filled his eyes. Suddenly, he scooped me up and left the bathroom. We didn't go far, just out to the living room, and he sat me down on the couch before getting on his knees in front of me. It reminded me of the first time we were together after Oli chased us both. He'd wrung so many orgasms from my body that I was sensitive for days afterward.

He pushed my legs further apart and settled between my thighs. Before starting, he reached up to rest a hand on my slightly swollen stomach, a scared and almost unsure expression flickering on his face. Then he directed his attention to my pussy. A slow lick of his tongue down my center was my only warning before he ate me out in earnest. I cried out his name as he played with my clit and fucked me with his skillful tongue.

My back bowed when he pulled back right before I fell into my orgasm, making me whimper and tug at his hair. I needed more. I tilted my hips and grabbed the back of his head to shove him into my pussy, grinding against him in retaliation.

"You've gotten bolder, pet. I'm a fan of it, but teasing has consequences. Eat me out like you mean it, and maybe our reunion will actually include an orgasm for you."

Bodhi whimpered against me before starting to tongue fuck me over and over again. Repositioning, I propped my feet up on the coffee table, giving me more leverage to keep riding his face while I cupped one of my breasts to play with my nipples. He slid his hands under my ass and pulled me further down, squeezing me hard enough that I knew I'd have bruises later. *Fuck yes, I missed this.*

When my orgasm got closer, I grabbed his hair and rode him harder, not caring if he could breathe. I fell into my orgasm, losing myself in pleasure while I cried out his name. When he tapped on my thigh, I loosened my hold, loving his shaky breath on my skin. The only thing that topped that was the sight of his face covered in my juices.

Sliding up my body, he smoothly thrust into me before pressing his lips to mine. I wrapped my arms around him and kissed him back. The kiss stayed slow and lazy while I savored the taste of myself on his tongue. His moans and whimpers made me grin, and I pulled back so there was just a whisper of space between us.

"You can come whenever you want, pet. Fill me up to remind me I'm yours."

"Shit," Bodhi whimpered, his rhythm faltering before he started pounding into me.

Those rougher strokes tipped him over the edge. We groaned each other's names as we rocked into each other, savoring the feel of *us*. He pressed a quick kiss to my lips before resting his cheek on my chest.

"I love you."

"I love you too, Bodhi," I replied warmly, absentmindedly running a hand through his hair.

Heavy footsteps caught my attention before someone cleared their throat behind me. With a big grin, I held Bodhi to me and tilted my head back. Alexei was standing there with a heated look in his eyes.

"Yes?" I asked, not the least bit ashamed. Bodhi shifted against me so he could see who had joined us.

"I hate to interrupt, but you have a call."

"Who?"

"Allen. He needs you to come down to the station tomorrow."

I hummed, thinking over what needed to be done. Thankfully, I felt much more clear headed now. "Tell him tomorrow at noon or so. I'll get in touch with Roderick to confirm when he can meet me there. Plus, Atlas and Oli should be back by then."

"And maybe someone will have located Christopher by then too," Bodhi tacked on.

"Maybe," I replied, my mind still not ready to think about someone I trusted betraying me like that.

"I'll let him know," Alexei replied softly before leaning over to press a kiss to my lips. He walked away, already on the phone, to give us another moment of privacy.

Suddenly, the front door slammed open. Maks' voice boomed, filling the house. "Nic! Razor is here, so get your ass out here."

Guess the real fun is about to begin.

Wrenn
Saturday

"What do you mean she's pregnant?!" Christopher asked, his face purple.

A huff of laughter escaped me, and searing pain rippled through my body as my probably broken ribs shifted and the tears from the bullet wound were pulled. Nic's aim was bad, so she hadn't managed to kill me, something I'd never forgive her for. My life had become nothing but pain since the moment he dragged me into this room—beatings, rape, torture. There wasn't an inch of me that he hadn't violated, but the worst part, the *very worst* part was that Thomas was made to watch it all.

His long hair was unkempt, hanging around his face as if he could block out what was happening around him. He had looked haunted, scared, but there was now a spark of shock and hope in his gaze at the mention of his sister.

Unlike me, he'll be safe around her. A shitty thought, but true nonetheless. The girl I had fallen in love with was long gone, and the moment she pulled the trigger, killing my brother, I knew just how different she was. Nic had warned me, hell, the men had told me as well, but I couldn't let go of the girl I remembered.

Christopher had left me alone in this room for a few hours after raping me for the first time. During that time, I had caught Thomas up on the fact that his sister was looking for him and made him memorize the names of her men or others he could trust. Because as much as I wanted to kill Nic right now, as much as I hated her, I wouldn't take it out on Thomas. I'd help him get away even if it cost me my life.

Even after everything, you still love her. I pushed that thought away. There was no way I could love her. I would hold that lie close until I couldn't anymore.

Smack.

Blood pooled in my mouth as my head whipped to the side, then rough hands grabbed my face, forcing me to look at Christopher.

"How are you so sure?"

"Pregnancy test. Doctor visits. Morning sickness," I mumbled as he shook me. There was no reason to hold back any of the information. I needed him angry. I needed him distracted to have my plan work out. *Just a little bit longer.*

"Finally," Christopher replied gleefully, and a horrible smile filled his face as he let me go. "I knew she would be able to breed again." *Again?* My thoughts must have been clear on my face because Christopher chuckled tauntingly. "She already has a child, Wrenn, a son actually. In fact, it's someone you know very well."

A slight wave of his hand indicated Thomas. The boy was sitting there, deathly pale, his wide eyes staring at Christopher. *What the actual fuck?!*

"Don't look so worried!" Christopher grinned at the boy. "I'm not your father. That was Joe's doing... Got

Nicholette and became obsessed. Miranda was always a fucking frigid bitch. Couldn't manage to have a baby, though she put her body through hell trying. Found a doctor who made all the legal documents be in her name, and there you have it... Miranda had you, not their nine year old daughter."

My stomach lurched, tears stinging my eyes as I thought of Nic. Did she know about this? If she did, she was one of the best actors I'd ever seen. She loved Thomas, but I'd had no idea, none, that he was actually her son.

"That can't be—" Thomas mumbled.

Christopher just laughed. "Of course it is. But don't worry, you'll be seeing her soon enough. Between finally confirming she's pregnant and everything that's happened, I'm going to get her. I'm done playing nice, and I'm *very* sick of waiting."

"This is nice?" I asked, unable to hold my tongue.

"You're still alive," he crooned, and out of the corner of my eye, I saw Thomas shifting. He was careful to limit his movements, making sure he didn't give away that his ropes had been loosened. Christopher had been sloppy in leaving us alone. He'd counted on my broken bones to stop me from being able to give Thomas any aid, but I'd swallowed the pain and forced myself over to the boy so I could work on his bindings.

I need to keep Christopher distracted so Thomas can get away.

"Nic isn't going to come just because you took me. I've told you that before."

"I remember seeing you together at the bar that night." He stepped closer to where I was strung up. My broken wrists had been screaming in pain since he wrapped rope around them, tying them to the top of two concrete pillars. "Flirting, talking... She cares."

"That was a while back, and we were just friends. After what happened, she isn't going to go out of her way for me. The best you're going to get is a thank you."

"She still thought of you, Wrenn, after all these years. Maybe it's not the love you wanted from her, but she does still love you in some way or she wouldn't have reacted at all."

"Either way, doesn't that just fucking kill you? She feels that way about me after all these years, but you're just some client who has to pay to get her to look your way."

He growled, backhanding me hard enough I saw stars. "Watch your fucking mouth and remember who you're talking to."

"Emotional," I taunted after taking a shaky breath. "She's with all these men, and you aren't even an afterthought. But *I* could come in and rock her entire world."

"You are nothing!" he screamed, and I flinched when spit hit my face. "Nothing but a useless cunt. Brought your brother in with those criminals, how else did you think that was going to play out? Then you were fucking gullible enough to be kidnapped. Useless."

"Maybe. Maybe you'll kill me, and I'll never get a chance to see what could be. But I won." I smiled, ignoring the sting caused by my split lip cracking open and starting to bleed again. Hysterical laughter fell from my lips as he stared at me, confused, then looked around. The air was filled with his curses when he realized that Thomas was gone. Nic's brother had used the opportunity I'd given him to run, and I hoped he made it. I hoped no one else got to him and hurt him.

As I faced the man responsible for stalking Nic, murdering countless women, and selling children for fucking profit, I knew I was going to die for this. A horrible, slow death.

I hate her.

I love her.

And now, I am finally going to be free of her.

Searing, sharp pain erupted between my legs as Christopher thrust a knife inside of me. My screams made my throat raw, and his taunts became distant echoes, mere ghosts of sound, while he fucked me with the blade, then his dick. Hard hands, pinches, and searing pain dominated what was left of my existence. I was bleeding to death, I knew that, and there was nothing I could do to stop his thrusts, to escape from the brutal rape that would become my final memories.

I forced myself to laugh at him, but then I thanked him for freeing me before the darkness took over.

Finally, I was done with Nicholette Graves.

Nicholette
Sunday

The roaring of engines, chains clattering together, and screams blended into a symphony. Then that was all overtaken by the satisfying tearing and wet squelch of meat plopping on the asphalt driveway as my men and Razor ripped Joe apart. It was everything I had ever wanted.

But instead of fully enjoying it, my mind kept coming back to the bombshell Joe had dropped. *Thomas is my son.* The numbers had hit me in the aftermath of Joe's death. I had only been nine when I had him. *Nine.* What the hell was wrong with him? What kind of sick fuck would take advantage of a fucking small child? And... Maeve said it looked like Thomas' was theirs. Paperwork and everything looked good. But with a trafficking ring it would be easy to get a legitimate doctor to forge those documents, at least that's what Blake and Em said when they came back to the house a few hours later. They were taking the night to regroup and keep looking for Christopher.

Ansel had kept himself busy, reaching out to his contacts. My other guys all stayed close, keeping an eye on me while we waited for Oli and Atlas to get back. My life was a complete fucking shitshow, and I would give *a lot* to have just a moment of fucking peace.

Guess that was why I found myself alone in the living room, flipping through channels to find something to watch. I had laid in bed for a few hours, but when sleep didn't come, I slipped out of the room. Sacha and Bodhi didn't move, so I left a note beside Sacha's phone.

What I really need is food. I pressed a hand to my stomach as it started to rumble. *Too bad there's no fucking delivery out here.*

"Can't sleep?" a tired voice asked, and I looked over my shoulder. Conrad was standing there with big circles under his eyes.

I shook my head. "Too much to process from today. You?"

"Nightmares." He didn't say anything else, but he didn't have to. I understood what it was like to be haunted by dreams that made it impossible to sleep.

"Want to join me?" I gestured at the TV. "I'm trying to find a good horror movie to watch. Oh, can you cook? I can't, and I didn't see any leftovers. I'm starving."

Conrad's face cleared a little bit, and a hint of a smile was here and gone before he started for the kitchen. "I'll see what's there. You find a movie?"

"Thank you!" I called out, switching my attention back to the tv. I flipped through a ton of options, but nothing really stood out so I settled on *Criminal Minds*. It was more of a police drama than I usually liked, but with so many interesting killers on the show, it would be enough to catch my attention. At least I hoped so.

"*Criminal Minds?*"

"I already watched all of *Hannibal*." I sighed as Conrad handed me a plate with a sandwich and chips. He settled down on a nearby chair, placing bowls of popcorn and chips on the coffee table. "The movies and the show. Everything else is some kind of action movie, or it's already ending. At least we can see some murders happening in this show."

"Which is a requirement?" he asked.

"Duh, otherwise we can't rank them or figure out if it's actually something that could happen."

"You do that?"

"Of course," I told him seriously, eating a chip. "You should have heard the back and forth when I watched *Saw* for the first time. It was... interesting."

"*Saw*?"

"Yeah, with Jigsaw? Nevermind. In my opinion, it's more of a gorefest than anything else."

I hit play and settled in to see some guy burning alive in a dorm room. *This could be fun.* We settled in and watched a few episodes, commenting back and forth about the murders. A poison episode made me really appreciate Con's knowledge, and I mentally filed away the fact that those were his speciality. *Could be useful later.*

It was silent for a while before Conrad suddenly spoke. "You said that you were a prostitute, a call girl..." His voice trailed off, but I stayed silent, waiting for him to continue. "And that you became personally acquainted with rape as a professional hazard."

"Yeah," I replied softly. "Fucking twisted, isn't it?"

"Did you ever get over it?"

"No," I told him honestly, shaking my head and chancing a look in his direction. He stared at me with haunted eyes that made me wish I could hug him. "I never got over it. I killed them. I pushed down the memories so I could function, but I never got over it. Not any of the times it happened. I think the person I used to be died. Parts of me were lost every time it happened, and now I'm someone new. If that makes sense?"

Conrad nodded slowly, a sheen of tears in his eyes. "I don't know how to do that. To be someone new."

I stared at him for a moment before softly replying, "You're already doing it. You *are* someone new. That takes time, Con, and nothing will make the violations fade from your mind. I found something that gives me back the feeling of power and embraced it—sex, killing, both together. It's a rush. Find something that works for you at your own pace. Like I said, I've had years and plenty of other trauma to deal with."

Conrad rubbed his fingers together, his silent need for nicotine clear. We both fell silent as we watched the show again.

"Thank you."

"If you need anything, someone to listen who you aren't fucking, just reach out. I'm always here, even if you just need someplace safe to be left alone."

Conrad whispered a rough thank you again before we lost ourselves in the show. I was curious about what had happened to him, but I wasn't going to pry. No, we just settled in. Over the few hours we watched the show, we became comfortable enough with each other that when I said something sarcastic, he threw popcorn at me in retaliation. I just smirked and popped it into my mouth, not sorry at all.

We were laughing at something on the screen when the front door opened. I heard familiar tired voices that instantly had me perking up. In walked Atlas and Oli, and the latter gave me an exhausted smile.

"Are we interrupting?" Right then, a scream from

someone on the screen made Atlas turn to the TV, but Oli just closed his eyes. "Why?"

"It's a cop show," I told him, grabbing his hand and urging him to sit beside me. "Nothing scary. There weren't any good movies on."

"That's not reassuring coming from you." Oli groaned, but he flopped down beside me and tugged me close to him.

"Only you could be so obsessed with killing people but hate horror movies," I teased him.

"That's more information than I needed to know," Atlas joked as he sat down on the arm of Con's chair. He carefully looked over the other man, who smiled up at him, and it reached all the way up to his blue eyes. Atlas gave him one of his own before sliding an arm around him, and they cuddled together on the chair.

"I mean, that's really just the tip of the iceberg," I started, but Oli interrupted me.

"If you keep talking, then the next time that happens, I'll just make you watch Bodhi and me have all the fun."

"I like watching," I told him gamely, and Oli muttered something about me being a pain in the ass before he grabbed the blanket from the back of the couch.

"Just shut up." Grinning, I leaned over and kissed him, snuggling into his side.

Atlas and Conrad talked softly until Con shifted around so he and Atlas were curled up together. The four of us fell asleep with the rising sun to the sounds of someone being electrocuted. I had to be up in a few hours, but right now it didn't matter.

For at least a little while, I had some peace.

Rhodes
Sunday

THE SMELL of ash and smoke was still heavy in the air as I walked around the remains of what had been my home for the past ten years. There had been nothing left of it besides the shells of buildings; everything inside of it had been destroyed. I scuffed a boot along the ground, thinking of my woman. She had been tucked in close to Sacha and Vas when I last saw her, and although I hadn't wanted to leave, I had a few things to take care of.

Well, one thing in particular.

Christopher.

A man I was going to kill with my bare fucking hands if I got the chance. He didn't deserve to breathe the same air as Nic and after what he did to the women here, to my Nic... he'll be lucky if all I do is kill him.

A customer who had become a friend of sorts, a confidant, betrayed me and everyone who mattered to me. I clenched my fists, wishing like hell I had something or someone to lash out at. If he had truly done this... He had taken away everything I had built for the Lords of Chaos, our safe place and headquarters. We'd have to be careful and make sure our presence was still felt in the city. No one was going to swoop in and steal our territory away because of this.

"Rhodes..." Razor's voice pulled me from my thoughts. I glanced over at the other man who met my hard stare with one of his own. "We'll rebuild."

"We will," I replied roughly, pulling out a cigarette and lighting it. I inhaled deeply, savoring the taste of it on my tongue before walking toward Razor. "Let's go back. I want to check out something before we go to Ansel's."

The place Nic had given me—a fresh start, a landing place until I figured out what the club was going to do. When she showed me the paperwork, I couldn't believe that she would just hand over the place. I hadn't told anyone else about it, wanting to make sure it would work for us before I announced anything.

"Excuse me," a small voice said, breaking the morning silence.

We stopped dead in our tracks, Razor's hand immediately found the gun on his hip as we eyed the young boy frozen a few feet away from us. He had a bloody and bruised face, and his tired blue eyes watched us from the shadows of a nearby alleyway. Fear came off of him in waves, and he was swaying on his feet.

"You should go, boy," Razor said first, his voice gentle despite the blunt command. "This isn't a safe place for you to be."

My eyes narrowed as he shifted his weight from one foot to the other, paling even more before he looked at the burned buildings behind us. "Are you— Are you the MC? Lords... something. I can't remember."

His voice cracked, sounding strained, as he focused on me in particular. He took a half step forward into the full light of the sun, and my heart skipped a beat. A flash of the picture Bodhi had found filled my mind, so I motioned at Razor to hold.

"What's your name?"

He bit his lip, and tears fell down one of his swollen cheeks. "Are you— Are you Rhodes? Wrenn told me— She told me to look for you or..."

"Yes, I'm Rhodes. Are you Thomas?" He nodded a few times, and Razor released a shaky breath, relaxing his stance. "Were you followed?"

"I don't know," he replied softly, wincing as he rubbed his throat. "I just... Where's Nic?"

"I can take you to her," I told him, offering my hand. I waited patiently, letting him come to me. After the abuse I could tell he'd suffered, I knew better than to be too physically assertive. Painstakingly, he walked to me, and every bruise that was revealed made my anger rise, but I kept my face blank, not wanting him to think it was directed at him. Nic would kill me if something happened to him.

When he placed a shaking hand in mine, I grasped it carefully, not wanting to hurt him more, and looked at Razor. "Get my bike somewhere safe. There's no way he'd make it on the back of one like he is."

"I'll call Blade to ride my bike and take yours back to Ansel's place. If that works for you?" Razor replied. I told him that was fine, and he stepped away to handle that.

I reached into my back pocket and called Ansel. He'd left before Joe was killed, and I would bet anything he was around Ashview, waiting to see what popped up in his search for the asshole that had betrayed us all. A few rings, then I was greeted with silence.

"I need a ride."

"What happened to your bike?" Ansel asked, sounding distracted.

"I also need a doctor," I told him, not bothering to answer his question. "I'm at the old compound. Come get us ASAP."

"Us?"

"I have Thomas."

There came a few curse words in German before the call ended.

"Wrenn is dead, isn't she?" Thomas broke the silence, and I looked down at him. His gaze was so solemn and innocent, with tears bright in his eyes. I couldn't find it in myself to lie to him no matter how hard the truth might be.

"Yes, she probably is."

Thomas swallowed hard and nodded a few times before falling silent. We didn't have to wait long before Ansel pulled up, and I got into the back with Thomas. No one spoke as Ansel got us on the road again, leaving the city and heading toward his home.

"The doctor is coming to the house?" I asked.

"Yes," Ansel replied, meeting my gaze in the rearview mirror. "I tried to call Nic, but she didn't answer her phone. So I guess we'll see what happens when we get there."

A small weight hit my chest at that point, and I looked down to see Thomas had fallen asleep, his body sliding with the turning of the car. I shifted him slightly and wrapped an arm around his shoulder so he wouldn't move more than was necessary. The poor kid deserved some peaceful sleep.

My heart felt heavy, full, and I knew we were so fucking screwed. Nic's brother... her son... was safe, but Wrenn was dead. Despite everything that had happened between them, I didn't think it would be easy news to deliver, and given the state this boy was in, he has gone through hell and back.

When my and Ansel's gazes met in the mirror, I knew he was thinking the same thing I was. This was going to lead Christopher right to us.

But this time, we'd be ready.

Nicholette
Sunday

Curled up with Oli on the couch, I only got an hour or two of sleep before I needed to pee. After that, I knew sleep was impossible, so I wandered into Ansel's study. Papers were scattered all over the place—inheritance documents from Maeve, the information she'd found out about my parents... who I thought were my parents, and background on Thomas.

Thomas.

I pressed a hand to my abdomen and tried to ignore how I could feel my stomach turning. The kid I loved with my whole fucking heart was my *son*, the result of both a rape and pregnancy that I didn't remember. Had I been drugged, or had my brain hidden this in the furthest dark recesses of my mind to protect itself and give me a chance at a normal life? My hands were shaking so badly I put the papers down, breathing deep to steady myself. My mind was still spinning. I knew that barely any time had passed since learning that heart-wrenching secret, but I had a feeling time couldn't make any of this better no matter how much had passed.

A knock on the door made me jolt, and I whipped my head up in time to see Oli in the doorway, watching me with concerned eyes that noticed too much.

"What's wrong?"

"You should be asleep," I admonished as I tried to catch my breath and slow my pounding heart.

"So should you." He walked over and wrapped a hand around my throat, squeezing just enough that I felt the strength in his hands. My breathing started to slow, and my heart gradually calmed as he rubbed his thumb over my pulse point. "This helps Bodhi when he's having a hard time calming down. I figured it might work with you too. What's going on, Nic? What did I miss?"

"We killed Joe. Found out a bunch of things I wasn't prepared for."

"Like Christopher?" Oli asked, his voice controlled. He maintained the steady grip around my neck, which was all the closeness I needed right now. It hadn't occurred to me that I should wake one of them up, that even though their presence wouldn't solve the problems we still needed to deal with, the comfort they could give me might make those obstacles seem a little less insurmountable. Given how much trouble I'd had sleeping without them, I should have realized that my body and my brain were well trained by now. My men had this secret to reaching the instinctual parts of me that wanted to feel and react, and it seemed like they all knew some way to rein in my crazy when I needed it.

"No. Thomas."

"Your brother?" Oli tilted his head, curiosity bright in his hazel eyes.

I swallowed hard, squeezing my eyes shut as I forced out an answer. "My son."

Immediately, the hand around my throat loosened, and I opened my eyes to see Oli going pale. He stumbled back, his ass hitting the desk . "Son?"

"My mom... Miranda..." I waved off my stumbling over what to call her. "She couldn't get pregnant. Had the hardest time. Then they got me... Apparently, Miranda *did* love me until I gave Joe something she never could—a child. I'll never know if it's true or not without a test but... Yeah, it was a lot."

Oli didn't say anything in response, so I cautiously took a step toward him, making sure he was still breathing. "Atlas and I opened the envelope. The one that Blake had. With the results."

"What did it say?" I asked as I reached out, my need to touch him overtaking my caution. He pulled me in, his hands on my hips and his head resting on my breasts.

"He's my brother." The words were so soft I wouldn't have heard them if he wasn't right in front of me.

"Is that a good thing?"

"Yes. No. I don't know," Oli rambled as I ran my fingers through his hair. "I have a lot of thoughts and feelings, and as fucked up as it is, I'm glad we have all of this shit with your stalker to deal with so I don't need to face this quite yet."

I chuckled, not above some dark humor to get through a hard time. "Understandable. Nothing like compartmentalizing to deal with when we can't run anymore, right?"

"There is *so* much to unpack in that statement." Bodhi's voice made us both look to the door where our lover was standing with an unsure expression on his face. "Sacha asked me to look for you. He got a call from Ansel."

"What's wrong? Is he okay?" I asked, concern

immediately hitting me. Bodhi's tone was careful, too careful, like he was afraid I would crack if I took one more hard hit.

He held up a hand and shook his head. "It sounded like he's fine, but I think he's on the way back. That's all I got before the call ended." He licked his lips, turning his attention to our boyfriend who was holding me still. "I didn't realize you were back."

"We stumbled in, and I passed out on the couch. Didn't get any real sleep since Thursday night before I left," Oli told Bodhi with a half smile.

Bodhi tsked at his boyfriend and shook his head in a silent reprimand. "You can't run off coffee forever."

"I wish I could," Oli and I said at the same time, making us all start laughing.

"Go find out what Sacha wants," Oli said, pushing me back. "You don't want to keep him waiting."

I blew him a kiss then pressed one to Bodhi's cheek on my way out. Hurrying through the hallway, I was just about to go upstairs when the front door opened.

"Nic?!"

I froze on the spot, my body unable to turn around or run away. *That voice.* The one I thought I'd never hear again. Thomas, my baby brother, the one guy who'd never let me down and loved without any reservation. He was alive, and, more importantly, he was *here.*

Hoping like hell I wouldn't mess this up, I forced myself to face the doorway, my tunnel vision zeroing in on my brother. He looked the same and yet so fucking different than the little kid I had seen last. He was taller now, but still just as slender as I remembered, and his eyes were the same blue. Long hair fell around his face, greasy and unwashed. It was so different from the short hair he'd had that my brain took a few seconds to really register everything else. There were bruises all over him, dried blood on his clothes, and swollen reminders where he'd obviously been hurt.

I'll kill him.

I'd break every damn bone in Christopher's body a thousand times over to make him pay for what he'd done to Thomas.

"Thomas?" My voice barely above a whisper, but then we were moving, our bodies speaking louder than my voice could. We rushed to grab each other. I didn't give a damn about anything else when he slammed into me, his arms tightly wound around me as he trembled. I squeezed him back, holding him close, and tried to hold back my tears. *Yeah, that's a pointless effort* Burying my face in his hair, I breathed deeply as tears fell without restraint.

My Thomas was alive, safe, and here in my arms. It was all I'd wanted since I left home at seventeen.

Footsteps filled the foyer, and I glanced up to find Ansel and Rhodes by the front door, watching us with intent expressions. "Where did you find him?" I managed, my voice sounding way more put together than I actually was.

"He found me at the old compound," Rhodes replied roughly, clearing his throat. "Fell asleep on the way here."

"The doctor will be here soon to check him over," Ansel tacked on. I nodded, running my hands through Thomas' hair. I faintly registered the sounds of the others joining us when Thomas' body stiffened the slightest bit like he was unsure if the newcomers would be safe. Sacha and Vas paused when they saw us, though they continued walking downstairs after the initial moment of surprise.

Thomas started murmuring things against me, so I knelt down, separating us just enough so I could see his face and wipe away his tears. "What's wrong?"

"He said—" He hiccuped and wiped at his face, leaving a smear of dirt across his cheek. "He did things—"

"Hey," I said gently, calmly, as I tried to smile. "We don't need to talk about that right now. Let's get you some space to clean up and get checked out, then you can catch us up."

"But I need to!" Thomas stubbornly refused to move, a scowl on his face. His brow furrowed as he glanced around at everyone. "Who are all of these people?"

"Friends," I told him. It wasn't the whole truth, but some things took time.

"He said they were more than friends," he replied, uncertainty flickering across his features. "He said—"

"Some fucking bullshit, I'm sure," Maksim muttered from somewhere, and Alexei whispered back for him to shut up.

"Can we talk somewhere? Just-Just us?"

His nerves had increased as we talked, anxiety making his fingers twitch, and I knew I'd do anything to help ease the worry and pain that he was feeling. Giving him a moment of privacy was the least I would do for him. Snagging his hand, I led him to the study I had just left. One set of footsteps followed us, but I didn't look back. Being truly alone wasn't really an option right now no matter how much privacy I wished to have for this reunion. Sure, I might have crept off to a room by myself while the others were sleeping, but I wouldn't take even that tiny risk with my brother's life now that I had him back.

"This isn't alone," Thomas replied shakily as I settled both of us on the couch. Sacha had taken up a spot by the door, a stoic expression on his face, and Vas appeared behind him.

"This is as alone as we get right now," I explained. "The

man who had you, he's coming for me. Being alone isn't safe." Thomas didn't say anything right away. He looked around, taking in the room then studying me. The expression in his eyes was way older than his thirteen years.

"He took me because of you." He said it softly, but fuck... if that didn't feel like a goddamn knife in my heart. I knew it was true, but hearing him say that to me made it really hit home. "To get you for himself. That's what he told me after he killed Mom."

I swallowed hard, "I'm sorry, Thomas, so sorry."

"He made me watch him rape and kill people after making them over to look like you. He called out your name when he—"

"Do you remember where you were held? Anything about it?" Vas cut in, his voice uncharacteristically soft.

"It was a warehouse... I think. Surrounded by a bunch of other buildings just like it. When I got away, I ran. I didn't look back or anything. I just wanted to get away."

"It's okay. That's fine," Vas assured him as he came closer, squatting down to look less intimidating. "Anything you remember is helpful."

"Wrenn is dead," Thomas said sadly. I closed my eyes and turned my face away, hoping to school my expression before anyone saw it.

Wrenn. I had loved her once, but while some of the bitterness of our time together had faded, it wasn't enough to make me love her again. My role in her death couldn't be downplayed. If I hadn't lost it and shot her, she might still be alive right now. *Though Thomas might not be.* That thought alone ensured I would never regret what I had done. "She told me where to find you and your boyfriends."

I choked on a laugh and looked at Vas and Sacha before

switching back to Thomas again. "That's weird hearing someone else say it."

"Are you saying we aren't?" Vas rumbled, all deliciously grumpy, as he glared at me. He wasn't actually angry though. A spark of amusement was bright in his brown eyes.

"Have I called you boyfriends before?" I mused aloud, smirking when I heard Oli yell out that I had. "Are they listening in right now? Really?"

"Of course they are." Sacha's lips twitched, but he managed to keep it together. Thomas just looked at all of us like we were crazy. *He hasn't seen anything yet.*

"You'll learn that they're all very high maintenance and need attention," I joked with the boy sitting beside me. "All of them."

"Excuse you?!" Vas growled.

Ignoring him, I continued. "But anything you can tell us about the man who had you would be a huge help. We need to know, Thomas. We have to stop him."

"You mean kill him?"

I searched his face, fear and nerves twisting together until I felt cold seep into my veins. Was he afraid of me? Afraid of Christopher? Both? If it was the former, what would I do when all of this was over? Give him up so he could live a normal life? I wasn't sure if I could do that, but how could I not if that was what he needed? Standing up, I put space between us and walked over to the desk, forcing myself to look at anything other than him.

"Tell us what you know, Thomas," I told him firmly. "We can worry about the details while you recover."

No one said anything for a minute, and I could feel the weight of their gazes on me. Then Thomas cleared his throat and started to fill us in from the beginning—being taken, beaten, and threatened. Wrenn's arrival and her telling him about me and the guys.

"And he knows you're pregnant," Thomas finally said, exhaustion making his quiet voice almost a whisper. "It's what she used to set him off and distract him so I could get away."

I pressed a shaky hand to my stomach as if that would help shield them, processing everything he had shared. "He's coming here then," I decided, staring up at Sacha and Vas. "Get him somewhere safe upstairs. I need to talk with the others."

"Nic—" Thomas started, reaching for me when I passed him, but I didn't look back. I couldn't. To see his fear directed at me... My walls were too fucking cracked right now to deal with that. It would destroy me.

"We have information," I said, walking past Sacha and Vas to where I thought the others were waiting. No one was in the hallway like I thought they would be, so I went out to the foyer only to come to a standstill. Oli was on the floor, blood pooling around him as he pressed a hand to his head. Bodhi was beside him trying to help. Before I could ask them what had happened, a hard hand clamped over my mouth from behind.

"Thomas left out the best parts." Christopher's usually upbeat and warm voice was now a cold and taunting whisper in my ear. "But not to worry, I think we're all going to get some things out in the open. Unlike the fucking bastards you're with now, I won't tolerate secrets. I own every fucking part of you."

"Christopher—" I tried to protest, but he squeezed my face hard enough that my eyes watered. The ache in my jaw forced a whimper past my lips even though I hated giving him any sign that he'd managed to hurt me.

"You'll learn your place soon enough, Nicholette," he promised me harshly. "But I think it's time we start with some goodbyes."

He lifted his other hand and aimed his gun, firing off a few shots before I managed to exhale.

"Bodhi!"

Nicholette
Sunday

Time slowed as I watched Bodhi topple to the floor. Oli moved to shield him with his own body the blood spilling out to pool around them both. Where the hell were the others?! Hopefully Sacha and Vas were hiding Thomas.

"I set up a few surprises for the others." Christopher pressed a soft kiss to my neck. "I don't want to be interrupted now that we're finally together."

I jerked away, stumbling back when he let me go. When I tried to approach Bodhi and Oli, both disturbingly silent, Christopher tsked and grabbed me, forcing me away from the two men I loved.

"Let me go, you sick fucking bastard!"

He backhanded me hard enough that blood filled my mouth and black spots speckled my vision. "You listen to me. You're *mine,* and you'll do as *I* say. Checking on the fucking trash isn't something you should worry about."

My mind was scrambling, trying to keep itself together so my guys and I could survive this. "You don't want secrets between us? What did you do to the others?"

"Security breaches along the property to occupy *Ansel.*"

His lips curled as he spat the German's name. "How the hell you got with that fucking freak of nature, I'll never know. He tortured his own daughter! You're pregnant, yet you're still with him despite knowing what he is capable of."

I swallowed hard when a hint of movement behind him revealed Ansel, a completely blank expression on his face. If he thought that was news to me, then he was in for a rude awakening. "I am."

"That's all you're going to say about it?!" Christopher's face was purple as he screamed in my face.

"You don't know the circumstances of what happened," I told him firmly, tilting my chin in defiance. "Besides, misgendering Blake isn't winning you any favors. Not to mention, isn't criticizing Ansel a bit of a pot-kettle situation given what you're involved in?"

"Me?" he hissed. "You want to judge me when you're spreading your legs for just anybody?"

A slight whimper revealed Thomas behind Sacha and Vas on the other side of the foyer. They must have gone the other way around, through the second level, to get to that position. Thank goodness they had focused on protecting my brother instead of leaving him vulnerable to get to me. Sacha's eyes were the coldest I'd ever seen. His eyes flicked to me, then Christopher, after he'd studied Bodhi and Oli's unmoving bodies on the floor.

Rhodes, Ansel, Alexei, and Maksim were off to the side, but Em, Blake, and their men were nowhere to be seen. Then I recalled Em telling Blake and the others they needed to head out super early tomorrow to go to Boston. Something business related had come up, and they wouldn't be back until tonight. *At least there's a few less people to keep track of or worry about.*

"I did what I had to do," I shot back, desperately

focusing on the here and now. "Besides, you were one of the clients paying thousands for a small bit of my attention. Do you really have the high ground here?"

"So did the others."

"Not all of them," I taunted him. "And not for long."

Christopher lashed out, pistol whipping me so hard I fell to the ground. I caught myself, the impact jarring to my hands and wrists, not wanting to harm the babies with the fall. "You think these men are perfect for you? Let me show you how wrong you are." He grabbed me then, hauling me up and holding me close as a body shield so the others wouldn't shoot. Christopher upped the ante by pressing the gun to my head.

"You're playing a dangerous game," Sacha said, speaking up for the first time. I shivered at the emptiness in the voice, and I looked up, trying to ignore the swelling on the side of my face and blood spilling onto my shirt.

"Ah, an audience! Good. I want you to be here when she finally realizes that she isn't meant to be with any of you. That it's been *me* all along."

"Never," Vas rumbled.

"Always," Christopher laughed, my skin crawling at the sound. "After all, that baby you're carrying is mine." I stilled as he continued. "Condoms are such delicate things. A few pricks through the packaging renders them useless, not much more than decoration, really. I calculated your days, your cycle, you know. Did you really think I randomly booked times with you? And the last time, hell, the last time *you* initiated the sex. Not me. Oh... Did you not tell them that?"

"I was doing my job. That's all you are. Nothing more," I retorted.

"Your *guys*, as you call them, they gave you shit for

keeping a second apartment, but did you know Sacha has had one the entire time? A secret little getaway that only Bodhi has been to, where they fucked while you were off trying to find your precious brother."

My head was pounding, my worry increasing as bile rose in my throat. *He must have really fucking hurt me when he hit me with the gun.* Mistaking my silence for shock, he kept going, probably trying to maximize what he saw as his victory.

"You already found out about Oli's secrets... if you want to call him that. I just called him a little faggot when I fucked him years ago." I threw up, but Christopher just laughed before he continued oversharing. *Why is it that bad guys love to hear themselves talk? Can't he just shut up for one fucking minute?*

"You all found my cameras, but not before I found out a bunch of interesting things about all of you."

"Is this really necessary?" Ansel asked, the bland tone of his voice sending shivers down my spine.

"Don't take another step further, or I'll blow her brains out." Christopher pushed the gun into my temple hard enough to make me whimper in pain, and everyone froze. His finger was on the trigger. One tiny movement, and I'd be dead. The closeness of our bodies meant that shooting him would kill me too, rendering my skilled killers helpless. "If I can't have her, no one can. I'll kill her and myself, then she'll be mine even in death."

"Can we get over the speech part of this shit already?" Maksim griped, lighting a cigarette as if this intense standoff wasn't even happening. "I have better things to do with my time than deal with you."

"Like fucking your brother?"

Alexei paled, but Maksim just inhaled, the red end of

his cigarette burning brightly before he replied. "Who I fuck is really none of your business."

"Brothers sharing you, brothers fucking brothers..." Christopher sneered at them in disgust. "Being with men older than your father, and the twinks over there... Well, they're not much of a problem anymore."

Oli and Bodhi hadn't moved at all since the shots were fired. My heart pounded, and tears fell once again as I prayed for them to be okay. *Whoever is out there, please... Please let them be okay.*

Please be okay.

Please be okay.

"I made him watch, you know," Christopher taunted, forcing my prayers to a halt. "I made Thomas watch me rape and kill those women. He heard me call out your name while I filled their corpses with my cum. Not to mention, I told him that little revelation you just had—that he isn't your brother. He's your son. Did you tell him how you found out?"

When I didn't respond, he jerked me around so I was face to face with Thomas. "I might have killed Miranda in front of him, but what did you do, Nic?" I swallowed hard as he shook me when I remained silent, my vision blurry. "Tell him!"

"I killed Joe," I said slowly. Fuck, I was hurt bad. There was no other explanation for how fuzzy my words sounded. "Watched them pull him apart like a rag doll."

"But that's just the tip of the iceberg, Thomas. Your sister, oh excuse me, your *mom* is one of the most prolific killers around here. Her body count rivals the hitman in this room. Though it's nowhere close to her body count as a whore. Fucked her way to the top by sneaking into the beds of men who had more standing and power than she ever could."

"That might apply to Maeve," I responded with a laugh, unable to keep myself from commenting, "but not to me. I slept with Maeve to get to the top, so that's not completely accurate. Everyone after that was a bonus."

"Maybe I'll let Thomas watch me fuck you before I kill him. I'll make them all watch before I force you to look on while I kill every single man here who thinks they can have you. I waited years, years! I dedicated myself to killing the scum that thought they could claim your body, and *this* is how you repaid me."

"I'll never be yours," I told him harshly. "Never."

I knew it wasn't what I should say. I was pushing someone who had killed lots of people to get ahold of me. This man had violated every right to privacy by stalking me and my boyfriends. I didn't care who fucked who or about people's pasts, but to have someone come in and lay that shit out in front of everyone... I glanced over at Alexei, who still looked pale, but he held himself stoically, watching Christopher's every move.

"But I haven't told you the best secret!" Christopher smirked and walked us over to nudge Bodhi with his boot. "Your little submissive, shy one here... He's the reason his sister is dead. Provoked his mother while on a bender then left his sister to take the brunt of Mommy's anger. The real monster has always been him."

"He was a child," I managed, training my eyes on Christopher once I saw Bodhi's hand twitch, his fingers slowly, oh so slowly, moving through the blood on the floor. Oli, who was on top of him, still hadn't moved, but I thought I detected the slightest rise and fall of his chest. I wanted to sob with relief, but even more than that, I wanted them to survive this, so I knew I had to stuff that desire down and focus on Christopher.

"Still murder, little Nic. You and these barbarians you chose to be with should know all about that."

"I'd choose them all over again too."

Christopher's once kind face became completely foreign to me when a sinister smile took over his expression. "You won't get that choice anymore. I'll help you make all your decisions from now on."

Before I knew what was happening, Oli's body rolled off of Bodhi. Oli was still out of it though, letting out a weak groan as Bodhi stood up, holding up what looked like Vas' hunting knife. *Where the hell did he get that from?* He was up, plunging it into Christopher's back, before anyone else could act. Vas moved then, grabbing the gun Christopher had dropped to make sure it didn't go off. I stumbled back and fell to the ground near Oli, black spots taking over my vision.

Christopher shrieked with pain and surprise, but Bodhi tugged the knife out and sank it into his body a second time. The older man's body fell to the ground as Bodhi was overtaken by rage and pain, stabbing the man over and over again. Somehow, Christopher was still alive, trying to dislodge Bodhi's hold on him, which was a fucking mistake. Bodhi slammed the knife home into Christopher's right eye, pushing the weapon so far the hilt hit his face.

When he couldn't pull the knife back out again, he turned to his fists, beating the shit out of Christopher's body until it was a bloody fucking mess. We all watched as he lost his shit, keeping our eyes on the still-bleeding bullet wounds in his arm, back, and leg. This was the anger Bodhi hid under his carefully controlled nature. I had no doubt that if he had been able to torture Christopher, he would have done it for days and days, taunting the man with death long before he gave it to him.

Once we were certain Christopher was dead, Sacha and Ansel stayed by Bodhi's side while Vas and Rhodes hurried to me. "Nic!"

"It's bad," I rasped, closing my eyes. The dizzying darkness I had been fighting off was starting to win our battle "Oli?"

I forced myself to open my eyes. Maks and Alexei were there, carefully checking Oli over with grim faces. "We need a hospital for all three of you. Now."

"Nic?!" Thomas' frantic, higher-pitched voice cut through everything. "Nic!"

"He needs to be kept safe." I reached up to Rhodes, and he looked down at me. "While they look me over and the others. Please, hotshot?"

"You're going to be fine, Nic," he rebuffed me, his trembling hand pressed to my cheek.

"A little head injury isn't going to take me down," I told him with a smile. "He hit like a little bitch, no force behind it at all. Maybe he should have watched you all work instead of tracking who was fucking who."

"Oh god, no jokes right now," Oli slurred from the ground nearby. "I can't fully appreciate them."

Thomas ran over and fell to his knees beside me, and the others let him pull me into his arms. I ran a hand through his hair to provide what comfort I could. He was shaking so much I was being jolted. "It's going to be okay, Thomas. I'm fine."

"Sacha," Maks said, his tone so controlled and bland you'd think he was bored, "if you don't pull Bodhi off of him, Ansel is going to have to scrape brain matter off the ceiling."

Bodhi rambled as Sacha and Ansel wrestled him away from Christopher, and I pressed a hand to my abdomen, hoping everything was okay with the babies.

Are they Christopher's?

That was my last thought before I lost consciousness.

Alexei
Tuesday

Nicholette ended up checked into the hospital due to her bad concussion and the fact that she was pregnant. Oliver and Bodhi had both been shot, but we'd been lucky. They'd both been hit in spots that led to alarming bleeding, but Bodhi's were just flesh wounds, while Oliver's were serious enough to warrant a few nights of observation. He was in the hospital with Nic, the two of them sharing a room, and they were driving the staff completely insane. Nic had been forcing him to watch horror movie after horror movie since he couldn't go anywhere to escape. He threatened her with increasingly violent sex in revenge, which just seemed to make her dig up even weirder shit. They were a strange pair, to be honest.

Bodhi came every day during visiting hours, his usually quiet nature even more reserved since he'd destroyed Christopher. There was really no other way to describe what he had done. It didn't even look like a body when he was done. Bodhi was shaken and taken aback by what he had done, and it was my personal theory that he was having trouble stuffing all that anger back inside of himself now that he'd let it out. Blake had gotten Robin to clean up the house, making sure nothing remained of the pieces even though they'd flown everywhere.

Bodhi wasn't the only one dealing with the aftereffects of everything. Christopher had outed me and Maksim, taking away the choice of when and how we'd do it. Of course, Maksim didn't care that others knew, but he had understood how much that control mattered to me. He didn't want to hide anymore, especially now that our relationship was common knowledge, but I needed some more time.

Shaking my head, I stepped into the shower, letting steam fog up the bathroom for a while. We were still staying at Ansel's place, all of us having taken over his space, but he didn't seem to mind. In fact, he seemed more amused and resigned than anything, especially after Maksim finally quit smoking indoors. Thomas had pointed out that it wouldn't be healthy for the babies, and Maksim had just muttered something about fucking pushy kids and walked outside to smoke.

Thomas was another piece of this fucked up family that had somehow fit perfectly. He was slowly finding his footing with the rest of us, but the kid definitely felt most comfortable around Rhodes. I'd occasionally heard him telling Rhodes about the things he'd seen or stuff Christopher had done... It was going to be a slow and rough road to some kind of normalcy for him, but he wouldn't be alone. Blake and Em went back to Boston, though they promised to pop by and annoy us whenever the need arose. A promise I was sure they would follow through on today.

"If you don't actually wash yourself, you're going to use up all the hot water." Maksim's dry voice jolted me from my thoughts. I looked through the glass shower door to see him watching me from the doorway.

"Lost in thought," I told him, hoping that would be the end of it, but this was Maksim. Things weren't over until he said they were.

Clothing rustled, then a few seconds later, cold air hit my back as he joined me in the shower, his hard body behind mine. His arms wound around my stomach, pulling me tight against him as he pressed a kiss to my back. Part of me wondered where this soft side of him was coming from since Maksim didn't do softness, but I didn't want to say something that broke the moment.

"No one cares that we're together, Alexei. No one has said shit since Christopher outed us," he whispered against my skin, his beard gently scratching the top of my shoulder. "Get out of that head of yours and let go."

"That's easier said than done," I told him. I wished like hell I could do that, knowing that would probably always be an issue for me, but I'd work on it. Staying in the circle of his arms, I turned to face him with a smile. "I do love you. You know that, right?"

"Of course I do," he replied, arching an eyebrow. "I wasn't worried about that changing because of that asshole."

I rolled my eyes. "You know most people would say it back."

"I've been with you for ten years, Alexei. Do you really have no idea?" Maksim stared at me like I was an idiot. "You are my safe space. The person I can go to that just lets me fucking be without demanding I exhaust myself. At the end of the day, you're the person I want to come home to and just be with. Maybe that's not the declaration you want, but it's one I mean with every part of me—"

I slanted my lips over his, needing to kiss him more than

I needed fucking air. Maksim wasn't like other people, he never would be, but I wouldn't want him to be. Love might not ever be on the table as something he could give to someone, me *or* Nic, but that didn't mean he didn't care. I could hear those words on his lips once every decade or never at all in the time we had left together, and my heart could still feel full. Maksim cared way more than most people realized or gave him credit for. Me being his safe space... I had never thought I meant that to him, but he was that for me too. I could let go with him, allowing him to take on the burdens of fucking everything that weighed on my shoulders and my mind.

Maksim kissed me back, not rushing or pushing for more. His hands flexed on my back before he pulled me even closer so that our hard cocks brushed together. He easily took control, keeping the pace slow even when I tried to speed it up.

When he did break our kiss, his lips traveled down my throat and chest, then lower as he got on his knees. My eyes were wide when he took my cock into his mouth. *Oh god.* His mouth was hot, and that wicked tongue of his knew every sensitive place on my cock. Angling my body to the right, I blocked the spray from hitting him so he didn't have to worry about that, and he took me deeper and deeper down his throat.

"Fuck." That one groan was all I could manage. My jaw tightened with my desperate effort to keep from coming.

He pulled off of me, teasing the head of my dick with his tongue. "Let go of that infamous self-control, brother. Or do you need more than my mouth to get you off?"

"Maksim," I ground out, rocking my hips forward, hoping he'd take me down his throat again.

"Not this time," Maksim said with a wicked gleam in his

blue gray eyes as he stood up. Droplets of water clung to his short hair, which somehow made him even more attractive. "Apparently, I need to show you what you mean to me, and we both know I'm shit with words. Bed. Now."

"We're going to miss going to the hospital."

"And I think our girlfriend, who was a whore, will understand why," Maksim retorted as he shut off the water. "Crawl for me. Degrade yourself for me until you're nothing but a cum dump for your brother's cock. I'll give you everything you need from me, Alexei."

A whimper fell from my lips as he lightly kissed me and traced his fingers over my leaking cock. Then I did exactly as he asked. I crawled out to the bedroom with him beside me and lost myself in the full power of his cruel attentions. Degraded and humiliated myself by crying out for more while he laughed at me. When he finally slid his cock inside me, I wept with relief, accepting his bruising pace until he was fucking me so hard I was sure anyone who passed by could hear us.

I came while cursing his name, savoring the sensation of his hot cum jetting inside me. He rocked his hips a while longer, fucking his seed deeper into me, and I helplessly shivered beneath him.

"That's how I feel about you, Alexei," he whispered into my ear, nipping the outer edge.

It seemed fucking perfect to me.

***

Nicholette
Tuesday

SACHA, Vas, and Bodhi picked us up from the hospital after days of being stuck there, though having Oli as my roommate made it much better than my last stay. When I asked where the others were, Vas cuddled me closer and refused to answer. Oli and Bodhi were curled up together on my other side, content to be together again.

In the rearview mirror, Sacha smirked at me. "Ansel said he had no doubt that his children were going to come today so he was staying home to make sure they didn't try to take anything. Thomas is helping Rhodes and Razor at the new compound you gave them. I'm pretty sure Alexei and Maksim were fucking loud enough that the entire house knew what they were doing."

"Hard to imagine Alexei as a bottom, though, to be fair, I can't picture Maksim submitting to anyone," Vas commented.

Oli snorted. "Yeah, you might want to rethink that given how many orgasms Alexei gave our girl the first time they were together."

"What does that mean?" Bodhi asked even though Vas muttered that he didn't want to know.

"Thirty-three," I answered, shivering with the memory of that night. I really needed him to take control of me again. Fuck, that would be hot as hell.

Sacha whistled as Vas bitched about getting details he didn't want. So, basically, it was a totally normal car ride with everyone. The only difference was having a new destination as our home. The guys were still keeping the Ashview apartment for work business, but it wasn't big enough for all of us, especially with the babies coming. I still needed to figure out what I was doing with the fortune that Maeve had left me, but that was a problem for later.

When we got back, Sacha and Vas helped Oli out of the

car as I headed up to the front door with Bodhi hovering behind me. Right before I could reach for it, someone opened it from the other side—Ansel. Without hesitation, I threw myself at him. He easily caught me, wrapping me up in his arms and pressing his face into my neck.

"I missed you," I told him.

"I came up there yesterday, Liebling," he reminded me with a hint of laughter in his voice.

"So?" I countered with a grin before he kissed me soundly. I hummed happily as we moved inside, settling down on the couch while the others slowly joined us. Alexei and Maksim came later. Everyone wasted no time, claiming we'd need to institute sex volume rules, much to Alexei's mortification. Maksim just leveled a look at them and asked if those applied to me as well because I was a screamer.

"But you all love my screams," I told them wide-eyed.

They kept giving each other shit until Rhodes and Thomas wandered in. Things with Thomas were still on shaky ground. We were happy to be together, but navigating his trauma, mine, and all the history we needed to untangle would take time. Allen had called to say that the murder case was being dropped. Apparently, there was new evidence that disputed the match from the DNA in my rape kit. I didn't plan to look at it too closely. No more questioning from the police was always a good thing in my book. The department even sent me a formal letter of apology due to Lewis' conduct during my case. Some things were better left in the past, so I was happy to close that door for now.

Rhodes sat down on my other side, and I leaned over to kiss him, happy to be back with everyone even as Vas and Maksim started yelling at each other. Some things would always stay the same no matter what life threw our way.

When Blake, their men, and Emmerich waltzed in a few hours later, Atlas immediately went to check on Oli while Ansel, Rhodes, and Emmerich started talking business. Sacha came over and sat beside me, wrapping his arms around me.

"I love you."

"I love you too, boss," I told him softly, smiling when he kissed the side of my head.

It took some time, but I'd found my family.

I was finally home.

Nicholette
Six months later

One cry, then another, filled the hospital room. Normally, that'd be cause for alarm, but this time it sent relief flooding through me. I'd done it. The doctor and nurses were cleaning them up and cradling them in my arms. A boy and a girl. They were perfect.

A soft kiss was pressed to my forehead. Rhodes was standing beside me, watching the babies with wonder-filled eyes.

"I'm okay, hotshot," I told him gently. "So are they."

He'd told me about his past, sharing the history that had made my pregnancy such a scary thing for him. The overprotectiveness he'd shown had put Sacha to shame, which was impressive in an almost smothering kind of way. It was an intense time, and I was ready to be free of that level of scrutiny from them. Their focus could now be turned to the children who had a large enough family that they'd probably get away with nothing... unless one of their dads was involved in whatever mischief they'd caused.

"Do you still want that DNA test?" the doctor asked.

I nodded in confirmation, and they assured me they had

saved part of the umbilical cord for that purpose. The others had already gone down to the lab to get blood drawn. Well, everyone but Ansel, who was sitting in the corner, and Rhodes, who hadn't left my bedside since I was admitted. The others had rotated being near me since Rhodes was constantly by my side, needing to know the babies and I were okay.

"Go get the blood draw, Rhodes. I'll be here when you get back," I told him gently but firmly.

He seemed hesitant until Ansel stood up and assured him that he would stay with me. Finally, he left the room. I looked down at the babies in my arms then up at Ansel when he ran a hand through my hair.

"What the hell do I do now?" I asked him, exhausted beyond belief.

Ansel smiled. "You do better than your parents before you. At least that was my goal. Sadly, that's all that I managed."

"Ansel—"

"I'm not perfect, Liebling, far from it. Trust me, I'm well aware of that fact. Luckily, you're not alone, nor do you have only me beside you. There are plenty of us to help you and each other out."

"They aren't yours by blood, but that doesn't make them any less yours in the ways that matter," I told him. "You're a part of this even though I warned you against it." He laughed lightly, but some of the tension I had seen in him started to loosen. "This is another chance to do it right. Hell, it's a two-for-one special. Though please don't let one of them grow up with Em's attitude. We'll never make it."

Ansel's smile reached his eyes this time, their steely gray warming up as he looked at the little ones in my arms. They were perfect, absolutely perfect.

"Can I come in?"

Thomas was hovering in the doorway, an unsure frown on his face. Ansel kissed my forehead as I told Thomas to come right in, then he stepped away so Thomas and I could be semi-alone for a minute. My brother came over and looked down at the babies, an unreadable look in his eyes.

"You did good, sis," he told him softly.

I blinked back tears and smiled at him. "Thanks."

We hadn't done the DNA test that would either confirm or disprove Joe's claim, and I wasn't sure I ever would. Thomas and I had talked about it, and he was more comfortable sticking with sis or sister for me, which I was fine with. Maybe one day we'd open that can of worms, but right now wasn't the time. We were figuring out a new start together, and so far we were doing well.

"How long will it take to get results?"

"Blake got someone on the inside to expedite it, so we should know by the end of the day," Ansel answered as he scrolled through his phone.

"Get ready for a lot of shit talking when those results get shared," I warned my brother, which just made him laugh.

BY LATE EVENING, I had been moved into a large recovery room, with all of my men squeezing into the space. It didn't help that we'd been visited by Emmerich, Blake, and their guys. The whole family was here to stay, and part of me wished Maeve was here to see this.

Sacha currently had the girl cradled to his chest, fast asleep in his arms, while Rhodes held our sleeping boy, both babies nestled in close to the men holding them. Bodhi and Oli had taken turns holding them, but neither had cuddled them for too long. Maksim had looked on while Alexei held them, which wasn't a surprise. Like any of his other connections, I knew Maks would need time to build it. He might not ever be the warm, fuzzy dad who offered cuddles or physical comfort, but he would protect these babies with his life and every ounce of viciousness inside him. For me, that was most important.

None of us had agreed on names yet. Until the battle of names began, I hadn't realized just how many options had been ruined by past associations, and with so many people involved, we had a lot of history to avoid. Needless to say, it didn't leave us many choices to pick from. We eventually decided that when we got the paternity results, the dad and I would make the final call on what our babies would be called.

Two brisk knocks came before the doctor opened the door, only to stop short at the sheer number of people in the room. "Only family is supposed to be here."

"We are family," Emmerich shot back. With an arched eyebrow, he pulled at his jacket to show off his gun.

"Oh my god, Em!" I quietly reprimanded as the doctor stepped back. "It's bad enough Vas almost got kicked out because of that earlier today."

"I did not!"

"You did! All because you thought the nurse wasn't moving fast enough—"

"You were in pain!"

I rolled my eyes. "I was having a baby! *Two* of them! We weren't on a time crunch." The dramatics of the delivery room wouldn't be forgotten anytime soon.

"Are those the results?" Bodhi asked, cutting through the arguments.

The doctor quickly said they were and shoved an envelope at Bodhi before rushing out of the room.

I sighed. "It will be a goddamn miracle if no one gets arrested today."

Bodhi brought over the envelope and handed it to me. With a deep breath, I ripped it open and read the paper once, twice, three times before I dropped it.

"What is it? Is it—"

"They aren't Christopher's," I said, the words slightly muffled by my hands rubbing my face. I could feel hysterical laughter threatening to escape, but I somehow managed to hold it together. "You all can't do anything by halves, can you?"

"What does that even mean?" Thomas asked.

"Who's the father?" Vas rumbled as I took a deep breath and picked up the paper again.

"Fathers," I corrected, making the room fall completely silent. "Each baby has a different father."

"What the actual fuck?" Emmerich murmured, dodging their sibling's swat as Blake told him to watch his language around the babies. "I think it's a fair question! Who else would this happen to?"

"What do the results say, Nic?" Sacha asked, trying to steer the conversation back on track.

"Rhodes," I announced, making the older man freeze, "and Bodhi." Bodhi would have fallen if Oli and Atlas hadn't been beside him, catching his arms to hold him up. "The boy is Bodhi's, and the girl is Rhodes' based on what this says."

We had one ragged breath of warning from Bodhi, then Oli had to talk him through a panic attack. Rhodes wasn't doing much better, but although he denied Ansel's offer to take the baby from him, he let his old friend guide him to sit on the edge of the bed.

Sacha pressed a kiss to the girl's head then handed her to me. All the non-biological fathers were unfazed by the results, and I was happy to see that not one of them looked upset that they weren't listed on the test results. Everyone in our group would be fathers to these kids; the DNA test didn't change that. I knew the shit-talking would start once the shock wore off, but that would all be in good fun. For now, I needed to concentrate on the dad who was about to pass out.

"Bodhi?"

"I don't think... I can't—"

"Come sit with me." I patted the bed, and after a few deep breaths, he stumbled over, collapsing beside me. His eyes darted between the pink bundle in my arms and the blue in Rhodes'.

"Let's leave them to it for a little while. I need a cigarette to process all of this," Maksim said, breaking the building tension.

"How about some vodka?" Em suggested, pointedly looking at Sacha, but the Russian in question rolled his eyes.

"I told you before, I'm not some stereotype."

"You said that last time, but that was probably the best vodka I've ever had," Emmerich joked.

Amidst Sacha and Em's banter, they all filed out of the room, leaving me, the bio-dads, and the babies behind.

"We need names."

Rhodes roughly cleared his throat, though it took him a few times before he could speak clearly. "How about Galina? It was my mother's name."

"Galina Iris?" I asked, looking down at our daughter in my arms.

"I like that, and I know Ansel will too." I looked up, and he kissed me, slowly and carefully, both of us aware of Bodhi beside us and the babies in our arms.

"Bodhi? Did you have any ideas for names?" He shook his head, uncertainty and remnants of panic in his eyes. "How about Sage? For your sister. I mean, unless you don't want..."

"I love that." His voice cracked as tears spilled down his face, but a smile was there. While small, it was bright and full of love. "Sage Wilder?"

"Perfect."

"What about last names?" I took a shaky breath.

"I think they should have yours, love." Rhodes nodded at me. "Take back your name and let our babies be your legacy, not those assholes."

"Besides, I can't imagine having to tell Vas the kids are taking *our* names," Bodhi said with a wry grin. "There are way too many people in this family for that kind of conversation, but everyone will be on board with them having yours."

I laughed, unable to hold it in. The two of them joined me, and the others soon came back, demanding to know what was so funny. All we managed was to choke out Vas' name between giggles. He didn't appreciate it, but the rest of us sure did.

Ansel, Blake, and Em all grew quiet when they learned our little girl's name, and there was some heavy emotion in Ansel's eyes when he took his turn holding her close with Rhodes beside him. Blake and Emmerich watched with curious and happy expressions as their dad interacted with the baby. I knew the history there was complicated and twisted, but hopefully this could be a fresh start for all of us.

Ansel was retiring from the Family, or at least stepping

back as much as one could from the mafia. Rhodes was re-establishing the Lords of Chaos' hold in Ashview, and Alexei and Maksim had bought another two clubs, in Boston this time, spreading their influence even further. Sacha and his team had new jobs pouring in, so by all accounts, our family's future was looking bright.

I had taken on my new roles as well. I was now a mother *and* the Madame, and I'd never felt more happy or fulfilled.

Who said women couldn't have it all?

That's the end of Nicholette's story— but don't worry, I'm sure you'll see her and her group around!

If you haven't checked out Blake's story, the Lies and Loves duet is part of the same criminal world and it's complete! If you love the high heat, morally gray characters, and the Family drama... you won't want to miss their story!

ABOUT THE AUTHOR

Suki Williams writes dark romance with all types of romantic pairings. She currently lives on the east coast with her family. She has always loved reading and writing and finally took the plunge to start indie publishing back in 2019.

The best way to stay up to date with her work is to join the reader group, sign up for her newsletter or check out her website, www.authorsukiwrites.com!

FOLLOW SUKI WILLIAMS

Link Tree:
https://linktr.ee/SukiWilliams

Reader Group:
Suki's House

Newsletter Sign Up

ALSO BY SUKI WILLIAMS

Queen of Hearts Trilogy

Hard Limits, Queen of Hearts Book 1

Safe Word, Queen of Hearts Book 2

Their Domme, Queen of Hearts Book 3

Lies and Loves Duet

Beauty of Corruption, Lies and Loves Book 1

Beauty of Betrayal, Lies and Loves Book 2

Standalone

Performed, Besties and Booze Book 3

Anthologies/Shared Worlds

Heartless Heroes

Chronicles of the Damned

Insidious, Enigma Society

Co-writes with Jarica James

The Forgotten Series

Nexus, Forgotten Prison Book 1

Broken, Forgotten Prison Book 2

Memory, Forgotten Prison Book 3

Reset, Forgotten Prison Book 4